About the Author

Lucie Wheeler lives in Essex with her husband and daughter, and her English Bull Terrier, Dame, who loves to sit under Lucie's desk as she writes and keep her feet warm. Never one to sit still, Lucie always has lots going on in her life. Currently, she's writing her novels alongside studying for a degree. She is also one of The Romaniacs.

Lucie loves reading, spending time with friends and eating chocolate – when she gets to do all three, she's a very happy lady!

@lucie_wheeler
www.facebook.com/luciewheelerpage
www.luciewheeler.co.uk

LUCIE WHEELER

The First Time Mums' Club

A division of HarperCollins*Publishers*
www.harpercollins.co.uk

Harper*Impulse*
an imprint of HarperCollins*Publishers* Ltd
1 London Bridge Street
London SE1 9GF

www.harpercollins.co.uk

This paperback edition 2017

First published in Great Britain in ebook format by
HarperCollins*Publishers* 2017

A catalogue record for this book
is available from the British Library

ISBN: 9780008216542

Set in Birka by
Palimpsest Book Production Limited, Falkirk, Stirlingshire

Printed and bound in the UK

For Gracie – you are the most precious thing in my whole world. Never give up on your dreams. You can achieve anything you want and I will always be right here beside you, believing in you.

And for Craig – thank you for working so hard and making it possible for me to take the time out to study and to write. Without your support, I wouldn't have had the chance to follow my dreams.

I love you both xx

PART ONE:

The First Trimester

Chapter 1

Ellie

'Come on, Ellie, how long are you going to be in there?'

'I'll be out in a minute,' she called back, pulling some toilet paper off the holder so that it made a noise and sounded authentic. She pulled her long blonde hair back into a ponytail so that it was off her neck – she was so hot, it made her feel sick.

'You've been in there ages, is everything okay?'

She had a little laugh to herself. Not because it was funny, more because she actually couldn't believe what she was doing. If someone had said to her years, even weeks, ago that this is what she would be doing on a Friday in November, she would have laughed in their face and told them not to be so stupid.

Yet, here she was. Locked in a bathroom at the hotel she was staying in for the photoshoot job she was on. The subtle cream walls were splashed with various shades of mocha, which did nothing but accentuate the sheer grandeur of the place. It was one of those places that had posh handwash and moisturiser for every basin – a far jump from Ellie's tiny flat in the centre of London, in which her bathroom rarely had a towel to dry her hands, let alone moisturiser.

She had hoped that it would have been at least another five minutes until Jenni, the photoshoot manager, noticed she was missing, though. Who was she kidding? People don't just forget that there is a make-up artist on set. 'Everything's fine. I'm just ... um ...' she frantically looked around the bathroom for inspiration and spotted some tweezers on the windowsill, 'plucking my eyebrows!' She creased her face as she cringed at her terrible attempt of lying.

'What? Why have you locked the door if you're just plucking your eyebrows? I've got Suzie out here waiting for her make-up for the photoshoot and you've picked now to lock yourself in a bathroom to pluck your eyebrows? I pay you to do other people's make-up, not sort your own face out!'

'I know, I'm ... uh ... doing it whilst I'm on the toilet – I must've eaten something dodgy.' She really was clutching at straws now. This is what her life had come to. She felt stupid but she had to do this. There was no other time and she couldn't face another day tearing herself apart inside with the constant worry and wondering about what the hell was going on – it had taken over her life. Yeah, sure, she could have done this at home, but she acted on impulse this morning at the chemist – her bag had felt like a lead weight ever since. She needed to just get rid of it and do it.

She heard Jenni exhale impatiently outside the door and stomp off. She listened to her footsteps quieten and then, finally, a door slammed.

'Eyebrows?' she said to herself and laughed. 'Bloody

plucking my eyebrows?' She looked up to the ceiling aghast and threw her hands up to her head to rub her cheeks.

Finally she turned her attention back to the task in hand; still another minute to go. This was the longest two minutes of her life. She should be out there, doing Suzie's make-up, laughing and joking on set and doing what she did best. She had been a make-up artist for about eight years now and she absolutely loved her job. The buzz she got from working with the models and photographers on set to help create some really beautiful masterpieces was pure indulgence. She could remember spending hours as a child, doing her own make-up with her mum's stash. Her and Zoe, who was three years older, would sneak into their mum's bedroom and take all her best make-up to practise with. The trouble they got into when Ellie once used their mum's MAC make-up to make Zoe look like a clown for her ninth birthday party. Their mum had thought Ellie used face paint and was full of praise and showing off about how talented her six-year-old was, and then she realised when she saw the lipstick barrel lying on the side, tip squashed down into mush from the pressure applied to create the crimson circles on Zoe's cheeks. The girls had joked that their mum's face went the same colour. She had her pocket money removed that week and she never used her mum's make-up again. That was when she started buying her own and Zoe was the perfect model to practise on. And now she got to do it for real, every day. Although she saved the clown faces for special occasions. And then there was art class at school. Ellie wasn't a grade-A student, but in art she totally aced it. When Zoe was bringing home straight A's in every subject and making their parents proud as punch, Ellie was bringing home an array of C's and D's and making their parents exhale in frustration that she *'wasn't more like Zoe.'* They didn't even acknowledge the A* in art because it wasn't a subject that they saw would get her anywhere in life.

Well, who's laughing now?

Her phone chimed to indicate a message and she swiped it up quickly for something to do with her hands. Minimising the stopwatch, she opened the message.

Hey. Sorry I haven't been in touch recently. I was just a bit freaked out about what happened between us that night.

You're not the only one, she thought as she scrolled down.

I don't want things to change between us. Are we OK?

She felt a strange feeling in her stomach as she read Chris's message. She had known Chris practically all her life. They'd grown up together on the same street and became firm friends at the tender age of six when Ellie stood up for Chris against some older boys, who were picking on him for having ginger hair. 'I like your hair,' she would often say to him. But that didn't stand up against the nasty taunts of *ginge* and *carrot top* that he frequently got from others. Not that he had that problem nowadays. His hair had darkened into a nice deep red as he grew older and it was actually shaved now anyway.

He had certainly grown into a gorgeous man, but they had stayed firm friends – most of the time. They occasionally strayed into dangerous territory, especially where drink was involved.

Throughout high school and starting their own careers, Chris and Ellie still hung out together and were regulars in each other's lives. Their friendship was on a completely different level to any other friendship she had, or probably ever would. The closeness between them would challenge a married couple of twenty years, yet that was all they ever remained as: friends. Because they didn't work as anything else.

Which made what happened the other night even worse. They should never have slept together again. They said after the last time that they wouldn't do it again because it was starting to affect their friendship. Being friends with benefits was a good laugh, but it made things complicated. She had watched him fall in love and have his heart broken – which had broken her own heart a little bit, too. Watching him fall deeper into despair and not being able to stop him. It had taken him years to get over what Chloe had done to him and Ellie had not wasted any time in making sure that that bitch knew exactly where she stood on the matter.

But what with a few too many Sambucas and a killer new dress that she'd bought, which clung to all the right places around her sleek, well-toned body, one thing had led to another and they'd found themselves in a hotel room at the function they had been at. She woke up the next day, frustrated at giving in to Chris again, so being the idiot that she was, she had just left. Just like that. She knew things were bad when he didn't contact her for a bit, but she had left it too long and then it became a *thing*. She tried so hard to not make a big deal out of it that, as a result of her being so blasé, she *did* make it a thing. Then she was too far in and couldn't come back from it. It was a weird feeling because up until then, any problems she'd ever had, she'd always gone straight to Chris. Problems in the male department – call Chris. Problems at work – call Chris. Bad period pains and she needed (yes, *needed*) chocolate ice cream at 11pm – yep, you got it, call Chris. And he was always there. Always. Never asking questions. Good old reliable Chris. They always came back from their awkwardness after sleeping together, but this time she felt different. She felt really emotional about it all and that fact alone pissed her off – she didn't *do* emotion.

So why was it so hard to talk to him now? She typed a response and pressed send.

Don't be silly, I didn't even notice. Been so busy with work and stuff.

That was a lie. She had thought about it. She thought of nothing else. A reply beeped back almost instantly.

Good. I don't want things to change between us, so don't go all weird on me now. We agreed – remember!

He added a geeky smiley. It did make her smile.

Oh please, don't flatter yourself. Now go away I'm working!

She went to press send, but hesitated. She went back into the message and added a kiss. Nodding to herself, she went to press send again but decided last minute to delete the kiss. Exhaling with frustration she added the kiss and pressed the send icon. Since when did she agonise over what to text him?

She got thumbs up in return. That was it. No kiss. But did it matter? She didn't know any more. Because as much as she wanted to act fine, she wasn't fine. It *had* made things weird. And she was about to find out why.

Her phone started beeping again and it was a split second before she realised it wasn't another text but the alarm. It was time.

She walked over to the windowsill on the other side of the bathroom and turned the white stick over.

'Shit,' she whispered, and began to cry.

* * * * *

Pippa

'The usual, Pip?'

Pippa shook her head as she took out her purse from the floral Cath Kidston bag she wore over one shoulder. 'No, I'm off the caffeine now. I'll take a decaf tea with soya milk, please.'

She paused as she saw Zoe's face in response to her request. 'What?'

'Decaf ... with soya? What's the reasoning?'

'I don't have to have a reason for trying something new, do I?' She pulled her deep-brown plait over her shoulder and began to play with the end, purely for something to do with her hands.

Zoe looked at her suspiciously and Pippa found it hard to keep the smile hidden that was already creeping across her face. The two women stood for a couple of minutes looking at each other, neither one of them wanting to be the first to break the stare. Pippa, with the smile creeping ever so slowly over her lips and Zoe, keeping her hard stare of suspicion.

Eventually Pippa cracked. 'Okay, fine. I am watching what I eat from now on.' She gave her that snippet, but that was all. She released the smile – she was enjoying this tease. The excitement was bubbling in the pit of her stomach, ready to explode from her in a torrent of words and squeals. But not yet, she needed to keep her cool and wait for the right moment.

'And why would you be doing that?' Zoe asked, and Pippa saw the corners of her mouth starting to turn up. She knew. She had blatantly guessed.

'Why do you think?'

'You're not?'

'Not what?'

'Stop it, you know what I mean!' Zoe was springing up and down on her feet like an excitable five-year-old that had just been told they were flying to Disneyland, her choppy blonde bob bouncing around her face.

Pippa squeaked and nodded.

'Oh my God, you're pregnant?' Zoe shouted, throwing her arms up and slapping them down onto her head.

Pippa immediately shushed her and looked around at the café full of customers. Laughing, she said, 'Alright, the whole world doesn't want to know.'

'Eeek! Pip!' Zoe rushed around from behind the counter and practically jumped into Pippa's arms. She squeezed her tight, squealing constantly in her ear. 'This is amazing news! When did you find out?'

'This morning. I did the test this morning and it was positive!'

'Have you told Jason? What did he say?'

Pippa opened her mouth to speak but Zoe held her hand up to silence her. 'Hang on, let me get you your drink and a chair and you can tell me all about it.' She rushed back behind the counter and set about making the tea. 'Oh shit,' she said as she fished the teabag out of the cup. 'That's not decaf. I tell you, I'm all over the place.' She turned to look at Pippa again and smiled. 'Pip, I'm so happy for you.'

'Thank you, I'm so happy for me too!' She really was. 'It bloody took its time but it finally happened.'

'I told you it would.' Zoe pulled the chair from the side and placed it up against the serving hatch. 'Sit here so you can tell me everything.'

Pippa gratefully took the chair and placed her bag down beside her. 'I know you did, but it was just taking so long, I really thought it was never going to happen for us. No amount of planning, sex scheduling, positioning, reading ... nothing was working.'

'Well no, I don't suppose reading would help to make a baby, Pip. You have to actually do the deed, not have your nose stuck inside a book. Unless you did it from behind, I suppose ...'

'Zoe! You know what I mean. I must've read like a million books about conceiving and tips to conceive and *how* to conceive ...'

'Again, sex pretty much does that job.'

'Well, you would think, but Jason and I were at it like rabbits at one point and it still never happened.' She became very aware of the elderly woman sitting on the table just to the left of her who had looked up at the mention of 'at it like rabbits' and seemed a little embarrassed. 'Sorry,' Pippa added, and turned back to Zoe, lowering her voice. 'I actually think we had sex nearly ten times one day.'

Zoe passed her the tea over the counter and creased her brow. 'Nearly?'

'Well, it kind of slipped in but the door went so we had to stop.' She glanced over her shoulder at the lady, who had decided enough was enough and was getting up to leave. 'Oh, I'm sorry; I didn't mean to put you off your food.'

The lady shook her head and left, muttering something about kids these days...

'Cheers, you're now costing me customers, thanks to your potty mouth.' Pippa began to apologise again but quickly realised Zoe was far from being serious. 'So, have you told Jason? What did he say? Is he as excited as you are?'

'I haven't told him yet. Look, I've got this.' She pulled a card out of her bag.

'Surprise!' Zoe read the swirly lettering that embossed the front of the card. Opening it she smiled, saying 'You're going to be a Daddy.'

'Isn't it lovely? Do you think he'll like it?'

'He bloody better! Couldn't you just, you know, ring him and tell him the good news?'

'No! I've waited seven years for this moment.'

'And how long have you had the card for?' Zoe smiled at her and Pippa felt embarrassed that they both knew what kind of answer she was going to give.

'About six years.'

Zoe laughed again and cut a slice of Bakewell tart from the counter. 'Here, you nutter, have this. It was made with love by a very special person.' She winked at her.

'Flattery will get you nowhere. Which reminds me, I've made a coffee and walnut cake in addition to your order this week as I had a load of walnuts left over from that wedding cake I made.'

'Amazing! I love coffee and walnut cake – can we just add that to the regular order anyway?'

'No problem, I'll drop it all in tomorrow afternoon as I've got doctors first thing. Have you got enough stuff to tide you over?' She looked into the display cabinet at the nearly empty containers that normally housed her cakes and pastries.

'Yeah, should be okay. I've still got some Victoria sponge out the back, too.' She pushed the plate with the Bakewell on it over the counter. 'Anyway, enough of work. Eat!'

'Oh no, I can't. I really need to watch what I eat from now on.' She slid the plate back towards her friend.

'Oh behave! It's a slice of cake and we are celebrating! You can be all strict with your food after you've had the baby, when you're trying to shift the baby weight.'

'Well, if we're celebrating, where's your slice?'

'That, Pip, is a good question.' She cut herself a piece. 'Oh my goodness, do you know what I just thought?'

Pippa looked at her with suspicion, 'What?' she asked, cautiously.

'Now that you are expecting, you can come to the mums' meetings here!'

Pippa smiled, feeling warm inside. Zoe didn't realise how long she had waited to hear those words. 'You're right. When do I start?' She couldn't hide the grin from her face.

'As soon as you are ready, my love.' Zoe shuffled behind the counter, 'Cheers,' she said, holding up her slice. 'To baby Pip!'

Pippa smiled as a warm, fuzzy feeling drizzled through her body. She tapped her cake with Zoe's. 'To baby Pip!'

* * * * *

Imogen

'Miss, can I get the paint out?'

Imogen snapped her attention to the little blond boy staring up at her from the table and realised she had been completely daydreaming. She glanced over to the class teacher, who was teaching phonics to some children on the carpet.

'When Mrs Anderson has finished her sounds, we will get the paint out. Let's wait for the others so they can join in, yes?'

The little boy ran off without even acknowledging their conversation.

A wave of nausea started to build up from Imogen's stomach and she felt the sweat begin to bead over her forehead. She needed to get to a bathroom, and quick! She tried to discreetly get Mrs Anderson's attention, but it failed and she soon found herself in a position she would never want to be in again, where she had no choice but to run out of the classroom with no warning whatsoever to the class teacher. She practically skidded around the corner of the corridor at the end of the hall, where she sprung into the staff toilets just in time to reach the toilet bowl. A tirade of mixed feelings erupted as she vomited. She took a moment to compose herself afterwards – and to make sure there wasn't any more – before standing to look at her reflection in the mirror.

She looked a mess. Whilst her wavy, light-brown hair was still in the ponytail she had placed it in just a couple of hours previously, there were numerous straggly sections that had dropped out around her face and were now stuck to her cheeks with the sweat from the hot flush she had just seconds before the vomiting started. Her eyes were red and bloodshot and her eyeliner had bled slightly into the fine lines around the edges of her eyes. Sporting a look that was a cross between someone who had just finished a marathon and a gothic clown, she spent a few minutes sorting her appearance before making her way back to the classroom.

'Mrs Anderson, she's back!' little Becca screeched as Imogen walked into the room.

Mrs Anderson came over to her, immediately looking worried and, if she was honest, a little pissed off. 'Everything okay?' she asked, cautiously eyeing her up and down.

'Yes, sorry. I just felt really sick all of a sudden.' She put her hands onto her hips to help convince her that she was okay.

Mrs Anderson eyed her up and down before saying, 'You don't look too great. Do you need to go home?'

She shook her head. 'No, I'll be fine. Just need to grab some water, that's all.'

'You don't need to be a hero, we all get sick. If you need to go, then go. I don't want the whole class coming down with a bug.'

Imogen closed her eyes for a second as two little boys ran past her screaming, one of them barging into her and causing a wave of nausea to wash over her again. 'I can't, you need me in here. There's no one to cover. I'll be fine, honest. I just need some water.' She felt another surge of acid in the back of her throat and frantically swallowed to hold it back.

'Imogen, that's not your problem. You can't help being ill. We can pull in another assistant from somewhere, just let Mr ...' It was too late. She had to run again. This was not a good feeling, she thought to herself, as she bolted back into the toilet. After round two had finished she admitted defeat and went home.

Walking through the front door and throwing her keys down into the bowl, she slumped onto the sofa and picked up her phone, pulling up Alice's number.

Had to come home, been sick twice this morning already.

Alice almost immediately called her back. 'What's wrong?'

'I was fine when I got up but I've been sick twice at work.' Just the thought of it made her stomach churn.

'Really?' The excitement in Alice's voice did not go missed. 'Well, that's great news!'

'Thanks. Glad to see my misery is causing you so much happiness.' She let out a feeble laugh and immediately stopped because of the feeling it gave her in her stomach.

'Sorry, baby, but you know what I mean. This could be it!'

Imogen shook her head. 'No, don't do that.'

'What?'

'Don't go getting your hopes up again. Not like last time.' The painful memories of previous attempts of checking and every time it being negative swam around her brain, making it feel cloudy.

'Oh come on. This is different. You don't normally feel sick, let alone actually be sick. This could be our month! Oh my God, I'm so excited. Have you done the test yet?'

'No.'

'What? Come on, don't be silly. Just do it already. You were going to do it tomorrow anyway, what's a day early?'

'Don't you want me to wait until you get home?'

'No way! It's 10.30 in the morning; I'll never be able to concentrate all day knowing this. Come on, just do it. It's in the cupboard.'

Imogen stood up, but immediately sat back down as a

wave of sickness began to descend again. 'Fine, I'll call you back.'

'Make sure you do. I've got a meeting in about fifteen minutes so I'm timing it. You've got ten minutes. Go!'

Imogen laughed. 'Okay, fine. Bye.'

'Love you! Bye!'

Imogen hung up with a little giggle to herself. She absolutely loved how excited Alice was. She always got so passionate about things, that's why Imogen fell in love with her.

Their relationship hadn't been an easy ride. Imogen's parents were not exactly supportive when she told them she was gay. Actually, unsupportive is probably an understatement. Imogen's mum cried. She cried for about two weeks every time she saw them. First they were tears of anger – although Imogen never quite understood why she was angry – and then tears of sadness.

'I'm never going to have grandchildren,' her mum would wail every time it was brought up. Which was a really silly way to look at things, but she had supposed that it was just her mum's way of dealing with the shock of it all. But no, things just continued to get worse. It went from never having grandchildren, to never going to her daughter's wedding – which she didn't – to 'what will the neighbours say?' It broke Imogen's heart to see her mother so distraught but equally, it made her angry, too. She wanted her family to be more like Alice's. Alice's parents embraced her sexuality and had been like surrogate parents to Imogen. They were truly amazing people and Imogen was glad to have that positivity in her life when there were already so many negative people trying to inflict upset on them. Like their neighbours, who insisted on shooting them disgusted looks every time they went out together.

Alice's view was very much *just let them get on with it*. She was an incredibly strong person, who didn't take any crap from anyone. Whereas Imogen was a worrier. She cared what people thought and what they said. Which was the sole reason it took her so long to eventually come out. She tried to act as if people's comments didn't bother her, but they did. A lot.

Thank God she had Alice. Her rock.

She pulled the test out of the shiny white bathroom cabinet and opened it up. She didn't need to read the instructions; it wasn't as though this was the first time she had done one of these.

She sat on the toilet and took a deep breath. 'Here goes,' she whispered, praying for a miracle. She wasn't sure she could handle another negative.

Chapter 2

'Ellie, what are you doing here?'

Zoe whipped her sister into a huge, warm embrace and Ellie instantly felt the urge to cry. She had held onto the emotion for the whole three-hour drive it had taken to get to her sister's café, but the second she had wrapped her arms around her, tears rapidly filled her eyes...

'Just wanted to see my sister, that's all,' she croaked, knowing full well that this line was not going to work on her.

Zoe pulled away from Ellie, looking at her in a way clearly indicating that she didn't buy the story. She still had her hands on Ellie's shoulders when she added, 'Really, Els, what's up?'

'I just needed to get away.'

She didn't need to say any more. Zoe smiled at her – you know, the kind of smile that said *Okay, you don't want to talk, that's fine* – and ushered her into the kitchen at the back of the café. 'Here, sit down and I'll make you a cuppa.'

Ellie took the proffered stool and instantly felt a rush of relief. Everything was going to be okay. She was here, her big sister would help her and everything would be okay. Zoe and Ellie's relationship was a close one. They hadn't been particularly close growing up, but once they got into their teens, their closeness began to grow. And when Zoe decided to fly the nest, she did it properly and moved what felt like a million miles away to Shropshire. It broke Ellie's heart, not that she showed it, and even though they spoke on the phone pretty much every day, she missed having her big sister just around the corner. When Ellie had flown the nest, she'd moved a hundred yards down the road from their family home. Whilst she was adventurous in the sense that she pursued her career as a make-up artist, slaving away for pretty much no money for hours every day just to get experience until she qualified, she still liked to be close to the family home. When their mum died, nearly ten years ago now, Ellie fell apart. Zoe had come back home to London – it had only been a few months since she had moved to Shropshire – and picked up all the pieces whilst Ellie went off the rails a little. Not a fact she was proud of but she needed to do it. It was her way of coping. Being the older sister had its unwritten responsibilities and Zoe stepped up whilst Ellie crumbled. But Ellie never forgave herself for that.

Yet, here she was again – running to Zoe to help pick up the pieces. She would never match up to her perfect sister, so why bother trying?

'So, come on. You clearly haven't driven 170-odd miles just to have a cuppa with me. What's going on?'

'Nothing major. Just needed a break and I figured I haven't seen you for a few months and it was time I came to you.' She shrugged to add effect to the *I'm fine, what's the big deal* persona she had created the second she entered the café.

Zoe didn't buy it, but instead of grilling her, she just

said, 'Hmm, fair enough. How long are you here for?'

Ellie hadn't thought that far ahead. When she saw the little pink line on the test, she'd panicked. She hadn't even said anything to the director of the shoot she was on, just grabbed her stuff and left. She had numerous calls on her phone throughout the car journey here and a few stroppy voicemails too. This was not going to be good for her reputation. But she didn't know what else to do. She couldn't run to her dad for help, he would go mad at her. Ellie was ever the disappointment to him. She was nothing like his Zoe. 'Why can't you be more like your sister,' he would throw at her in the years following their mum's death. Because Zoe, whilst she mourned, took it as a springboard and catapulted herself into work, opening up the café and making it a success. Whereas Ellie struggled to stick at a job and then decided to take up being a make-up artist – much to the dismay of her father. Their relationship broke down and she barely spoke to him now.

And normally, in a situation like this, she would go to Chris for advice. But that was off the table, too.

So here she was. In Shropshire and indirectly calling out to Zoe for help. She just needed to pluck up the courage to actually tell her.

'I don't know yet. I've taken a little break from work and I thought I'd come and explore the countryside. See what all the fuss is about!' she smiled at Zoe, a big fat fake one, and sipped the tea. 'Ah man, Zoe, you do seriously make a wicked cup of tea. I've missed these!'

'Why, thank you. Do you know what you're missing, though?'

Ellie shook her head.

'A slice of cake. Bakewell or Victoria sponge?'

Ellie thought for a second; there was only one reply to this question at a time like this. 'Both.'

* * * * *

Pippa had just finished boxing up all the cakes for tomorrow's delivery to Zoe when Jason walked in the front door. She jumped in surprise at the sound of the door slamming and knocked a box of cupcakes onto the floor.

'Damn it!' she cursed, hurriedly picking them up and inspecting the damage. 'Great!' All but one cupcake out of the box of twelve, had split open, causing a frosting crime scene. She dumped the box on the side and grabbed a bowl from the cupboard. She could whip up a batch of cupcakes with her eyes closed, but she had looked forward to having a sit-down after her hectic day today, she was so tired. In all the pregnancy books she had read – which was a lot – right about now the baby would be the size of a lentil – how was something that small making her feel so shattered?

Jason strolled past the kitchen door without even popping his head in to say hello. Pippa knew instinctively that this must mean he hadn't had a good day at work. She glanced at the clock; he wasn't due home for another hour yet. She placed the bowl down onto the side and made her way into the living room.

'Hi honey, you're home early?' He was slumped on the sofa, already flicking through the channels. He didn't answer. She walked over to him and sat down next to him, placing a hand on his knee. He wasn't a big man but, at the same time, he wasn't slim. But that's what Pippa had always loved about him, having a bit of meat to hold onto. Except that recently he had started to lose weight. Not enough to change his appearance massively, but enough to be noticeable. She knew he had been stressed at work lately because his whole attitude had started to be short and distance. And now it was clearly having an effect on his weight. 'Everything okay?'

'Fine,' was his reply. He didn't move to indicate he had felt her hand.

'What's happened?' She tried not to take his bad mood personally, but she couldn't help it. His sharpness stabbed at her emotions like a knife and she felt the tears prickle behind her eyes as frustration showed its face.

He exhaled impatiently and stood up. 'Just a bad day.'

'Well, talk to me. I'm your wife, that's what I'm here for.' Same argument, different day.

He turned to look at her in frustration, hands brushing through his short, cropped brown hair. 'Why? You're hardly going to be able to help me. I come home to chill out, not bring my work home and spend hours talking about it. See, this is what you don't understand. You skip off every day to your silly little job baking cakes and talking to women when I'm at work slogging my guts out to bring home a decent wage. This house, the bills ... those clothes you're wearing. It's all because of *my* job. *My* hard work. So when I've had a bad day, the least you can do is let me chill out and not annoy the hell out of me!'

'Jason ...' she started to talk but the tears had now filled her eyes and she hiccupped as one rolled down her cheek.

He looked at her and for a fleeting moment she saw

irritation in his expression, before he exhaled. 'I'm sorry, it's just been a really shitty day at the office and I'd rather not talk about it.' He put his arm around her and hugged her close, stroking along her back as she snuggled into his chest. 'Come on, don't cry. I didn't mean to take it out on you. You know I don't mean all that.'

She sniffed back the tears. 'I just hate seeing you like this. Every day for the last few weeks, you've been coming home miserable.' She felt disappointment settle as she knew her whole revelation of being pregnant was not going to go as planned now. 'And you know I try my hardest to earn more. I'm trying my best and I promise I will try harder to make more money so that I can help out more. I'm getting there.' She hated this argument. They bickered regularly and every single time the argument came back to money and how she didn't contribute as much as he did. And she felt really shit about it.

'I know, I'm sorry. It's just things are pretty hectic and today Betty walked out, leaving me with no receptionist and a shed load of meetings planned for next week ...'

'Oh no!' she gasped. 'Why did she walk out?' Pippa liked Betty.

'Who knows? She said she'd had enough of being treated the way she was and that she was done. She just stood up and left. Just like that. No word of warning, no letter of resignation, just ... gone.'

'Honey, I'm sorry.' She rubbed his arm, but again, he didn't react. 'But maybe I can cheer you up?'

A smile immediately crept across his face as he sat back down on the sofa and leaned into her, sliding his hand along her thigh and nuzzling into her neck. 'No, wait, I didn't mean that,' Pippa smiled as she gently pushed him off. 'Wait here, I've got something that might make you smile.' She jumped up and ran into the kitchen, opening her handbag and rummaging for the card.

'Shall I just meet you upstairs?' he called out, innuendo screaming from his comment.

'No, wait there. I'm coming.' She grabbed the card and in one swift movement, slid it behind her back to hide. She walked into the living room with the biggest smile plastered across her cheeks. She couldn't wait to see his face. 'Are you ready?'

'As I'll ever be,' came the response and he held out his hands.

She placed the card into them and squeaked like a mouse as she sat down next to him again. 'Go on, open it.'

'It's not my birthday, Pip.' He eyed the card suspiciously.

'It's not a birthday card.'

He looked at her in confusion. 'Well, what is it, then?'

'Just open it and find out!'

He thumbed the envelope open and stared at the *Surprise!* text. Another glance to her with knitted eyebrows indicated just how baffled he was.

'Go on ...' she prompted. The excitement was just too much. Swarms of butterflies circled inside her tummy as the anticipation grew. Seven years she had waited for this moment. Seven years she had spent reading textbooks and looking online and planning every second of her dream pregnancy and now was the time.

He opened the card and read the words. Silence. He didn't move for what felt like minutes, though it was probably only a few seconds. Slowly he looked up at her. 'Are you serious?'

She nodded, hardly able to contain her excitement. 'Yes.'

He looked back down to the card and then placed his head in his hands. Pippa instantly switched from elation to disappointment. 'What's wrong? Aren't you happy?'

He hesitated before saying, 'Of course I am.'

'Well, it doesn't look like you are.' The tears were welling again.

He shook his head. 'I am. It's just not great timing, with everything going on at work. But it's fine, we'll get through it. It's fine.'

Pippa couldn't hide her disappointment. She took a deep breath, trying to stop the tears from falling. This wasn't how this scenario was meant to play out. In her head he had been up and screaming with elation. Jumping around, holding her tight and saying how he couldn't believe, after this many years, that he was finally about to become a daddy.

But no. He didn't do any of that. He hadn't even given her a hug. She slid along the sofa towards him and held out her arms.

'Sorry baby, come here.' He pulled her in for the cuddle she longed for but it didn't feel sincere. It felt forced, like he didn't mean it. 'We'll get through this, it'll be fine. I just need to work out what I'm going to do at work. But it'll be fine.'

But she didn't feel fine. She felt cheated. This was supposed to be their life-changing moment.

And it had fallen flat on its face.

Chapter 3

Ellie looked around the café and took it all in. She hadn't been up here for absolutely ages and was really quite impressed with how far Zoe had come. She let her eyes run over every inch as she sipped at the third cup of tea Zoe had placed in front of her now that she was sitting at a table in the corner. When Zoe had taken the café on, it was the most miserable- looking building you could imagine. Paint peeling from the walls, a dingy kitchen that needed some serious TLC and a broken window. But now, looking at it, Ellie couldn't believe how amazing it looked.

She absolutely loved the way Zoe had kept things so simple but it gave such a punch. The walls were kept an off-cream colour, but she had explosions of vibrant pinks and greens to accentuate. Light fittings, the serving hatch and bookshelves, all splashed with colour, kept the room feeling bright and exciting. There was a new addition since the last time she was here too, in the form of a little section in one corner, which housed a few shelving units and a table filled with things to purchase. Ellie stood and took a stroll over to it to browse. The shelves were full of little bits and pieces, bespoke, unique, one-of-a-kind-type objects. She chose a little figurine of two girls playing with some building blocks and was immediately transported back to being four years old and playing with Zoe. She missed those days. When had life become so complicated?

It was the teatime rush and there were swarms of people buzzing around and lining up waiting to be served. Ellie had offered to help her sister but was told, categorically, to sit down, have some more tea and relax. Thankful for the excuse to not talk about what was going on in her life, she took the chance and did as she was asked.

Weaving her way back to the table she was sitting at, Ellie took her phone out and saw that she had fourteen missed calls, two voicemails and three text messages. She was glad she had put it onto silent when she got here. She knew Jenni wouldn't let up about the job. She quickly flicked through the texts first. Nothing of interest: just two from work and one from her neighbour asking about the milkman. She led such an interesting life. Next, she scrolled the missed-call list. Pretty much what she expected. Jenni ... Jenni ... Jenni ... oh...

She looked at his name. Why had he tried to call her? Did he know? He couldn't know, she hadn't told anyone. She felt a wave of nausea creep up and swallowed it down, trying to stop the impending fear creeping up. She hesitated before clicking onto the voicemail and tentatively listening.

'*Ellie, its Jenni,*' Relief flooded her body quicker than a hot shower. '*I don't know what is going on with you today but you need to sort yourself out and call me back. I need to know whether I need a new make-up artist for the shoots I have you booked for next week. Call me as soon as you get this, please.'*

She wasn't happy. But then again, neither would Ellie be if someone she had booked for work just up and left without an explanation. She listened as her phone told her she had another new message.

'Els, it's me.' She held her breath as she listened to Chris's silky voice. *'Why aren't you answering my calls? You said you wouldn't be weird. Come on, pick up.'*

She placed her phone on the table and dropped her head into her hands, her straightened hair falling over her shoulders and brushing the tabletop. What had she got herself into?

'Well, that doesn't look like someone who is fine.'

Ellie snapped her head up to look at her sister. She laughed nervously, to buy herself some precious seconds of thinking time. 'I'm just tired after the long drive, that's all.'

Zoe placed a plate in front of Ellie that had a cheese-and-tomato panini with salad and crisps on the side. 'Maybe this will help perk you up.' She followed with a can of Coke and a straw.

'Thanks, sis.'

'No problem. Eat up and when I've shut up shop I'll take you upstairs to sort your stuff. I figure you have stuff with you ... in the car?'

Oh right, stuff. That would've come in handy 'Um ... actually ...' The thought hadn't crossed her mind until now. She didn't bring anything because she just got in the car and drove. Whereas in the past her impulsiveness had brought her many exciting adventures, sometimes it simply backfired.

'It's fine. I've got everything you'll need.' She placed a hand on Ellie's shoulder and gave it a squeeze. 'You eat up and we'll have a chat when we go upstairs. I've only got a few more bits to do, so I won't be long.'

Ellie smiled her thanks and took a bite from her panini. She wasn't looking forward to this conversation.

* * * * *

'Imogen, where are you?'

She immediately jumped up from the sofa and ran to the hallway to greet Alice. As she rounded the corner of the stairs, she saw the flowers first.

'Oh my God, where are *you?*' she joked, peering around the huge bunch of flowers to see Alice's face. 'These are humungous!'

'Only the best for my beautiful girl.' She handed the flowers to Imogen and leant in for a kiss. Imogen smiled as Alice's soft lips brushed delicately onto hers.

'They're gorgeous, Alice, thank you.' She looked at the array of pinks and green and instantly fell in love with the vibrant yellow sunflower in the centre of the arrangement.

'And I got this for me – but you can't have any, Mummy.' Alice held up the bottle of champagne and Imogen didn't care at all. Not one bit. Because she was carrying their first baby. The baby they had longed so many years for. The baby they had spent weeks crying over when the test results had showed a negative time after time.

'Guess I'll have to get used to not drinking for the next

nine months, eh?' She rolled her eyes dramatically, but really she couldn't care less about this fact.

'It's okay, I'll hold the fort and take on your drinking for you.'

'Come on, sit down. Put your feet up and I'll start the dinner.' Imogen turned to walk away when Alice shouted,

'Wait!' Imogen froze as Alice stopped her with her hand and walked back out of the front door.

'Where are you going?' She leaned forward and tried to see what she was doing. She watched Alice get another bag out of the boot of her car and return. The smell of vinegar hit her nose as she entered into the hallway and Imogen smiled. 'Chippy?'

'Well, you can't join me with the champagne, so I figured you have to celebrate somehow.'

'You, Alice, are amazing.'

'Do you think you can stomach it? How are you feeling now?'

They walked into the kitchen together and Alice grabbed two plates from the cupboard as Imogen found a home for her beautiful bouquet. 'I feel okay, it comes in waves. Let's get this down me before the next wave comes.' Imogen grabbed the ketchup and a glass for Alice's champagne whilst Alice took the food through to the dining table.

'So, how was work?' Imogen asked, delving into the chips as she spoke, their salty taste working wonders on her nausea. It had been ages since she'd eaten a takeaway. They had been trying to be super-healthy whilst trying to conceive, as the consultant had asked them to make sure everything was as good as they could make it to ensure optimum conceiving chances. So Imogen had strictly watched what and how much she ate, trying to get her body to its best so as not to cause any unnecessary problems. But how she had longed for chips from the chippy for months. And Alice knew this. So the fact she'd brought these in today simply showed Imogen the exact reason why she loved her so much. Her thoughtfulness was impeccable and it really mattered. It's the little things that mean the most and Alice was very good at getting those little things spot on.

'It was actually quite a good day. We completed some house sales and remember that house we put up last week that had been on with our rivals for months? Well, we sold it today!' She pulled her long, brown hair back into a ponytail and then continued to eat.

'You're joking! How do you do it?'

'Because we are brilliant.' Alice puffed out her chest and Imogen laughed. 'Seriously, though, that house spent months up with another agent, but we managed to sell it in four days! I'm so proud of the team.'

'That's great news. So we have a few things to celebrate, then?'

'Damn right. Have you told your mum?'

Imogen was waiting to see how long it would take her to ask. She had thought of nothing else all day. Every time she even thought of ringing her mum she felt sick – and that wasn't even the nausea. That was sheer panic. She knew exactly how her mum was going to react.

'Not yet.'

Alice leant forward and squeezed Imogen's hand. 'It'll be okay, you know that?'

She shrugged. Suddenly she wasn't hungry any more.

'Imogen, listen. Whatever happens, you will always have me, okay? I will never let you down and I am not going anywhere. This baby will have us both and it will be loved, no matter what other people want to say to us or behind our backs.'

'I know.' She did know. 'It's just hard. I know what she will say. She gets me all worked up, right under my skin. She knows what she is doing.'

'She might be fine. She's finally getting the grandchild she thought she would never have. She might surprise you and be excited.' Alice tried to put on a confident face but they both knew that was highly unlikely.

Imogen snorted. 'Yeah, and pigs might fly.'

'Come on, what's the worst that might happen?'

Imogen let all the thoughts crowd into her head. Her mum might disown her, feeling so ashamed that her daughter was having a baby with another woman that she couldn't bear to even look or talk to her any more, so she might decide to cut all ties and leave Imogen without parents, because her dad sure wouldn't stand up to her mum. Or maybe she'd get really angry and end up shouting abuse down the phone to her. Or worst still, become so upset that Imogen had been a disappointment of a daughter and not what she had *brought her up to be* as she had said on many occasions, and spend the whole time crying down the phone, making Imogen feel like the biggest regret of her mother's life.

But instead of saying all this, she simply replied, 'I guess I'm just not ready to say anything to her yet. Let's wait until we have seen the doctor and everything is okay.' She tried to avoid Alice's stare. 'Please?' she added.

'Okay, if that's what you want to do, then I'll support you.' Alice stood and slipped out of her suit jacket, revealing her perfectly formed petite body, which Imogen loved. Alice was a confident, powerful, assertive woman, wrapped up in a beautiful petite package.

'Have you told *your* mum yet?'

Alice shook her head. 'I thought we might go and visit them this weekend and tell them in person?'

Alice's parent lived about half an hour away and Imogen thought about travelling in a car whilst feeling sick, but decided that she needed to feel some support around her. Alice's parents were amazing. They were sure to be over the moon and she needed to surround herself with positivity at this moment in time. 'Sounds like a great idea.'

'Great, I'll call after dinner to see when they're free.'

'Okay and we need to call the clinic. Tell them we've had a positive test.'

Alice laughed and shook her head.

'What?' Imogen couldn't help but smile along, even though she had no idea what Alice was smiling at.

'I just can't believe it, Imogen. We are going to be parents!'

Chapter 4

'Okay, so you've been here about six hours. We've spoken about my work, your work, Dad, my new boyfriend and all the latest soaps we've both watched over the last week.' Zoe was staring at her and Ellie struggled to keep the eye contact. She knew this was coming. She knew she would have to speak to Zoe and tell her what was happening, but she just didn't want to. It wasn't that she didn't want to speak to Zoe; she didn't want to speak to *anyone*. She wanted to curl up in a ball and pretend this wasn't happening.

But it was.

'Come on, spill. What's the real reason you are here?'

'What? I can't just rock up and spend time with my sister every once in a while?' Ellie played the hurt-sister card but it was having zero effect on Zoe and she simply stuck with her hard stare and disbelief. 'Okay, fine,' Ellie conceded, 'I need your help.'

'Okay, and what exactly do you need help with? Money?'

'No! When have I ever asked you for money?' She was offended that her sister thought she would drive all this way just to ask her for money. Plus, she made good money now that she was doing higher-profile jobs with her make-up. Although that probably wasn't set to last now. Not once word got around that she was unreliable and would just stroll off set whenever she felt like it. She made a mental note to make sure she rang Jenni this weekend to try to repair some of the damage to her reputation before it plummeted.

'Well, what, then?'

She hesitated and tried to think of a way to word it. How could she tell her sister not only that she was pregnant but who the dad was? She was never going to believe her. And then all the questions would start and Ellie wasn't even sure she knew the answers.

'Are you in some sort of trouble?' Zoe looked worried.

'No, well, not exactly.' She exhaled, 'Kind of.'

'Okay, whatever it is, we can sort it, okay? It will be fine. But you need to tell me what's happening – I can't help you if you don't tell me.' Ellie felt a twinge of irritation at the way Zoe was speaking, as if she was her mum. Whilst it was nice to have Zoe to turn to, when she spoke like that it only reminded Ellie that her mum wasn't there. And no one could fill that gap, no matter how much Zoe tried.

She threw her hands up and dropped them down into her lap with a *here goes* gesture and said, 'I'm pregnant.'

There, she had said it. It was the first time she had said it, too. Out loud. She had been over this conversation a million times in her head as she made the long car journey to the café, but as soon as those words came rushing out of her mouth, she felt the uncontrollable urge to burst into tears. Whether it was sadness or relief that she had told someone who could help her, but her eyes filled with gloom and she let the one tear fall over the edge and escape down her cheek. 'I'm sorry,' she added as an afterthought, although she didn't know why she was apologising.

'Oh, Els, don't be sorry!' Zoe immediately jumped up from the other end of the sofa in the flat above the café where Zoe lived and was right by her side, arms around her and rubbing her back as Ellie began to sob. 'Why didn't you tell me sooner? You don't have to keep something like this bottled up. How long have you known?'

'I only found out this morning,' she mumbled into Zoe's shoulder.

'Wow, okay.' Zoe squeezed her harder as she continued to sob. 'Come on, it's going to be okay. You can do this.'

Ellie pulled back in surprise. 'What do you mean, I can do this? How am I going to do this? I'm not ready to be a mum. I've got my career; my flat is too small to have a baby ... Zoe, I'm not even in a relationship!' Sheer panic was rising fast inside her chest and she realised that she hadn't actually thought of any of this until just now.

'Ellie,' she pulled her back and looked straight into her eyes. 'It will be okay. I promise.'

She nodded to show that she had heard her, not that she agreed with her.

'Now, take a deep breath and calm down.'

She did as she was asked and, actually, once she pushed aside the impending feeling of dread, she actually felt a little relieved to have got it off her chest. She was no longer alone in this battle. She had Zoe and she would help her. She had to.

'Now, first things first.' Zoe stood up and went to the kettle. 'A nice cuppa and a choccie biscuit sorts out everything.' Zoe then threw over a box of tissues, which landed on the sofa next to Ellie. 'And wipe your eyes; we are going to sort this out together. Okay?'

She nodded and grabbed a tissue.

'Oh wait!' Ellie snapped her head up to look at Zoe, startled by the sudden increase in volume in Zoe's voice. 'Whose is it, then?'

'What?' Ellie replied, buying herself yet more time.

'Whose is it, if you aren't in a relationship at the moment?'

Ellie shook her head and dropped eye contact. How could she tell her who the baby's dad was? Whilst Ellie and Zoe were close, no one really knew the kind of relationship she and Chris had. It had worked for them for years. But people wouldn't understand, especially her sister, who knew Chris very well.

'Do I know him? I do, don't I?' Zoe's face lit up. 'Oh my God, is it that guy you were seeing from the film?'

Ellie creased her face in disgust. 'God, no! He was nice to look at but he was lousy in bed.'

'Being lousy doesn't stop you getting pregnant, though.'

'That's true.' Ellie drew another tissue from the box and wiped her face dry. She had not cried this much for years. She didn't do crying. It was weak. And she wasn't weak. Although she felt it at times, she couldn't let her outer self show this. When people saw you were weak, they took advantage of that and she wasn't one to be taken advantage of. It was her against the world – with Zoe, of course. But they lived so far apart,

Ellie felt alone a lot of the time, especially since their dad was not interested in her or anything she did. Unless she was Zoe, she couldn't live up to what he wanted from her. So it was easier to just let go and get on with her life. She didn't need him. She didn't need anyone.

'Was it that guy you started seeing a few months ago, the guy Chris set you up with from the pub?'

She tensed at hearing his name. Ellie remembered her dates with that guy; he had clearly stated he wanted nothing but fun and being annoyed at Chris for whatever reason it was at that time, she had agreed. But she found herself unable to go through with the type of relationship he wanted and ended it. It was only a matter of weeks after that that she and Chris had slept together again.

'So ...' Zoe held out her hands, waiting for a reply.

'Nope, not him.'

'Oh come on, why won't you tell me?' She slammed her hands on the sofa in frustration, briefly showing a more immature side.

'Okay, fine. But I don't want any comments.' Ellie pointed at her sister, warning her.

'Why would I make a comment?'

'Because I know you and I know what you will say.'

'I promise I won't make a comment.' She froze, expectantly waiting for Ellie to speak.

'It's Chris.'

Zoe gasped and then clamped her hand over her mouth.

'You said you wouldn't say anything!'

Ellie watched as Zoe frantically shook her head, still keeping her hand tight over her mouth. It was as if she was desperately holding in the words that wanted to spill out of her mouth. Ellie could see the smile that was splayed across her face, even behind her hand.

They stood there in silence for a minute and then Ellie added. 'Okay, fine. I can't stand the silence. Just say something.'

Zoe dropped her hand and revealed the warmest, biggest smile. 'Els, this is amazing!'

'How's that now?' She knew Zoe would react like this. That's why she didn't want to tell her. She didn't want this to cloud her judgement about what she should do next.

'Because, it's Chris! He is going to be the best dad! You're like, best friends!'

'I know; that's why this is so weird! It's Chris, for God's sake. We don't do things like having a baby! We are supposed to be out, getting drunk, eating junk food and watching reruns of *Friends* until 4am.' She felt a tingle inside as she relived it – the number of Saturday nights they spent doing exactly that.

'That's a good point, how did this happen?' Zoe walked back to the sofa and plonked herself down next to Ellie, bringing her legs up and crossing them underneath her as if she was about to get some really juicy gossip. Which, to be fair, she probably was.

Ellie skipped past the fact that they had done the whole sex thing a few times now and just referred to the latest time – which Zoe clearly thought was a one-off. 'He came with me to a product-launch night I was invited to go to a couple of months ago. It was a free bar, we had too much to drink, I had bought a new dress ... you get the gist.'

'This is crazy. What does he say about it all?' Ellie looked at her sister and pulled a face. 'You haven't told him? Ellie!' She playfully pushed her arm as she berated her.

'What? I panicked and I literally jumped in the car and drove here.' Great, now she was feeling guilty as well as emotional and very, very tired.

'So he doesn't even know? You have to tell him.'

'What? No!' The panic was back. 'Zoe, I can't just call him up and say hey, you know that night we shagged, well, turns out I'm pregnant!' She rolled her eyes. 'Imagine what he would do. Imagine what he would say! He'd run a bloody mile!'

'Would he, though? Ellie, that guy loves you to pieces.'

She shook her head. 'No, he doesn't, not like that.'

'He bloody does. You two are perfect for each other; you're both just too bloody stubborn to admit it!'

'That's not true.'

'Oh whatever. Fact is, you are pregnant and you *do* have to tell him.'

She knew Zoe was right. But she wasn't about to admit that to her face. She just needed some time to figure out what the hell was she going to do next?

Chapter 5

The little bell above the door of the café tinkled as Pippa walked through, armed with numerous boxes – and many more in the van outside. She was greeted by Zoe as she quickly ran over to swipe the boxes from her clutches. 'Should you be carrying all this yourself, Pip?' Zoe manoeuvred the shop floor with ease, winding in and out of the tables with her tiny frame and long legs, boxes balanced high.

'Zoe, I'm pregnant, not ill. I think I can manage a few cake boxes.' She laughed at her friend's concern and retrieved more boxes from the back of her little van.

'Here, take a seat. I want to talk to you about something.'

Pippa handed over the final few boxes and sat down at the counter. 'Everything okay?'

She watched Zoe as she looked over her shoulder, back into the kitchen, and then leant in to say in a quiet voice. 'My sister turned up yesterday.'

'Oh, that's nice. Did you know she was coming?' She took in the whispering and constant checking over her shoulder that Zoe was doing and added, 'Are you afraid the FBI are following you?'

'What? No! I don't want Ellie to hear me.'

Pippa laughed. 'Okay. So why is your sister visiting a big secret?'

'It's not a secret, but she will go mad if she thinks I'm talking about her.'

Pippa watched as Zoe set about slicing the cakes she had just delivered and put them out on display. 'You want me to help slice? Then you can tell me whatever it is that's got you acting so weird.' She stood and joined Zoe on the other side, pulling a lemon meringue from its box and slicing through the vibrant-yellow creation. It was actually quite therapeutic watching the blade slowly drag through the mixture, forming straight lines of perfection. 'So how long is your sister here for? Is she okay?'

'Not really. She's got herself into a bit of a situation and she wants me to help. But I just don't know what to do for the best.'

'Well, what's the situation? Maybe I can help.' She was willing to do anything that would take her mind off what was going on at home. Jason had still been acting weird when he got up for work this morning and left without even saying goodbye. Announcing her pregnancy – that the two of them had waited so long for – should be such an exciting time. Yet she couldn't help but feel Jason was more upset than elated. She had spent hours last night after Jason went to bed scouring the internet, looking for ways to increase her business potential and bring in more money, but the thought that the baby would be here in less than a year was constantly biting away at the back of her mind.

'She's just found out she's pregnant.'

'Oh wow! That's great news. There must be something in the water, eh!' Pippa laughed but immediately sensed that Zoe wasn't in the mood for jokes. 'You're not happy she's pregnant?'

'It's not that! I'm over the bloody moon. I'm going to be an aunty, it's amazing.'

'So, what's wrong?'

Zoe put down the knife she was using to cut the brownies and exhaled agitatedly. 'I don't know if she is going to keep it.'

Pippa felt as if she had been punched in the stomach. The wind was temporarily knocked out of her and she tried her best to not show how devastating those words were to her. As someone who had tried for a baby for so many years and struggled so much to conceive, the thought of someone terminating a pregnancy just like that was haunting. But this was Zoe's sister and she needed to be supportive and non-judgemental. 'Wow, that is a huge decision. What makes you think that – did she actually say she wants to get rid of it?'

'Yeah, she's terrified. She's clearly panicking and not realising what she's saying. I know my sister and I know how she deals with things when times get hard, and I'm just so worried she is going to go off the rails again and do something stupid. You see, the guy whose baby it is, Chris, he's such a nice guy! He and Ellie have been best friends ever since I can remember. Growing up they were always together – like two peas in a pod.'

'So, are they together?'

Zoe shook her head. 'No, but they should be. He loves her to pieces and I know she feels the same, but they keep up this whole 'we're just friends' thing and it's stupid. Everyone around them can see how in love they are, everyone apart from them.'

'And now she's pregnant with his baby?'

'Yup! Crazy one-night stand, as far as I understand.'

'Have you tried just explaining to her what you're worried about?'

'We had the longest chat last night; she said she doesn't know what she's going to do and that she just needed time to think. That's why she's come up here, to get away from it all. Chris doesn't know yet – although I did say to her that she has to tell him – and she is *very* hormonal. This, for Ellie, isn't a good thing because she can't handle emotions. She doesn't just cry and let it all out like the rest of us do; she's like another species. She bottles it all up and it ends up having a detrimental effect on either her mind or her body. When Mum died, she completely lost it and I struggled to keep her head above the water, so to speak.' Zoe had stopped slicing now and was full-on facing Pippa, concern etched over every part of her face. 'Pip, I'm just worried she'll do something stupid and regret it for the rest of her life.'

Pippa knew exactly what Zoe was talking about and leaned over to give her just a single squeeze of her hand, just to let her know.

'I never told her about what happened to me, and I can't tell her now, it's too far down the line. But the thought of her not having this baby, it's heart-breaking. I don't know what to do to convince her to just stop and think.'

'Unfortunately, it's her decision, I'm afraid. All you can do is be there for her. I'm sure she won't do anything without thinking it through.'

Zoe gave a little laugh before saying, 'You don't know my sister.' Her head snapped round to the kitchen door as it opened.

Pippa followed her glance to the door and saw Ellie walk in. She hadn't met Ellie in person before and the first thing she noticed was her beautiful, long blonde hair cascading over her shoulder and the full face of make-up. Whilst Pippa had more of a natural look, Ellie's make- up was stunning, flawless. She oozed perfection and even with the jogging bottoms and t-shirt she was sporting, she looked glamorous. It must run in the family, as Zoe always looked chic and effortless. She wore less make-up than her sister but hers was a natural beauty and she carried it off very well.

'Morning! How are you feeling today?' Zoe chirped in her normal cheery voice that she used on everyone. Pippa was one of the only people to ever see Zoe stressed or miserable. They had been friends for some time now, but recently their friendship had become quite a close one. Zoe was opening up a lot more to Pippa and she was glad to have a friend to talk to. Not that Pippa opened up completely to anyone. If anyone knew how her home life had been more recently, they would think badly not only of Jason, but of her for staying with him. And that was more hassle than it was worth. Nobody needed to know about things at home. She knew her friends would talk her out of the marriage and now that they had a baby on the way, there was no way she was going to walk away. No matter what he did – or had done in the past. As far as anyone was concerned, she and Jason had a wonderful marriage and a baby on the way. End of story.

'I'm okay.' Ellie glanced over to Pippa so she smiled, hoping it looked normal and not full of sympathy. 'Hi,' she added to Pippa.

'Oh, Ellie, this is my friend Pippa. She's the lady who does all my cakes.'

'Oh, so you're who I have to thank for the most amazing Bakewell I've ever had.'

Pippa blushed, 'Aw, thank you. I'm glad you liked it.'

'Pippa makes the most amazing cakes. I remember when she first came in the shop and offered her services. She brought in a tray of samples the next day and, oh my God, I was in love.'

Pippa beamed at the memory. She had only just started out her baking business from home and was so nervous about drumming up enough business to stay afloat and make it work. But she had actually done all right over the years, considering she'd built it from nothing. Well, that's what she thought. After six months of trading, Jason had persuaded her to give up her job at the bakery she worked in and go it alone completely, so she could throw herself fully into it. It worked and she expanded a little in that time, but it was never enough for him and he was always making comments about how he was holding things together all the time. But she kept plodding along with a smile on her face because of people like Zoe, who told her she was doing amazing things. When things were falling apart behind the scenes, Pippa was able to still project this image of perfection, with her business going from strength to strength. Albeit in baby steps.

But now that there was a baby on the way, she was worried that she wouldn't be able to keep this image up. She couldn't handle people talking about her behind her back. And she was prepared to do anything to make sure that didn't happen.

* * * * *

Imogen watched out of the window as the world passed by. They were on their way to Alice's parents' house and she was so incredibly nervous, the nausea she was already suffering from had increased tenfold. She didn't understand why she was nervous. She knew deep down that Alice's parents would be nothing but elated over this news. This was her mother's doing. Every time she was about to do anything big like this, her mother's words of disappointment hung over her like a wet blanket, pushing down onto her lungs, making her feel claustrophobic. Nothing she could do would please her mum, because the only thing she saw in Imogen was the fact that she was gay. Nothing else seemed to matter. And as much as Imogen embraced the fact that she was in love with a woman, there was still that small part of her that her mum was able to attack with just a few words, which made her confidence come crashing down. All she ever wanted was her mum's approval. Clearly that was too much to ask for.

'Are you okay? You look a bit peaky?' Alice glanced over to her as she drove and then rested her hand on top of Imogen's.

'I'm fine. Just feeling a big sick, that's all.' She placed her other hand in the pocket of her hoodie, resting it on her stomach.

'It's going to be okay; you know that, don't you?'

She didn't know that. There were so many things that could go wrong both with this pregnancy and everything else that it entailed. And her mum. Just thinking about her mum brought on so much anxiety. 'I really admire you, Alice.'

Alice laughed in response. 'Really? Why?'

'You're just so positive about everything. You see the good that can come out of every situation; nothing ever fazes you.' She wished she could be more like Alice.

'Oh, come on, Ims, you know that's not true.' Alice kept glancing over to her as she drove.

'It is! You never worry about things; you just get on with it and make things happen. You don't worry about what other people think and you just breeze through life, enjoying it.' Anxiety settled in the pit of her stomach and she recognised the feeling instantly. Having suffered with anxiety attacks in the past due to stress, she knew the warning signs. She concentrated on her breathing and looked out of the window so that Alice couldn't see panic in her eyes. She kind of wished she hadn't worn the hoodie now as she felt a bead of sweat trickle down her chest. She rolled her sleeves up, exhaling.

'Listen. You are an incredibly strong woman. You have so much to be happy about; you don't even need to entertain anyone else who wants to be negative in your life. You have me, and we have this baby – that is all you will ever need.'

She nodded but didn't answer. She could feel her heart rate increasing, pounding, reverberating through every inch of her skin. The high-pitched noise ringing in her ears as she desperately tried to slow her breathing. Don't do this, not now, she told herself. She concentrated on the spot of dirt that she could see on the window. She needed to channel all her energy into this spot, focus, bring everything down a level and breathe. In through her nose; out through her mouth. She needed to do this as discreetly as she could; she couldn't let Alice see that this anxiety was making a comeback. And because of her mum, yet again. All she ever wanted was to have that close mother-daughter relationship that others had with their mums. And now she was pregnant, it just highlighted the fact that she didn't have this with her mum. She would never have that mother-daughter best-friend relationship – and that hurt more than anything.

But she couldn't go through what she did before when the anxiety got too much. It took over her life and caused so many problems both in her relationship and at work. She was determined not to let that happen again. She just needed to focus.

Thankfully Alice had taken her silence as thoughtfulness and was giving her a few minutes. Imogen leant over and turned the volume dial on the music up a little, letting the song wash over her. She didn't recognise the song but the heavy guitar solo was too much for her brain, it made her feel erratic and stressed. She flicked the button and selected the next station. A gentle, but upbeat song was playing and she instantly felt a little lighter. She left it playing and leant her head on the headrest of her chair, closing her eyes and steadying her breathing. She could do this. She just needed to take things one step at a time. Get through the here and now and she could sort the mum issue out when she felt stronger.

She felt Alice's hand again on hers and she wrapped her fingers around hers, taking comfort in knowing she'd always have her Alice.

* * * * *

'I can't believe how busy this place gets.' Ellie turned the dishwasher on for another cycle and began to stack away the plates she had just unloaded. 'I mean, seriously, when do you get a chance to have a cuppa yourself?'

Zoe laughed. 'Don't be silly. I am here to make other people tea and coffee, not drink it myself.' She was busy plating up a panini and slid the plate along to the serving hatch, already pulling out some bread for the next order.

'Is it always this manic?'

'On a Saturday at lunchtime, yeah.'

'That's crazy.' Ellie closed the cupboard and wiped the tops with antibacterial spray. 'I mean, it's great and all, but it's crazy!'

'What can I say? People love my sandwiches.' Zoe was a total natural at working, constantly moving her hands and running here and there, but looking as cool and calm as a cucumber as she did so.

'You were always good in the kitchen, to be fair. Me, I couldn't boil an egg without ruining it. Remember that time I was making cheese on toast for us all because Mum said it was about time I started doing the lunch and I totally forgot about it and started watching that model programme?'

'Oh God, you nearly burnt down the house!'

Ellie laughed fondly. 'I know! But she never asked me to do lunch again – winning!' she sang.

'Well,' Zoe said as she slid a plate of salad and some prawns towards her sister. 'You'd better learn some basics fast, sis, because you're not staying here rent-free without lifting a finger. Prawn and avocado salad on there, please.'

Ellie looked at the ingredients in front to her. 'Prawn and avocado salad,' she repeated, almost to herself, nodding. 'Fair enough, no cooking required – I can do that.'

'Of course you can. Stop always putting yourself down.' Zoe threw a tea towel at her.

'Well, when you've grown up with Little Miss Perfect over there it's hard to stand out.'

'Oh believe me, Els, you stand out all right.' Zoe chopped some lettuce and said, almost under her breath, 'And Miss Perfect, I ain't!'

Two hours later and they finally got to take a five-minute break. Ellie slumped into a chair and sipped at her tea. 'Oh, my goodness, this is pure heaven. How do you do that every day?'

'Well, to be fair, it isn't that crazy every second of every day. Saturdays are busy. That's just the way things are in a café. Although, saying that, I am very lucky, we do get a steady stream of customers in every day. There are quieter periods during the week, but generally, it's doing okay.'

'You've really made this work. You've done so well.' She felt a smile of pride sneak over her lips.

'Thanks, sis. It hasn't been easy, but I got there in the end. Dad was brilliant with helping me start up and, I have to give him his due, he's always been around ever since.'

Zoe knew what she was doing. 'Yeah, thanks for rubbing it in.' She felt a surge of annoyance at the mention of her dad. Everyone knew that he worshipped Zoe and his princess could do no wrong. Ellie couldn't do anything right when it came to her father. Not that she cared what he thought.

'Oh, be quiet! I'm not rubbing it in. I'm just saying, he's not as bad as you like to make out he is.'

'Zoe, the man couldn't give two shits about me. As far as he is concerned, he only has one daughter.'

'That's not true and you know it!' Zoe's voice was stern, but she wasn't angry.

'Of course it is. When Mum died, all he cared about was making sure you were okay. He wasn't interested in what I had to say.' She tried not to let the jealousy show, but she could feel the feelings from her childhood rear their ugly heads. She tried to push them back down into the box she kept them tightly locked in.

'Ellie, that's because you didn't have anything you *wanted* to say. You were so hell-bent on self-destruction that you didn't even talk to any of us. Dad had a hard time too.'

'I spoke to you, didn't I?' She could feel the emotion already creeping up her throat, making it feel sticky and restricted.

'Yeah, only because you had no choice.'

'No, because you made time for me. He didn't even care.'

'Come on, you're being silly. Stop making yourself the victim all the time. It was a hard time for us all. You can't hold that against him for the rest of his life. You're being selfish. Are you telling me that you would rather stay stubborn and have no parents than make amends and make the most of the parent you do still have?' Zoe had leant forward now into Ellie's face, making her argument more prominent.

Ellie stood up as a bolt of frustration shot through her body. 'Are we really having this conversation? I came here because I wanted help from my sister, not because I wanted the third degree about why my dad doesn't care about me.' She stormed towards the kitchen door that led out to the back of the café shop.

'Oh, for goodness sake, he *does* care about you.' She threw her hands up. 'Where are you going?'

'Out.' And she slammed the door behind her as she left. She had no idea where she was going to go, but she needed to go somewhere. There was no way she was going to cry over something as silly as her dad.

* * * * *

'Okay, this is it. Are you ready?'

Imogen smiled at Alice as she nodded. 'As ready as I'll ever be.'

She had spent the remainder of the car journey calming herself, using various techniques she had learnt previously to deal with her anxiety. Thankfully it hadn't developed into anything she couldn't handle. She put it down to the additional hormones that were whizzing around her body at the moment. Her poor body had been through so much recently, what with all the testing and medical interventions, it was no wonder she felt a bit alien to it.

They exited the car and made their way to the front door of Alice's parents' house. It was a beautiful detached bungalow with the most adorable little front garden. Whilst the front of the house was fairly close to the country lane it was built on, the back garden more than made up for it, stretching back as far as Imogen could see, reaching the woods that lay beyond. Alice's parents took pride in their bungalow and this was clear to see from the well-kept gardens and immaculate furnishings within. Imogen remembered the first time she had been here years ago. Stunned by the modern refurbishment Alice's parents had undertaken shortly after they'd moved in, the bungalow felt fresh, bright and free-flowing. Having down-sized after Alice and her brother moved out, her parents had bought a smaller home, but had completely gutted it and transformed it into what they wanted. They had even built an annexe in the garden for when their children came to stay. Whilst Alice and Imogen only lived half an hour down the road, Alice's brother had moved abroad and so, when he came to stay with his family, they were able to have some privacy but be close to their parents. It was the loving family that Imogen has always wished for, but had never really had. Even more reason to make sure her baby would have the upbringing she didn't and Alice was more than up for the job.

Imogen felt nervous, but more of an excited nervousness. Alice parents were lovely and they totally embraced them and their relationship. The girls could be themselves whenever they were round there and it was like a breath of fresh air.

Alice rang the doorbell and bounced on her feet excitedly. 'Here goes.' She gave a little squeal to emphasise her excitement.

'Alice, Imogen, come in!' Alice's mum was tall and slender and she had the most beautiful long, chestnut hair, which she always wore in a plait. Older than Imogen's parents, Alice's parents were both retired and having run their own business for many years, were in a very good financial position. She ushered the girls in and greeted them both with a hug and a kiss. 'Your father is in the garden sparking up the barbecue.'

'Oh nice! You should've said you were going to do a barbecue, we would've brought some food with us.'

'Oh, it was a last-minute thing, you know your father. He has these good ideas and you have to strike while it's hot. Plus we didn't know the weather was going to be like this, so we're doing it before the rain comes. We've got plenty of food anyway.' She turned to Imogen. 'Are you okay, sweetie, you look a little peaky today?'

Imogen was stumped for a response, concentrating so hard on not blurting out their good news just yet, she froze and couldn't think of a reply that wasn't 'I'm pregnant!'

'She's fine, she's just tired, that's all,' Alice chipped in and Imogen smiled in thanks as Alice's mum walked off into the kitchen shouting, *you'll need a cardy on though, Alice – the wind is chilly.*

'I don't know why that happened,' she whispered as she followed Alice through to the conservatory.

'It's fine. We will tell them in a minute and get it out, so you don't have to keep it in.' Alice smiled lovingly at Imogen, her big brown eyes creasing around the edges as she did so. 'You're such a weirdo, I love it.'

They walked out into the brightly lit conservatory and through into the garden, where she could see Alice's dad standing broadly over the barbecue, placing various slabs of meat onto the grill.

'Hey, Dad,' Alice called out as she approached him. 'Any excuse for a barbecue, hey? What's cooking?'

'There's my girl.' He stepped away from the barbecue and pulled her into a huge embrace, kissing her forehead. 'And there's my other girl.' He repeated the same for Imogen. From the word go, Alice's parents had treated Imogen like a second daughter.

'Hi, how are you?' she asked as she pulled out a chair from the table and sat down.

'Yes, I'm good. Been tinkering with that car I showed you both last week, you know, the Stag?'

Imogen loved how passionate Alice's dad was about cars. Alice had grown up with going to car auctions with her dad and helping him fix up old cars to sell on. More recently, he had been branching out into classic cars and a Triumph Stag was one of his favourites. He was so excited when he found this one last week, he had called Alice up and the pair of them had talked cars for almost an hour. Imogen didn't understand the fascination, but she respected his passion and always engaged in conversation with him about his latest challenge whenever they met up.

'How's it going? Is it up and running yet?' Imogen asked, feeling happy at the inclusion.

'Oh, it's a blinder. I'll show you both after we've eaten. Here, Alice, you'll take it for a spin, see how she runs?'

'Course, Dad.' Alice was going back and forth into the kitchen to help her mum bring out some food for the table. 'You don't mind, do you, Ims?'

'Course she doesn't mind. We can have a girly chat whilst you two are off doing your father-daughter-car thingy.'

Imogen laughed at Alice's mum's struggle with defining their quality time.

'Well, that's sorted, then.'

Because Alice had been a real daddy's girl growing up – and still was – her mum had taken Imogen under her wing from the word go and she could tell that Alice's mum secretly loved doing more girly things with her and talking about celebrities and clothes shopping and all your stereotypical 'girl' things. As much as Imogen and Alice were not your stereotypical gay couple, when it came to things like shopping and celebrities, Alice couldn't give a monkeys, whereas her mum loved a gossip with Imogen.

'Did you see that programme last night about the plastic surgery? That woman's nose!' Alice's mum's face was hilarious; the shock made her eyebrows rise and practically touch her hairline. She continued to pour out some juice for Imogen. 'I mean, I know when we all get a bit older some of us like to get some help in the looks department. Hell, I wouldn't say no to a few fillers here and there,' she laughed, 'but that nose job was horrendous!'

'I didn't see it. Not sure I have the guts to have surgery for anything. Imagine if it went wrong – especially on your face!'

'You don't need surgery, my lovely. You are perfect as you are.'

'I'll second that!' Alice said from behind Imogen and she jumped in surprise.

'You scared the life out of me; I thought you were in the kitchen.'

Alice placed the salad bowl in the centre of the table and laughed. 'Sorry.'

When Alice had finished bringing all the food out and she had sat down at the table to join everyone else, she looked at Imogen and gave the slightest nod. Imogen nodded in return. They had agreed this little secret-code exchange before they'd left. Their way of letting each other know that they were ready to do the big announcement. Imogen took a deep breath.

'Mum, Dad, we have some news.'

Imogen watched as Alice's mum's face began to light up. She had guessed already. Although, when someone says they have news, and they are already married, it is automatically your next thought. Alice's dad, however, was still oblivious.

'We are having a baby!'

Alice's mum was already squealing and had jumped up instantly, pulling her daughter in for a huge hug. 'Oh, my God, girls, that's amazing news!'

'Well, bloody hell!' Alice's dad, stood up. 'Come here!' He

pulled Alice from her mum's grasp and squeezed her into another.

Imogen didn't have much time to take it in because Alice's mum was now pulling her up, wrapping her arms around her and saying, 'Imogen, this is the best news!'

'Thanks, we can't quite believe it ourselves.'

And here was her dad, pulling Imogen in for a cuddle.

They all took their seats back at the table.

'When did this all happen? I mean, how long have you known?' Alice's mum was now sobbing. She took the tissue her husband was holding out for her and dabbed her eyes.

'Imogen took the test yesterday morning. She got sent home from work because she was throwing up and she called me and then took the test and it was positive!'

Pride swelled in her chest as she listened to Alice retell the story. Alice was so excited and happy, the words were just tumbling out of her mouth and Imogen felt so emotional knowing that she was a part of the reason for making Alice so happy.

'This calls for a celebration. I'll get the special champagne out from the garage.' Alice's dad pointed at Imogen as he left the table. 'Not for you, mind, you can have some orange juice.' He winked at her and she laughed as she saluted him.

This was exactly how telling your parents should go.

Chapter 6

Pippa waited another half an hour before she picked up her phone and began to type. She hated it when he made her feel like this. It wasn't as though she was an obsessive wife who needed to know where her husband was at every point during every day, but recently he had been so distracted when he was at home, she couldn't help but wonder where he was when he wasn't with her. This morning he had got up early and left, after telling her yesterday that he had some things to do at the office today and that he wouldn't be too long. Even though it was a Saturday, she had been okay with it because she thought he wouldn't be too long, as he had said. But it was now nearly five and he was still not home. She had tried everything to distract herself from the thoughts that had been accumulating in her mind. She couldn't push out the images from before and what it had amounted to. Surely he wouldn't do that to her again?

After doing her normal delivery to the café first thing, she had traipsed around town, picking up a few things for her bakes next week, some pregnancy essentials (which she had secretly really enjoyed doing after waiting so long to finally be able to buy them) and dinner for this evening, which she had decided would be a little celebration dinner following their amazing news yesterday. And finally, returning home to an empty house, she decided to clean the kitchen.

Cleaning was her go-to thing to do when she was stressed. *A tidy house; a tidy mind* was her motto. It was also the way, her friends had learned, that everyone kept tabs on how Pippa was feeling. They knew that when the house was sparkling, Pippa had something on her mind or was feeling stressed about work-related things – not that she would ever admit to it. She took pride in everyone thinking she was the perfect housewife and business owner. Funnily enough, no one ever questioned her marriage. She supposed that was because, on the surface, Pippa had a fairytale marriage. She and Jason had met in high school and got together when they were just fifteen. They split up for a bit when Jason had got itchy feet about being tied down and she had caught him texting another woman. She later found out he had been having an affair with her. But after a few years apart, he came back to her, claiming to have got it out of his system. He missed her and wanted to settle down and they had got married the following year. Jason had been at his job at the communications company since he started when he was seventeen and had worked his way up the career ladder to manager. Of course, when he started, he was simply an assistant to the assistant of the regional manager. Their friends would joke that he was an assistant's assistant and would tease him about having such a mediocre job. But he worked hard and had now worked up to being regional manager himself. He worked long hours, but it was financially rewarding and meant they could buy their dream home out in the Shropshire countryside that they had both always dreamed of. It also meant that they were financially stable enough so that Pippa could take a step back from work temporarily when she had the baby. This had been the case for quite some time now, but she just hadn't fallen pregnant. But now, she had finally conquered that stage and was now well on her way to fulfilling their dreams and starting the family she had always wanted.

Except, behind the perfect marriage image that she and Jason portrayed, things were falling apart. He was spending more and more time at work recently and she hardly got to see him. He would come home stressed and, as a result, they would argue and whenever he had time at home, or if they went on holiday, after a couple of days of niceties, he would become distracted and distant and she felt she had to fight for his attention away from his mobile phone. 'It's work stuff' he would tell her, 'I can't just leave them at the office fending for themselves without me; the place would fall apart if I wasn't there.' Which was lovely, knowing how important he was to the company, but when you are out for a romantic meal on holiday and your husband keeps whipping out his phone, it is hardly the romantic dinner a girl dreams of.

How's it going? Will you be much longer? Xx

She sent the message and waited another half an hour before trying to call. Voicemail. She left a message for him to call her when he got it and finally, at six-thirty, she heard from him.

'Hi, sweetheart, sorry I took so long. Things have been manic here. I swear, without me, this place would go under!'

'Well they are incredibly lucky to have such a hardworking employee. I didn't think it was going to take so long today. I thought you would be home by midday.' She was being totally honest when she said this. When he said to her yesterday that he had to go in and sort some things out, she thought two, maybe three, hours maximum, and then they could go out and spend some quality time together. He had been working so much recently, it was actually a miracle she had even fallen pregnant. Had they not had that crazy weekend last month, she would have claimed miraculous conception or even tested the theory of *'there must be something in the air'*.

'Yeah, well, so did I, but as soon as I sorted one problem out, another one materialised.'

'Is it that Patrick again?'

'Yeah, the guy is a liability.'

She sighed. This bloke who worked there, Patrick, seemed to be at the bottom of everything that got messed up at Jason's work. Pippa was a very forgiving person, but this Patrick was really starting to get on her nerves. 'How comes he hasn't been fired by now? This guy has been causing you so much extra work; surely he's had his quota of mistakes by now?'

'You would think, but it's out of my hands. I've told the guys up in head office about him but apparently he's really good at his job, in general, so they seem to overlook all these little mistakes he's making. It doesn't seem to matter that it creates a whole barrage of work for other people.'

'So it's not just you, there are other people that have to go in of a weekend to catch up?'

'Yeah, there's a few of us here. The guy has a lot to answer for, causing this much additional work.'

Pippa gave up. There was clearly no point in this conversation. She really disliked this Patrick for taking up so much of their free time together. She could only hope that the guy would trip himself up sooner or later and she would get her husband back. 'Anyway, never mind that, are you coming home now?'

'Yeah, I'll be home soon.'

'I'll wait for you then. I bought some bits in town today. I thought we could have a nice dinner together, you know, to celebrate?'

'Sounds great. I'll call you when I leave.'

Pippa hung up and after looking at the time, decided to put the dinner on hold. She went upstairs and pulled open her wardrobe. It had been a few weeks since they'd had some quality time together. She pulled out a little black dress and her make-up bag and quickly typed a text.

Let's make this a night to remember and go out to celebrate. Text me when you leave and I'll meet you at the station xx

She typed another message to Zoe.

Do you want to meet up for some celebratory dinner with me and Jason? You can bring the new boyfriend?

* * * * *

Pippa had been sitting on the sofa watching the clock for the past hour. Every minute that went by, her mood worsened. First irritation (he's always bloody late), then frustration (why can't he be on time, just once), then anger (he's taking the piss) and now, worry (oh my God, what if something has happened?) She took one last glance at the clock as it ticked over to 11pm and then pressed call on her phone.

It took Jason two separate calls before he finally picked up.

'Pip?' he called out, shouting over the loud music in the background.

'Jason? Is everything okay?'

'What? Oh yeah, fine. You?'

A surge of rage bolted through her body. 'Where are you?'

'What? I can't hear you properly, hang on.' She listened as the music gradually died down to a dull hum in the background. 'That's better, what's up?'

'Where are you?' She was now pacing the living room.

'I'm at the Bull and Hound; they've got live music in tonight. The band is fucking awesome!'

'What are you doing there? I sent you a text asking you to let me know when you were on your way home.' She was throwing her arms about as she spoke, not caring that he couldn't see her. 'I arranged for Zoe and her new boyfriend to meet us – I told you this!'

'I know and I will. I'm not leaving yet, so I haven't texted. Jeez, chill the fuck out.'

'Why have you gone to the pub? I got dressed up; I thought

we were going to celebrate tonight?' The anger was subsiding but Pippa found herself getting emotional now. Bloody hormones.

'I *am* celebrating. What's the big deal?'

Annoyance dripped through her tone. 'I meant, together!'

'Well come down here, then.' He had clearly started to make his way back into the pub as the music was getting louder again.

'Jason, I don't want to be in a pub full of drunken people and loud music. I thought we could celebrate together, you know, a meal or something.' Like she was going to let everyone see Jason treat her like shit because he was drunk. No chance. She needed it to be just him and her when he was like this. She didn't want to give anyone fuel for gossip.

'What?'

'Go back outside, it's too loud!' She was shouting now. She hated it when he had a drink. He was supposed to be cutting down now that she was pregnant. Guess there was no chance of that happening.

'Listen, I'll be home by midnight and I'll bring in a takeaway, yeah? We can have our meal then.' He then raised his voice to be heard over the music, calling out to a friend, 'Yeah, get me another one. Same again!'

'Jason, please. Just come home.' She knew what he was like when he drank too much and she really didn't want to have to deal with him later on.

'Oh get off my case, Pip; I'm having a few drinks with mates. I'll be home at midnight.'

And with that, he hung up. And Pippa knew he wouldn't

be home at midnight, so she took herself upstairs and after getting changed out of her dress and taking her make-up off, she got into bed and let the tears fall, where no one could see her. She looked through her phone messages to Zoe, cancelling the meet because of 'nausea'. She hated it when Jason's selfishness meant she had to cancel things and lie to her friends. If she didn't want this baby so much, she would just walk out the door and never come back. She hated the financial hold he had on her.

Chapter 7

'Morning, sleepy head.'

Ellie opened her eyes as a stream of sunlight shot into the room as a result of Zoe opening the living-room curtains. She groaned and pulled the cover up over her face.

'Here, I made you a coffee. It's decaf, mind.'

'Why?' Ellie's voice was muffled by the cover.

'Because you need to reduce the amount of caffeine you are drinking. It's not good for the baby.'

Ellie pulled the cover off and sat up a little, making room on the end of the sofa for Zoe to sit down. 'No, I mean, why did you bring me a coffee?'

'Listen,' Zoe perched on the edge of the sofa not far from Ellie's feet and passed the cup. 'I am sorry about yesterday. I didn't mean to upset you with all that talk about Dad. I just wanted to make you see that he's not a monster and it would be good for you to have him around, you know, especially now.'

The reality of why she was here at her sister's came crashing back down and she was forced to think about everything again. She sipped at her coffee for something to do, it tasted bitter.

'You know that I will always be here for you and that I

will do everything I can to make things okay, but just don't forget about Dad. I know he misses having you around and I miss having my family. It's bad enough Mum not being here, but having to see you and Dad separately all the time drives me crazy. We should be sticking together, not pushing each other away. It makes it really hard on me – I hate having to choose all the time.'

'I'm not asking you to choose.'

'You kind of are, Ellie. You two not being able to be in the same room together without creating tension means I have to split myself. It's not fair on me. Plus I know Dad would want to be involved with you having a baby – he'd love to have a grandchild!'

Ellie shook her head. 'Let's not get too carried away.'

Zoe huffed. 'Honesty, it's like talking to a brick wall sometimes.'

Ellie shrugged, reverting to acting like a child. Sometimes when she and Zoe were together she found herself behaving as she would've done at eleven years old, having her annoying fourteen-year-old sister around.

'How comes you slept on the sofa and not in the spare room?' Zoe peered at her over her coffee cup.

Ellie avoided eye contact. 'I was watching a film and I must've fallen asleep.'

'Fair enough. So, I've been thinking. We need to sort a plan out so that we know what we are doing and how we are going to do it. First things first, you need to tell Chris.'

Ellie groaned and dropped her head back so that it rested on the back of the sofa. 'Not this again.'

'Come on, you owe it to him to tell him. What have you got to lose?'

'Err, let me think. My best friend, my job, my freedom ... my sanity!' She listed them on her free hand, one finger at a time.

'Oh you're such a drama queen. You will not lose your sanity and the rest we can sort out. You can't just hide away at my place and pretend nothing is happening. You need to go and see a doctor, get the ball rolling with a midwife, put things in place ready for when the baby comes ...'

Ellie felt her chest tighten listening to all this talk about the baby. 'Look, I haven't even decided what I am going to do yet. There's no point in involving Chris in this until I know what I am doing.'

'What you are doing? Ellie, you're not going to do anything stupid, are you?' Zoe eyed her suspiciously and Ellie had to turn away again.

'I don't know what I am going to do. I need time to think. It's all happening too fast and I've got work appointments next week to sort out and I need to do a new order for this film I am doing next month and—'

'Ellie, I am afraid that's life. When shit gets thrown at you, you have to suck it up and deal with it. Not brush it under the carpet and hope that it will go away. And this definitely won't go away; this will become more and more prominent in your life, so you need to work out what you are doing. I will help you. You don't have to go through this alone, but you *do* have to tell Chris.'

She knew she had to tell Chris, but she was so scared of

losing him. 'Zoe, what happened between me and Chris – it was a mistake. A huge mistake that should never have happened.' And it shouldn't have happened all the other times too. What was she thinking? Nobody can have a sexual relationship without the possibility of it getting complicated. She wished she had learnt this lesson before she got pregnant.

'But it did!'

'Don't I bloody know it!'

There was a long pause, where both girls didn't know what to say next. Ellie thumbed the mug and stared down into the shiny brown liquid. She knew her sister would be like this. Maybe, subconsciously, that's why she came up here. She needed her sister to take control of the situation and tell her what she needed to do. This is exactly what she did when their mum died. She pulled Ellie back onto the straight and narrow and yet here she was again, nearly ten years later, and asking her sister to do the same. Would she ever learn? The thought of her being such a burden weighed down in her stomach and she felt guilty. 'I'm sorry,' she mumbled, taking another sip of coffee.

'What are you sorry for?' Zoe had now leant back and had her feet up on the coffee table, her long legs bare, with just a small pair of bed shorts on.

'For always being such a mess. For always relying on you to pick up the pieces when I make a mistake ... for being a crap sister.'

'Don't be silly, you aren't a crap sister.'

'I bloody feel like one. It's never the other way around, is it? It's never you coming to me and needing help to sort *your* life out. You're so confident and clever and ... just ... Zoe. You never make mistakes; you never do anything wrong.' Zoe looked away from Ellie and seemed a little uncomfortable. She was playing with her cup and looked awkward. 'What's wrong?' Ellie asked, eyeing her sister suspiciously.

'Nothing.' She didn't look at her.

'Well, it doesn't look like nothing.' Ellie nudged her with her foot from under the cover.

'Ellie, everyone makes mistakes. Even me.'

'What's that supposed to mean? You're Little Miss Perfect, you don't make mistakes. Everything seems to fall into your lap and you make things happen.'

Zoe turned her head to look at Ellie, her expression more serious than she had been for ages. 'Everything doesn't just fall into my lap. I work bloody hard for everything that I have.'

'I didn't mean it like that. I'm just saying, some people are really lucky in life and others, well, others seem to get all the bad luck. Like me.'

'I get bad luck too. I have my moments of weakness and I *do* things wrong. It's not what happens to you in life; it's how you deal with things. That's the difference.'

Ellie eyed her suspiciously. Zoe looked uncomfortable, sad. 'What aren't you telling me?'

'What do you mean?' The colour had drained out a little from her face.

'You're not telling me something. Why do you keep saying how you aren't perfect, how you get things wrong?' She paused, but didn't drop her gaze. Zoe, however, wouldn't look at her. 'Zoe? What aren't you telling me?' she pressed.

Zoe exhaled and shuffled in her seat, turning round to face Ellie front-on. 'Listen, I don't want you to get rid of the baby. I think you will regret it for the rest of your life.' She looked away. 'I did.'

Ellie felt her stomach flip. The air suddenly became tight and she felt her throat close slightly with anxiety. 'What do you mean, *'you did'*?'

'Ellie, things happen in life that you can't control and sometimes you have to make a decision based on what you *can* control.'

'I don't understand.' She kind of understood, but she didn't want to.

'I have been pregnant before.' The silence in the air that followed this revelation was both uncomfortable and strange. Zoe looked back up at her. 'I didn't have a choice. It was a volatile relationship and I had got myself into a situation I couldn't get out of. And then I found myself pregnant.'

'Shit,' Ellie whispered as she reached across the sofa and held Zoe's hand.

'I couldn't bring a baby into that environment. I had spent months gearing up to leaving him because he was,' she swallowed, 'he was physical with me.'

'Zoe ...' Ellie breathed out. She felt distraught for her sister, but underneath a bubble of anger was beginning to brew.

'It's fine. I'm not with him now.' She tried to laugh, but it came out strained.

'So you got an abortion?'

'I'm not proud of my decision and I regret it every single day. But I just couldn't bring a baby into that. I was worried sick that he would hurt the baby and then I would be the worst mum in the world because I couldn't stop it happening.'

'Oh Zoe, why didn't you tell me?'

She shook her head. 'It doesn't matter. I didn't want anyone else to know. I was ashamed of being so weak to let things get to that stage.'

'It's not weak, Zoe. For Christ sake, it's him who should be feeling shitty, not you!' She felt the anger building. 'Who was he?'

'It doesn't matter—'

'It does bloody matter; he deserves to be in prison for what he did.' Her voice was shaky, but controlled. For now.

'Ellie, it doesn't matter. It was years ago and I'm okay. He can't hurt me any more; I'm a different person to who I was back then. I'm stronger.'

'When was it?' She shuffled in her seat, still making sure she held Zoe's hand, not letting go of her. She never wanted to let go of her. She should have been here for her when it happened and she didn't think she could ever forgive herself for not.

'Not long after Mum died.'

Ellie gasped, feeling the tears spring to her eyes.

'I wasn't coping very well and he came along and was so charming. I think he could sense that I was weak. He said all the right things I needed to hear and I let my guard down. It took me about six months to realise that I was in too deep and had become reliant on him. He knew it too. So he started to get heavy-handed if I didn't do what he wanted and it just went downhill.'

'Oh God, Zoe. Why didn't you tell me, or Dad? He would've gone mad.'

'That's exactly why I didn't tell him. But then I found out I was pregnant and that night we had an argument and he pushed me and I fell down the stairs.'

'Oh my God, when you broke your arm!' It was a statement rather than a question. Ellie remembered when Zoe came to visit and she had her arm in a cast. 'You said you fell down the stairs.'

'And I did. I just … had a little help.' She looked down into her lap, clearly ashamed. 'Ellie, I couldn't bring a baby into that.'

'I know. You did the right thing.' She rubbed her thumb over Zoe's hand.

'Didn't feel like the right thing.'

'I can't believe you went through all that on your own.'

'I didn't want anyone to see how stupid I had been.' She coughed and composed herself, 'Listen, all I'm saying is that you need to think long and hard before doing anything stupid. Because what you decide now will affect you for the rest of your life. Whatever you decide, just make sure it's the right decision for you.'

'Is that what you think we would've thought? That you had been stupid? Zoe, you are a lot of things, but stupid isn't one of them.'

'I got myself into that situation, didn't I? That was stupid.'

'No, that was grief. It does fucked-up things to your mind. I should know – it royally fucked up mine.' She felt a glimmer of relief that she now knew she wasn't the only one to have let it get to her, though. When she thought Zoe was handling life perfectly well, underneath she was crumbling too. And as horrible as that was, it was comforting to know.

'I can't blame grief for my poor mistakes.'

'Yes you bloody can. Zoe, you are not a machine – you cannot programme yourself to just erase things. You are human.'

'Yes, but you have to take responsibility for your actions in life and that relationship was one bad decision after another – it was as if I was possessed. I could see myself spiralling further into despair, but I felt powerless to do anything about it. Until it was too late.' She looked into her lap, ashamed.

'Honey, you are allowed to make mistakes. It's okay. Feel free to take the baton from me for a bit – I'm in my overdraft from the Bank of Mistakes!' The girls both laughed and it helped to lighten the air. Ellie smiled. It was the first time in her whole life that she had seen that her big sister was not the perfect human being she had made her out to be. Whilst that was clearly a hard concept for her sister to deal with, it did make Ellie feel closer to her. As though a barrier had lifted out of the way – they weren't so different after all.

All too quickly, though, their conversation drifted back to Ellie and the latest mistake she had made. After hearing her sister's story, she knew that she couldn't get rid of this baby. Deep down she never wanted to anyway.

'I just don't know what to do. I don't want to get rid of the baby – I don't know that that was even what I was thinking – but I am terrified. I can't be a mum. I can barely look after myself!' She huffed and put her head in her hands. 'How would you deal with this situation?' Even though she knew her sister was no longer *perfect*, she was more perfect than Ellie would ever be.

'You know what I would do first?' Ellie's phone began to ring just as Zoe opened her mouth to speak. Both girls looked at the phone flashing on the coffee table with the one name Ellie didn't want to see. Zoe pointed at it. 'That. That is what I would do first.' She stood up and squeezed Ellie's knee. 'Come on, you need to talk to him. He deserves to know.' Zoe stood to leave, but Ellie sprung up and pulled her in for a hug. She squeezed her so tight.

'I am so sorry you had to go through all that without me, Zoe. I promise I will always be here for you. No matter what.'

Zoe squeezed her back and then pulled away, looking Ellie in the eyes. 'I know you will. Now do the right thing.' She squeezed Ellie's shoulder and left the living room, closing the door so she could give Ellie the privacy she needed to get this phone call out of the way.

Ellie picked up her mobile and took a shaky intake of breath before pressing the answer key. 'Hi Chris.'

'About bloody time! Where the hell have you been?'

'Sorry, things are just a bit manic at the moment. I'm at my sister's. Needed a break.' Her heart was racing so fast. She took another sip of coffee to calm her nerves.

'At your sister's? In Shropshire? When did that happen?'

'Friday.'

Chris paused. 'So why do you need a break. Surely work isn't going that badly?'

'No, work was fine. Is fine,' she corrected quickly. 'I just, have some stuff going on and I needed some time to, you know, sort my head.'

'Have you stopped being weird with me now?' He laughed and Ellie felt a surge of affection for him. She missed him.

'I wasn't being weird.' This conversation was probably one of the most awkward conversations they had ever had. She was avoiding the big elephant in the room and she needed to tell him. Thing is, the words just weren't coming out. She physically couldn't say the one thing she so desperately needed to say. Before she knew it, she blurted out, 'Can we meet?'

'Meet up? In Shropshire? I can't come all that way today, Els, I have an early start tomorrow and a million meetings planned.'

'Right ...' Disappointment dripped from that one word and Chris obviously picked up on it.

'Is everything okay? You *are* being weird.'

'Yes, its fine. I'm fine.'

'Look, how about this? We meet halfway? Go for some lunch somewhere in Milton Keynes?'

Ellie thought about this for a second and then replied, 'Actually, that's not a bad idea. What time?'

'Well, I need to jump in the shower and that, so let's say one? I'll google a place and text you where to meet me.'

'Okay. No problem. See you in a few hours.'

'Oh, Ellie?'

She stopped pacing. 'Yes?'

'Try and cheer up. It's not the end of the world.'

No, she thought. But it may as well be.

* * * * *

'Do you know what I fancy?' Imogen put down her menu and looked at Alice thoughtfully.

'Me?' Came the reply with a cheeky grin. Her hair was down today, as opposed to being scraped back, which was how she usually wore it for work, and she looked so beautiful. With a cute little t-shirt under a jacket and tight jeans, Alice looked casual but really pretty.

Imogen laughed. 'Yes, of course. But I did mean foodwise.'

'I know, I'm just messing. What do you fancy? It's not going to be some weird concoction is it? I'm sure that doesn't start this early.'

'No,' Imogen shook her head. 'Nothing weird ... yet. I really fancy a prawn sandwich.'

Alice turned her nose up in disgust. 'Urgh, I can't stand prawns. Especially not in bread. I mean, what is *that* about? The weird consistency of the slimy prawns on the dry bread ... nope, can't do it.' She shook her head.

'Slimy? No wonder you don't like it if you are using slimy prawns!' Imogen grimaced, shivering slightly at the thought.

'You know what I mean. They're all slippery and ... and ...' she searched for the right word, using her hand as if that would help her brain, and settled for 'fleshy.'

'You're making my prawn sandwich sound like a horror movie,' Imogen giggled and picked up the menu again. 'Maybe I'll go for something else. It doesn't sound as appealing now.'

'Sorry, I won't ruin your next choice.' She smiled lovingly.

'Hi ladies, are you ready to order?'

'I am, are you ready, Ims?' Alice flashed the woman a smile before settling back on Imogen.

She nodded at Alice but indicated that she should go first, to give herself some more time to look.

'I'll just have a BLT with a cup of tea, please.' She handed back the menu.

'No problem, and for you?' The woman looked at Imogen with a beautiful, big smile, the lines around her eyes creasing as she did. She had a simple t-shirt with khaki jeggings on and an apron tied around her waist that had splatters of something brown on. She had her hair tied back into a tiny bun with a few strands loose around her face and she just looked the epitome of friendly.

'I'll just have a cheese and ham panini please, with a cappuccino.'

'No problem, ladies. I'll be back in a minute with your drinks and if you need anything else, just give me a shout. My name is Zoe.' She gave another big smile and walked off.

'Thank you, we will.' Alice watched Zoe leave and Imogen felt a stab of jealousy. She kept it hidden, though. She knew she was being stupid. She was always the one to feel insecure in their relationship, even though Alice would continually reassure her that no one would ever come close to what they had. It was an insecurity that she guessed stemmed from her mum and the way she had always criticised her and never accepted her just for who she was.

'So this place is nice. When did you come in here?' Imogen had never even seen this café before.

'Someone at work was talking about it the other day and they recommended it to me. Said I should bring you here. I had a quick peek at it on the internet and it looked nice.

Thought it would be a nice treat to have some lunch out today. We need to make the most of it before the baby comes!'

Imogen couldn't stop the smile from appearing on her face as Alice spoke about the baby. Their baby. She dreamt about the weekend strolls and spending time together as a family of three. She didn't even mind about the late-night feeds and constant crying. Well, not yet, anyway. She might be spouting a different story this time next year. 'I still can't believe it,' she said, catching Alice's eye and feeling warmth course through her body.

'I know. It's crazy. How are you actually feeling in yourself, though? Any more nausea today? You seemed pretty rough this morning?'

'Yeah, it comes and goes. It's not too bad today, actually. I just hope I manage to get lunch inside me before it starts again.'

'Well, if you can't finish your lunch, I'm sure I can help you. Especially now that you've seen sense and abandoned the idea of slime in bread. You do look good today, though. Positively glowing!' Alice stood up. 'Just going to run to the loo.' She placed her hand on Imogen's shoulder as she went past her and gave it a squeeze. It was the little things like that that still sent shivers down Imogen's spine. She loved how Alice didn't have to say anything; sometimes just a simple squeeze of the hand on her shoulder could say a thousand words. Their connection was special. Never before had she felt the feelings she did when she was with Alice. She couldn't describe it. Alice made her feel complete. She felt as if she could face the world as long as she had Alice by her side.

This was why she had texted her mum the other day. She didn't tell her about the baby; she just made the connection. Their relationship was a difficult one. Imogen couldn't always tell what sort of mood her mum was going to be in and how she was going to take her messages. She had received a stroppy message back when she texted so she and Alice had agreed that maybe it was best to keep a distance from her for now. Alice didn't want Imogen to be stressed out unnecessarily and she saw the texts from Imogen's mum as completely unnecessary. She didn't think there was any point in Imogen trying to get her mum to understand because, quite frankly, that was never going to happen. Imogen had her and that was all she needed, according to Alice.

But, whilst Alice was away in the toilet, Imogen pulled out her phone as it beeped. She had another message from her mum. She had been receiving these stupid messages ever since she had made the first move and she didn't know what to do. She couldn't tell Alice, she didn't need that kind of stress at the moment. Alice would get upset and then confront her mum and it would become a whole big thing, like last time. So she kept it all to herself and she tried her best to smooth the situation, but the fact was, her mum was never going to approve of their relationship and she would always be a problem. She should've listened to Alice rather than partake in this back-and-forth battle of words. If she let the poison seep into her relationship, it would fall apart. Not that they weren't a strong unit, but the venom-laced messages she was starting to get would surely be a cause for anger on Alice's part and Imogen didn't need to be arguing with her too. As understanding as Alice was, she just didn't know what it was like to not have her mum around. So things were just best kept quiet. And whilst she felt less bothered by these texts more recently, now that she was expecting, it gave the situation a bitter sweet tinge.

She clicked on the message icon and opened it up.

Imogen, please, don't ignore me. Like I said before, we can help you. You can come and stay with us until you get back on your feet and she won't even know you're here.

She, was Alice. Imogen's mum couldn't bring herself to even say Alice's name now. It had been about six months since she had last seen her mum in person, and that was such a bad experience, Imogen had steered clear ever since, just exchanging messages and phone calls to keep the peace as much as she could whenever her mum was having a *good* day. At the end of the day, she was her mum and she didn't want to just not have her around. She had thought things would get better with time, once her mum realised just how much in love she and Alice were. Maybe she would even accept their relationship. But it hadn't happened yet. And now she had a baby to throw into the mix. She couldn't help but think that cutting all ties would be the best answer for her and the baby. Except, she didn't want to. She wanted her mum. She so desperately wanted to have the supportive mum that everyone else had. She should be sharing messages of elation about the baby with her, rather than nasty name–

calling, argumentative ones. It was a constant battle she fought internally with herself.

Alice joined her back at the table just as Zoe brought over their drinks.

'Here you go, ladies, your food won't be too much longer.'

'Thanks,' Alice muttered as she sat down and slid Imogen's cappuccino over to her. 'Sugar?'

Imogen nodded and slipped her phone back into her bag.

'You okay?' Alice looked at her in confusion. 'You seem a little off.'

'I'm fine, just tired, that's all.'

There was no way a text from her mum was going to ruin their day together. Not in a million years. She would deal with that later.

Chapter 8

Ellie let her eyes wander around the restaurant, taking in the calm, rustic feel that the wooden beams and vaulted ceiling projected. The dark browns and deep, golden colours made her feel strangely at ease, as though she was wrapped up in a blanket of tranquillity. Because it was a weekend lunchtime, she had assumed that the restaurant would be busy, bustling with lunch-time trade. But instead, she was seated in a far corner with the surrounding tables empty. She watched the waiting staff as they attended to the tables opposite to where she had been seated; zipping between the kitchen and the customers, carrying different-sized plates and bowls as they scooted around.

There was one big table of ten people over by the far wall. A birthday, Ellie had deciphered, because of the huge '40' balloon bobbing away in the centre. A continuous stream of laughter kept Ellie feeling more relaxed and made the differ-ence between her staying seated and running a mile. She watched the large table more closely and her attention was caught by a woman at one end who was holding a young baby – the actual reason she was sitting here in the first place hit her again. She had to tell Chris.

Fear began to seep into her mind as she watched the woman eating with one hand and cradling the baby in the other. She looked happy; that fact alone helped to alleviate some of the distress that was fast building in her mind. The woman was laughing and joking like the rest of them whilst this baby just slept peacefully in her arms. Her interaction hadn't been compromised. Ellie let herself think about what it would be like for her to actually have this baby. Maybe it would be okay. Maybe this was a blessing in disguise and a baby was what Ellie's life had been lacking. If she let herself think about it – actually think about it – there was a tiny part of her that was a little bit excited about the prospect of being a mum. Ellie was just starting to relax slightly when movement by the door caught her eye.

It was Chris.

All traces of acceptance melted away and were replaced, again, by terror. She watched him enter and close the door behind him, shaking the raindrops from his head. She hadn't even noticed that it was now raining and she briefly turned her head to the window for confirmation. Sure enough, huge droplets were wiggling down the window, forming pools at the base.

Chris stood at the entrance talking to the staff when his glance snaked over to where Ellie was sitting. A huge smile crept instantly across his face as he saw her and he lifted one arm up in a kind of salute wave.

'Alright?' he said as he bent down to kiss her on the cheek. The explosion of his aftershave hit her instantly and she was transported to the last time she had smelt it that strongly, when they were frantically kissing and undressing each other in that hotel room. His soft hands tracing her body as he ripped off *that* dress ... the sole reason she was here now settled firmly in the forefront of her mind.

'Yeah, you?' she managed to squeak out. If it was this hard to do the small-talk, she had no idea how she was going to discuss the one thing she was here to discuss.

Chris pulled the chair out and sat down, running his hand over his wet head as he did so and then wiping the excess moisture off on his jeans. Now that he had shaved his head, you could hardly see the natural red colour he was; it looked more like brown now. He had chosen to wear jeans with a beige long-sleeved jumper, which now sported darker spots as the raindrops soaked through. 'All the way here the weather has been fine and the second I pull up and get out, the bloody heavens open.'

Ellie managed to force out a laugh. She quickly sipped at her water, purely for something to do with her hands. She hated how uneasy this was already. He pulled his chair in, brushing off his jumper as much as he could and then giving in to the fact that he was going to be a little wet. 'Have you been waiting here long?'

'Not too long. I was a little early anyway so ...' she trailed off, unsure where that sentence was going.

'Is everything okay? You seem a little distracted?' Chris was staring at her with his deep- blue eyes and she could see the moisture from the rain glistening on his skin. He had the most gorgeous skin tone, Ellie had always been jealous of how beautiful his skin was. She was the type to suffer from breakouts every so often and relied hugely on make-up to create the flawless look he had. His smooth complexion would be the envy of a lot of women.

'Yeah I'm fine. Just a little tired, that's all.'

He raised his eyebrows at her. 'Ellie, how long have we known each other?'

'God,' she exhaled to buy herself some time, moving her eyes away from his because she knew where this was going. 'Like, a million years.'

'Exactly. But to be more precise, the best part of twenty-four years.' He smiled and it was beautiful.

'Bloody hell, when you say it like that it sounds crazy.'

'True. But what I am saying is that someone can't know another person for that long and not know if something is up. Plus, given the fact that you have just upped and gone to stay with your sister, who lives three hours away, at the drop of a hat, no warning, no planning ... You abandoned your photoshoot on Friday and didn't even tell anyone where you were going.' He looked at her, square in the eyes, and she pulled her glance away, distracting it with another sip of the water. 'So, don't tell me that it is just tiredness. I know you, Els.'

They sat in silence for a few seconds before the waiter interrupted with a 'Hi guys, would you like to order some drinks?'

'Yes please,' Chris responded, before Ellie had a chance to. 'We will have a bottle of Chardonnay please ...'

'No!' Ellie blurted out before realising what this would look like. 'I mean, I can't, and I'm ... driving.'

'That's never stopped you having a couple of glasses before. It's with a meal, Els, it'll be fine.'

'No. I don't want any wine. No ... thank you.' She was making a right hash of this. 'Can I just have a Coke please?' she asked the waiter, who at this point was glancing back and forth between the pair of them, a confused expression on his face.

'Okay, fair enough. I'll just have a glass of the Chardonnay, then, please. And a still water.'

'No problem and have you guys had a chance to look at the menu or would you like a few minutes?'

Ellie looked up at Chris, who seemed to be studying her face with interest. He was onto her, she knew it. She felt uncomfortable and mumbled, 'Few minutes, please,' before dropping her gaze back to the menu just for something to do with her eyes.

The waiter left and as she looked up she saw that Chris hadn't budged and was still looking at her, confusion etched on his face.

'The salmon sounds lovely,' she said, a little too upbeat to be believable. He was never going to fall for this *I'm fine* charade. What was she thinking? She shouldn't have come here. She felt pressured already and she hadn't even said anything yet.

Chris leaned across the table and took Ellie's hand into his. She didn't struggle and let him hold it. A surge of nausea erupted at the feel of his touch. Not because he repulsed her, quite the opposite. She was annoyed at herself for feeling like this. He was her friend, what was she doing? It must be the hormones. He held her hand for about a minute and then asked, 'What's wrong?' as he stroked the top of her hand with his thumb. His hands felt warm and soft and she wished that they weren't sitting in a restaurant but somewhere more private. Then she pushed that thought as far away from her mind as she could. This was *Chris*. She pulled her hand away, a little more roughly than she had meant to, and replied. 'Nothing, honestly, I'm just tired. I think I might be coming down with something. I've been working long hours recently and it's all caught up with me.' She realised she had probably given about ten more answers than she actually needed to give.

Chris looked offended at the sharpness of both her reply and the retraction of her hand but he didn't say anything. He just gave one of those smiles; the ones where you can tell it is fake but the other person doesn't know what else to do, and picked his menu up to browse.

'I'll have the ribeye steak, please, medium rare, with twice-cooked chips and coleslaw,' Chris said to the waiter, who was busy scrawling down his order.

'And for you, madam?'

'I'll have the salmon, please, with new potatoes and veg.' She passed over her menu and discreetly took a deep breath. She wasn't ready to do this. Not at all. Maybe she didn't have to tell him today. There was plenty of time. Maybe she should just enjoy seeing him, have some lunch, enjoy her break at her sister's and deal with all this crap when she returned home.

Yes. That sounded like a much better idea.

'So,' Chris began, 'What's going on at work? How come you walked out?'

'How did you know about that, anyway? I meant to ask you before.'

'That woman who was running the shoot contacted me to see if I knew where you had gone as she couldn't get hold of you.'

'How the hell did she know to contact you?'

'I guess she must've asked Rob for it – I spoke to Rob about getting you the shoot job, remember?'

Realisation dawned. 'Oh, of course. Yeah, sorry about that. Didn't mean to mess up on a job you helped me get.' She pulled a face, clenching her teeth. 'Bad friend!' she cursed herself.

'It's okay, I'll let you off. After all, you're paying for lunch.'

'What? No chance. It's your turn!'

'Yes, but I would've picked somewhere a lot closer to home. Taking into consideration the amount of time I have had to drive to get to you to take you for lunch, I think it's only fair you pick up this one ...' He had a glint in his eye and the beginnings of a cheeky smile creeping across his face.

'Yeah, yeah, whatever. Always trying to skive out of your turn, you.' She smiled and took a sip of her water. Was she actually flirting with him? Is this what she did now?

'Well, what do you expect? Being mates with a famous make-up artist must have some perks, surely?'

'I'm hardly famous.' She couldn't take her eyes from his face. The creases around his eyes deepened as he laughed. He made her feel so completely at ease. This is what she needed.

Complete normality. Back to how things were before that night. Before everything changed.

'Well, you will be one day. With your talent, I'm surprised you aren't working on A-list celebs yet.' She paused for a minute as the feeling of warmth and pride crept over her skin. 'What?' he asked, smiling.

'Do you really mean that?'

'Of course I do. Els, you are very talented. I mean, naturally I don't know from personal experience, but from the stuff I hear and see you are pretty good at your job. You wouldn't be working on the jobs you are if you weren't. Give yourself some credit. Is that why you walked out? Because you didn't feel like you were good enough?' She noticed his hand move towards his glass and she couldn't help but think about how much she wanted his hand to hold hers again. It really unsettled her.

'No ...' she trailed off.

'Well, what is it? Are we going to skirt around the issue or are you going to tell me why we are sitting in a restaurant in Milton Keynes instead of somewhere where we both live?'

Ellie sipped at her water to try and buy herself yet more time. They were enjoying themselves just talking. She had started to feel normal again, just for a second, and was forgetting the madness that had been the last couple of days. It had been so nice to just be her, laughing and joking with Chris, as if they didn't have a care in the world. Two friends enjoying life and having a laugh. This, ironically, was the reason they were in this mess.

'I thought this would make a nice change from our normal

routine of lunch ... no?' Her joking did not have the desired effect she thought it would and Chris raised his eyebrow slightly at her.

'Okay fine.' But then she paused. The settled state of her stomach very quickly became a washing machine on spin cycle. The breakfast she had enjoyed so much this morning was threatening to join her again and she wasn't sure that this would be the best outcome for any party involved. 'Actually, do you mind if I run to the loo quickly?'

'As long as you don't climb out of the window and leave me with the bill.' Chris smiled at her and the effect on her insides made her think that maybe it wasn't just the nerves making her feel peaky. She shook the thought from her mind almost instantly. She was being stupid! Chris shouldn't have this effect on her insides.

'Do you seriously think my arse would fit out of one of those windows?'

'Fair point. I think we are safe.'

Ellie threw her napkin at him as she stood. 'Idiot,' she mumbled through a grin and made her way to the toilet.

When inside, she sat on the toilet (seat down) and took a deep breath. 'What the hell!' she whispered as she dropped her head into her hands. This was so much harder than she thought it would be. Why couldn't she just say to him what was going on. She took her phone from her pocket and opened WhatsApp, typing a message to Zoe.

FFS I can't do this!

Instantly a reply pinged back.

What do you mean? You've been there ages, haven't you told him yet?

She shook her head as she typed.

I can't

Ellie's phone vibrated again.

Ellie, just explain to him what is going on. He deserves to know. Man up!

It was only a matter of seconds before her phone rang. She answered instantly. 'Zoe, help me. I can't do this!' She gasped for breath as she felt the nerves overwhelm her.

'Pull yourself together, Ellie. You can and you will. You just need to take a minute to compose yourself.'

Ellie sat on the toilet and closed her eyes, pressing the phone to her ear. She felt squashed by the clinically white walls and bleach-tinged toilet smell. Zoe was talking to her but she found it hard to decipher the words and meaning of what she was saying. It must be the nerves, clouding her mind.

'Are you okay?' came a voice from outside her cubicle. It was then she realised she was gasping still. More hyperventilating, actually. What the hell was going on? She unlocked the door and opened it, face to face with a concerned-looking woman wearing a worried expression. 'Do you need some help?'

Ellie felt the emotion catch in her throat that took her by surprise. She wasn't expecting to have such an attack of nerves when the time came to speak out. Yeah sure, she knew she would be nervous, but this overwhelming feeling that was starting to descend was nothing like she had ever felt before. She was doing the right thing, she kept telling herself over and over.

'Ellie!' Zoe's voice pierced her mind as she shrieked down the phone. 'What's happening, are you okay?'

The woman looked at the phone perched in Ellie's hand as she stumbled backwards and resumed her seat on the toilet, resting her head in her trembling hands, nearly dropping the phone. The woman scooted forward and kneeled at Ellie's feet, taking the phone from Ellie's hand.

'Hello?' the woman said.

Ellie couldn't make sense of what was going on and simply rocked as a high-pitched sound pulsated through her ears. She then had an almighty urge to be sick. It came on so suddenly and she jumped up, shoving the woman away from her as she slammed the door shut and flicked the lock. She spun round and threw herself onto her knees on the floor and hugged the toilet bowl, retching so hard her eyes watered.

Never before had she felt so confused, scared and alone as she did right now. She needed to get out of here. She couldn't stay within the confines of these walls any longer. She felt as if the world around her was closing in, the walls dragging ever closer to push against her. She could almost feel the air being forced out of her lungs. She found it hard to breathe and her eyes were going fuzzy. She blinked continuously, trying to clear her vision. 'Oh God,' she whispered as she stood up. She stumbled over to the door and began to fumble the lock. She couldn't unlock it. She seemed to be locked in. She frantically pulled at the lever, catching her finger in the lock as it slid back into its holster. A mix of pain from her finger and sheer relief, she let the tears fall as she exited the toilet. Stumbling forward precipitously, just to make sure she was actually out of there, she fell into the sink and began to sob. She didn't care that there was a woman next to her, staring at her in worried confusion; she didn't care that she must look like a total idiot. She also didn't care that Zoe was going to be worried sick on the other end of her phone, wondering what the hell was happening!

The woman immediately ran over to Ellie, throwing a friendly arm around her shoulders. 'Oh my goodness, what's wrong? Do you need an ambulance?'

Ellie threw out a few random words in between sobs and, uncharacteristically, rested her head on this stranger's shoulder and cried her heart out.

'Shh, it's okay,' the woman comforted, rubbing Ellie's shoulder. 'Would you like me to call someone?'

There was only one person she wanted at this moment in time, and the realisation made her feel sick again. But she couldn't hide it any more. She needed to face up to the situation. She raised her hand and pointed towards the door, indicating the restaurant as the tears began to fall more heavily again. She simply squeaked, 'Chris,'

Chapter 9

'So come on then, spill.' Pippa stirred the tea that Zoe had passed her over the counter and picked up a bourbon biscuit to dunk.

'What do you want to know?' Zoe was busy wiping down the sides but Pippa could see the smile on her face.

'Anything and everything. Where did he take you? What did you eat? What did you wear and, most importantly, did he stay over?' Pippa winked.

'Pip!' Zoe gasped, looking at her, shocked.

'I don't even know where that came from. I'm blaming the hormones.' She flushed a little.

Zoe laughed and leant on the counter. 'Well, after you cancelled he suggested we go to that new Mexican place on the other side of the High Street – the one with the red canopy outside?' Pippa nodded her acknowledgement. 'So we went there and the food, oh my goodness, Pip, it was divine.'

'I'm not a Mexican lover – plus Jason doesn't eat it, so it works out well for us.' She was still really angry at him and the mention of his name prompted a sense of irritation inside her.

'Oh, maybe don't go there, then. But we really enjoyed it.'

'Did you stay there all evening?'

'No, we then went on to that bar on the corner of Walker Street?'

Pippa gasped. 'Oh, I really want to go there. Hasn't it recently been refurbished?' It had been so long since Pippa had had a girly night out. It was always Jason going out with her staying home to bake.

'Yeah, new owners. It's really nice in there, and they were doing two-for-one on cocktails until 11pm.' Zoe took Pippa's plate, which had the bourbons on, and slipped it onto the side with the other dirty dishes, ready to go out back. 'When you've had that baby we will sort a girls' night out. To celebrate.'

Pippa smiled in agreement, but secretly knew that Jason wouldn't be happy about it. 'So did Gregg come back for some coffee afterwards or ...' she trailed off, a smile springing to her lips.

'No,' Zoe said, rolling her eyes. 'Ellie's here, isn't she, so I can hardly take him back to mine.'

'What about his?'

'Are you pimping me out, Pip?'

Pippa laughed and sprayed her tea over the counter. 'Oh no, I'm sorry,' she giggled.

'It was the word *pimp*, wasn't it?' Zoe chuckled and wiped up the spray from the counter. 'I didn't go back to his, not sure I'm ready for that sort of commitment yet. Just enjoying the whole dating thing right now.'

'That's all well and good, but make sure you don't punish

yourself just because you don't want to rely on anyone. I know what you're like; you will be beating yourself up over the past and keeping him at a distance. Not everyone is like ...' she trailed off, not wanting to say that guy's name and wondering whether she was right to be turning the conversation back to that time in Zoe's life. Zoe looked a little uncomfortable at the mention of this. 'Look,' Pippa placed her hand on top of her friend's to gain her attention. 'I don't want to make you think of that time, but just remember that you deserve to be happy. Don't tar every guy with the same brush – let nice things happen.'

Zoe nodded and smiled. 'I know, and I'm not tarring anyone with that, I'm just making sure everything is right before I go that one step further. We've only been dating a couple of months – it's still early days yet.'

'But you do like him?' Pippa asked, a smile snaking across her mouth because she already knew the answer. Judging by the way Zoe had been speaking about him recently, she knew she was head over heels.

Zoe laughed and nudged Pippa gently. 'Oh, be quiet, we sound like schoolgirls. Now drink up because I have a new coffee syrup I want you to try for me.' She went to walk away and shouted over her shoulder, 'Don't worry, its decaf!'

* * * * *

'Els!'

Chris came rushing into the women's toilet, locating her almost instantly on the floor by the sink, sobbing. His knees buckled as he immediately dropped to the floor, throwing his arms around Ellie's shoulders and practically pulling her onto his lap.

'Shh, it's okay. Come on, calm down.' He pulled her hair away from her face and smoothed it down her back, letting his hand slide gently along her spine and then slowly back up again, how he always did to calm her down.

'I don't know what happened. I just came in and she was hyperventilating in there.' Ellie kept her eyes firmly squeezed shut as she listened to the woman talking, her sobbing calming to a quiet hiccup as Chris's calming strokes along her back began to take hold. Ellie thought back to the time she was sitting on Chris's sofa in his flat when her mum had died and he just held her. No words. Just held her for hours, stroking up and down her spine and kissing her occasionally on the top of her head. He had this way with her like no other person; he could calm her with just one touch. It was an amazing connection they had. And now she was going to fuck it all up by telling him she had gone and got herself pregnant. If she lost him too, she didn't know what she would do.

'Els?' She felt his chest pull away from hers slightly as he tried to look down at her. 'How are you feeling?'

She looked up at him, unable to describe how she felt. Because, in all honesty, she didn't actually know what the hell just happened to her. She pleaded with her eyes for him to help her. One of the great things about being so connected to someone was that she knew she only had to look at him and he would know what to do. Except, this time he had no idea what secret she was harbouring. How the words that

104

were going to have to come out of her mouth would turn his whole life upside down. What scared her more was that she was starting to think she wanted this baby.

'Els, I can't help you if you don't talk to me. Please,' he lifted his hand and brushed his thumb down her cheek. 'I'm worried about you.'

She felt her chin quiver and threaten to give way to the tsunami of emotion ready to explode again. 'I'm sorry.' She managed to squeak out.

He looked heartbroken. As though he felt completely useless and unable to fathom what it was he was supposed to actually do to make her better.

She sat up, away from his tight grasp and let his hands drop slightly into her lap, pulling at her fingers to cup into his. 'I don't know what to do,' she finally said.

'If you don't tell me, I can't help you.' He shrugged and willed her to talk. After a moment he squeezed her hand. 'Shall we go back to the table and get a coffee? Then you can tell me exactly what the hell is going on?'

She nervously looked at him. His face was a cross between love and concern, and seriousness. He wasn't going to let her leave this time without coming clean. It was now or never.

Chapter 10

After what felt like a million years, Ellie was sitting back at the table in the restaurant she had chosen to meet Chris at.

'I bet I look a mess, don't I?' She said, rubbing her hands over her tear-stained face.

Chris walked around the table with a glass of water he had just collected from the bar and stood facing Ellie, not yet taking his seat. She couldn't look at him. Her whole body tensed up and she physically hurt. She didn't want to look at him. Didn't want him to see her face. Didn't want to be here. He sat down in the chair that he had recently vacated, but then seemed to change his mind and stood up. Ellie was afraid he was going to walk away, so she snapped her head up and said, 'Chris, wait!' He didn't stop, but instead of walking away, he strolled right around to her side of the table and sat down next to her, pulling her in for the biggest hug, wrapping his arms around her waist and squeezing her tight.

Ellie felt a bolt of emotion overcome her and, without being able to control herself, she burst into tears again. Just the feeling of Chris's arms around her again, someone she trusted, someone she knew loved her, someone who was always there for her, she hugged him back and never wanted to let him go.

'Oh, Els, what is going on?' he asked as he stroked the back of her head. 'Shh, come on. It's okay. I'm here now and whatever it is, we can sort it out. I promise.'

She could smell his aftershave again. It was the one he always wore; she could identify it in a heartbeat. He smelt sweet and manly and up until now, she just thought it was his smell. But now, now it smelt different. It was the same aftershave, she was sure of that, but this time it smelt stronger. Not as if he was wearing more, but as though she smelt it through a new nose. It was a weird sensation.

After a few moments, her crying calmed to a soft blub and she pulled back from his shoulder, trying to hide her face in her hands out of sheer embarrassment.

'What are you doing?' he asked, and it was clear he was smiling; she could hear the smile in his voice.

'I look a mess.' She dropped her head into her hands and wished now, more than ever, that she had her make-up supplies with her.

'Don't be stupid. You look fine.'

Defiantly she snapped her head up and looked at him, raising her eyebrow in a challenging way as if to say *go on; tell me I look fine now*.

He laughed, and it was the loveliest sound she had heard in a long time. His silky voice emitting this beautiful, happy sound. She wished she could bottle it and keep it forever. Because she knew, after today, that there probably wouldn't be much laughter between them – it would probably be all stress and nappies and money-talk.

'Honestly, you're fine. A little blotchy here and there, but mostly your normal, beautiful self.'

Ellie pushed him on his arm and rolled her eyes. She didn't take compliments at the best of times, least of all from Chris.

'Here,' Chris gave her a tissue from his pocket.

'It's not covered in your snot is it?' she eyed it suspiciously, hiccupping as she tried to steady her breathing.

'No, but I'm pretty sure it's about to be covered in yours, by the look of your face.'

'Hey!' she quickly put the tissue up to her face.

'I'm joking,' he replied. 'You're fine ... honest.'

She used the tissue to clean herself up a bit and regain a normal breathing pattern again. Chris had stood up to go back over to the counter, so she used this time to check her face in her mirror. She was right; she did look a complete state. Her face was patchy with red splodges; her eyes puffy as though she had really bad hay fever and her top lip looked a little swollen where she had been constantly crying and rubbing her nose. It was not a pretty sight. She wet the corner of the tissue with the tip of her tongue, to try and wipe away some of the mascara that had spread down one of her cheeks. Really, she needed to take all her make-up off and start again. She felt vulnerable sitting in public with her face like this.

He came back to the table, holding a latte for himself and a chocolate milkshake for Ellie. 'What's that for?' she asked, unable to stop the smile from spreading across her face.

'Well, if there was ever a time for chocolate milkshake, I

reckon now would be it.' He put it on the table, kissed her on the top of her head and sat down opposite. He watched her as she took a sip. The creaminess from the ice cream melted in her mouth as she swallowed the amazing chocolatey flavour. 'Good?'

'Mmm, epic.'

'So, come on, what the hell is going on with you? Because I'm not going to lie, this wants to be good otherwise I have just spent the last God knows how long sat on the floor in the ladies' toilet for no reason.'

Ellie turned up the corners of her mouth at his comment, but then shook her head and looked into the glass of frothy brown liquid.

'Nope, not having all this again Ellie. You can't just walk out of a shoot, drive hours away to your sisters, ask to meet me, act weird, hardly text me, miss my calls, meet me for lunch in bloody Milton Keynes, have a complete meltdown in the ladies loo ... and tell me nothing is wrong.'

Ellis stared at Chris, her eyes wide, taking it all in. 'Wow, when you say it like that it does sound a bit like I'm a loony.'

'No, you've always been a loony. This, however, is completely out of character – and you know it.'

She nodded as the realisation dawned on her. She had to tell him or risk losing him forever. And actually, she thought to herself, by telling she might lose him forever too, so either way, she could potentially ruin their friendship – so what did she have to lose?

He paused for a minute and then said sadly, 'Is it me? Have I done something wrong?'

She took his hands in hers across the table, her face contorted with sorrow. 'No Chris, it's not you. You have done nothing but be there for me.'

He leaned in closer so that their faces were just inches apart. His eyes staring into hers, never wavering. His thumb gently rubbing the top of her hand whilst his knee, leaning against hers under the table, bounced up and down in anticipation.

This was it. It was now or never. She took a deep breath and did what she had been dreading.

'Chris ... I'm pregnant.'

Chapter 11

The breeze whipped at Imogen's face as she walked past the duck pond in the park, hand in hand with Alice. This was one of her favourite places to be. She frequently came here after work to walk around the pond, watching the children feeding the ducks on their way home from school after having spent half an hour in the park. Occasionally she would sit on the bench by the park and just listen. Listen to the sound of the children screaming and laughing as they jumped around on the play equipment. No fear, just pure elation and adventure. It was one of her favourite sounds – happiness and innocence all wrapped up in an exciting little package of wonderment. And now, finally, she was going to experience that first hand.

'What you thinking about?' Alice asked, snapping Imogen out of her daydream and back to reality.

'How much fun it's going to be to bring the baby to the park and to feed the ducks.'

'I literally cannot tell you how excited I am, Ims. It's just the best feeling in the world.'

'I know. But until we see the doctor, I don't think we should get too excited. I just want to know everything is okay.'

'I know, but I can feel it. It's all going to be fine.'

'Don't, Alice.' Imogen looked out over the pond at the little boy with his father, throwing small pieces of ripped-up bread into the water. 'As hard as it has been each time we tried and it failed, we never had it, so it was manageable. But this time, it's there. We do have it – I couldn't bear it if anything happened.'

Alice stopped suddenly and pulled Imogen around to face her. 'Hey, why are you talking like that? Her tone was kind and gentle. 'Everything is going to be fine. I promise.'

'You can't promise this, Alice. It's not in our hands.'

'Why would anything go wrong?' She paused and then added. 'You need to allow yourself to enjoy this moment, Ims. Stop thinking of the negative and enjoy the excitement.'

Imogen started walking again and gently pulled Alice's hand to encourage her to follow. 'I just don't want to get my hopes up and then something happens and I have to ... come back from it. I don't think I could come back from something like that.'

'Baby, you're worrying over nothing at the moment. Let's just wait and see what the doctor says tomorrow and, hopefully, then you'll allow yourself to be happy.'

Imogen nodded.

'I just want to tell the world.'

'Does it not worry you, though ... what people will say?' She couldn't look at Alice as she asked because she knew what Alice would say.

'No, it doesn't. And it shouldn't worry you either.' Her response was a little sterner than last time. Imogen knew this topic frustrated Alice. She couldn't understand why Imogen let it bother her so much.

'I can't help it, you know. It just gets to me.'

'But we are adults now. We are entitled to do what we want and be with who we want to be with. There is no law against same-sex relationships and there isn't one for those couples having babies either. Those people who have a problem with it – it's their problem. Not ours. The more you let their words seep into your brain, the more it will mess you up. You need to stand strong with your head held high.'

'It's easy for you to say, you've got people behind you.'

'Imogen, you have me and you have my family. You can't let people like your mother ruin your life. If she cared about you then she would love you no matter what.'

'That's not fair and you know it.'

They went quiet and as they continued to walk, the air between them tense. With every step she took, Imogen regretted bringing this up. This was supposed to be a nice calm stroll through the park before dinner and now it was turning into a heated discussion between the pair of them. She just wished Alice would try to understand. But Alice was very strong-minded and when it came to defending her sexuality, she was very passionate about it.

'Has your mum been messaging you again, then?' Alice asked, and Imogen could hear the tension in her tone.

'No,' she lied, and instantly regretted it. But it wasn't worth the argument.

'Good, because we don't need her stressing you out.'

'She doesn't mean it, you know.'

'Ims, don't make excuses for her. She chooses to be the way she is with you and with me, and this whole situation. She has the choice to be okay with it and to be a part of our lives.'

'But she's sick, she can't help it.' Imogen always went on the defensive with her mum. Even after everything she had put Imogen through; she couldn't help but long to have that relationship with her.

She stopped walking and sat Imogen down with her on the bench they were passing. 'Bipolar Disorder is an illness and she may not be able to help it. But she has been given medication to help her and she doesn't take it. The doctors offered her therapy to help – she didn't take that either.'

Imogen exhaled, defeated.

'There's only so much we can do, but she chooses to let these episodes rule her life and she takes it out on you. And that's not fair.' Alice cupped Imogen's hand in hers.

'I just want to be able to help her, to make things easier.'

'I know you do, but we have tried. She's not willing to let us help – she wants you to leave me and go back to living with her so you can go back to doing everything for her.' She paused and then tentatively asked, 'That isn't what you want, is it?'

'No, of course not. Alice, I love you so much. I'm just finding it really hard not having Mum around, you know, now that we have the baby coming.'

Alice pulled her in for a hug and kissed her forehead. 'Things will be fine. I promise I will work my arse off to make sure you and this baby have the best life. And you know you'll always have my mum.'

'I know,' Imogen said, but inside her heart sunk. Alice's mum wasn't the same – she wanted her mum.

But it looked as if that was never going to happen.

Chapter 12

'Chris?' Ellie looked back at her friend who was sitting open-mouthed, having not moved for the last few minutes. His beautiful blue eyes were wide in disbelief as he stared back at her. Her heart pulsated rapidly, pumping her blood so quickly around her body that she was becoming a little fuzzy-headed. She looked around the restaurant, certain that everyone must be able to hear the pounding in her chest, which was causing her to hear a loud ringing noise in her ears. She could feel her skin becoming clammy as she began to sweat. After a quick glance around, she looked back at Chris whose gaze had now dropped slightly as he tried to take in this new information. Ellie shook his hand slightly to get his attention back to her. 'Chris? Say something ... please.'

He looked back at her, gazing into her eyes. He closed his mouth and shook his head in disbelief. 'Pregnant?' he practically whispered the word to her. Tears filled her eyes again as she nodded. Chris seemed to snap out of whatever it was as he saw her getting upset again. He stood up and immediately, joined her back on the other side of the table, once again, putting his arm around her and giving her that much-needed reassurance. 'Shit,' he breathed.

'I'm sorry, Chris, I—'

'Shh, it's okay. We will get through this. It's fine. Why didn't you bloody tell me sooner?'

'I don't know.' She did know. But she could hardly tell him that she was worried he would do a runner. That this would be the end of their friendship. That she didn't want to have a baby. There was no real reason to think he would do any of those things. He's a nice guy. But panic was making her brain fry and she could no longer decipher between thoughts that were rational and thoughts that weren't. She was a mess – plain and simple.

'Well, we need to sort things out and make sure that the guy pulls his weight and doesn't leave you to do everything.'

'But ... Chris ...'

'No, Ellie, you can't be being all Mrs Independent on this like you usually do with things, the guy has a responsibility too – it takes two to make a baby. Has he been supportive?'

Ellie tried to talk, but all that came out was a mix of stutters and half-words. She thought she had done the hardest part; she didn't expect Chris to get the total wrong end of the stick.

'Who is he?' Chris looked a little angry as he asked and this threw Ellie off-course.

'What?' She croaked.

'Who's the dad? Because if he thinks he's going to just leave you with all this to deal with on your own, he's got another think coming.'

'Chris ... listen to me.' He turned his head, catching her eyes square-on. She felt as if she was going to buckle under the surge of panic, which seared through her chest right at that moment. He looked just like the Chris she remembered. The protective, loving, always-there-for-her Chris who she was so fond of. Right now he was fighting her corner, but would he continue to do so once he found out the truth? She didn't have a choice in the matter. She had to tell him. 'It's ... it's ...' she stumbled and dropped her gaze.

'Oh my God,' he whispered. 'It's mine, isn't it?'

She held on to the quiver in her chin as she nodded.

'Fuck,' she heard him say under his breath, moving towards her and pulling her in for a hug. He exhaled heavily. Whilst he was there for her physically, she couldn't shake off the feeling that, emotionally, he was a little empty right now. She wanted to gauge what he was thinking but instead chose to stay quiet and wait for him to talk. It took a little longer than she felt comfortable with, but eventually he spoke. 'Els, this is huge.'

'I know,' she squeaked.

Silence again. She wanted to ask him if he was going to run a mile. She wanted to beg him not to leave her. But realistically, she didn't know what was going to happen. And she wasn't the type of girl to beg for anything. She didn't need anyone.

Her phone beeped. It was a message from Zoe.

Please just let me know that you are okay?

'Shit, I forgot to text Zoe.' She typed a quick reply, just saying that she was fine and that she was talking to Chris. She placed her phone back in her bag and resumed picking at her nails for something to do.

Chris coughed, either to clear his throat or get Ellie's attention. Either way, she looked up. 'I need to just, you know, take this in.' He smiled at her but she could see the strain behind it.

'I don't expect anything from you, Chris. You know that don't you?' She felt her barriers shoot up as if they were spring-loaded. The first sign of worry and, yep, up they go.

He glanced at her with a look on his face as if she had hurt his feelings. 'I'm not going to just abandon you, Ellie. I'm not an arsehole.'

'I know you're not!' She leaned back, offended that he would think that of her. 'I'm just saying, I didn't come here to tell you to make you do anything you didn't want to.'

'You didn't come here to tell me at all, if you're being honest' he said, under his breath. But she heard him. She also heard the strain in his voice.

'But I did tell you.' She defended herself.

He gave a little snort, but then tried to cover it up. 'I don't want to argue with you. We have bigger things to worry about right now.'

She went to retaliate, but decided not to. Right now, all she wanted to do was leave.

* * * * *

Imogen picked up her phone from the counter when Alice went in the bath and typed out a message.

Mum, it's me. Just wanted to check all was okay?

She felt guilty straight away for doing it behind Alice's back, but after their conversation today she really just wanted to speak to her mum. Maybe if she tried harder to make her mum understand, things would be easier. And then she could show Alice that all was okay and everyone would be happy. She loved Alice to pieces, but one thing Alice wasn't very good at was understanding from her point of view about the whole Mum situation. It was easy for her, she had amazing parents. But Imogen grew up in a difficult household plagued with anxiety and depression and as much as Alice said she understood how hard it was, she didn't – not really.

But that wasn't her fault. And it didn't make Imogen love her any less. It just meant that for things like this, and whilst she was sorting herself out, it was best to keep these things quiet.

But instead of texting back, her mum called.

'Hello?' Imogen said quietly, trying not to sound as if she was trying to whisper.

'Imogen, it's Mum.'

'Hi.'

There was a pause. It felt awkward. She listened to her mum's breathing down the phone; it was sort of jittery, as though she was crying.

'Mum? Is everything okay?'

'It's so nice to hear from you, sweetheart, are you coming home yet?' She was clearly upset. It broke Imogen's heart to hear her mum like this, and she had had many calls and texts over the years with her mum either crying or shouting at her, for whatever reason.

'No Mum, I live here. With Alice. You know this.'

'But I promise you, you will be happier back here with me. You won't have to deal with people looking at you funny or talking about you behind your back. We can sort this. You can start again.'

'I don't want to start again. I love Alice and I want to be here with her. I don't care if people talk behind my back – that's their problem, not mine.' She relayed what Alice had said to her earlier, wishing she felt as strong as she made out.

'So why did you text, then, if you don't want to get away?'

'Because I wanted to make sure you were okay. After the last time we spoke you were pretty upset and then I haven't heard from you – I was worried. I don't set out to upset you, Mum. I just want you to understand, to see, that we are really happy and I want you to be a part of that.'

'You know I can't do that.'

'But why?' she pleaded.

'Because what will people think, Imogen? What will they say about me? What they already say about you.'

'Why do you care so much? Surely my happiness means more to you than what other people think and do? No?' She willed in her mind for her mum to just see what she was saying. 'Things could be so different if you just accepted that I am married to Alice and—'

'I can't!'

They both sat in silence for a minute and then Imogen heard Alice come out of the bathroom and begin to descend the stairs.

'Listen, Mum, I have to go. Just think about it, okay? Please.' She waited for a response, but her mum just ended the call.

'Alright?' Alice said as she walked into the kitchen. 'Want a cuppa?'

Imogen smiled and nodded. She was afraid if she tried to speak, tears would come out instead.

Chapter 13

'Whose fucking bad idea was that?' Ellie shrieked as she stormed into her sister's flat. She slumped down immediately onto the sofa, next to Zoe, and placed her hands over her eyes dramatically. It was mostly for effect, but also because she truly couldn't believe what her life had become over the last few days.

'Does this need coffee?' Zoe asked, but didn't move.

Ellie threw her arms back down at her sides and turned her head to face her sister. 'Honestly, what the fuck is going on in my life?'

Zoe laughed and squeezed Ellie's knee. 'Do you know what, sis? I ask myself that question plenty of times.' She stood up and walked to the kitchen, flicking the kettle on. Ellie could still hear her perfectly because the flat was so tiny. 'So, come on, spill.'

'I don't even know where to begin.'

'The beginning is always a good start,' Zoe retorted.

'Haha, very funny', Ellie said under her breath. 'Well, I told him. He knows he is the dad. And,' she paused as she relived his expression, 'I guess he will be there for me.' She sighed and looked out of the window beside her, looking at the lights from the shop cascading down onto the footpath outside and losing herself in the brightness.

After a few minutes, Zoe returned to the room with two cups of something hot and a packet of biscuits under her arm. 'Here, take these.' She passed the cookies to Ellie and dropped into the sofa beside her. 'So he's okay?'

Ellie shrugged.

'He's going to help you?'

A sigh. 'I guess so.' She paused as she let the thoughts from today wash over her. 'Zoe, I just don't want him to feel pressured into being something he doesn't want to be.' She sipped her hot chocolate and tried to blink back the tears.

'What do you mean?'

Ellie swallowed hard before saying, 'I just don't want our friendship to suffer because of a mistake we made. I love Chris to bits and if I lose what we have because of a drunken shag, I would never forgive myself. Our friendship means so much to me and I will do anything to make sure that it is kept safe.' She waited for a response but didn't get anything. She looked at Zoe, who was playing with her nail varnish. 'Do you see what I mean?'

Zoe looked up. Her face was full of sorrow and, what Ellie could only describe as bittersweet happiness.

'Els, I'm afraid your friendship *will* have to change because of this. There's nothing you can do about that.'

Ellie huffed and looked back at the window. Fucking great, she thought as she sipped her tea.

'It'll be okay,' Zoe must've used her sister senses and realised how low Ellie was feeling right now because she reached over and pulled Ellie into a hug. 'I know this is really shit for you at the moment, but trust me, it'll work out.'

Ellie pulled away. 'How?'

Zoe looked startled. 'What?'

'How?' Ellie pressed. 'How will this all be hunky dory?' The sarcasm dripped from her voice like honey, lacing every syllable leaking from her mouth.

'Because it will.'

'Oh, thank God for that. It'll be okay, *because it will*', that's okay, then.'

'Stop it!' Zoe pushed Ellie's shoulder, not hard, but hard enough for her to realise that she wasn't messing around. 'You aren't going to get anywhere by feeling sorry for yourself!'

A moment passed whilst the two sisters glared at each other, waiting for one to give up and drop the gaze. Subsequently, this time, it was Zoe.

'Els, it *will* be okay because it *has* to be! You can't just brush it under the carpet because things got too tough. Life is hard, you have to deal with it – end of!'

'How?' Ellie shrieked, before letting a stray tear, which betrayed her, slide down her cheek. 'Zoe, I can't do it.'

Zoe stood and walked towards her, taking her hands into hers. 'Why can't you?'

Ellie took a moment to compose herself and then raised her gaze. Not all the way to Zoe's, she wasn't ready for that, but enough to lift her chin. 'I'm not like Mum,' was all she said, before taking her hands back and walking back to the sofa, keeping the distance between them.

Zoe's face creased in confusion as she said, 'What? I don't get it? What's that supposed to mean?'

Ellie threw her cardigan on the sofa and whipped up her mug of hot chocolate. She stopped in the doorway and said, 'I can't be the mum that our mum was. I will never live up to what she would've wanted, to what mums should be. I'm crap! I can barely look after myself, let alone another living being. Chris says he will be there but I can tell he's freaking out.'

'Is he not allowed to freak out too?' Zoe pressed. 'Look at you! You're totally having a meltdown about it – maybe think about him too. You've known for a few days – he has literally just found out. So why can't he freak out?' She was shouting at Ellie in frustration now.

'I just can't do it, okay?' Ellie slammed the door behind her as she walked to the bedroom. She knew she was being irrational, but it was the only way she knew how to be right now.

* * * * *

Ellie woke up to the sound of her phone vibrating on her bedside table in the spare room. She rubbed her eyes and leant across to pick it up. Chris's name was flashing at her and it took her a moment to see that he was video-calling her. She groaned and answered but turned the camera so that it was facing the ceiling instead of her face.

'Do you realise how late it is?' she answered the call with.

'I know, I'm sorry. I just felt like we left things strained today and I wanted to talk to you.' He frowned. 'Why can I only see your ceiling?'

Ellie giggled. 'Because, it is 11.30 at night and I currently have no make-up on, bed hair and the most unflattering pyjamas because I have to borrow Zoe's and she doesn't have the same taste in nightwear as I do.'

'Oh give over! Just turn the camera round. I'm not going to lie here and talk to your ceiling.'

Ellie groaned, 'Fine, but one comment about the state of my face and I'm switching you back round, understood?'

'Loud and clear,' he replied and she could see a smile sneak across his lips.

She turned the camera around, but not before doing a quick flick with her hair so that she didn't look completely hideous. 'There, happy now?' She looked at him as he nodded and smiled fully.

'That's better.' There was a pause. 'How are you feeling?'

'Bit shit, to be honest.' Well, there was no point in lying. 'You?'

'Pretty much the same,' he replied. 'This is so huge, Els.'

'I know, Chris. I'm sorry to spring this on you; I know this isn't what either of us wanted.'

'Why are you apologising? We both decided to go through with ...' he seemed to hesitate, unable to decide on what word to use and then settled on 'it'.

Ellie laughed. 'You sound like a kid who doesn't want to say the 'S' word.'

Now he laughed and as he did, he lifted his arm up and rested it on his forehead. He was lying in bed without a shirt on and just a pair of bottoms – although from the angle, she couldn't see if it was shorts or trousers, just that it had a waistband. She tried not to react to the fact that he was topless; it wasn't as though she hadn't seen it all before. But this time it all just seemed so different. Everything had changed; nothing felt normal any more.

'I just want you to know that I am here and I am not going to let you do this alone. We just need to come up with a plan, a strategy, and we can make this work.'

'Make it work?' she questioned. Was he telling her he wanted to be more than friends? Maybe this was the start of a proper relationship. Ellie wasn't even sure if that was what she wanted. She felt as if her mind wasn't her own any more – she didn't know what she wanted. It was all just so confusing.

'Yeah, we can sort out maintenance, and share custody – whatever you want. I will be here for you. And ... well ... the baby.'

She felt a little disappointment settle as she realised he meant making things work logically, not romantically. 'I just feel so confused.'

'About what?' He shuffled on the bed and unknowingly revealed a little more body. Ellie could see the waistband of his bottoms shift slightly lower and she found she couldn't take her eyes off it. When she realised what she was doing she snapped her vision away, looking at the alarm clock on the side table, her cheeks flushing.

'Just about everything. It's all so complicated. I don't want to fuck up your life – or mine. I just need to get my head around it and work out what to do.'

'That's understandable, Els. It's a massive change. My head has been all over the place this evening. I feel like I might be hormonal!' He laughed.

Ellie cracked a smile this time and they spent a good minute just smiling at each other. She looked at him on the screen and felt as though she could see right into his soul. He made her feel as if they were the only two people on this earth and all she wanted to do was be there on the bed with him, snuggled into his chest, feeling the warmth of his skin against her. It felt so good on that fateful night when all this happened. He had this way of making her feel as if she was the only person in his world who mattered.

'Chris ...' she began, but then paused. What was she expecting to happen now? For her to declare her love to him and him to pull her into his arms and declare it back? It was a stupid idea. They were too far into the friend zone to become anything more – it would be weird.

'Els, we can do this. Okay? You are my best mate and I know we can bring this child up to be loved and feel special – we don't have to be together for that to happen.'

Well, that was it, decision made. 'I guess so.'

'So we are doing it?' he asked.

'We are doing it,' she repeated.

He smiled the biggest grin she had seen from him in a long time. 'Awesome. Well, get some sleep and rest up. And I'll call you soon.'

'Okay,' she squeaked, trying not to let the emotion show. 'Night, Chris.'

'Night, Els.'

She ended the call and wiped the tears from her eyes with the back of her hand. That was it, then. They were raising this baby together – as friends.

What could possibly go wrong?

Chapter 14

'Are you not talking to me, then?' Pippa ignored Jason's comment and continued mixing the batter for the peanut-butter cake she was trying out. 'Come on, Pip, I said I was sorry.' He slipped his hands onto her waist from behind and tried to nuzzle into her neck. Pippa shook him off almost instantly and went to the pantry. She didn't actually need anything from in there, but she had to get his hands off her. She was still fuming about how he behaved at the weekend. It was times like this that she was overcome with feelings that she tried so desperately to hide. Not just from others, but from herself, too. She had made the decision that she was going to stick by Jason and have a future with him, not go back over old ground all the time. But when he got underneath her skin, she struggled to stick to her decision. It wasn't as if she had a choice, though. If she wanted this baby and the family life she was so desperate for, she would have to learn to brush off moments like the weekend. She needed to pick her fights and this one wasn't one worth choosing. Knowing that didn't stop the frustration building up inside, though.

'What more can I do?' His voice was a little more urgent now; a cross between desperation and frustration.

'Nothing,' was her chosen reply.

'Nothing? So, what? I just wait until you decide you can talk to me again? Is that it?' Frustration had clearly won the battle. 'It's been three days!'

Pippa spun round to face him. 'Yes, Jason, that's exactly what you do. Because, what else can you do? Can you change what you did? No. Can you turn back time and not do it? No.'

'Oh, for crying out loud. So I went for a few drinks with my mates. Big deal.' He had taken his suit jacket off when he returned home from work that evening and removed his tie. He actually looked scruffy rather than the usual relaxed look. Or was that just because she was angry at him?

'We were supposed to be celebrating … together!' she added, as she saw Jason's mouth open to reply. 'But instead, you chose to go and get drunk with your friends and not even tell me. I had to call you to see where you were. I was all dressed up …' she could feel the anger beginning to bubble up. Jason's face softened as he saw how worked up Pippa was becoming. He moved closer to her and tried to pull her in for a cuddle. 'Don't,' she said, looking away.

'Pip, stop it. Come on.'

'You promised you would cut down on the drinking. You know it makes you unbearable to be around.'

Jason shifted uncomfortably on his feet. 'Yeah, I know. I'm sorry.'

'I can't be around you when you are like that. We've got a

baby on the way and you should be trying your hardest to make things good at home, not go out your way to piss me off and create tension.' Times like this she felt like his mum and she hated that.

'Pip, I know! Alright? I said I'm sorry. What more do you want?' He exhaled and walked to the window, saying quietly, 'Jeez, bloody baby stuff is getting on my nerves already.'

Pippa went to retaliate but chose not to. If she did, then this would all blow up into a huge argument and she might say or do something she would regret. She just needed to knuckle down with work, get herself some independence and make sure her baby was safe and loved. Whether Jason was a part of that plan in the long run, she wasn't so sure any more, but right now she needed the support. He turned back from the window, having calmed himself a little, and walked over to her, seemingly testing the water with a smile. She sighed and let him wrap his arms around her as she buried her face into his shoulder. She could feel his hands rubbing up and down her back, squeezing her harder the more she relaxed. 'I'm sorry,' he said gently. 'I shouldn't have been an idiot. Let me make it up to you?'

She nodded without lifting her face. It felt so nice to be held. Jason hadn't held her like this for ages. It was all arguments and rushing around and being stressed from work; he never had time to just hold her without knowing it was going to lead to something. This is what she missed. The intimacy. The feeling of being wanted. The love.

'How about I take you out for dinner tonight? Your choice?'

'I don't really feel like it, to be honest.' She wiped the tear from her eyes and turned back to the cake mix. She felt exhausted from the tirade of emotions he frequently unleashed in her. It was draining being his wife sometimes.

'Come on, please? Let me make it up to you?' His hands were back on her waist.

She didn't have the strength to continue going round in circles with him so she nodded. 'But first I need to finish this cake.'

* * * * *

'Okay, hear me out before you say no.'

Ellie looked at her sister suspiciously. 'Why do I feel as if I am not going to like what you are about to say?'

'You will, it'll be fine. Just hear me out before you answer. Listen to the *whole* thing.' Ellie nodded her acceptance of the terms and made herself comfortable on the stall she was sitting on, propped up against the serving hatch in the café. There weren't many people in at the moment, so Ellie had been chatting to her sister on and off all morning.

'Okay, so, I was thinking that whilst you are up here and you aren't sure how long you'll be staying ... it would be good for you to make some friends. People in a ... um ... similar situation to you. So,' she held up her hand to stop Ellie from talking, 'I was thinking you might like to join the pregnancy club thingy here at the café I run every week. Other pregnant mums get together to chat, share tips, tell their stories: sort of a mummy community. Then you might feel a little better about everything and you can see that it isn't as scary as you think. They're a great bunch and my friend is starting too, so you won't be the only new-comer.'

There was a pause and Ellie asked, 'Are you finished?'

Zoe nodded, a huge excitable smile spread over her face.

'Okay. I've listened, I didn't interrupt … but, no.'

Zoe's face dropped. 'What do you mean, 'no'?'

'I'm not up for it, Zo. Why do I want to sit around with a load of pregnant people talking baby stuff?' She dismissed it with her hand as she ate her sandwich.

'Because YOU are pregnant, Ellie. It would be nice for you to chat to other people in the same situation as you.' She swung the tea towel over her shoulder and crossed her arms.

'But they're not in the same situation, Zoe. How many other people get pregnant by their best friend on a one-night stand that went horribly wrong?'

'You aren't the only person in the world this has happened to, Ellie. Stop being so dramatic.'

'Maybe not, but I am not interested in making small-talk with people I don't know about something I don't care about.' She shrugged it off. Why Zoe thought this would be something that Ellie would entertain, she didn't know. It was stupid. The whole situation was stupid.

'Something you don't care about? Ellie, that's your baby inside there.' She pointed to Ellie's stomach, as if she didn't know what she was talking about. 'Is this what it's going to be like all the time now? Chris isn't an arsehole, he will stick by you.'

'I know he will. It's fine. Just leave it.' She picked up and flicked through the magazine on the counter, not taking in anything, simply scanning the printed material.

'Well, it is hard to just leave it when you are always so stroppy about it all. Maybe you two should meet up again and sort out a plan? Instead of you always running away from it all like you always do. You haven't got to do this all alone; there are people around you who want to help.'

Ellie rolled her eyes. 'We *have* sorted out a plan. We are going to bring this baby up and just stay friends. It's all going to be hunky bloody dory, okay!' Except she wasn't okay because she didn't want to just be friends. And this fact annoyed her more than anything. But she'd be damned if she was about to tell anyone how she felt about Chris. She caved and gave in to the idea so that Zoe would get off her case – she wasn't in the mood today. 'Okay, fine, let's do the mummy club thing.'

Zoe squeaked and clapped her hands together. 'Really? That's great news – you and Chris are going to make amazing parents! And I was hoping you would agree to the group. Pippa is starting too. We could have a special cake offer just for then – I'll talk to Pip – and you will get to meet some lovely ladies.' Ellie could see that Zoe was running away with ideas already.

'Can't wait,' Ellie said, with more enthusiasm than she felt.

Zoe huffed. 'Well, can I just say that I am *loving* your mood swings right now – you're lucky you're giving me a niece or nephew because, in all honesty, that's what keeping me from slapping some sense into you.'

Just as Ellie was about to drink her tea, her phone rang. She glanced at the flashing screen and saw Chris's name. Every part of her body tingled with apprehension as she contemplated answering. Would she always feel like this every time he rang, because she wasn't sure she was up for that.

'Aren't you going to pick up?'

She snapped her attention to Zoe. She really didn't want to answer. To have to pretend all was fine and she was loving life. Urgh!

'Look, I'll go make myself busy, you speak to Chris. Just ... you know ... be nice. Don't take your bad mood out on him.' Zoe raised a knowing eyebrow and then glided off into the kitchen.

Ellie picked up her phone and swiped to answer, taking a deep breath and, using her breeziest voice, she said, 'Alright Chris?'

'Yeah I'm okay, how are you?' He sounded strange already.

'You know ... feeling fat and trying not to pee every two seconds.' She cringed. She was trying to be cool about things, but she was just making it awkward.

'You weirdo,' he replied, and she could hear the smile on his face. He chuckled down the phone and Ellie filled with fondness as she smiled.

'I'll always be weird, Chris. That's why you love me.'

'I love you in spite of that.' Normally a comment like that would be funny, but now, everything seemed different. *They* seemed different.

There was a long silence, which felt as if it lasted a lifetime. Finally Chris said, 'Els, when are you coming home? I hate that you are so far away.'

'I don't know, soon maybe.' She played with the edge of the magazine page on the counter, rolling the paper between her fingers,

'Just a maybe?'

141

'Come on, you've been without me for a lot longer than a few days.' She realised that she really liked having him so concerned about her. It made her feel important. As if she was someone worth worrying about. He was sweet.

'Yes, true, but this time is different.' There was a long, awkward silence following his comment as the pair of them thought about just how true that comment was. 'You are so far away and so much is happening and I want to be there for you. It's just ...' he trailed off and Ellie waited for him to talk. To say anything. Finally he said, 'Just know that I am always here for you.'

'You know you mean the world to me, right?' As she said the words her heart was pumping so hard.

'As do you to me,' he replied.

But she couldn't. As much as she wanted to declare her love for him and they live happily ever after, that just wasn't going to be their love story. Instead she said, 'We'll sort something out. But right now I'm tired. Not used to having all this time off work – I'm sure it'll drive me mad soon, but right now, got to say, I'm loving the chilling.' She laughed nervously. 'I'll speak to you soon?'

It was a question but not one she actually wanted answering. Her life was majorly fucked up and she didn't have a clue as to what she was going to do about it. She had some serious thinking to do. She exhaled. 'Bye Chris.'

She heard him exhale too. But then silence, before he said, 'Yeah, okay, see you, Els.'

Chapter 15

Imogen looked at the leaflet again and read out the swirly letters under her breath: *The First Time Mums' Club.* It sounded like exactly what she needed; a chance to meet others going through the same as her. Alice had given her this leaflet the other day when she had got in from work. 'I think you'll love it,' she had said, 'It's a great way to make some friends before the baby comes. Plus, it's at that nice café we went to. They hold it there every week, apparently, and Jules at work says her friend went to it and loved it.'

Imogen had agreed straight away. Whilst she had her friends, no one else seemed to be interested in having babies. Imogen had longed for a baby since she was little. She was one of those children who knew, growing up, that she was born to be a mum. When she met Alice, everything fell into place. She had stumbled from one relationship to another, with both sexes, never feeling fulfilled, and then along came Alice with her gorgeous long, dark hair and deep-chestnut eyes and she fell in love. When Alice had expressed her desire for children, too, Imogen felt her life was complete. But it had not been an easy ride.

But, here she was, carrying their first child and about to embark on a new journey as a mummy. Dreams really can come true.

'Hopefully you'll meet some lovely ladies and you will feel a bit more supported,' Alice had said. Imogen knew what she actually meant, though – if Imogen made some friends then maybe she wouldn't be so fussed about her mum. She could read Alice like a book, but she did appreciate the sentiment and knew she was only trying to help.

She pushed the door of the café open and ventured inside. It was very quiet, with just one person sitting at a high table by the window and three people sitting around a table on the far side. She walked over to the counter and spoke to the woman whom she recognised from her previous visit.

'Hi, can I help?' Zoe asked.

'Yes, I picked up this leaflet about a mums' club group. Am I in the right place?'

'You sure are. Please, take a seat with the other women over there. We are just waiting for a few more to turn up, then we will begin. Can I get you a drink to take over?'

Imogen nodded and asked for a cappuccino. Taking her drink along with her, she introduced herself to the woman on the table. 'Hi, I'm Imogen. Do you mind if I join you?'

Two of the women smiled and replied with 'of course,' as they shuffled their chairs along. The other woman just looked at Imogen. No expression other than sheer boredom. She sat down and set her cup onto the table.

Around fifteen minutes later, the woman from the café joined the table and waited for the remaining people to sit down. The numbers had multiplied in that time and there were now numerous people crammed around a few tables that had been pushed closer together, although still separate.

'Hello ladies, nice to see you and welcome to a couple of new faces I can see. I'm so glad you could come along today. I am sure you will all agree that parenthood is a scary concept, albeit exciting, and when I started this group I had thought that it would be a great idea to do something like this for our town so that we can make new friends and help each other along the way. Pregnancy can sometimes be a lonely place if you maybe have a partner who works long hours, or family who live far away, so we like to think that this is our little family. So, please, those of you who are new, do chat to everyone and listen to each others' stories, because we are all in the same boat.' Zoe grabbed her coffee from the counter. 'I will check in with you all as I go round the tables and make sure I come and say hi to any new faces.'

Zoe walked over to the table that Imogen had sat at and pulled up another chair. She smiled at Imogen and she instantly felt reassured. 'Okay, so let's welcome this lovely lady to our group. Sorry, what was your name?'

'Imogen,' she replied, feeling numerous sets of eyes turn to look at her.

'Hi Imogen. It's so lovely to have you here. So that we aren't bombarding you with questions straight off, I will start the ball rolling with introductions around the table, so that you know a little about us too.' She sipped her coffee. 'My name is Zoe and I run this café. I am thirty-three years old and when I am not working, I love to read and watch soaps on the TV.'

There were some noises that suggested some of the women around the table also enjoyed watching soaps.

'I am not pregnant, but I wanted to start up a group like this to help others, especially those who aren't from around here, make friends and not have to go through pregnancy alone. I had wanted to start some sort of mummy group in the café anyway and this was suggested to me by a friend ages ago. The idea stewed for a while and then I took the plunge and did it.' Zoe then looked at Imogen and gave her an encouraging smile.

A couple of the other ladies at the table next to them spoke up, saying their names and what their backgrounds were. Everyone seemed so nice and genuinely interested in listening to each other.

'This group has been a godsend,' one of the ladies was saying. 'My husband works away in the army and my parents live back at home in China, so I didn't really have many people around me when we moved here. I started coming to this group and I have made some wonderful friends – friends for life.' She smiled at the group of women on her table and Imogen found herself smiling along. Just listening to these women was making all her worries melt away into her cup of cappuccino. She was laughing along and chipping in comments. She felt the most relaxed she had felt in ages. But then came the time when it was her turn to talk to the group. She felt her nerves creep back up. She wasn't ready to tell this bunch of strangers her life story; hers wasn't as lovely as theirs, what with her crazy mother. But she was never going to make friends if she didn't try.

'Hi everyone. My name is Imogen and I am thirty years old. I am a part-time teaching assistant at Riverside Primary, and I am about six weeks' pregnant. Early days, but I was too excited, so I thought I would take the plunge and come to the group.' She paused and looked around at the expectant faces. 'That's pretty much it.' She gave a nervous laugh.

'That's great. I can see you're nervous, but please don't worry. We are all friends here.' She smiled.

Imogen nodded and desperately wanted the focus to shift from her. Whilst she was open about her sexuality now, she was still plagued with nerves whenever she met someone new, and was expected to tell her story. She never used to be. But then, seeing the way her mum reacted almost left her with a fear of telling people. Most people were absolutely fine. But she still had the nerves whenever it came up with people she didn't know. She couldn't read them and that made her apprehensive.

'Are you married?' Zoe asked.

And there it was. She knew it was coming. She hesitated and then nodded, 'Yes, I've been married for three years now.'

'Aw, a nice new marriage.' The woman opposite her said. She had long, brown hair, like Alice's, and was really pretty in a simple way. 'And what's your husband's name?'

Imogen's heart was pounding so hard against her chest she was sure the others would be able to hear it. 'Err ... well, my wife's name is Alice.'

The table fell silent for just a second and Zoe quickly added, 'Oh my God, I am so sorry. Look at us just assuming like that. I feel terrible!'

'Please, don't. It's okay, really. Everyone does.' She looked around the table and was faced with genuine smiles. No weird looks, no whispering. These were all right people, she concluded. She felt a little more relaxed.

'So how long have you known your wife?'

'We've been together for nearly five years now.'

'Aw, that's so lovely.' The woman opposite smiled reassuringly at Imogen, for which she was so grateful.

'So, how did you fall pregnant?' Everyone around the table whipped their head to look at the woman – who was clearly bored up until this point – in disbelief. 'What?' She asked, 'It's a valid question.'

'It's okay,' Imogen said, smiling at everyone and trying not to laugh.

'Ellie is my sister – she's new today too – she can be a little direct sometimes,' Zoe said, trying to ease the moment.

'Err hello, I *am* still here.' Ellie said, holding out her hands.

'Don't we know it!' The table laughed at Zoe's comment.

'Honestly, it's fine. I'd rather people say it how it is than talk about me behind my back.'

'Do you get a lot of that, then?' Imogen nodded at Zoe sadly. 'People can be so horrible sometimes. But you don't have to worry about that with us; we are all friends here and we want you to feel happy and comfortable to tell us what you want. Don't feel pressured.'

'Thank you. Its fine. I'm happy to tell you.'

'So, how does it work?' Ellie settled back in her chair ready for the story.

Imogen looked at the interested faces around the table and felt a sudden rush of nerves...

'You don't have to tell us anything you don't want us to know.' Zoe leant across the table and stroked Imogen's hand. She must've looked like a rabbit in headlights for her to have said something.

'Honestly, it's fine. I just don't know where to begin, that's all.' She could feel her hands becoming clammy. She wasn't used to being the one who divulged the ins and outs of their relationship. That was Alice's domain. She would know exactly what to say in this sort of situation, whereas Imogen felt completely out of her depth. But, she was going to become a mum so she needed to learn to deal with these sorts of questions. 'Alice and I had been together for about two years when we first started talking about our future and what we wanted. I was very lucky to find someone as amazing as Alice – she really is my rock.'

'Where do you even go to find out about your options? I wouldn't know where to begin.' Ellie was leaning on the table, clearly enthralled already by the conversation.

'I guess you would be looking for an answer a lot more substantial than ... Google?'

Laughter erupted at the table, but then as they seemed to notice Imogen's face, one by one they stopped. 'Oh, you're serious?' The brunette added.

'Well, kind of, yeah. You see, we were the same, we didn't know where to begin looking so we did what everyone does when they have a question, we asked Google!'

'And did Google have the answer?' Zoe probed, sipping at her cup.

'Yes and no. There was a mass of information out there and

I just became overwhelmed with it all. Then Alice came home from work one evening saying she had heard about a seminar that was taking place the following month at a clinic in London which seemed really interesting, so I agreed to go. We went the following month and I was truly amazed at how much there was to offer same-sex couples.' She paused to take a sip of her cappuccino, feeling her apprehension ease slightly the more she spoke about her story. The others seemed so interested and it made her feel wanted, included ... like one of them.

'So, you told them that you were a couple and they were okay with it?'

'Ellie! For God's sake!' Zoe threw a look to her sister.

'Honestly,' Imogen held her hand up to Zoe to reassure her. 'It really is okay. You would be surprised, well you might be, I don't know you well enough yet, but they were so welcoming and treated us like every other person in the room. This particular clinic was so inclusive and they promote themselves as being the clinic of choice for same-sex couples, so we knew we were in the right place. They told us what all our options were – this was without either of us having gone through any tests or anything, so they were speaking overall, not just for us in particular – and we went away feeling so totally elated knowing it was possible and we could do it.'

'I tried IVF a while back,' the woman opposite said as she broke off a piece of Bakewell tart and placed it in her mouth.

'Really, did it work out for you?' Imogen then flushed red at her stupid question. 'Sorry! Of course it worked out.' She indicated to the woman's stomach and drooped a little in her chair from sheer embarrassment.

'Oh, no, that's not how I got pregnant. This was a pure miracle.' She rubbed her tummy and Imogen felt a little better.

'So, what happened with the IVF?'

'It just didn't work. That's the be-all and end-all of it, I'm afraid. I guess yours did?'

'Yeah, eventually. It wasn't the first thing we tried, though. We opted for other treatments but they just didn't work out for us.'

Ellie shuffled in her seat, getting more comfortable and powered over another round of questions that amounted to her pretty much asking about the different treatments and how they were executed. 'So you just turn up, they squirt the sperm inside you and you go home?'

Imogen couldn't stifle her laugh, 'Pretty much. That was for the IUI treatment. It wasn't for us – far too impersonal for what we wanted. But I guess it works for some people and it does work, so that's the main thing. But it didn't for us.'

'What does IUI actually mean?'

Imogen smiled at the interest Ellie was showing. She liked Ellie. She didn't hold any bars. If she wanted to know something, she simply asked. There was no misreading that one. 'IUI is basically artificial insemination. It's called intrauterine insemination.'

'Wow, this stuff just blows my mind. It's amazing what can be done nowadays. So, the artificial thing didn't work, what did you do next?'

'We ended up with just straightforward IVF.'

'I remember when Jason and I went through IVF; it's not

exactly what I would call straightforward.' The woman, who she now knew was called Pippa, raised her eyebrows at Zoe, who clearly knew what she had been through.

'Well, you know what I mean, straightforward in the sense that it was just us and them. No complications, no egg-sharing – although we did want to do that – just us and IVF.'

'I remember all the blood tests and injections,' Pippa reminisced.

'Oh my God, I remember the injections!' Zoe interrupted, shaking her head at the memory. 'I would be round Pippa's,' she addressed Imogen, 'and all of a sudden her phone alarm would go off and she would be like 'it's injection time' and she would whip out the needle and stab it into her stomach. Just like that. Like it was the most normal thing in the world!'

Pippa laughed. 'I remember seeing Zoe's face the first time I did it.'

Zoe shook her head and shivered as she relived it. 'Honestly, it was like a horror movie.'

As the conversation about Pippa's pregnancy unwound, Imogen sat back in her chair and secretly praised herself. She had done it. She got it out of the way and revealed who she was and she felt great. But she had done enough sharing now and was thankful when Zoe pushed the conversation further around the table to take the attention off her.

* * * * *

'My name is Ellie and I'm an alcoholic.' Zoe exhaled and gave Ellie a stern look. She glanced around the table of expectant mums and laughed. 'I'm only joking. Lighten up.'

'Okay, let's start again, shall we?' Zoe raised her eyebrows, an expression that screamed *don't ruin this!* 'Other people have introduced themselves. It's your turn.'

'Okay, fine. My name is Ellie but I'm not an alcoholic. Well, not unless you count the amount of bottles of wine I can get through with the girls on a night out ... before I was pregnant, that is,' she hastily added, just to make sure those people on the next table, who were currently frowning, didn't call social services on her before she even popped this little one out.

'Tell us a little bit about yourself? Maybe not so much about the alcohol side ... maybe, hobbies?'

Ellie used every ounce of self-control to not retaliate with a sarcastic comment. This was a huge ask of her, seeing as sarcasm was her natural go-to in any uncomfortable situation. She felt better when it was other people talking, but now it was her turn, she was forced to think about her messed-up situation.

'I was only joking. I make jokes when I'm nervous. It's a talent, I assure you.' A deep breath. 'Okay. My name is Ellie and I am thirty years old. Turned the big three-oh about six months ago and celebrated in usual fashion with my friends and BOOM,' she clapped her hands together, making a few people jump, 'Six months later, here I am with a bun in the oven.' She cringed inwardly at her use of language as a few of the other mums gave looks to each other. 'Again, I'm joking. Clearly this isn't a six-month bump. I'm about ten weeks' pregnant.' She didn't fit in with this crowd – she stood out like a sore thumb. Nausea suddenly crept up from her stomach and settled nicely in the base of her throat, causing a surge of heat to erupt all over. Damn hot flushes.

'I think maybe we should keep the momentum going around the group. Thanks for sharing, Ellie.' Zoe's face said something completely different from the words coming out of her mouth. Ellie frowned at her as the woman next to her was giving her introductory speech. 'What?' Ellie mouthed to her sister. Zoe shook her head and indicated for Ellie to listen.

'Tell us a little about your journey to pregnancy, Jane.' Zoe was a natural at this. Yet another thing she was perfect at.

'Of course. Well, my husband and I like to do things as naturally as possible and we did a lot of research into natural ways to fall pregnant. We found a lot of very interesting things we could do to increase our chances of falling straight away. I think the one thing that worked the most for us was that every time we finished making love, I would put my body into the best position I could to conceive. And BOOM, here I am.' The woman glanced at Ellie as she said the last bit and curled the corners of her mouth into what looked like a smug smile.

Ellie's mouth dropped open slightly at the sheer shock of this woman's blatant piss-taking. But no one around her seemed to see it. Either that or they all chose to ignore it.

'What a lovely story. It is always best to do things as naturally as possible and let nature do its thing, hey?'

The women around Jane nodded in agreement, with sickly smiles on their faces.

'What if you can't do it naturally, though? Surely those who need a little help shouldn't feel bad for doing so?' Ellie asked, riled by this woman's clear disregard for anything other than what she believed. Especially after some people had just spoken about needing extra help.

'Well, if it's meant to be, then it'll happen.'

Ellie exhaled in disbelief. 'What? That's rubbish!'

'Ellie, let's keep things nice, please.' Zoe was looking at her in disappointment. 'We value everyone's comments at this group and I would appreciate you doing the same, please.'

'I am quite offended that you feel the need to target me like this.' Jane moved her gaze to the Zoe. 'I just wanted to share my story, to help others.'

'It's fine. Please continue.' Zoe gave one last warning look at Ellie and then smiled for the woman to continue.

Ellie made a noise and leant back in her chair. She actually couldn't believe this was happening. She watched the two ladies go back and forth with conversation, but she couldn't concentrate. Anger was bubbling up from the pit of her stomach and all she wanted to do was get up and leave. But she didn't want this woman to know she had affected her. She was normally a confident woman with a somewhat hard exterior. She never let on to anyone if they had upset or offended her. That's just the person she was. As soon as you let someone know they have got one over you, that's it. No going back. She lived by that. But ever since she fell pregnant, she was unable to uphold this confident exterior all the time and she found many things did actually affect her. Bloody hormones, she thought to herself, as she discreetly took some deep breaths to pull back the emotion that was building. Being pregnant was such a stressful time for Ellie. Her friends had always told her how dismissive she was of new things and how she should at least try sometimes. So here she was, trying.

Sometimes she tried very hard.

'I am sure I speak for a lot of the others when I say how fascinated I am by this posing routine you speak of.'

Posing routine? What had she missed?

'It's very simple, yet completely effective. I don't think I would have got pregnant without doing this every night.'

Jane was still talking then.

'Would you show us some of your poses?'

'Oh, of course.' She stood up to take centre stage in the middle of the café and Zoe immediately stood to fetch a mat from the side of the café, dragging it into the centre as a precaution. The mums' club wasn't the only club Zoe entertained here. She also had a yoga club and a seniors' afternoon tea club.

'First, you want to get into a headstand,' she said, as she effortlessly bent forward and sprung her body up into said headstand.

Ellie had to admit that she was slightly impressed by the ease of this. Not that she would let on, though. Not to this woman, anyway.

'Then you bring the soles of your feet together and pull them down towards you, so that your knees are outwards. Sort of an upside-down genie. Then,' the woman lifted and dropped her legs so that it made a pumping action, 'You want to pump your legs like this whilst making a puffing sound.'

Puff, puff, puff...

'After every three puffs, you want to stretch your legs up straight, to the ceiling, and make this sound ... yeoow!'

Ellie snorted before she had a chance to stop it escaping. She held up her hand in apology and tried to keep a straight face.

'You need to do this seven times, repeating each cycle.'

Puff, puff, puff, yeoow, puff, puff, puff, yeoow...

Ellie looked around the room, an array of amused faces were watching Jane with interest. If anyone walked into the café now, they would be in for a treat!

Puff, puff, puff, yeooowwwwwwww

She held the last note for ages and everyone clapped. Slowly she lowered herself to the group and sat back on her heels. 'And that, my friends, is how you fall pregnant.'

'Nothing to do with the sex you had before doing that, eh?' Ellie said under her breath and shook her head in disbelief.

'Jane, thank you so much for sharing that with us. What a wonderful insight to your pregnancy journey.' Zoe smiled at the next person. 'Pip?'

'Hi everyone, I'm Pippa and I am thirty-three years old. I am married to my husband, Jason, who is thirty-six, and we are finally pregnant with our first baby. I'm eight weeks on Friday. We had a difficult time falling pregnant, so it has been one hell of a journey already, but we got there and we are so excited.'

'Maybe you should've tried the pumping pose!' Ellie said to Pippa under her breath and Pippa smiled, clearly trying to hide her amusement. Ellie felt a little relaxed knowing someone else here shared her thoughts about this woman.

After the session had finished, Ellie walked up to Zoe as she was tidying away. 'What's the deal, then?'

Zoe looked confused, but didn't stop moving around. 'What do you mean?'

'Well, that woman was proper rude to me and you didn't say anything. What's that about?'

'Ellie, that woman is the daughter of the guy who I bought this place with – I can't upset her.'

'Are you for real? What happened to the Zoe who wouldn't take any crap from anyone? You just turn around and let her speak to people like that just because you don't want to upset her.'

'Ellie, grow up! This is business. Don't take everything so personally.' Zoe disappeared behind the counter.

Ellie picked up her bag and stormed through the kitchen. 'Nice to know you've got my back, Zo.' She called over her shoulder. 'Mum would want us to be sticking together, not letting other people chat shit.'

Zoe rounded the corner of the kitchen door and walked right up to Ellie at speed, anger drawn over her face. 'Why have you got to bring Mum into this?'

'Why not?' Ellie threw back defiantly, even though now she had said it she knew it was a low blow.

'What has Mum got to do with any of this? I am doing the best I can, Ellie. It's not easy for me. I had to do all this business malarkey by myself, I didn't have Mum and Dad was a wreck. I was on my own and I did the best I could. So if it means me having to be nice to this guy's daughter so it keeps things ticking over nicely, then that's what I'll do. You're a big girl, Ellie; you can stand up for yourself. I shouldn't have to hold your hand – I'm not Mum!'

The air was tight between them and Ellie could feel a tirade of emotions bubbling in the pit of her stomach. 'You think it's been easy for me either? I lost Mum too, you know. I had to struggle too.'

'I know you did, Ellie, and have I ever questioned any of it?'

'Well, no, but ...'

'Ellie, maybe you should concentrate on your own life at the moment instead of trying to pick mine apart.' Zoe glared at her. 'What has made you so angry today? This group was supposed to be a nice thing for you to do and you've been short-tempered all day.'

Ellie shrugged and threw a 'nothing' at Zoe as she picked up her handbag.

'Well, you're bloody moody for a 'nothing'.' Zoe picked up the tea towel off the side and walked back to the café floor.

Ellie pulled her phone out of her bag and again read the text message she had received from Chris earlier on today.

Hey you. Just checking in – all okay? I will call you tomorrow as I'm off out with Emily this afternoon so I can't talk. Wish me luck! Xx

She practically threw the phone back into her bag and went upstairs. She really regretted telling Chris to go on that date now.

* * * * *

159

'How did it go?' Alice entered the living room and plonked herself down onto the sofa in an exhausted heap.

'Yeah, it was good. Busy day?'

'Ah, tell me about it. I just seemed to have appointment after appointment today. I haven't stopped.'

Imogen stood from her position on the sofa and positioned herself in front of where Alice was sitting. She scooped up Alice's foot in her hands and began to massage it. 'How's that?'

'Ah, Im, that's amazing.' She closed her eyes and dropped her head back. After a minute she snapped her head back up and whipped her foot away. 'Wait, you shouldn't be scrunched up on the floor like that. I should be the one massaging your feet. Here, sit back down.'

'Alice, it's fine,' Imogen giggled. 'What are you like?'

By now, Alice had already stood up so she slid down and joined Imogen on the floor. Taking her hand into hers and gazing into her eyes, she smiled. 'How are you feeling today?'

'I'm okay.' Imogen tried to keep the eye contact as she said the words, not fully believing them herself, so there was no way it would fool Alice. Her suspicion was confirmed when Alice lifted just one eyebrow in disbelief. 'What?' She bought herself some more time.

'You don't look okay. What's wrong?'

'Nothing is wrong.' She shrugged and smiled to add weight to her words.

'Imogen ...'

She exhaled, but kept smiling, to soften the blow a little of what she was about to say. 'It's nothing, honest. I just had a bit of a text war with Mum.'

Alice shuffled on the floor to get more comfortable. 'What do you mean?'

Imogen inhaled deeply before saying, 'I know you said to just leave her, but I texted her the other day and she's been sending stroppy messages to me. So I've told her I don't want to hear from her any more,' she trailed off, feeling ashamed. 'Sorry, I know you said to leave it and I didn't.'

'Why are you sorry? You don't ever have to apologise to me.' She lightly stroked the top of Imogen's hand. 'It isn't easy when you don't have parents around. I understand that. When you've not had the support from your family, your loved ones, it will haunt you forever. And in situations like that, you will desperately want to try to salvage some sort of relationship, especially now we have this little one on the way.' She stroked her hand across Imogen's stomach. 'But your mum is never going to accept us. So maybe this time it would be best to just break the connection for good?'

'I know,' she felt as if she had betrayed Alice. 'It's just hard.'

Alice moved forward and pulled Imogen into her arms, squeezing her tight in an embrace that was full of love and safety. 'I know it is hard. But this is you, Imogen. You shouldn't have to hide away from being who you are. We aren't a freak show. We aren't murderers. We aren't even flaunting it in people's faces. We are just two people who love each other and no one should make you feel like you can't be honest. They are the ones who have the problem, not us.'

Alice made it sound so easy. She oozed confidence and pride and always had done from the moment they first met. 'I wish I could be more like you,' Imogen snuggled into the embrace more, wrapping her arms around Alice and melting into her body as if they were just one person.

'I don't,' Alice replied, and pulled Imogen's face up slightly to look at hers. 'Because I love you for who *you* are. You are caring, kind, gentle, loving ... you always put other people before you and you are the most beautiful person I know – inside and out. I wouldn't change you for the world.'

Imogen closed her eyes as Alice's lips brushed against hers. Soft and smooth, her lips gently caressed Imogen's, playfully prising them apart with her tongue. Imogen relaxed into Alice's arms, letting her control which way she went. Sliding over so that their bodies were fully entwined with one another, moving in sync perfectly. Alice's gentle kisses on the lips soon moved across towards her neck. Imogen arched her head back to fully expose the sensitive skin underneath her jaw – Alice knew this was her favourite place to be kissed and wasted no time in showing Imogen exactly how much she loved her, tracing her tongue over Imogen's skin, sending shivers down her spine.

'You don't ever need to change who you are, okay?' Alice whispered into Imogen's ear. She could feel her hot breath over her ear and it did amazing things to her insides. She felt super- sensitive to every touch right now. She nodded, letting the smile spread over her face.

'Come on ...' Alice stood and took Imogen's hand.

'Where are we going?'

'I want you to dance with me.' Alice turned the music up on the TV and Imogen instantly recognised the song.

'Our wedding song?' She smiled.

Alice pulled her close, resting her forehead onto Imogen's

and gently beginning to sway. 'It's a sign. Any song could come on the TV at any time, but now, as you're feeling stressed, this one just happened to start playing. What does that tell you?'

'That it is a huge coincidence,' she replied, moving her hips alongside Alice's, feeling as if they were one body.

'No, baby, it means that no matter what, you will always have me. I will be by your side every single day and we will get through anything anyone has to throw at us because we love each other so much.' She brushed her lips across Imogen's and Imogen felt her knees weaken slightly. Alice placed her arms completely around her body, encapsulating her. Their bodies glided for a moment, sliding over the music, as if they were floating on air. Imogen could feel only Alice, holding her close and making every ounce of worry melt away. The melodic notes swirling around her head as she let Alice guide her steps back and forth, resting her head on her shoulder.

'Come on,' Alice said, taking her hand, 'I want to show you just how much I love you.' She gave her a cheeky smile and walked her upstairs.

Chapter 16

'Okay, are you ready?'

Imogen looked at Alice for reassurance as the sonographer inserted the internal camera for their first scan. This had been the moment they had been looking forward to for ages. And the moment they had been dreading. Because this would tell them if everything was okay with their baby. This moment would tell them if their latest attempt had worked properly; it would change their lives forever. Imogen now began to have second thoughts about going to the mums' club on Wednesday, thinking maybe it wasn't such a good idea. What if something was wrong? She should've waited. She was anxious. Alice squeezed Imogen's hand and smiled encouragingly.

'Yes, I'm ready.' She took a deep breath as the camera was inserted. It felt strange but it didn't hurt. She had been so worried in the run-up to this appointment, how she would cope with the invasive procedure, but she found herself relaxing a lot more than she had thought. Because of the type of treatment they had, they were told that their first scan at six weeks would be an internal one, so they were able to prepare a little for it.

The sonographer started clicking away on the computer as she tried to get a better picture. It felt as if she was quiet for ages and Alice's cool exterior started to crack and Imogen could tell she was anxious too. But in true Alice-style, when she noticed Imogen looking at her, she smiled reassuringly and put on a brave face. 'You okay?' she asked quietly. 'You're not in pain, are you?'

'No, I'm fine.' She returned the smile and looked back at the sonographer. 'Is everything okay?' She tried to hide the tremble in her voice, the anticipation becoming too much.

'Yes, I'm just trying to get the measurements at the moment. I won't be a second and then you can see.' The sonographer quickly smiled at her and then continued clicking away. After a moment, she removed the camera and stood up. 'I won't be a moment; I just want to get my colleague in to check something.' She quickly left the room.

Immediately Imogen sat up, staring wide-eyed at Alice, who also looked a little concerned, although she seemed to be trying to hide it. 'Alice ...' She couldn't find any other words, her lip trembling.

'It's okay. I'm sure it is perfectly normal practice to double-check things. Especially people who have conceived through something like IVF. They are just being thorough. I'm sure it is nothing to worry about.' She smiled, but it didn't reach her eyes.

'Alice, what if ... something's wrong with it?' She could barely bring herself to say the words. This was the furthest they had ever got in the process. It had cost them an absolute fortune to attempt it for the third time and this was their last chance. They couldn't afford it a fourth time and plus, Imogen wasn't sure she had the courage and stability to go through the emotional roller-coaster that was IVF again. So this really was it. And now, it looked like this may not even be *it*.

'Nothing will be wrong, they are just being thorough, and that's all. Everything will be okay, I promise.'

'How can you promise?' Imogen lay back down on the bed and lifted both arms up to her face, resting her forearms over her eyes to stop the tears. 'You can't make promises like that. You don't know!'

'Ims, come on. You need to be strong. Don't go getting yourself worked up over something that hasn't even happened yet.' Alice pulled her arms away from her face and kissed the hand she was holding. 'It'll be okay.'

The door opened and the sonographer returned with another woman. 'Sorry to have kept you waiting,' the second woman said and she sat herself down, the first sonographer standing behind her, watching over her shoulder as she worked. 'I'm just going to pop this in again, Imogen, okay?' She had such a reassuring face and Imogen found herself nodding and opening her legs again.

'Okay, let's have a look, then.' She began clicking away and Imogen felt slightly reassured by this woman's tone of voice. It was smooth and light and, she thought to herself, surely this isn't a voice that could give her bad news. But then she doubted herself and thought maybe a soft, friendly voice like that was perfect for giving bad news. Maybe that's why she called her in, to break it to them gently. She felt her heartrate increase as the words swarmed in her mind.

'Is there a problem?'

Imogen heard Alice's voice over her panicked thoughts and was glad she asked the question.

'Oh no, not at all.' She turned the screen to face them. 'If you have a look on here, you can see the amniotic sac and there,' she pointed to a spot on the screen, 'There is a baby.'

'Oh!' Imogen said as she exhaled in relief. 'There's the baby, Alice.'

'I see it!' She squeezed Imogen's hand.

'And here,' the sonographer moved the curser and clicked, 'is the other baby.'

Imogen pulled her eyebrows together. 'What did you say?'

The woman smiled. 'There's your other baby ... it's twins.'

Imogen turned her head to Alice, who was sitting, open-mouthed, staring at the screen. 'Two?' Imogen asked. 'Twins?'

'Uh-huh, congratulations.'

'Oh my God.' It came out like a whisper and she felt Alice's grip squeeze as she lifted her hand and kissed it. 'Alice ... twins!'

'I know!'

'And the heartbeat for twin one ...' Imogen held her breath as she listened. At first there was nothing, but then she heard it. The low hum of the heartbeat.

'Oh my God.' Tears were welling up and she had to blink to clear her vision so she could look at the screen, watching the flutter as the heart beat.

'And twin two ...' the sonographer searched and clicked a few times, but nothing happened. She tried again. Nothing. She creased her brow as she clicked a few different things and

Imogen looked at Alice, who was clearly panicking too. She couldn't hide it this time. Imogen felt her own heartbeat increase as she began to drop from her elation. 'Imogen, could you just turn slightly onto your left side, only very slightly.' She did as she was asked, terror tearing through her body. 'That's perfect, and hold it there.' Imogen stayed, propped on her side, not daring to move. Alice took her hand again and stroked it, miming to her that everything was going to be okay. But Imogen didn't believe her. She knew it was too good to be true falling with one, let alone two. The chances were slim to have one baby successfully, having two, well, that was just asking for too much. She should be thankful that one of them had a heartbeat. A lot of people didn't even get that choice, and previously she had been one of those. So she should be grateful.

'Alice?' she whispered, as a stray tear slide down her nose and onto the bed.

'It's okay. Stay strong. I'm here.' She bent down and kissed her on the forehead, which, nice as it was, seemed to open a floodgate and another tear slid down.

And then there it was. Unmistakeable and strong.

'And there's twin two.'

'Really?' Imogen lifted her head and turned to the screen.

'Really.' The sonographer smiled. 'Both babies are healthy and so we can refer you to the NHS and your pregnancy will be under the usual midwifery team.'

'Alice!' Imogen said as she burst into tears.

'I know, baby, I know.' Alice bent down and enveloped Imogen in a hug. 'We're going to be mummies!'

Chapter 17

Pippa finished drizzling the lemon icing onto the cake and then placed it on the rack to set. Over the last few days things had become increasingly strained at home and every day she seemed to be arguing with Jason. This was not the marriage she had longed for. Pippa was distracted from her thoughts when the front-door bell rang. Wiping her hands on her apron, she quickly ran to the door.

'Zoe, what are you doing here? Was something wrong with my delivery?'

'What, no, don't be silly. There's never anything wrong with your orders – you are the queen of organisation.' Zoe wiped her feet as she entered the hallway.

'Is everything okay, then?' Pippa eyed her suspiciously and then remembered the buns in the oven. 'Oh crap, I've got a bun in the oven!' She ran back to the kitchen, sliding on the floor as she rounded the corner.

'I hope that's not how you broke the news to Jason!' Zoe called back, entering the kitchen as she laughed at her own joke.

'I reckon that was more what Jason thought when I did tell him.' She raised her eyebrows.

'What? You're joking, right?' Pippa shook her head. 'Ah, Pip ...'

'It's okay,' she interrupted before Zoe could voice her pity, 'He'll come around to the idea. I didn't choose the best time to tell him, that's all.' She loosened the bun from the tin and flipped it out onto the cooling rack. 'And anyway, what was I expecting? Him to be jumping around like a girl, screeching and whooping? He's a man. He doesn't show excitement in the same way as we do, hey?' She didn't wait for an answer as she saw the raised-eyebrow look on Zoe's face. Desperate to shift the focus away from her flailing marriage, she said, 'Anyway, enough jibber jabber about me, what brings you round here? Something wrong?'

Zoe immediately looked uncomfortable and began shuffling in her seat. 'Okay, well, I have kind of done something stupid. Well, not exactly done something stupid. I am about to do something stupid.' She paused. 'Not really stupid, exactly, just ... well ...'

'Zoe?' Pippa held up her hand to stop the rambling. 'What is going on exactly?'

Zoe dropped her hands in defeat. 'I've asked Chris to meet me ... I'm going to try and get them together.' She immediately pulled a face, which clearly showed that she knew she was wading into dangerous territory.

'Zoe!'

'I know, I know, it's not my place to meddle. But Pip, Ellie is not doing it and I think the only person who will convince her that everything will be all right is him.'

'Zoe, it's a really bad idea.' She didn't know Ellie that well, but from what she did know, she knew this wasn't one of Zoe's better ideas.

'Come on, look at the bigger picture. He will come and talk sense into her. I know he will be happy about it. This could be their chance to finally become one.' She opened her arms as if she had just solved the biggest mystery in one fell swoop. 'Easy, right?'

Pippa shook her head. 'It's not going to work, Zoe. You're messing with fate. If they are meant to be, then things will work out. Ellie will do it in her own time and things will be what they're meant to be.'

Exhaling hard, Zoe slumped onto a stool by the breakfast bar, picking up one of the cupcakes that were cooling on the side. Pippa tried hard to conceal her unease. Watching Zoe eating one of those meant the amount would be eleven, not twelve, cupcakes. She didn't bake in uneven numbers. She shook her head slightly, as if it would make the uncomfortable thought exit her brain. Needless to say, this didn't work. Zoe huffed as she finished off the cupcake. 'Pip, if I don't do something, I think Ellie might go off the rails again and I can't watch her go through that again.'

Pippa sat down on the stool next to her and took her hand. 'But it isn't your responsibility to make that decision for her. As hard as it might be, it's her baby.' Pippa watched as the tears began to fill her friend's eyes. She rubbed her thumb over Zoe's hand in comfort, feeling the burden of sadness descend upon her.

'She just feels scared and trapped. She's putting on a brave face, but her mood swings are horrendous. I can see she is really struggling with it and I want to help her. If I can just make her see that she isn't alone, then maybe—'

'You can't tell her what to do; she needs to make her own mistakes.'

'I know that, but ...' She trailed off.

They sat in silence for a few minutes before Pippa finally said the one thing that they were both thinking. 'Zoe, you can't keep blaming yourself for the abortion. You did what you had to do. You didn't have a choice. The only person who blames you for that is you. You can't save everyone else to make up for it.' Zoe flinched at the mention of the abortion and Pippa felt awful for bringing it up. 'I'm sorry.'

'I just don't want her to feel sad – this should be an exciting, magical time for her. For both of them.'

'As much as you don't want to hear this, Ellie is an adult and I don't think it will go down well if you tell her and Chris what to do. You have to let her deal with this, otherwise she will not only hate you but her relationship with Chris will definitely be over'

Zoe nodded and wiped the tears from her eyes. 'You're right. I'll tell him I can't make it.'

'I think it's for the best. I thought they had sorted things out anyway – weren't they doing it together, but as friends?'

'Yeah, but I just don't think it is what either of them want.' Zoe looked at her and Pippa pulled a face. 'Okay, fine. I will back off.'

'Good. Now, would you like some cake, seeing as you've already helped yourself to my cupcake batch?'

'I thought you'd never ask.'

The front door slammed as Jason stormed in, walking past the kitchen and straight into the living room. Pippa's heart began to race as the panic seared through her at lightning speed. Jason didn't know Zoe was here and she didn't want him to come in, all guns blazing, ready for a row. 'I'll be back in a minute,' Pippa smiled, as she left Zoe in the kitchen and closed the door behind her. She tucked her head round the living-room door and could see Jason rummaging through the post. 'Everything okay?'

He spun round in alarm. 'Pip! What you doing here? I thought you were out.'

'No,' she said, her tone charged with suspicion. 'Why?'

'I didn't see the van outside, so thought you were out delivering.' He continued to rummage.

'What are you looking for?' she questioned, very aware that Zoe was just a few feet away.

'Nothing!' His sharp response surprised her.

'If you tell me what it is, I can help you.' She tried to keep her voice light and airy so that Zoe wouldn't hear.

'For crying out loud, Pip, I said leave it! I don't need your help.'

Anger bubbled inside her. She took a breath and said, through clenched teeth, 'There's no need to shout at me. I am just trying to help.'

He spun round and glared at her, mimicking her clenched teeth, he said, 'I don't need your help.'

'What is wrong with you?' She spat the words at him, but then straightened up as she heard the kitchen door open. Zoe walked out and entered the living room, first smiling at Pippa and then looking at Jason.

'All right Jason?'

He didn't respond and Pippa felt a little piece of her die

inside. She glanced at Zoe nervously and laughed it off. 'Deaf as a doorpost when he's concentrating.' Another nervous laugh. She daren't look directly at her because she knew she wasn't buying it.

'All right Jason!' Zoe called, a little louder this time and Pippa cringed as Jason ignored her yet again. She looked at her friend this time and pleaded with her eyes not to push this. Zoe clearly read the signal because she didn't say anything else. Jason stood up, having located a letter he was looking for and walked out of the room, past them both, without a word. Pippa's face blazed as the embarrassment filtered through.

'I won't be home for dinner,' Jason called as he left, slamming the door behind him.

There was an awkward silence for what felt like forever. Pippa clapped her hands together for something to do and simply said, 'I'd better check on the cupcakes.' And she left the room as quickly as she could. But Zoe didn't want to play ball. She followed Pippa into the kitchen and stood in the doorway with her arms crossed. Pippa tried to avoid her gaze and busied herself with the cakes, moving them from one board to another to look as if she was doing something. But she couldn't do this forever and eventually turned around and faced Zoe with her eyebrow raised.

'You finished?' she asked, using an expression that pretty much said don't even try to bullshit me. Pippa nodded. 'Okay, now make another cuppa; I think we need to talk, don't you?'

* * * * *

'Penny for your thoughts?'

Ellie jumped and clasped her hand to her chest, feeling her heartbeat pulsating. She turned to face the voice. The one voice she could always rely on. The one voice that once used to make her laugh with simply one word, but now made her confused and a little sad. Turning to Chris, she forced a smile, trying to hide the fear that was bubbling up in her stomach. 'What are you doing here?' she managed to squeak out.

Chris plonked himself down next to her on the grassy verge and plastered on a silly smile that he always did for her. She likened it to a mix of goofiness and pure cheese. She secretly loved it, but recoiled in her usual fashion and scrunched her face up. 'My God, how do you ever get dates with that face?'

'Because, my dear, they can't resist my wonderful charm. I mean, who could, to be fair?' He held out his arms wide and winked at her. Whilst this would, under normal circumstances, make her cringe, this time, because of all that was going on, she couldn't help but smile fondly at him. She instantly shook the thought out of her mind and pulled herself back into the reality of the moment. Here she was, sitting on the side of a hill in Shropshire, 200 odd miles from her home, pregnant and a big question mark over whether she had a job to go home to. The wind was biting at her cheeks, stinging. She pulled her sister's jacket closer, tucking her chin inside, leaving just her nose and eyes free.

'Are you still with us or should I have a nap?' Chris was looking at her with his goofy smile, but Ellie could see the genuine compassion behind his eyes, which had a hint of confusion wrapped up in it too.

'I'm sorry, I was miles away.' She looked at the ground and then towards the horizon in front of her. Basically she looked anywhere she could that wasn't directly at Chris.

'So I can see.' He shuffled a little closer to her, zipping his coat up.

'So how was your date?' Ellie asked, trying to sound as cool as she could.

'Yeah it went well. She wants to see me again next week, so I can't have been that horrendous to look at.'

'Either that or she has problems with her eyesight. You didn't wear that horrendous pink shirt, did you?'

Chris laughed and recoiled in mock surprise. 'You mean to tell me you don't like my date shirt? It has worked on plenty of women, let me tell you that.'

'Oh, of course. Because you are currently in a long-term relationship. I keep forgetting that.'

Chris playfully pushed her sideways and she dropped to the ground as laughter erupted from her mouth. 'Hey!' she giggled.

'Look, maybe the shirt worked wonders but I just haven't found the woman for me yet. Nothing wrong with looking for someone who isn't a psycho, or married ... or—'

'A blonde?'

Chris looked at her. 'What? I don't always go for the same type of woman?'

'Yes you do! I have never seen you date, or fancy, someone who isn't brunette.' A twinge of jealousy shot through her as they spoke about Chris's dating scene.

'That's utter rubbish. I have dated a blonde before ...' he

trailed off as he looked into the distance, clearly trying to think of such a time.

'Forget it, Chris, you're never going to win this fight. I know for a fact that you have only ever dated brunettes.' She knew that because there had been more than one occasion when she wanted to dye her hair just to get Chris to notice her. To stop seeing her as a friend and see her as a potential date. But he never did. He didn't see her in that way and it took her years to work out that this wasn't just because she was blonde. They were too firmly into the friend-zone.

He laughed but Ellie's smile didn't reach her eyes. Just hearing him talk about his dates made her feel sick. She sat in silence as she looked out over the fields. The view of the countryside from this position was beautiful.

After a minute, Chris asked, 'You want to tell me what's really going on in that head of yours?'

She sat in silence for another minute or two, not knowing what to say to him, which in itself was a new feeling for her. He was a complete gentleman and gave her that time to compose her thoughts, not once interrupting or asking her to hurry up. She could see him out of the corner of her eye, picking at the grass and throwing it away when the piece he was playing with was too small.

Finally she took a deep breath and said, 'Why are you here, Chris?'

'Why do you think?' He looked at her as he spoke. She knew this because she could see out of the corner of her eye, not because she was looking at him. She couldn't bring herself to look at him directly. She was worried that if she did, he would see straight through her and look into her eyes, through into her soul and be able to tell all the feelings she was harbouring inside. Instead she simply shrugged, behaving like a stroppy toddler who had been told they couldn't watch any more TV.

'I'm here because I am worried about you, Ellie. Your sister texted me and asked me to come down because she was worried about you and she wanted to talk to me. But then I drive past here, see your car pulled up and see you sitting on a hill, in the middle of a field. ' He gave her a look. 'You got to admit Els, it's a little weird.'

Anger bubbled up inside her as she realised what Zoe was up to, meddling in her business. But then the reality hit her and she understood. Zoe wanted the best for her, she always did. But what was the best thing in this situation? She was so confused. Chris leaned forward to get her attention again. She pushed her anger towards her sister aside and gave in to the fact that he wasn't going to accept any bullshit stories. Instead she tried to play it down. 'There's nothing to be worried about. I'm fine.' She tried to laugh it off, but even she could tell that she was lying, so there was no way this was going to get past Chris.

'Hmm, a likely story. Ellie, you seem to forget that I am normally your partner in crime for things, so I know all your secret tricks of the trade. I can tell when you're lying, or bending the truth or, more importantly, when you're not okay.'

She shrugged.

'Look, I know I acted a bit weird when you told me, but you have to understand that this was a huge surprise for me – it was the last thing I thought you would be saying to me over lunch. I never expected to be sitting down with you discussing the fact that you were pregnant with my child. It scared the shit out of me, if I'm honest.'

'I never asked you for anything.'

'I know that! But what did you expect would happen? That I would say 'oh sorry, Ellie, shit happens, better luck next time' and just leave you to it?'

'Well, no, but ... I just don't want you thinking that now you have this tie to me that you have to be involved in.'

'Look, this situation is a bit crap, we both know that. Neither of us went into that evening wanting to have children,. Having kids never even crossed my mind at this moment in my life – and I know it didn't yours either. But the truth of the matter is this is actually happening and we can't just brush it under the carpet. I need to sort stuff out with work, There will be money to pay you and a complete lifestyle change. But, well, that's what we will have to do.' He didn't look sincere as he said it; more scared than anything. 'I know I didn't react the best way and this isn't how either of us planned to settle down and start a family, but it will be fine – we will be fine. You just have to stop pushing me away.'

Ellie shuffled on her bum, feeling claustrophobic with the intensity of the conversation. She needed to steer away from all this. 'Does this mean that you are going to wait on me hand and foot ... you still owe me from having me over after that party in September!'

Chris burst into laughter at the memory. 'I had you going for days.'

'You're such an idiot. One bump to the head and you played

me like a ... a ... oh I don't even know what the saying is, but you definitely had me going.'

'And it went on for days, do you remember? I had you making tea and cooking dinner for almost a week before you cottoned on that I was having a laugh.'

'Yes, I do remember. So you still owe me a week of being my slave.' She picked up a daisy from the grass and began to thread it through another.

'Is that right? And what would you have me doing as your slave? Feeding you grapes, fanning you with some big leaves ...'

'That would be just the beginning.'

'Oh really?' He lay down on the grass, extending his arms above his head to support his neck. 'So come on, humour me, what would your day entail if I was your slave.'

'Isn't it conversations like this that got us into this mess in the first place?' Ellie giggled as she remembered back to *that* night. She took a few minutes to think as she continued with her daisy chain, threading each delicate stalk into another and then smoothing them out to see her creation as she worked. 'Well, it would definitely entail you bringing me lots of chocolate – because every great day has chocolate in it – and maybe glasses of prosecco on demand.' She sidestepped the fact that she couldn't actually drink at the moment. 'And you would give me back massages as I watched reruns of *Friends* on the TV.'

'Would I be allowed to watch them with you or are you going to be strict and whip my arse if I stopped massaging you.'

'Oh, you would definitely get whipped.' She gave a little smile to herself as she said the words and Chris burst into loud laughter and pulled his hands up to his face to cover his shaking head. 'Man, Ell's, you really know how to talk to a guy.'

She smirked to herself, feeling pleased that she was still the owner of her sharp, witty humour. She was also smiling to herself because this conversation was proof itself that she and Chris could get past this. They could be their normal selves. Go back to being just ... well ... Chris and Ellie.

'How long are you planning to stay at your sister's – you've been here like two weeks already!'

'I don't know. I quite like it up here, away from everything.'

'Away from me?' This time it was Chris, who couldn't give any eye contact.

'No, Chris, not away from you. I just ... I don't know, I guess I'm just looking at my life and wondering what I have to show for it.'

'You have lots to show. You made a fantastic career for yourself, you're self-sufficient, and you are an amazing friend, beautiful ...' he trailed off as Ellie shook her head. 'What?'

'It's not enough, Chris. I'm thirty years old with no relationship, still renting a dingy one-bed place ...'

He clearly saw the look on her face because he then added, 'The Ellie I know wouldn't care about those things.'

The Ellie he knew also wouldn't be falling for him. She shrugged. 'I just don't know what my purpose in life is and I'm feeling rubbish about it all. Maybe it's about time I grew up.'

'Ellie, it's not as simple as that, and you know it.'

They sat in silence for a minute and then she said, 'I think I'm going to stay up here for Christmas and then start the New Year fresh. Sort my life out, you know?'

'I don't understand what you need to sort out, but okay. Just don't ignore me. Just because you are up here, doesn't mean we can't still be in touch. I know you're obviously having a bit of a mid-life crisis,' he smirked at her, 'but just know that I will always be here, okay? It's my baby too. Sooner or later we will have to talk about this. It's not going to go away.'

She nodded and fixed her stare to the river below as Chris continued to lie on the grass. She felt as if she was constantly wading against the tide, trying to get her head above the water but drowning under the tsunami of life and its constant traumas. She would get Christmas out of the way and next year things would be different. She wasn't sure how yet, but they would. They had to be. She looked at Chris, lying on the ground with his eyes closed. He looked so peaceful, as if life never fazed him, but all she could think about was how much she wanted to kiss him. And that feeling was so alien to her, she squashed it deep down inside her and covered it with a blanket. She needed to pull herself together.

'Chris?'

'Yeah?'

'I'm sorry for being weird and for everything else. I just need a break, you know? I promise I'll sort myself out and you can slap me out of it.'

He sat up and placed his arm around her shoulders, squeezing her tight and pulling her into his shoulder as he gently kissed the top of her head. 'Don't apologise. The fact that you are a little weirdo is the whole reason why I love you so much.'

Chapter 18

'So, come on, spill.' Zoe looked at Pippa sternly, crossing her arms and clearly taking no more bullshit. Pippa shuffled around in the kitchen, taking longer than necessary to wipe the sides down and pack her cake utensils away. This was not a conversation she wanted to have. Not now. Not ever. If only Jason had just stopped being a pig for one second, this would never have happened. She put the last of the utensils in to soak in the sink and plonked herself down onto the chair opposite Zoe at the breakfast bar. Folding her hands around the warm mug of coffee, she let her shoulders slump for the first time in forever.

'Just don't go on about it, okay? It's nothing.' Even though she knew Zoe wouldn't accept this, she still felt the need to try and protect her dignity. To try and project this image that, up until now, she had managed to keep up.

Zoe shook her head. 'Nope. Not happening, Pip.'

Pippa exhaled. 'Honestly, it's nothing. He's clearly just had a bad day and is a bit off. Haven't you ever had a day where you don't want to talk to anyone? It's normal. He's just stressed. There's a lot going on at work at the moment and he's been feeling the pressure and ...' Pippa stopped as Zoe raised her hand up to silence her. 'What?'

'Pip, I am not stupid. I am also not the kind of friend to sit back and not say anything when I feel like something is up.' They sat in silence for a minute, neither one knowing what to say. Eventually Zoe said, 'Are things not good between you two?' Pippa hesitated. If she spoke about it now then there was no taking things back. Zoe reached over and placed her hand on top of hers. 'You know you can trust me. I promise anything you say will be kept between us.' She gave Pippa a warming smile and it made her want to cry.

She took a deep breath. 'Things have been ... hard, recently.'

'Okay, in what way?'

'He's been working lots and coming home stressed out. He takes it out on me – not physically,' she added quickly before that thought entered Zoe's mind. 'He gets stroppy or shouts, or he hits the drink. But that just makes it worse because I then get the shouting when he's drunk and the stroppiness tenfold when he's sobering up.'

'Oh, Pip, I had no idea. I'm sorry.'

Pippa laughed. 'Why are you sorry? You haven't done anything.'

'I know, but I feel bad that you've been having a rubbish time and dealing with it on your own. You should've told me.'

'It's no big deal.' She shrugged and tried to brush it off, but now she was saying the words out loud, she was starting to realise how miserable things had become lately.

'So, when you told him about the baby ...' Zoe trailed off as Pippa nodded.

'He wasn't too happy. He seemed more stressed than happy.'

Sadness rose from the pit of her stomach and set up camp in her chest.

'Why would he go through IVF with you if he didn't want a baby?'

'He does want a baby. Well, he says he does. And he did when we were going through the process, he's just, more recently, seemed a bit distant from everything. Well, everything apart from work.'

'And have you spoken to him about how much he's working?' She stood up and flicked the kettle back on.

Pippa nodded. 'Yeah, but what can you do? If there's work that needs doing, it has to be done. I can't have him falling behind or getting the sack because then where will that leave us when the baby comes? We need that income. I will have to take a break from work when I have the baby, so his income will be our only source of money. He needs that job – we both do.' She drunk the remainder of her coffee and passed Zoe the cup.

'But Pip, you two can't carry on like this. What about when the baby comes? Is he going to continue to shout and drink whilst you take care of the baby and recover from childbirth?' Zoe's voice had become more urgent, almost begging Pippa to see her side of the argument. But Pippa couldn't.

'There's nothing I can do about it, Zoe.'

'Of course there is! You tell him to shape up or ship out!' Zoe thrust her thumb over her shoulder, reiterating the throwing-him-out part.

Pippa laughed sadly. 'I can't do that.'

'Why?' Zoe plonked herself back down on the chair opposite, facing Pippa squarely.

'Zoe, I'm not like you. I can't be on my own. I'm not strong enough. I don't have the ability to be this strong, independent woman that you are. I wish I did, I really do. You make it look so easy, but I can't do it.'

'Rubbish!' Zoe banged her hand on the table. 'Of course you can bloody do it! That man doesn't own you, and he certainly doesn't own the right to whether you are happy or not.' She leaned in closer, looking right in Pippa's eye. 'Honey, if you aren't happy, you need to either tell him, or leave him.'

Pippa felt sick. This was all too personal for her liking. She didn't do opening up to people. And now Zoe was on the inside and she would think badly of her ... she should never have opened up. 'I'm happy, honestly. Once the baby comes, things will be fine. I know they will. I'm just being a baby about it all – must be the hormones or something.'

'But Pip—'

'Zoe, listen to me. This baby means more to me than anything in the world; I don't have another chance at this. I have no more savings; I can't pay for any more treatment. I am not bringing this baby up in a broken marriage – it needs its mummy and daddy and I will do everything to make that okay. So please, don't keep on. I've made my decision and I'm staying. End of.' She stood up. 'Now, if you'll excuse me, I need to pee for the hundredth time today.' She smiled warmly at Zoe to try and show her gratitude for her caring so much. As she walked past, Pippa stopped and hugged Zoe from behind very quickly, and then turned to go to the bathroom as fast as she could. She'd already failed by opening up to Zoe about all this crap; she wasn't about to let her see her cry over it too.

Chapter 19

'How are you feeling?'

Ellie glanced over at her sister, who was sitting on the chair directly next to her. She was finding it difficult to describe just how she was feeling. Terror was curdled up with anxiety, worry and panic. There was a small part of her that was a little excited about seeing the baby for the first time, but nerves were definitely the dominating feeling right now. She pushed a smile out and replied, 'I'm all right.'

'What time is Chris getting here? I hope he makes it in time.'

'He should be here by now.' Ellie looked at the clock on the wall: 10.27.

'Are you excited to see the baby?' Zoe was trying really hard to make this experience a positive one and Ellie actually really appreciated it. When Zoe suggested she register as a temporary patient at the local doctors so things could get underway, Ellie was initially reluctant, but actually it made sense. As did all of Zoe's good ideas.

Ellie's phone vibrated.

I'm just parking the car – I'll be two minutes! Don't go in without me!

Ellie typed back a simple, 'Okay' and put the phone back into her pocket. 'Chris is just parking the car.' Zoe nodded as she flicked through the four-year-old magazine from the table. Moments later, Chris went running past the door.

'Chris!' Ellie called out, letting a little giggle escape her mouth. She waited a second and then his head suddenly appeared round the doorframe.

'There you are!' He walked over to her and kissed her on the cheek, then going to Zoe and doing the same. 'The receptionist sent me up here but said it was the room opposite the lifts.'

Ellie pointed to the lifts at the other end of the room.

'Ohhhh ...'

Ellie laughed. 'You idiot. At least you're here now. They haven't called us in yet.' Ellie smiled. She was secretly so glad he was here. As nice as it was that Zoe said she would come with her for the scan, having Chris here meant a great deal.

'How are you feeling?' Chris asked, slipping into the chair on Ellie's other side.

'I'm all right,' she repeated. 'Desperate for a wee, though.'

'Can you not quickly go? I'm sure they'll wait.' Chris looked around the room as he spoke, clearly trying to locate a toilet. 'Look, over there.' He pointed.

'I can't, I have to fill up my bladder so the picture is clearer.' Chris looked at her, shocked, with a little smile. 'I know, get me! Knowing all my baby shit.' They laughed, both clearly as nervous as one another but neither wanting to show it.

'Ellie Samson?' The nurse called out, and every inch of Ellie's body tensed.

Chris leaned over and took her hand. 'Come on, it'll be okay.' He smiled and Ellie nodded – more for herself than anything else.

'I'll wait out here,' Zoe said, bringing Ellie temporarily out of her shock.

'What? No, you can come in too.'

'Ellie, it's fine. You have Chris with you – have this moment just you two. I'll see the picture.' Zoe nodded and encouraged Ellie to go.

When inside the room, Ellie could feel her heartbeat galloping. She repeatedly glanced over at Chris, who kept nodding and smiling. She was so glad he was here.

'Okay, if you want to take a seat on the bed, and you can sit here.' She indicated a chair to Chris next to the bed. 'And let's meet your baby.'

Half an hour later, Ellie was in the waiting room watching Zoe coo over the picture.

'Oh my goodness, it's so perfect,' she just kept saying.

'And look, there's its nose ...' Chris was leaning over her shoulder, playing the excited daddy very well. Ellie watched his face as he showed Zoe the picture. He was absolutely over the moon. Ellie was too. Everything was okay with the baby. 'Estimated due date of June 29th,' Chris was saying.

'Oh my goodness, this makes it all seem so real now.' Zoe stood up and grabbed her car keys. 'Right, I'm just going to pop to the loo and then we can get going.'

Once Zoe had disappeared into the toilet, Chris walked

over to Ellie and, without saying anything, pulled her close to him and hugged her. She buried her face into his chest and let him completely enfold her in the hug.

'Well done, Mummy,' he said, and kissed her on the head. And she wanted to stay there forever.

PART TWO:

The Second Trimester

Chapter 20

'IT'S CHRIIIIISTMAAAAAASSSS!'
Imogen jumped out of bed to the sound of Christmas songs ringing out loudly from the bungalow. It took her a moment before she remembered that she was staying at Alice's parents' house this year and they had decided to sleep over on Christmas Eve so that they didn't have to make the journey on Christmas morning. After opening the curtains she moved back over to the bed and planted a gentle kiss on Alice's lips, waking her up with a smile.

'Good morning, beautiful. Is it that time already?'

'Yep, it's Christmas!' Imogen bounced up and down on the bed.

'You're like a kid at Christmas, Ims: our children are going to love Christmas.' She rubbed her eyes and dropped her head back onto the pillow.

'Guess what?' She squealed excitedly. Clapping her hands together.

Alice smiled fondly. 'I don't know, what?'

'I may have bought a little something for the babies ...' Imogen coyly looked over her shoulder in a bid to make herself look as innocent as possible. They had said they wouldn't buy anything yet.

'Ims ...' Alice warned, but her tone was light.

'I know, I know, but I just saw these and they were the cutest little things.' Her voice rose to a higher pitch as she spoke. 'Look.' She whipped the bag from under the bed and handed it to Alice. She watched excitedly as Alice unwrapped the yellow tissue paper to reveal two beautiful cream bunnies.

'Oh, they're beautiful!' Alice picked up one and stroked her thumb over the fur. 'They're so soft.'

'I know. I saw them the other day and just couldn't resist getting them. I know we said we weren't going to jinx it by buying things now but, just these won't hurt.' She plastered a huge smile on her face to try and win Alice back over.

'You, madam, are a pain in the bum!' She tapped Imogen on the nose and then lay back down on the bed.

'Come on, come on, get up. I want to give you my present.' Imogen pulled the covers off Alice, revealing just a pair of very short shorts and a bra. 'You might want to chuck some clothes on too, before you go over to the bungalow.'

'I was hoping we could have a little cuddle in bed before going over.' Alice winked and tapped the bed beside her. This was definitely a perk to staying in the annex.

'But your parents ...' Imogen looked towards the door and back but couldn't stop the grin from spreading.

'They won't bother us, it's still early.'

'They're playing Christmas songs.'

'Yeah I know, but that just means that Mum is baking. She'll be doing the Christmas scones for breakfast. We have at least an hour before we need to be over there. Come on, come back to bed.'

Imogen didn't miss the twinkle in her eye and she jumped back into bed, giggling. 'But only quickly, I don't want your mum thinking we are staying in here all day.'

Alice pulled her close and began kissing her neck. 'Don't worry, this won't take long.' And she giggled as she pulled the cover over their heads.

* * * * *

'Jason, come on. How long are you going to be?' Pippa stabbed at the potatoes and dropped them onto the plates with frustration. It didn't go unnoticed and Jason's mum tutted.

'You know, if you bake them in goose fat they come out a lot nicer than those ones you're serving.'

Pippa clenched her teeth together and held on to the comment she was tempted to throw back at Jason's mother. Ever since she arrived the day before yesterday, she had been criticising everything that Pippa was doing. She couldn't cook properly, she didn't fold the clothes in the right way, she used too much washing-up liquid, she didn't do enough for her son – there was literally nothing Pippa could do to make his mother happy. So when she had spent all morning in the kitchen, slaving away, making a Christmas dinner that was worthy of his mother's taste buds – all whilst being pregnant and finishing off the Christmas orders she had to bake – and his mother still felt the need to comment, Pippa was starting to struggle with not retaliating. She always felt the loss more at this time of the year more than ever. It was the tenth year without her mum and the fourth year without her dad and it didn't get any easier to handle.

It didn't help matters that Jason had spent the entire morning glued to his phone with his feet up in the living room, Christmas films on in the background. She had called him about twenty minutes ago and asked him to set the table ready for when she dished up, but he was still yet to surface.

'Jason!'

'Oh leave him! He works hard all year round, he should be relaxing over the Christmas period. You can lay the table, surely?'

'Oh yeah, I'll just bloody do everything, shall I? Stick a broom up my arse and sweep the floor as I do everything else. It's okay, I'm only pregnant with your grandchild.' As much as she wanted to say all of that to his mum, she opted for muttering this under her breath. So when she replied, 'Sorry dear?' and looked up from the crossword she was doing on the dining-room table, Pippa just smiled and said, 'Nothing.'

She continued plating up and then laid the table herself. Calling Jason in when dinner was on the table. He came in almost instantly. 'Oh, so you can hear me when it's time to eat, then.'

'Sorry, Pip, I was sorting work stuff.' He sat down and put his mobile on the table.

'On Christmas Day?'

'Yeah,' was his reply, but he didn't look at her. She hated how much he was stuck on his phone lately. She felt as if she was in a three-way marriage. It wasn't just that, though. She felt guilty too. And his mum never let her forget.

'Well, he works hard, doesn't he? Whilst you're making your cakes, Jason's slogging his guts out keeping a roof over your head. You should be grateful, not having a go all the time.'

Pippa glared at her. 'I *am* grateful,' she said, through gritted teeth.

His mum made a *humph* noise and set about sorting her napkin out. Pippa looked over at Jason, who had now picked up his phone again and was tapping away at the screen. 'Can't we have a 'no phones at the table' rule, just this once? It would be nice to have a family meal and chat.' Pippa put everyone's meals in front of them and then sat down herself as Jason huffed and put his phone in his pocket. She supposed that was better than nothing.

The meal dragged. Talking to Jason when he was so distracted was hard enough lately, but trying to talk to his mum, who found fault in everything, was even worse. She found herself opting to stay quiet and just eat. She had been dreading Christmas Day for exactly this reason. When Jason had suggested inviting his mum over this year, Pippa cringed. They didn't normally have her over as she always went to friends with her husband and Pippa and Jason spent it just the two of them. Normally they would relax together and spend quality time with each other. But because his mum was here this year, Pippa hadn't relaxed from the second she got up. She tried really hard to engage his mother in conversation, but when she constantly moaned about how Pippa was not good enough at anything, she kind of gave up.

'How is Charlie?' Pippa asked, trying one last attempt at

breaking the awkward silence. 'He's fine, I suppose. Thanks for bringing that up!' His mother snapped back.

Charlie was Jason's dad. He was actually okay to get along with but he and Jason's mum recently split up – which was why she was here and not at the usual friend's house this Christmas. They had parted on amicable terms, which was why Pippa thought it was safe to talk about it. Clearly not.

'I'm sorry, I just thought—'

'That's the thing, though, Pippa, isn't it. You don't always think. Sometimes it is best to just stay quiet, dear, isn't it? Maybe you should try it.'

Pippa recoiled in surprise at the rudeness of his mum. Thankfully Jason stepped up before Pippa did.

'Come on, Mum, don't be like that. She was only asking how Dad was.' He smiled over at Pippa reassuringly and it settled her. She was pleasantly surprised that he had backed her up. It was a nice move; one that he didn't carry out often.

'I just don't wish for that topic to be brought up whilst I am eating. Is that too much to ask?'

Both Pippa and Jason stayed quiet. Sometimes, with his mother, silence was the better option. As soon as he had finished his meal, Jason stood up and excused himself from the table and Pippa caught him taking his phone out of his pocket as soon as he left the room, tapping away on it with a smile on his face. His mum then stood and walked out, making her way to the living room, saying, 'It's about time that film was starting, isn't it?'

'I'll do the washing up, then,' she called after them both and began to clear the table, placing the plates into the sink a little more roughly than she needed to. She took her phone out of her handbag on the side and sent Zoe a text.

Merry Christmas to you and Ellie. Hope you're having a better day than I am!

She added an angry emoji and waited for a reply, pouring herself a coffee. Well, if you can't beat them, join them. At least she had the scan to look forward to on Friday.

* * * * *

'Merry Christmas, Sis.' Ellie's eyes snapped open as Zoe knelt down next to the sofa, where she was lying. She had to blink a few times to clear her vision, taking her hand and wiping the moisture from her chin as she sat up. 'Well, isn't that a pretty sight?'

'I must've fallen asleep. What time is it?'

'Hammertime!' Zoe shook her head questioningly, 'No, not awake enough to joke?' She looked at her watch, 'It's just after eight.'

'Eight? Wow, I think I've slept for most of the day.' She pulled her feet off the sofa to make room for Zoe to sit down. 'Why are you here? I thought you were staying at Dad's tonight?'

'I couldn't leave you sitting here alone on Christmas night, plus Dad had some friends invite him over for the evening, so I said I would come home. Spend it with you.'

'You didn't have to do that.' Ellie still felt a little guilty for not going with Zoe to visit their Dad on Christmas Day, but she stood by what she said this morning – he hadn't made any extra effort to see her, just as she hadn't with him. So what was the point?

'I know I didn't, but I wanted to.'

'Hmm,' Ellie had nothing to say to that. She wasn't up for engaging in a long and meaningful conversation about why she and her dad didn't sort things out, which was clearly the angle Zoe was taking. 'So, what did you get me?' She took the present Zoe had on her lap and began to unwrap.

'You'll have to wait and see. I hope you like it.'

Zoe sat expectantly as Ellie tore the Christmas paper apart and unfolded the tissue paper. 'I feel bad that I didn't get you anything, but, well, you know, I'm a bit strapped for cash at the moment.'

'It's fine, you're already giving me the best present by being here with me.'

'Oh, someone's had a glass of wine.' Ellie pushed Zoe as she giggled. 'I'm only joking; it's nice to be here with you too. It's just a shame it's under shitty circumstances.' As she spoke she pulled out the present that was encased inside the beautiful pale-cream tissue paper. She held it up as she took it in. The tiny yellow jumpsuit felt soft on her skin. It had a picture of a teddy bear on one side and across the front it said *if you think I'm cute, you should see my Aunty!*

'Isn't it great? I saw it last week and just had to get it.'

'Wow.'

'What? You don't like it? I can take it back – I kept the receipt.'

Ellie laughed softly. 'Shut up, you wally. It's beautiful.'

'Oh, thank God for that. I just had to get it. I can just imagine little one in it – totally rocking the teddy-bear look.' Zoe clapped her hands together. 'I literally cannot contain my excitement when I think about it.'

Ellie shuffled on the sofa to get more comfortable, pulling the blanket up around her shoulders. 'Did you tell Dad?' she asked, not looking at her sister.

'Yes,' Zoe replied.

'And ...'

'He was shocked, but I think he will come round to the idea.' Now Zoe wasn't looking at her.

'He's disappointed in me?' Ellie asked the question, but regardless of what Zoe would say, she knew her dad would be. Zoe would try and sugarcoat it, but she knew her dad, she knew he would be saying *I told you she would waste her life*.

'No, he's just in shock. He's upset you didn't tell him your-self. He wanted me to ask you to go and see him.'

'Zoe, I can't.'

'Ellie, come on. I'll come with you, and if it gets too much, we'll leave.' Zoe's face was lit up with hope. All she ever wanted was for them all to be a happy family. But Ellie knew it wouldn't be the fairytale she wished for.

'I'm not ready for it. Not right now. I'm all hormonal as it is. I can't deal with Dad and his disapproving looks at me.'

'He won't—'

'I'll think about it, okay?' She cut off.

'Also, I've been thinking ...' Zoe turned to face her, hands in her lap.

203

'Here we go.'

'We need to sort out what you are going to do – long term. As much as I love you staying here, you have your flat and bills and your job ...' she trailed off. 'We need to get the ball rolling.'

'What do you mean?'

'Well, you don't have any ties back home – apart from Chris, which we can sort – so you're staying here with me, for good.'

'Zoe, I don't know. Like you said, I've got work to do, no clothes here ...'

'Work can wait. You're freelance, right?' Ellie nodded. 'Well, you can set up some freelance work here. We'll advertise in the shop and we can go back to yours together and grab some stuff.'

'Zoe, I can't just up and leave. What will I do about the flat?'

'You're only renting it, give notice.' Zoe sat down.

'Notice? Zoe I can't move up here.' Ellie sat to join her.

'Why not? What's holding you in London?' Zoe said the words as if it was a no-brainer. As if it was just that easy to up and move.

'Well, what about Dad, then?' Ellie knew this was clutching at straws, but the thought of moving her whole life seemed absolutely absurd. Although in answer to her sister's question, she couldn't actually think of a valid reason as to why this couldn't happen.

'Oh come on, really? You're pulling the Dad card now?' Zoe raised an eyebrow and at that moment she looked just like their mum. Ellie wasn't prepared for the feelings that washed over her and she was momentarily stunned. What would her mum be saying to her at this moment in time? She didn't know. But she did know one thing; she would want her daughters to stick together.

'You're right.'

'Come on, this is your chance at a new start. New baby, new life. You can do this.' She moved across the sofa and put her arm around Ellie's shoulders.

Ellie shook her head. 'Zoe, I'm scared.' It came out as barely a whisper but the full force of the words hit her.

'I know you are but you don't have to be. I am here and I will always be here, okay? I'm not going anywhere.' She pulled Ellie in for an embrace and Ellie let the droplets of emotion trickle down her cheek.

Barely a minute passed when Ellie's phone began to ring and she pulled away from Zoe abruptly in surprise as she felt the vibration in her pocket. She pulled it out and they both looked down at the name flashing on her screen.

'Why don't you tell him the good news?'

'We haven't decided anything yet. Stop rushing me.' After a few minutes, the phone stopped ringing and was followed by the beep of a voicemail.

'Hey Els, just wishing you and the baby a Merry Christmas. I'll call you tomorrow.'

Ellie smiled and quickly put her phone on the coffee table, dropping the jumpsuit back inside the wrapping bundle and laying it on the floor. 'So, what do you say? Girly chick flick and popcorn?

'I'll go one better.' Zoe jumped up and ran into the kitchen, returning seconds later with a tub of Ben and Jerry's ice cream and two spoons.

'Now, that is what I call heaven.' And she shuffled under the duvet, feeling quietly contented.

Chapter 21

'Hi,' Imogen said, as she manoeuvred her way around the tables in the café to the one at the back, where the others were sitting. 'Room for a little one?' She liked these women. Out of everyone who went to these meetings, Imogen felt the most comfortable with them. After having only been to a few, she was starting to feel like part of this little group of women. She looked forward to catching up with them each week and had actually missed not coming over Christmas.

'Of course.' Zoe ushered her to a seat around the other side. 'You don't have to ask permission, my lovely; you're always welcome at our table.'

Imogen took the chair and smiled her thanks. With all the stuff that had been going on recently, she was relieved to have some new friends who she could see every week and who knew very little about what was going on in her life. Alice had been mega-busy at work in the run-up to Christmas and now was back at work, dealing with the January rush. She was seeing less of her at the moment, which did nothing for her stress levels.

'Okay ladies, welcome back. I hope you all had a lovely

Christmas and enjoyed indulging in lots of chocolate, seeing as we can't enjoy the festive tipples. And on the topic of food, I thought this week's conversation starter should be cravings.'

Imogen watched as Zoe took the lead at the front of the café. She really admired Zoe. Such a strong, independent woman. She had her café; she was beautiful and clearly acing life! Just being around Zoe made Imogen feel empowered. If she was honest, it was this group of ladies that kept her coming each week. She hadn't really fully bonded with this little group yet, more like sitting on the sidelines and chipping in as and when, but having this weekly solace from all the shit she was still getting from her mum was keeping her sane.

'Oh my God, I have seriously been craving those banana chip thingies.' Pippa was rummaging in her bag as she spoke and then whipped out a sandwich bag full of said banana chips. 'I seriously cannot go out anywhere without knowing they are in my bag.'

'I can't stand those.' Imogen turned up her nose at the bag and actually felt a little nausea when the banana smell wafted her way.

'How can you not like these? They're amazing.' She threw a few into her mouth before putting the bag away.

'Well, I just remember one time at work one of the kids had these as a snack and was sick afterwards and now every time I see them I just think of that.'

'Oh no! No, don't ruin it for me – I've got like a lifetime's supply of these at home. I practically re-mortgaged the house just to pay for my habit.'

Imogen laughed as Zoe re-joined the table. 'What did I miss?'

'Banana chips make Imogen feel sick and apparently make children vomit and I need to re-mortgage my house to pay for my banana addiction.' Pippa looked up at Zoe with a dead-straight face, shaking her head in mock despair over what she had just discovered and Imogen couldn't help but give the game away by laughing. 'Oh Imogen, you were supposed to play along.'

'I'm sorry,' she said through giggles, 'I just couldn't keep a straight face, and Zoe's reaction was a picture!' She turned to Zoe, 'You looked so confused.'

'I still am, a little.'

'Don't worry; I just need you to bail me out when I get caught for stealing money to feed my addiction.'

'To ... bananas?' Zoe looked from one girl to the other as they descended into fits of giggles. 'Okay, I'm just going to move along the conversation to something a little more ... shall we say ... sane.' She placed two coffees on the table. 'Who wants cake?'

'Have you got banana cake?' Imogen managed to get out before spiralling into yet more laughter, spurred on by Pippa's reaction. The pair of them had tears streaming down their faces and had caught the attention of the other people in the café too.

Zoe sat down with them and a smile spread across her face. 'Okay, clearly you two are on something and I want in!'

Imogen dabbed at her eyes with a napkin. 'Sorry, I don't know what's got into me. I haven't had much sleep – I blame the tiredness.'

'I don't have an excuse,' Pippa added, 'I just found it really funny.'

'Well, it's nice to see you both so happy.'

'Hey, look.' Pippa pulled out an envelope from her bag, revealing her scan picture.

'Oh, let me see!' Imogen took the picture and studied it. 'This is amazing. I can't wait to have another one of mine. Got my twelve-week one on Friday. So excited!'

'Is Alice going with you?' Pippa asked.

'Yeah, she's booked the afternoon off.' Imogen handed the photo to Zoe.

She laughed as she took the photo. 'This is so exciting. I can't believe you're going to have a little baby. Just think, Christmas this year you'll all have extra mouths to feed.'

'I know! And you will be an Aunty!' Realisation dawned on Pippa. 'Hey, where's Ellie? Isn't she joining us today?'

'Who knows, Pip. I can't keep up with her and her hormones at the moment. One minute she's fine and I really enjoy having her around, the next minute she's having a strop about God knows what and she storms off.'

'She'll settle down with the hormones. Just give her time.'

'Yeah, I know. She was fine last week, but then this morning was really moody. It's like living with her as a teenager again.'

'Has she decided how long she's staying for yet?' Pippa sipped at her drink.

'Well, I asked her to stay – for good. She keeps changing her mind. I don't think, given the situation, it would be a good idea for her to be all the way back in London, so I hope she does stay. Despite her being annoying, it has been nice to have her around every day.'

Imogen's phone beeped and she quickly swiped the message away. It wasn't missed by the others and they both stared at her, confused. 'You okay?' Zoe asked.

'Yeah, fine.' Why did she have to text now?

'Why did you swipe your phone like that – you got something to hide?' Zoe said it in jest, but Imogen felt as if she had guilt written all over her face. She didn't respond and Zoe looked worried. 'Hey, I was only joking. I didn't mean to offend you. It was just funny that you moved so quickly.'

'Sorry, I just hate my phone going off in the middle of stuff. Habit ... you know.' She picked the phone up and excused herself to the toilet, leaving the others at the table looking baffled by her strange behaviour. As she got into the cubicle she opened up the message from her mum:

> *I heard something today which makes me very upset.*
> *I told the person that you wouldn't do this to me.*
> *Please tell me it isn't true – please tell me you aren't*
> *having a baby with that woman.*

* * * * *

That evening Pippa found herself sitting on the sofa next to Jason, who had been asleep for the past hour. She typed a quick text to Zoe:

Can you believe it? He works all the hours under the sun and then when he finally does come home, he's bloody asleep within minutes of starting a film!

Zoe responded almost instantly.

Hold his nose and cover his mouth – that'll soon wake him up!!

She added a laughing emoji and Pippa had to stop herself from laughing so that she didn't wake him up. Because, truth be told, having him asleep now meant that what she was about to do would be a hell of a lot easier.

She slid herself off the sofa and padded gently across the room, glancing back when she reached the door to check that he was still asleep. Mouth wide open and head lolled back against the wall – yep, she was safe. She went out into the kitchen, where Jason's phone was sitting on charge on the counter. The cold tiles under her bare feet made her shiver involuntarily as she walked over them. She checked over her shoulder one last time before picking his phone up. She felt guilty already. She knew she shouldn't be doing this, but something wasn't right. And after going through it all before, she was afraid it was happening again. She thought back to when they were together before and the moment she discovered he was messaging another woman.

'I'm sorry, babe, it's not what you think.' He had said to her as she held the phone up, questioning who Katie was.

'What am I thinking?' she had challenged him. Not really

212

wanting to hear the answer but knowing full well that she had to.

'You're thinking that I'm having an affair with her. You're thinking that I have been going behind your back.' The panic on his face was horrendous. She could remember feeling utter disgrace looking at him and feeling a little guilty for making him feel so bad.

'And I'm wrong, am I?' Whilst she needed to ask that question, that was what eventually ended their relationship all those years ago as he admitted everything and dropped to his knees sobbing. She hadn't the strength back then to stand up to him – she still didn't now – so she had simply dropped to the floor with him, joining him in the tears. However, the days that followed that were so hard that she decided to walk out and with the support of her dad behind her, she left him.

But she didn't have her dad here any more. He had been her rock, her saviour. She was his princess and she knew that whenever anything went wrong, he was always there beside her to support her. Even when she decided to take Jason back, although unhappy, her dad could see how much she loved him and he supported her. Their relationship had become really strong when her mum had passed away and they became inseparable. But when her dad died too, Pippa felt as if she had lost the last part of her strength. And now, all these years later, she was back in this situation with Jason, where he was working late all the time, glued to his phone the rest of the time and behaving distant with her, and she was so scared that he was doing it to her again.

She reached the counter and unlocked his phone, using the

pin she had seen him doing earlier and went straight to his messages. Scrolling through the list, nothing seemed amiss. Just a few texts from his mates at the football ground and some from Patrick at work. She didn't bother going into any of the messages, just kept scrolling until she came across names she didn't recognise, or names that were female. But there was nothing. She wasn't sure if she felt relieved or disappointed. Not that she wanted to find anything bad on his phone, but she was sure that something was up, and now she just felt like an idiot. She tried his picture gallery and then his call list. But still nothing. She felt as if she was losing her mind.

'What do you think you are doing?'

Pippa jumped so high that she dropped the phone and grabbed onto the counter for support. 'For crying out loud, Jason, you scared the crap out of me!'

'Were you looking through my phone?' His face was contorted with anger and Pippa felt a wave of shame wash over her.

'I ... um ... no.'

'Don't lie to me!' He snatched his phone off the floor and held it up to her face. 'Find anything interesting did you?' He was furious and she totally understood why. She hadn't found anything and now she felt like the worst wife in the world. She shook her head. 'Why the fuck did you think you needed to go through my phone?'

'I'm sorry, I didn't mean to—'

'What? The phone just happened to fall into your hands and open up did it?' His face began to turn red and his eyes scrunched up in anger.

'Well no, but—' she was shaking.

'Save it! I don't want to hear your pathetic excuses. You're bang out of order for doing this. I've done nothing but love you and provide for you and this is how you repay me.'

She started to panic and her eyes began to fill. This just seemed to aggravate Jason as he yelled out, 'Oh save the tears, Pip. You're the one who stepped out of line here, not me! We're having a baby – what do you take me for?'

'I just thought ...' she trailed off. She didn't know what her response was going to be.

'What did you think? That I would do it again?'

She felt a surge of annoyance spark as he mocked her. 'Well actually, yes! And can you blame me? You've been acting so distant lately and working all the time, what am I supposed to think?' Her heart was pounding in her chest, the anticipation of confronting him like this making her feel panicked. She hadn't expected to be having this row tonight.

Jason slammed his hand down on the counter. 'Pip, I am working loads to support our family – that baby!' He jabbed his finger in the air towards her stomach and she recoiled in shock. 'You don't expect that we can survive on your piddly little wage that you bring in from your little cake business, do you?' His eyes were narrowed as he dared her to disagree.

'I am trying my best, Jason. You were the one who told me to give up my job and do it full time. You said you would support me, that you wanted me to follow my dreams.' The words stung as she remembered.

'Yes, well ... I guess I thought you would make it bigger

than you have.' He moved his eye contact, unable to look her in the eye as he said the words.

Disappointment dropped down heavily into her chest. 'Why didn't you say any of this before? Why not tell me you weren't happy with how I am running my business?'

'Because what good would that do? You'll just get upset or have a strop and I'm not up for that, Pip. I just want to do my work and come home and have a bottle of wine watching the telly. Is that too much to ask?'

She didn't say anything about his alcohol comment because she didn't want to fuel the argument. But she couldn't help but feel deflated that he still revolved everything around drink. 'I can try harder, I'll do some marketing and—'

'What, for all of five minutes before the baby comes? What good is that going to do? You won't be able to stick to your plans, so why bother?'

Pippa's mouth dropped open a little at his abruptness. 'Well, what do you want me to say, Jason? I don't feel like I am saying the words you want to hear, so tell me – what is it you want?' Panic was pulsing through her veins. She could feel her marriage slipping away, thread by thread, and if that happened, where would she be? Alone, with a baby and a piddly little cake business to support her.

He turned and stormed up the hallway towards the front door.

'Jason wait,' she wailed, chasing after him, 'where are you going?'

'Out!'

'But Jason—'

He spun around on his heels and stopped just inches away from her face. Speaking calmly he simply said, 'I can't believe you. I work my arse off for you and this is how you repay me.' And after a pause to ensure full impact of his words hit home, he turned and left, leaving Pippa to wonder if her husband was coming home ever again.

* * * * *

The next morning, Pippa woke early to the sound of the front door slamming. She jumped out of bed as quickly as she could and raced downstairs, following the noise of crashing and banging in the kitchen. As she walked in, she could see Jason stumbling about, seemingly trying to make some food.

'Jason?' she asked, tentatively.

He spun round and his face lit up with happiness. 'There she is. There's my girl.' He stumbled over and threw his arms around her waist, pulling her in for a hug. Pippa had to hold her breath to stop breathing in the stale stench of alcohol. She patted his back and then tried to peel him off. 'Good night was it?' She asked.

'What? Oh, yeah. I had a few beers.' He moved back to the counter. 'Fancy a sandwich?'

'No, I'm okay thanks.' She paused before saying, 'Listen, Jason, I'm sorry about last night. I didn't mean to—'

He held up his hands. 'It's okay. It's fine. You know why?'

She shook her head.

'Because I've been an arsehole before and I understand why you are thinking the worst.'

She wasn't sure how to take him today. 'Look, I know I've been an idiot in the past but, let's just forget last night happened. Yeah?' He went to lean on the side but missed it and stumbled backwards. He burst into laughter. 'Did you just see that? I missed the table.' He held his stomach as he laughed silently. 'Classic!'

Pippa hated seeing him in this state. It made a difference from the shouting drunk he had been previously, but in a way, this was worse. She tied up her robe and turned to leave.

'Hey, where you going?' He was pointing at her.

'I'm going to take a shower. I think you need to eat something then sleep it off.' She tried to force a smile on her face and then left.

As she walked up the stairs she pulled out her phone and saw she had been added to a WhatsApp group by Zoe.

Zoe: Hi girls. I need your help with something. Are you free to meet up today?

Imogen: Yes, I can meet up. What time?

Zoe: Can you come to the café, I'm working today? I need to wait until Ellie is out, though, as I don't want her to hear.

Imogen: Is Ellie not in this group chat?

Zoe: No, just me, you and Pip.

Imogen: Okay, I'll pop in around ten-ish, will that work?

Zoe: Fab. Pip?

Pippa read the messages and smiled. Even though her life seemed to be falling apart at home, it was nice that she had these girls. They had built up their little friendship group over the last couple of months and she was really grateful to have them. Because the way things were back here, she was close to breaking point. Having these girls gave her a reason to keep fighting and put that brave face on. No matter how much she was drowning under the surface. No one needed to know that.

Pippa: I'll be there. See you then xx

She quickly switched on the shower and looked at her face in the mirror. She was pale and had dark circles under her eyes, where she had, yet again, cried herself to sleep. And no matter how much she told herself that she was doing the right thing by persisting, she couldn't help but think of her dad and how disappointed he would be to see her unhappy but not doing anything about it. Why was she with him? She wasn't so sure any more.

Chapter 22

'You've been acting really weird over the last couple of weeks. Actually,' Alice corrected herself, 'since before Christmas, is everything okay?'

Imogen played with the teaspoon on the table in front of her, avoiding Alice's eye contact. The café was beginning to get busy, but Imogen was thankful of the distraction. Although every time the door opened, signalled by the gentle tinkle of the bell, a gust of wind would blow in, making Imogen shiver. She didn't care, though. It gave her something to focus on. She had been trying so hard recently to push all her worries to the back of her mind and just get on with actually enjoying being pregnant, but she couldn't get away from the nasty messages her mum had been sending her. She had ignored that last message and had since received a barrage of demanding texts. But if she told Alice then she would be stressed and it would impact the pair of them. Imogen was ashamed that her family were the ones causing problems and as much as she wanted to just cut loose, she found she couldn't.

'Yeah, I'm fine, just really tired with this pregnancy, that's all.' She couldn't look at her, not when she lied. She would definitely give it away if she did – she was a terrible liar. Which up until now, she was actually proud of. It wasn't a good trait to have, so to be so bad at it was a good thing! Which was why the way she was behaving was making her feel ill. This wasn't her, she didn't lie.

'Are you sure that's all? You know I'm here, don't you. I feel like recently you've been distant from me and I'm worried.' Alice held her hand and gave it a squeeze. But instead of feeling reassured and loved, Imogen felt guilty. She still hadn't told Alice that the doctor had signed her off work just before Christmas because of stress and she was terrified of being found out. But because she had taken so long to admit it, she was now too far in and if Alice found out she had been lying, she would never forgive her. She should've said earlier and now it was out of control.

'I'm fine.' She forced a smile. 'Can't wait for the scan tomorrow.'

'I know, I've booked the morning off work, but I have to go back after lunch, unfortunately. Are you glad you booked today off? It's a nice idea having the day before the scan off – means you'll be nicely relaxed by tomorrow.'

'Yeah well, seeing as I have Fridays off anyway, I thought I would make a long weekend of it.' Nothing to do with the fact that she was no longer allowed to work – doctor's orders!

'Hey, you okay? How you feeling today?' Zoe placed down the two teas the girls had ordered.

'Yeah I'm okay. This is Alice.' She gestured with her hand to her wife and was pleased when Alice took the lead in the conversation.

'Hi, it's nice to finally meet you. Imogen really enjoys coming to the mums' club meetings you do here. I'm so glad she's found some great friends here.'

Zoe joined them at the table, taking up the spare seat opposite Imogen. 'Yeah, I actually can't believe how popular it became in such a short time. It's crazy. I must admit, I think I enjoy them more than anyone.' She smiled at Imogen, but something in her face changed. Maybe she could tell Imogen wasn't right.

'Well, there must've been a demand for it; you did well to jump on it before anyone else did.'

'Yeah, I know. So will you be able to make any of the meetings? Would be lovely for you to meet the others. You're more than welcome.' She kept glancing back at Imogen, which made her feel really uncomfortable. Imogen forced a smile, which she hoped looked genuine.

'Oh I wish I could, but I only managed to pop out today because I had a viewing to do and the woman cancelled last minute. Normally it's crazy busy at the office, so I work through my lunch most days. I was actually really surprised to bump into this one outside; I thought she was at work. But a pleasant surprise it was and she persuaded me to stop for a cuppa. I never could resist her puppy-dog eyes.' She glanced over at Imogen, her face full of love for her. Again, Imogen tried to produce a smile but she felt it was forced.

'Well, it was nice to meet you. I'd better get on.' Zoe smiled at them both and then left.

After they had finished their tea, Alice gave Imogen a kiss goodbye and left for the office, leaving Imogen at the table alone. She took this chance to read the text that had pinged into her inbox halfway through her tea which she had been avoiding reading whilst Alice was still there. And, sure enough, it was another text from her mum.

She had to read the message twice to make sure she was actually seeing things as they were.

I don't know what you're playing at but it's not funny. Two women cannot have a baby. It's irresponsible and selfish and all you are doing is setting that poor child up for a life of teasing and being the butt of everyone's joke. If you have any decency left in your body you will end this stupidity. You have brought shame onto our family and I will not tolerate it. Stop thinking of yourself and think of someone else for a change.

She scrolled back and forth through the message, blinking through the haze to make out the harsh words her mother had thrown at her this time. She was so engrossed in the message that she didn't hear Zoe creeping up behind her. The first she knew of it was feeling the chair next to her move backwards to allow Zoe to slip in. 'Hey you,' she said as she took up the seat. 'Everything okay?'

Imogen quickly shut down the message on the screen, wondering if Zoe had managed to see any of what was written. God, she hoped not. She was so ashamed of her family, she didn't want to have to admit to anyone that she was related to such horrible people. She plastered on a smile and replied, 'Yeah, course, why wouldn't it be?'

'Well,' Zoe said as she leaned back in her chair. 'Ever since Alice left a few minutes ago, you have been staring at your phone, looking like you are about to cry. And now that I think about it, you've been off for a little while. The last couple of times I have seen you you've been quiet and ... well ... you look sad.' Zoe held out her hands, palms up and added, 'It's not rocket science. What's up?'

She prepared herself to tell another lie, but stopped in her tracks. She couldn't do this any more. She couldn't bear the brunt of everything going on and stay sane; it was driving her nuts – even the doctors said that. She took a deep breath and prepared herself to let Zoe in. 'Okay, I'm not okay.'

'Do you want to talk about it?'

She didn't answer. She wanted to say yes, but her mouth wouldn't let her. She eventually said, 'I feel guilty.'

'For what?'

Zoe's voice was soft and calm and made Imogen feel more at ease than she had felt all morning. She took a moment to look around the café. It wasn't busy, which wasn't surprising seeing as it was nearing lunchtime on a weekday and everyone would be either at work or school, or at home preparing for lunch. The café was quieter in the mornings than after lunch, which was probably why Zoe wanted to meet them. It had taken Imogen by surprise when she'd seen Alice outside, so she had to think on her feet and invite her for coffee. 'I should be talking to Alice.' She felt the guilt drop down further into her stomach as she said her name. She really should be talking to Alice. She shouldn't be here. Yet she couldn't bring herself to leave.

'Has something happened? Is it the babies?'

'No, the babies are fine.'

'Imogen, sweetheart, you're not really making any sense.' Zoe took her hand and gently placed it inside her two. Imogen exhaled a little, feeling frustrated with both herself and the situation. ' You know, you can talk to me in confidence. I won't ever talk about it to anyone. I'm like a kind of vicar of the café world; pretend this table is my confession box. I'm bound by the terms of the café, it discreetly says in the café handbook that any client wishing to divulge sensitive information can do so on any table assuming nobody else is in earshot and the proprietor – that's me – does a pinkie-swear to keep all information confidential between themselves and the ... um ... information-giver ...' she pulled a face at her bad use of language, but then held out her hand, which she had fisted, keeping her little finger jutting out, ready to honourably take the pinkie oath. Imogen couldn't help but laugh, at which Zoe crossed her heart solemnly and nodded, reiterating her promise to her friend.

'Well, how can I not speak to you now that you've made all that effort to make up all that rubbish just for me?'

'No, no, not rubbish. It's the café-oath. Everyone has to do it.' She shrugged in a nonchalant way and wiggled her little finger again. Imogen smiled and joined her finger with Zoë's, wrapping it round and following Zoe's movement to bond this oath. 'So now, you see, I am bound by the laws. I cannot repeat any information you give me. This stays between us unless you decide to extend the knowledge further.' She smiled and Imogen couldn't help but warm to Zoe even more.

'You must have a vat of information swirling around inside of you with the number of people who come in here. How do you even get any work done?'

Zoe flicked her hair over her shoulder, mimicking an airhead and said, 'Dahhling, I'm a natural.'

After a few giggles and the very awkward silence that followed, Imogen finally said, 'The doctor signed me off work with stress.' Zoe nodded to show she had heard her revelation and she added, reluctantly, 'I haven't told Alice.'

'Okay and what's the reason for that?'

'I don't want to worry her. She's so stressed with work and the babies and everything, even though she never shows it, but I just don't want to be another burden for her.'

'And is that what you think you would be; a burden?' Imogen shrugged and Zoe continued. 'Do you not think she would rather know, so she could help you?'

'It's not fair to put more on her shoulders.'

'So where does she think you are during the day?'

'At work.'

'Have you told her you are?' Imogen couldn't hide the guilt on her face and Zoe added, 'I see.'

'I'm a really bad person, aren't I?' Maybe her mum was right.

'No, not at all. Hey, listen to me,' Zoe put her finger under Imogen's chin and lifted her head just enough so that they regained eye contact. 'You're not a bad person, okay? You are one of the nicest, kindest people I have met in a long time. So don't you go thinking that you are anything but.'

'You don't have to say that.'

'I know I don't, but I mean it.' Another silence before Zoe asked, 'Why has he signed you off with stress? Is it anything I can help with?'

'No.'

'Surely Alice can help? She wouldn't want you to be stressed out and not tell her.'

Imogen acted on impulse whilst she still had the confidence and simply opened her mum's message on her phone and slid it across the table for Zoe to read. She looked at Imogen with slight confusion as she picked up the phone and read. It felt weird. Half like it was a weight off her shoulders to share this with someone, and half betrayal of Alice. Because, realistically, she should be the one she was sharing this with.

'Wow, I take it this isn't the first message your mum has sent you like this.' Imogen shook her head. 'And Alice doesn't know about this?' Another shake. 'I can see why you wouldn't want to share this with her, but honestly, she should know what is going on. She would want to help you. Does she know your mum feels like this?'

'She knows Mum isn't really on board with the whole lesbian thing and she knows that Mum has sent me texts before, but we spoke and agreed that I wouldn't reply and fuel the argument. I suffered with really bad anxiety attacks a while back because of stuff Mum was saying and Alice was so annoyed. That's why she wants me to not see Mum any more. I told her I cut off from her recently. She doesn't know Mum is still sending me these.' She pointed at her phone in frustration. 'Zoe, I can't show her, it would break her heart to hear my mum speak about her like that. And I promised I wouldn't message her any more. And then I lied, and now I'm too far into it and I don't want Alice to think I am a liar ... it's just a mess!'

'And what about how she's speaking to you? That isn't right.' She leaned in so that her face was closer to Imogen's, making her point clear.

'I know, but Mum will never change.'

'That doesn't mean you have to put up with this sort of abuse. Don't you think it would be better to cut away? Can't you change your number?' Zoe looked over her shoulder as some customers entered the café talking loudly between themselves and taking up seats at a table by the door.

'That wouldn't help. She knows where I live. If she can't contact me via the phone, she might turn up at the house. And I *really* don't want that.'

'So, what are you going to do? Keep receiving these horrible messages from her? It's making you ill. You need to think about the effect this has on your body and ...' she trailed off, clearly not wanting to say it. Imogen knew what she meant, though.

'The babies?'

Zoe's eyes were sad. 'Listen, I'm not about to sit here and preach to you – you obviously get enough of that from your mum. But I just want you to think about yourself. You are so lovely, Imogen, and you always think of other people first, but maybe it's about time you thought about you. You're a grown woman. If your mum isn't going to support you to be happy, then you don't need that sort of negativity in your life.'

'But she's my ...' she couldn't say it, the emotion caught in her throat and she stopped talking.

'I know, sweetheart. But you have Alice and you have us. You never know, she might come round to it when the babies are here?' Imogen wasn't so sure. 'Hang on, I'll just serve these customers and we can think of what we are going to do. Plus I want to talk to you about tomorrow's surprise for Ellie, if you're still around to help?' Zoe gave her a squeeze on the shoulder before she made her way over to the group who had just come in.

Chapter 23

'So you're here to stay for a bit, then? You decided to listen to me?' Zoe smirked as she placed the cutlery away from the dishwasher and Ellie couldn't help but roll her eyes. 'It's only taken you nearly a week to come round to the idea.'

'Yes okay, you were right, I was wrong, blah, blah, blah!' She gathered up the plates and put them in the cupboard. She had to admit, being here with her sister and doing mundane things like unloading the dishwasher together was actually really nice. When the shop was closed and it was just the two of them, in the flat, doing stuff like this, she realised how much she missed having her sister around all the time.

'I'm only messing with you, you know that. I'm just glad you decided to take me up on the offer.'

'Yeah, well, I don't have many other options at the moment, do I?'

Zoe closed the dishwasher door and looked at Ellie. 'Thanks for that, Sis. Nice to feel loved.'

'Zoe—'

She held up her hand in protest. 'It's okay, I'm joking. So how are you feeling today? Any more nausea?'

'Oh God, that was horrendous last week. I honestly felt like I wanted to curl up and die.' She instinctively touched her stomach.

'Bit dramatic.' Zoe shrugged.

'Oh yeah? Well until you are throwing up every five minutes, your opinion doesn't count.'

The knocker sounded and Zoe jumped to answer it before Ellie even had a chance to think. 'Woah, easy girl. What's the rush?'

'I've kind of got a little bit of a surprise for you.' She called over her shoulder as she exited the kitchen.

Ellie's stomach turned over in anticipation. 'What do you mean a surprise?'

'You'll see.'

'What? I don't want to see, I want to know – Zoe?' She heard the front door open and the familiar voices of Pippa and Imogen floated through into the kitchen. Within seconds the pair of them appeared in the doorway looking suspicious. 'Why do I feel like something is going on?'

Zoe popped her head around the doorframe, appearing as a floating head between Imogen and Pippa's torsos. 'Wellllll ...'

'Zoe ...' Ellie warned.

'Thing is, Sis, we've been talking and the girls agree that you should move up here ... permanently.'

'What?' she picked up the tea towel to dry her hands. 'Come on, we've—'

'Just hear us out.' Zoe moved into the room fully and the others took up positions either side of her. 'You don't have anything holding you where you are living at the moment. I know you've got your job, but you can find work up here and you can work at the café until things settle down. I could do with a hand some days.'

Pippa took out a piece of paper from her pocket and unfolded it. 'We've found a list of possible job opportunities that you might like and we've also put down some ideas for something self-employed so that there's more flexibility when the baby comes.' She handed the paper to Ellie, who took it slowly, eyeing up her friends in confusion, with her mouth slightly open. As she turned the paper around to look at it, Imogen stepped forward.

'We've also got a list of flats that are vacant at the moment, but we all agreed that maybe you might be better off staying here with Zoe until after the baby is born and you have some regular money coming in, but if you really didn't want to be here then there are some other options available at the moment.'

Zoe knelt down in front of the sofa and placed her hands on Ellie's knees. 'But I would really like it if you stayed here with me. I want to be a big part in this baby's life, Ellie. You and I have lived so far apart for too long and I miss you. Having you around these last couple of months has been amazing and it has made me realise how much I miss having my little sister around.'

'Wow, Zoe, I don't know what to say.'

'Say yes.' She looked so happy at the thought of having Ellie back in her life every day.

'Zoe, it's not that simple. It's one thing taking an extended holiday and putting all my bills, work ... my life on hold. But

I can't just uproot and move here for good.' She rested the small of her back on the counter.

'Why can't you? We've worked everything out, it can be done, Ellie. What reason do you have to stay where you are?'

Zoe challenged Ellie and for the first time she actually couldn't think of a good enough reason. She had spent so long working herself into the ground before this all happened so she didn't have a huge amount of friends back home – mostly colleagues who hung out with her because of who she was, not because they cared about her. And then there was her dad.

'I guess.' She looked at the three of them and smiled. 'I can't believe you have all gone to so much trouble to do all of this. Why?'

Imogen smiled. 'Because we're friends and that's what friends do.'

'And there's one more thing.' Zoe held up a finger.

'Zoe! Seriously, I can't take all of these surprises. This one better be a male stripper or I'm going home right now.'

'Well, you're kind of right.' She looked to the other girls, who both nodded.

'What! You've actually got a stripper?'

'Not exactly, but you are going home right now.'

Ellie pulled a face. 'I don't get it.'

'The girls have not just come over to help me to convince you to stay; we're going on a road trip.' Ellie looked from one girl to another. Pippa stepped forward and held out her hand.

'Come on ... we're going to get your stuff.'

'My stuff?'

'Yep. It's moving day and the only help you have are two pregnant ladies and a woman on a mission.' Zoe jumped up and grabbed her keys. 'Last one to the car buys the McDonalds.'

Chapter 24

'Just keep an eye out for me, please!' Ellie was feeling extremely nervous and frustrated all at once. She continued to rummage around in her bedroom, throwing in clothes, shoes, bedding ... anything she could get her hands on, into black sacks. Had she had more time, this might have been a little more glamorous, with leaving parties and good-luck cards and maybe even a suitcase or three! But she didn't have the luxury of time. Zoe had to be back by 4pm to close up the café and relieve Sarah, who was helping out today as a last-minute thing. And there were only the four of them to pack. As she threw the various items into black sacks, she couldn't help but worry that maybe she was making the wrong decision. She was forced to make a decision, but who knows if this was the right one.

'Ellie!'

'What?' She poked her head out of her bedroom door, looking directly at Zoe, who was still stationed in the front doorway of the flat.

'This is silly, I should be helping you pack, not sitting here like an idiot.'

'Zoe, I don't want to see Chris, okay? Not until I've sorted myself out and he can see that I can make this work. I want to show him properly, in my own time, that I am determined to make this transition for us an easy one. But if he gets wind that I'm here, he will be round here like a shot and he will be upset that I haven't told him and that I won't be down the road any more. So just do what I ask and keep an eye out for him. I'm almost done here.' That was the sad thing. After just two hours, they had already nearly finished packing up her life. Two hours to put all her worldly possessions into black sacks. It wasn't until now that she realised just how much growing up and settling down she needed to do. At thirty years old, why was she still living off takeaways and going out to get drunk. No boyfriend, no family, yet here she was, pregnant and going to stay at her sister's. Times were going to change and Ellie, as much as she wouldn't admit it, felt a twinge of excitement at that fact.

'Ellie, come on. Just let me help, he's not coming.'

'Fine, but if he turns up when you're not watching out for him—'

She was interrupted by the sound of the doorbell. Both girls looked at each other with wide eyes. 'I bloody told you!' Ellie whispered, glancing to the front door, which was now closed.

'It might not be him.' Imogen tried her best to calm the situation, but inside Ellie was panicking.

'Pfft, yeah okay.'

'It's fine, just let me deal with it.' Zoe held her hands up to Ellie and walked the few steps back to the front door.

Ellie listened intently as she stood up against her bedroom door, which was now closed and serving as the barrier between her and Chris. 'What the hell is he doing here anyway?' she said to the other two girls, who had ceased all packing and were sitting on the floor, poised to take action should they need to.

Pippa continued putting the DVD's she was packing into the holdall as she said, 'It'll be okay. Maybe he's come to see you.'

'Or maybe he needs to collect something – does he have any stuff here?'

'No, he's not my boyfriend'

'I know. I just meant he might have left stuff here from a night out or something ... I don't know ...' Imogen trailed off and Ellie felt bad.

'Sorry, I didn't mean to snap. She didn't have to wait long before her bedroom door opened slowly and Zoe came back in. 'Err, Els, it's for you.'

'Well clearly! I'd be surprised if someone knocked on my bloody door asking for the Queen.' Zoe didn't respond, but seemed to look confused. 'Who is it?'

'Who do you think?' Zoe pulled a face that said *I'm sorry* as she walked over to the bed and sheepishly picked up a bag to fill.

Ellie walked out into the living room. Chris had his back to her and was looking out of the window. He looked relaxed and calm, and had a little smile playing on his lips, which developed into a full-blown grin when he spotted Ellie.

'Els! You okay?' He walked over to her and gave her a hug, kissing her cheek. 'What you doing back here? You never said you were home.'

'Sit down with me, Chris,' she said as she walked over to the sofa.

'What's wrong?' His face full of concern. 'Is it the baby?'

Ellie smiled. She hadn't seen this side to him before but she really liked it.

'No, the baby is fine – playing trampolines with my bladder, but fine.'

He smiled fondly at her.

'Chris, listen. I need to tell you something.' She shuffled around, not able to get comfortable, unsure whether it was because of the baby or her nerves. 'I'm moving in with Zoe.' She glanced up to gauge an initial reaction from his face.

He didn't say anything, but his face looked hurt. As though she had offended him.

'What?' she asked.

'Why are you moving away, Els? Don't you want me to be part of this?'

'Of course I do! 'She couldn't bear to see his hurt face. 'I just need to have my sister round right now – she's been a massive help so far and it would be good to have her close by when the baby comes.'

'So you're moving up there, for good? What about me?'

'You can still be there. We can come to you, and you can come up to see us ...'

'Ellie, this is stupid. Why do you need to move four hours away? It's my baby too; I should be able to see it every day.' His face had gone from hurt to pissed off. Ellie didn't like this face as much as the last.

'Chris, listen to me. I'm struggling with this whole pregnancy

240

thing. As much as I have come to terms with the fact that I am pregnant, I am still finding the whole thing really hard.'

'Then let me help you! It's down to me – as the dad – not Zoe!'

'What is wrong with you? I am trying to make a better life for myself and the baby. I have sorted out staying at Zoe's for now and then when the baby is here, I will get a place of my own. I'm going to start freelancing with my make-up so that I can fit it around the baby and Zoe will help with that. This means I don't completely lose my identity and I can still work. I have worked my arse off to get where I am with my job, I can't just give it up.' The words were just spilling out of her mouth now; she was desperate for him to understand. 'I can't stay here, Chris, there's nothing for me here any more.'

He stood up. 'Nothing for you? It doesn't matter that I am here, huh? There's nothing at all for you here?' He spat the words out angrily.

Ellie stood too. 'Chris, you know that's not what I meant. I can't carry on with my life here; it doesn't fit with having a baby. None of my friends have children; I go out all the time ... it all has to change. And I don't feel comfortable staying here and making those changes. I have made friends up in Shropshire, they're in the same situation I am ... it's nice to have proper friends for once, not just clients who want to butter me up for free make-up.' The words came out without Ellie even realising that she was thinking about things like that. She hadn't realised how much of an impact having the girls around her now had been.

Chris softened a little after hearing her out. 'I just hate

that you'll be so far away. I won't get to see you all the time.'

'You can see the baby as much as you want to – we can make it work. Just look at it this way, you'll have the baby but you still get to do all the fun things like going out after work and at weekends ...'

'Is that what you think I care about?' He was angry again.

'You're taking this all the wrong way—'

'No, I hear you loud and clear, Els.' He turned to walk out, but then stopped. 'Do you know, I walked past here today and saw your car outside and I was so happy, because I thought you were coming home.'

'Chris ...'

'No, forget it. You just get on with it.' And he stormed out, leaving Ellie standing in the centre of her living room wondering what the hell had just happened.

After a minute, Zoe and the girls crept into the room looking sheepish.

'Everything okay?' Zoe asked.

'Fine,' Ellie replied, wiping her face quickly, gathering up a bag from the floor by the sofa and throwing the TV remote into it.

'Look, if you want we can—'

'Zoe, I'm not in the mood to talk, okay? Let's just get packed and get the hell out of here. We can pick up a cake on the way home for Pippa's birthday tomorrow.' She grabbed a cushion with the other hand and marched into the hallway. 'I'm taking this out to the car. Let's get this shit hole packed up and get on the road in the next half hour. I don't want to be here any more.'

Chapter 25

I'm going to be late tonight. Patrick didn't show up today so have had to take on his workload. Will see you in the morning x

Pippa stared at the text and felt the disappointment settle in her stomach like a lead balloon. That was the third time this week that Jason had had to work late. She typed back 'okay' and sent it. No kisses or anything. She wanted him to know that she wasn't happy about this but then she immediately felt guilty. It wasn't his fault.

'Why the glum face?' Zoe asked, passing her a cup of tea with some biscuits on the side.

'It's just Jason.'

'What's he done now?'

'Nothing really. It's not his fault; he just has to work late again tonight, that's all.' She shrugged it off. Now that she had opened up to Zoe, she felt able to make these comments to her.

'Again? Didn't he work late one evening at the beginning of the week?' Zoe turned to the counter to pick up the tray of cupcakes and set them down on the middle of the table.

'Yeah, Monday and Tuesday,' she huffed. 'And he forgot my birthday last week.'

'And he's working late again tonight?'

Pippa shrugged. 'I don't know, there's a guy at work who isn't pulling his weight and keeps not showing up for work, so Jason and the others have to pick up the slack and get it done on top of their workload.' She picked up her spoon and stirred the warm, light-brown liquid.

'Well, that doesn't seem fair. Can't they just replace this guy – he sounds like a liability.'

'You're telling me. I suggested that for the millionth time the other week but Jason reckons it's out of his hands, so what can I do?' She sipped her tea, trying to ignore the disappointment settling in her stomach.

'Well that's rubbish. You can't keep going on like this, Pip!'

She held her hand up and dismissed the comment. 'It's fine. Like I said, what can I do? I thought he had something planned for my birthday because when I was at Ellie's helping you guys to pack, he texted me saying he had a surprise. But then the next day he had to work late and when he finally got home he apologised, saying he forgot. He got me some chocolates the next day.'

'Are you serious? That's not on.' Zoe looked angry.

'It's not like I expected anything extravagant, just, you know, him remembering.' She took a deep breath before admitting, 'Things have been getting worse at home.'

'Really?' Zoe sat down.

Pippa shook her head. 'I checked his phone a couple of weeks ago.'

'And?' She seemed shocked at this revelation.

'He caught me; it was horrible. He made me feel so bad, but I couldn't help but think something might be going on – he's always working.'

'What about when the baby comes, though, you're going to need him to be around, not slogging his guts out at work because of some colleague not doing his job properly.'

'I know that, Zoe!' She immediately realised her overreaction to the comment. 'Sorry, I'm just tired, that's all.'

Zoe placed her arm around her friend and squeezed. 'Hey, it's okay. It's what I'm here for. Let's have a nice afternoon here and you can have dinner at mine tonight; save you cooking.'

'Sounds like a plan. What time is it?'

Zoe looked at her watch. 'Quarter to three. I'll go get the rest of the cakes, everyone should be here soon.'

Ten minutes later and Pippa was joined at her usual table with Ellie and Imogen and then, after doing her usual thing of greeting everyone personally, Zoe floated back over to their table. 'How's it going, ladies?' Zoe asked, pulling up a chair.

'Good thanks,' Imogen said and then gestured to the rest of the room. 'This mums' club seems to be really taking off, hey?'

'Do you know what? I'm so surprised. I wasn't expecting such a big turnout. When I started it there were only a few ladies – the last couple of months we seem to have had an influx of people.'

Pippa looked around the room. 'I remember thinking that everyone around here was already a mum and I was finding it so hard to fall pregnant, but now, here we are with a café full of women who are yet to experience the wonders of parenthood.'

'How amazing is that?' Zoe held out her hands and the girls nodded in agreement. 'Although I find it hard to believe that I am the only place offering a mums' club around here,' she continued as she refilled their teacups.

'Maybe the other places are just mums' club; it might be the fact that yours is a *'first time'* mums' club that is drawing them in. I know I feel much more comfortable here than I would in a meeting with people who had had children before.' Pippa subconsciously placed a protective hand over her stomach as she spoke. Something she had found herself doing more often, ever since her bump became more protruding.

'I second that,' Imogen agreed. 'I love the fact that no one here has experienced anything like this before, so when I feel like I have a stupid question, you can guarantee the other women have either thought about the question before or have the answer from finding out from others. But I feel like I can always ask.'

'Like when Ellie asked if babies do anything else other than eat and poo!' Zoe ducked as Ellie swiped her arm. 'Alright, I'm sorry. That was uncalled for. Right, I think it's question time, *I'll be back.*' Zoe added the last line in with her best Arnold Schwarzenegger accent.

Pippa watched her best friend walk into the middle of the room and gain everyone's attention by ringing a bell. 'Okay, ladies, I hope you have all had a fantastic week since we last met. Now that we have the hellos out the way, it is time for this week's topic.' She pulled the bucket from under the counter and held it out to Pippa. 'Here we go, Pip, your turn this week to choose.'

She reached into the bucket and pulled out her question choice. She opened it up and read it out loud to the café. 'Who has played a big part in your journey to falling pregnant and why?'

The noise in the room immediately rose a few decibels as everyone began to start their stories. Zoe slipped back into her seat next to Pippa and said, 'Okay, who is going to start this week?'

'I take it we are looking for a deeper answer than 'the father of the baby because he shagged me and without him I wouldn't be pregnant'?'

'Ellie!'

Pippa tried not to spit out her mouthful of tea as she snorted in response to Ellie's comment. She loved how direct she was.

'What?' Ellie replied. 'You asked who has played a big part – aside from the mums; I'm guessing dads have played a huge part. In some cases, maybe huge is the right word, too.' She winked as the girls giggled.

'I know what you meant, but this question is more than that. Why don't you try to dig a little deeper?'

Zoe looked frustratedly at her sister, so Pippa tried to relax the mood again.

'I'm going to mix things up a bit by saying that Zoe has actually played a huge part in my journey, actually.'

'Aw, Pip, that's sweet.'

'It's true.' She turned to the others. 'I found it hard to fall pregnant. It wasn't an easy job for me and it took a long time. Zoe was always the person I went to for advice, to make me laugh, for a cuddle when yet another month went by and I still wasn't pregnant.'

'I know that feeling,' Imogen agreed.

'Did you get a lot of support from your family when you were going through IVF? I can't imagine anyone having to go through it alone; it's such a hard time.' Pippa thought about how useless Jason had actually been during that time.

'My family weren't around much, but I had Alice. That's all I needed.'

Pippa noticed that Imogen kind of shut down the question, so didn't probe any further.

The rest of the meeting went by in a blur of laughter and tea – just what Pippa needed.

* * * * *

The following evening, Alice got home fairly early for her, the clock ticking over to 6pm. 'Hey beautiful, how was work?'

Imogen hated that question at the moment. She hated lying to Alice, but she didn't feel she had a choice. She was in too far and things would be too complicated to try and unravel now. She would have to tell her about the constant messages still coming in from her mum and it would just be too horrible and totally unnecessary. She could handle this. She plastered on a false smile and replied, 'not bad'. If she kept her answers short, she wouldn't have to cover one lie with another. She hated that her mum had made her into a liar. Never before had she lied to Alice and it felt awful.

'I bet you're glad you don't work Wednesdays or Fridays at the moment?' Alice set about making some dinner as she spoke.

'What do you mean?' Imogen felt nervous. Did she know? Why say something like that?

'Well, you look really tired. I just meant that if you had to work full time and carry those babies, you'd be feeling even worse than you do now.' Alice stopped what she was doing and looked over to her. 'That's all I meant. Are you sure you're okay?'

'I'm fine.' Now would be the perfect opportunity to tell her. She would understand; it would be fine. She reassured herself constantly as Alice continued to make the tea, chatting about work. 'Alice?'

'Yeah?'

Her phone beeped in her pocket and she took it out, recognising the number as her mum's.

'Never mind.'

Alice looked confused. 'Sure?'

Imogen nodded and smiled. 'I'm just going to jump in the bath before dinner. I won't be long.'

Chapter 26

Pippa decided to walk into town today for the mums' club. It was a beautiful day. The sun was shining and the sky was clear, meaning it was uncharacteristically warm for the last day in January and she just didn't fancy sitting inside her van. She didn't have any orders to take into the café, so there was no reason why she shouldn't embrace the unusual warm weather and walk. As she strolled through the side streets that led to the café, she let her mind wander to how things were at home. The more time went on, the more she questioned why she was with Jason. He made her unhappy more times than he made her smile. But every time she came close to saying anything, she was reminded – sometimes by him – of how hard he worked to support Pippa and now the baby, ready for when it comes. She didn't earn enough to make any sort of dent in the bills or mortgage, so he had had to work extra hard lately because there were things to buy for the baby as well as clothes – she was rapidly growing out of her own!

But this morning, with every step she took, she became angrier and angrier at how much work Patrick was putting onto Jason. She was sure that the stress from that guy was having a knock-on effect, which resulted in Jason taking it out on Pippa. She wished he would just disappear.

The walk didn't actually take her that long, which took her by surprise and before she knew it she was at the duck pond, just a few steps away from Zoe's café.

'Pip!'

She turned around to see Imogen walking towards her from the other side of the street. She waved in response and shouted, 'Hey, you all right?' The sun was hot on her face and she undid her coat to freshen up and try to calm the hot flush creeping over her.

Imogen nodded as she approached. 'Yeah not too bad. You walked in today?'

'Yeah, thought I'd get some fresh air. I'm just going to call Jason; I'll be in in a minute.' She fished her phone out of her bag and pressed call on his name. She couldn't help but think about their argument yesterday and in the time she had taken to walk into town, she had built up the courage to call the office and give them what for. It wasn't fair that Jason had to pick up the slack all the time. Well, not any more. Jason might be too nice to say anything, but she was a highly hormonal woman and she was going to take advantage of that. She wasn't taking any shit today.

She waited for what felt like forever, when finally a female voice picked up. 'Hello, Betty speaking, how can I help you?' Betty? Jason said she had resigned. What was she still doing there? 'Hello?' the voice pulled her back into the moment.

'Oh sorry, um, did you say that was Betty?'

'Yes, how may I help you?'

'I thought ... um,' she thought for a second and concluded, 'I'm sorry, I think I must've got the wrong end of the stick. You see, I thought you had resigned.'

Betty laughed, which in turn made Pippa a little uneasy. 'No, no, I'm still here. May I help you with anything?'

'Oh sorry, I should've said, it's Pippa, Jason's wife.'

Another laugh from Betty, although this time it seemed a little nervous. Her tone changed slightly and she became more frantic in her speech. 'Oh, sorry! I didn't ... um ... realise it was you. Jason's not here at the moment.'

'It's okay. I didn't really call to speak to him. I wanted to speak with Mr Jacobs, actually, about Patrick.' Her confidence began to wane; she was thrown off by Betty answering the phone.

'Mr Jacobs isn't here either, I'm afraid. Would you like to leave a message for him and I can ask him to call you back when he gets in?'

Pippa started to realise how silly she must sound. Telling tales on another staff member. She stepped down from her mission feeling stupid. 'No, it's fine. Maybe it's a good thing.'

'Is there a problem with Patrick's work that he did before? I only ask because we've had a few people complain about him.'

'Really?' Well, at least she wasn't the only one thinking badly of this Patrick guy. 'That's interesting. But no, this is more to do with the work he isn't doing right now.'

A pause. 'I'm sorry, you've lost me, Pippa.'

'Patrick. He's not pulling his weight. It's not fair on Jason to have to take up the slack to cover for him. Just because

253

he's the boss's son doesn't mean he gets to freeload on everyone else.' There, she'd said it. No turning back now.

'I don't understand, Pippa, Patrick isn't here any more.'

Pippa paused as she took in this information. 'What? I don't understand.' She leaned against the railings that surrounded the duck pond, involuntarily shuddering as her hand touched the hard metal bars. None of this made sense.

'Patrick, he resigned months ago. He doesn't even work here any more.'

Chapter 27

Ellie, Zoe and Imogen all looked at each other and then back at Pippa as she calmed herself down. Zoe was the first to speak. 'How are you feeling now?'

Pippa didn't speak, but instead took another sip of her water and exhaled. She couldn't find the words at the moment. Her mind was awash with a million questions making her feel dizzy and unsteady. She could feel the heat coursing through her veins as her face flushed with frustration.

'You aren't going to faint are you? You still look really pale.' Ellie was over the far side of the table but still looked as if she wanted to move further away just in case Pippa keeled over.

Pippa shook her head and put the water down. She looked up at her friends. 'Hear me out okay? And tell me what you think? I'm worried that I am going stir-crazy with pregnancy hormones and I need you all to tell me I am being stupid and that I need to chill the fuck out, because, quite frankly, I'm freaking out!' Pippa steadied her breathing; she couldn't believe she was crumbling like this in front of other people. She hated the fact that she was slowly but surely losing the control that she had of what people saw. More and more, as this pregnancy progressed, she was failing herself and letting her guard down and that alone was enough to make her want to scream. She was losing control and she didn't like it.

'Honey, calm down all right? We are here and we are listening.' Zoe pushed another glass of water across the table which was followed by Ellie sliding over a packet of chocolate hobnobs.

'It's Jason.' She clenched her teeth as she prepared herself for the ultimate revelation of trust in these girls.

'Okay ...' They listened with intent.

'I think he's having an affair.' Pippa's voice quivered with emotion and she swallowed down the lump that was fast forming in the back of her throat. That's it. Her perception of perfection shattered in six words.

'Are you serious?' Imogen gasped, looking as though she was about to be sick. 'How can you be sure?'

'I just called his office and Patrick doesn't even work there any more.' Her eyes wide in disbelief, she paused for the reaction from the girls.

'Honey, who is Patrick?' Imogen asked the question they all were thinking.

Zoe stepped in as Pippa steadied her quivering chin. 'For months now, Jason has said that this Patrick guy at his work wasn't pulling his weight and so Jason had to pick up the slack. He's been working late all the time and even some weekends. Blaming it all on Patrick.'

'And I called up today to give the boss a piece of my mind because, you know, we have a baby on the way and I can't have him working all these extra hours and not being at home with me and the baby.' A small hiccup escaped her mouth as the words tumbled out. 'But I called and Betty said that Patrick hasn't worked there for months.'

'Oh Pip.' Imogen moved her chair closer.

'And that's not it. He told me Betty had resigned. But she hasn't, she's still there. I don't even get why he would say that.'

'Pip, you need to calm yourself down and breathe. This isn't doing you, or the baby, any good. Let me get the meeting started and get you some more water and we will sort this out, okay?' Zoe bent down so that Pippa's face was level with hers. 'Pip? I promise you, we will sort this out, okay?' Zoe rushed off to start the session and pick out this week's topic-starter.

Imogen looked at Ellie, who in turn shrugged. Pippa knew they wanted to help, but no one seemed to know what to say. If she was honest, she didn't even know what to say or do. 'I'm sorry, girls, I've totally ruined this week's meeting. I swear, I didn't want to bring this all up. I just ... it just took me by surprise and I felt myself getting all light-headed and before I knew it I was here and ... and ...'

'Shh, Pip, it's okay. You don't have anything to be sorry about; it's that lowlife of a husband of yours. He has got some serious explaining to do. When we get our hands on him ...' Ellie trailed off.

'I don't want you to do anything.' Pippa started to feel guilty for bringing this all up with everyone, especially these two, who she didn't know as well. What was she doing? Everyone was going to know that she was falling apart behind the scenes. This was the last thing she wanted. Although, in amidst all of this, she did have to admit that it was nice to see everyone fighting her corner. Yes, they hadn't known each other that long but there was most definitely some sort of bond that they had formed and seeing them jump to her defence like this made the whole situation a little easier to bear.

'Are you kidding? You're not going to let him get away with this are you?'

'I don't think it's our place to get involved. I mean, of course we are here for you, Pippa, but, at the end of the day, this is your choice. You tell us what you want to happen.' Imogen was very good at keeping things calm.

'I don't know what I want to happen,' she said, feeling more and more deflated the longer she sat there. She felt a bit stupid, if she was honest. Everything had seemed to come to a head and happened so fast, but now she had the time to digest what was happening, she wasn't sure what she needed to do and how exactly she was going to do it. 'Maybe there is an explanation. Maybe I overreacted.' The look she got from both girls clearly said that neither of them believed nor accepted what she had said.

She didn't have too much time to think about it because her phone began to flash and vibrate. She watched Jason's name flashing and, every time the phone lit up, displaying his name, she felt a surge of nausea. Sheer panic rose from the pit of her stomach and she frantically looked at the girls for support. No matter how much she wanted to pretend she was okay, fact of the matter was, she was terrified that the thoughts in her head were the truth. She stared back at the phone, unable to move.

'Are you going to speak to him?' Zoe had returned to the table and Pippa took some relief from the fact that the general hubbub in the café had increased just a notch so that their discussions were nicely hidden between the conversations that floated around the room.

'What am I going to say?'

'Tell him he's a total bastard and you want him out!'

'Ellie! If you don't have anything helpful to say, then stay quiet,' Zoe hissed.

'What? How is that not helpful? She doesn't need a lowlife like that in her life when she is about to have his baby.'

Pippa watched this exchange between the sisters and, on impulse, snatched up her phone and pressed answer. 'Hello?' The second she spoke, silence fell around the table and all three girls diverted their attention to her and what was about to happen.

'All right baby, what took you so long?'

Just hearing his voice made her skin crawl. She didn't know what it was, but he sounded weird, as if he wasn't himself. She couldn't put her finger on what exactly made him sound so weird. 'I was, um. I'm at mums' club.' She kept her eyes diverted to the table, fiddling with a small wrapper from the biscuits for something to do with her hands. She couldn't look at the others. If she did she was worried she would give it all away. She didn't want him to know something was up. Not until she knew what she was feeling. Right now she felt as though she was wading through a hazy fog and all she could think about was when she could make this all stop and go back to feeling normal.

'Oh sorry, I forgot it was mums' club today.' The line went quiet and for the first time in the whole time they had been together as a couple, Pippa was at a loss as to what to say to her husband. Thankfully he broke the silence. 'Are you okay?' He sounded nervous. Did he know something was up?

'I'm fine. Why wouldn't I be?' She silently dared him to say something, to give away what she feared. But he didn't.

'No reason. Just checking on how my lovely wife is. Listen, I'll be home early tonight.'

Pippa screwed her face up, 'What? I thought you were working late tonight?' The girls looked at her, in just as much confusion. They could only hear her side of the conversation and were left to wonder what he was saying in return.

'Yeah, I was, but I managed to get out of it.' He laughed and it sounded forced.

That was really out of character for him. He never managed to 'get out of it' when it came to work. Why the sudden change now? She was annoyed at herself for questioning him in her mind. 'Okay, great. I'll see you tonight, then.'

'Okay baby, love you.'

She retaliated in the only way she could at this moment in time. 'You too.' She placed the mobile down on the table in front of her and kept her eyes fixed on the screen.

'Well?' Zoe pressed.

'He's not working late tonight any more.' Her tone was steady. She felt completely exhausted from the last few minutes. It was as though she had run an emotional marathon and now all she wanted to do was sleep. Except she knew she wouldn't be able to. Her mind was already picking apart the last ten years of their relationship.

'That's weird, how come?'

Pippa looked up at Zoe and shrugged. 'Who knows? Anyway, enough about me, what's the question for this week?'

'Pip, we don't have to do this. If you want me to take you home, I can.'

'No, Zoe, its fine. I'm fine. I'll sort this my own way. There will be a simple explanation; I just got het up with my pregnancy hormones and got carried away. You girls must be the same. It's fine. I'm fine.' She realised she was repeating herself and stopped talking.

'Pip—'

'I said I'm fine!' she responded, a little too harshly than she meant as her barriers sprung up, reinstating their place around her image. She looked around the table at the girls – her friends – and felt shit. 'I'm sorry, let's just drop it ... please?'

They looked at each other and admitted defeat. 'Okay,' Zoe finally said, 'But just remember that we are here, okay? Don't think you're on your own to deal with this. Let us help you.'

'I don't need any help. I'll speak to him tonight. I'm sure there's a simple explanation.' She excused herself to the toilet and walked as fast – and as normally – as she could so that she still appeared to be calm and unbothered by the last half hour. But inside she was panicking. What the hell was going on?

* * * * *

Pippa sat on the edge of her bed, staring into space. She felt empty. She felt cold. But most of all, she felt confused.

She glanced around the bedroom – their bedroom – and all she could see was evidence that they had been unhappy for a while. No pictures around of them laughing and cuddling. No slinky nightwear ready to put on for a night of passion. Just a bedside full of books and herbal remedies on one side and the remote on the other, which summed them up as a couple. The bedroom was functional. They had wanted a baby for so long, all the magic had evaporated from this room and had it become a visual to-do list of events. Trying certain times of the month, certain positions – before, during and after sex – certain natural products that helped women to conceive. It wasn't fun any more. And it was only now, looking around at their sorry state of a bedroom, that Pippa realised how frantic she must've become on those last months before they did finally conceive. She had turned having sex into a regimented, planned duty. It wouldn't surprise her if she had pushed him away.

All these years they had been a couple and never before had he made her feel so confused about who they were, and even who she was. Not even after last time. She wasn't the type of person who checked her husband's texts, or went through his pockets, or hired out a secret detective to follow him to and from work, detailing every second of his existence. That wasn't her. Yes, she had suffered with self-doubt in the past, which, to be fair, was his fault to begin with, but she never inflicted her worries onto him. It was her issue.

She had decided to move past what happened before and start afresh.

But lately, things had been different. He had turned her into this person and she didn't like it. She heard the door open and then close from downstairs, signalling Jason's return. 'Pip?' he called out from the hallway.

'I'm in here,' she replied, feeling all of a sudden at a loss for anything to do with her hands. She coughed to clear her throat and perk herself up. Jason strolled into their bedroom just minutes later holding a beautiful bouquet of flowers. A colourful mix of oranges, yellows and pinks – she couldn't help but smile at him as he presented them to her, followed by a gentle kiss on the head. Maybe she had been overreacting.

'Oh Jason, they're beautiful! What have I done to deserve these?'

'It's more a case of, what have *I* done ...'

The happiness was short-lived and Pippa felt a weight drop into her stomach as he sat down beside her. 'What do you mean?' she managed to choke out, still trying to sound relatively calm and normal when inside she was screaming and fighting against the urge to run away.

'Baby, I've not been totally honest with you.'

Oh my God, here it is, she thought to herself and dropped her eye contact. She couldn't look at him. He was about to tell her that he'd been seeing someone else, she could feel it. The thoughts in her head became frantic and she struggled to clear her mind of the haze long enough to hear what he was saying. She could see his lips moving but she couldn't make sense of what he was saying. She now had a ringing sensation in her ear, replicating the pumping of her heart. Surely her head would explode before she was able to calm herself. And what effect would this have on the baby? She had read in lots of magazines that stress can affect the baby massively and here she was, inflicting her poor unborn child with a truckload of stress and...

'Pip? Did you hear me?'

She snapped her eyes up to Jason, who was now smiling at her. What had she missed? Surely he wouldn't be smiling at her if he had just told her that he had been having an affair. She knew he had a weird sense of humour, but surely even he couldn't be this strange.

'Pip?'

'What ... um ... sorry, you lost me. What did you say?'

'I was just saying that I know you have been stressing a lot recently with the amount of work I have taken on and Betty told me that she had spoken to you and you were calling up about Patrick.'

She nodded to show him she was still with him. Where was he going with this?

'And I know I have seemed a little off recently, but I want you to know that it has nothing to do with you and that I love you. I know you will be thinking the worst and you're wrong.'

She opened her mouth to speak, but no words came out. What was she supposed to say to that?

'Baby, listen. I know have been working loads recently.'

'I know, I know,' she finally said, 'Patrick.'

'No baby, not Patrick.' She knew that anyway, though, didn't she? Was he about to come clean for lying? 'Patrick left a while back. I used him as an excuse because I didn't think you would ever question it and I didn't want to talk about the real reason why I have been working loads. But ... well, you did question it.'

'What was I supposed to do, Jason, just sit back and lose my husband to his job? I hardly ever see you.' She was pleading with him to understand.

'I know! But that's what I am trying to explain.'

'Jason, you're not making any sense.' A dull ache began to creep up inside her skull and make its presence known. She could feel the headache brewing and from past experiences knew she had about thirty minutes before the migraine completely took hold.

'Okay. Yes, I've been working lots but it isn't because of Patrick. It's because I am struggling a little bit.' He looked at the ground.

'Struggling? With what?'

'With the whole baby thing.'

She felt as if she had been slapped in the face. 'What do you mean? Me being pregnant?' He nodded. 'What?' It came out like a whisper.

He jumped up straight away and came closer to her, kneeling on the floor in front of where she was sitting and putting his hands around hers. 'But I'm working on it. I promise, it'll be okay. When the baby is here, I'm sure I'll feel different. It was just hard to take the news initially and I guess I just went off the rails a bit ...'

'Jason, we decided to have this baby together – you agreed

you wanted a baby.' She couldn't believe she was having this conversation. 'We spoke about it for ages!' Her voice was lifting up a notch now.

'I know we did. I guess I just panicked when it actually happened.'

'And you're telling me this *now*? What do you expect me to do?'

'Nothing!' He was up on his feet, brushing his hands through his hair in frustration. 'I just wanted to be honest with you about how I am feeling – surely I should be able to talk to you about this. You're my wife, for Christ sake!'

'Yes, I am your pregnant wife! For fuck's sake, Jason!' She stood up and stormed towards the door.

'Baby, please don't leave it like this. I was just trying to be honest with you. I'm going to try harder, I promise. I'll make it up to you.'

She stood in the doorway looking at him. She didn't know what she felt: anger, frustration, betrayal … all of them? 'I don't know what you want me to do.'

'I want you to just … say it's okay and we can move forward from this.' His eyes pleaded with her for forgiveness.

'Jason, do you want this baby?' The words make her feel sick just asking them. What was she going to do if he said no? Everything that she was scared of was now becoming a possibility – being a single parent and having to do everything alone.

He hesitated. 'Yes, I do.'

'You don't sound too sure.'

He strode over to her and took her hands once again into

his. 'I do. I just had a blip, but I'm on board and ready. I'm sorry I put you through this. I will try harder.'

Pippa nodded and then made her excuses so she could get some fresh air. She needed to walk this conversation off.

'Can I come with you?' he asked.

'I just want to have some me time, if that's okay?' She needed to breathe.

'No worries.' Pippa turned to walk. 'Pip?'

She looked over her shoulder.

'I'm sorry.'

She looked back at him but she felt as if she was looking at a stranger. He wasn't the Jason she fell in love with and married. Every time they argued and even when he strayed before, she still loved him and they got through it. But this ... this made her feel so completely out of her skin. She spoke softly, barely able to raise her voice loud enough to be heard. She tried to push out the words, fighting against the dragging feeling that was pressing down on her chest.

'Having a baby means everything to me, Jason. It's my life.' He stepped forward, but she held her hand up to stop him. 'I have dreamt of this for as long as I can remember and you were always right behind me. Every step of the way. You wanted this as badly as I did – at least, I thought you did.'

'Pip, please.' He looked as if he was going to cry, but it had no effect on her any more. And that frightened her.

'And now ...' her chin quivered as she fought against the emotion. 'Now you're telling me you don't want this.' She looked down at her tummy as she rubbed her hand over the bump.

'Baby, listen to me, I do want this, I just needed to tell you how I was feeling.' He was pleading with her now. But she brushed him off.

'I need to just have some space. I'm going for a walk.' She turned to the bedroom door and walked out, quickly. She needed to get outside, get some air. Her world was slowly falling apart and she had no idea how to fix it any more.

Chapter 28

'Hey you.'

Ellie tensed up as she heard Chris's voice. Zoe gave her one last look and then left them to it, which Ellie was grateful for. It was hard enough that she has to sort things out with Chris, after their argument at her flat a couple of weeks ago, without having an audience for it, too.

Chris hovered in the doorway of Zoe's flat, seemingly unsure of what to do. She didn't miss the fact that he looked tired. But, annoyingly, even though he was clearly stressed and not sleeping, he still looked gorgeous. His t-shirt tight against body teamed with the jogging bottoms he had thrown on this morning was a really nice combination; Ellie found herself looking at his chest, but then realised that she was staring and whipped her eyes away. 'You going to stand there all day or shall I put the kettle on?'

He looked a little uncomfortable, but after a moment gave in to a smile and walked into the room, closing the door behind him. The air between them was awkward, which felt strange because, out of everyone Ellie had ever known, Chris was always the one she felt most comfortable with. But now she couldn't even remember a time when there hadn't been an awkward atmosphere between them. This pregnancy felt like a lifetime.

'So ...' he began.

'So ...' she replied.

'Listen,' Chris said as he walked into the kitchen after Ellie. 'I'm really sorry about the way I behaved at yours the other week. I shouldn't have shouted at you.'

Ellie smiled at him. 'It's okay. I should've told you earlier about me moving up here. It's just we had only just decided and I wanted to get myself sorted before I told you, so that you would see that everything was fine and I was coping fine up here.'

'I don't doubt that you will cope fine, Els. You're a tough little cookie; you can do pretty much anything.' He smiled at her and her heart jumped for joy. Things were okay.

'Yeah, well, I do have a plan. Despite what you may think, Zoe and I have sorted out a plan of action and things are going to be okay.'

Chris took the coffee from Ellie and walked back into the living room, so Ellie followed closely behind, taking up her seat on the sofa next to him.

'So ...' he looked at her expectantly.

'What?'

'This master plan of yours?' He smirked and Ellie poked her tongue out.

'Right, so, I am going to stay here with Zoe until the baby comes. I have given notice to my landlord and, all being well, I should have my security deposit back from him within the next two weeks – this will help with paying my way for a month or so.'

'You know, you don't have to worry about money, Els. I would never let you struggle.'

'I know you wouldn't, but it's not your responsibility – I'm not your responsibility.'

'But—'

'Chris, its fine. I've been sorting out different things and I am going to set up my freelance work here. I've been working on the flyers to put up around town – here, take a look.' Ellie jumped up and walked over to the laptop in the corner, pulling out some sheets of paper from underneath. She handed one to Chris and sat down expectantly. 'Well?'

He smiled. 'These look great.' He placed it on the coffee table. 'So this is it? This is what you're going to do?'

'What do you mean, this is it? Isn't 'it' good enough?'

'That isn't what I meant. I mean, this is the plan? You're happy with the plan?'

She nodded. 'Yes. I can freelance here and work in the café for now, and then when the baby is here I will build up a little business, doing the make-up as a mobile venture.' She took in his wary expression. 'You don't like the plan?'

'Of course I do. You built up your reputation before, I know you can do it again. You realise up here it won't be as busy as when you are in London? Things aren't as fast-paced out here.'

'I know that, but with the baby here I won't be able to keep up with the fast-paced lifestyle.' She rubbed her belly as she felt a twinge of pain.

'But you love the fast-paced world of doing photoshoots and films. You are always rushing from one place to another, doing this, that and everything in between. Are you sure you will be happy with slowing down?'

'Chris, I don't have a choice, do I? I can hardly just have the baby and then go back to living how I was. It won't work. Things have to change. *I* have to change.'

He leaned forward excitedly and took her hands into his lap. 'But you don't have to change. If you stay in London with me, you can carry on with what you do and we can work things out so that we can both keep doing what we love.'

She frowned. 'Chris, it's not as simple as that.'

'It is. You just aren't giving it a chance.'

She squeezed his hands and smiled. 'You are so lovely. And I really appreciate you trying to think of me. But this is what I *want* to do. It is time for me to take charge of the situation and be an adult. I do have to change – but that's okay.'

There was a brief silence that followed. Chris continued to focus his attention on their hands, intertwined with one another on his lap. After a moment, he said, 'Since when did you become an adult?'

She laughed fondly. 'I'm afraid it's the hormones. They force me to realise that I have to grow up.'

'And what about me?'

'What about you?'

'Where do I fit in?'

Ellie shrugged. Because realistically, it had taken her so long to get her own head around this situation, to get herself there, she had to shut off from everything else and think about what she wanted. 'I just need to do this, Chris. For me – you know?'

He nodded and stood up, grabbing his coat from the side.

'Where are you going?' She shuffled on the sofa to standing and followed him out to the hallway.

'I should get back home. I said I would meet the lads down the pub so ...' he trailed off.

'Chris?' she called as he walked out of the door. 'Are you still coming with me for the second scan next week?'

He paused and then looked over his shoulder at her, a sad smile displayed across his face. 'Course. Wouldn't miss it for the world.' And he left.

Ellie walked back into the flat and closed the door, and within a couple of minutes, Zoe appeared in the doorway.

'Has he gone already?' she looked confused.

'Yeah,' Ellie replied, flopping back down onto the sofa.

'Did you sort things out?'

'Yeah,' came her reply again.

'Are you going to elaborate or shall I just keep asking questions until you have explained everything?' Zoe dropped down onto the sofa next to her and put her arm around her shoulders as a tear dripped down Ellie's cheek. 'Hey, what's wrong?'

'I just feel like I can't do anything right.'

'Why? What did he say about the make-up business?'

'Oh nothing, he said it was great.'

'So ... what's got you upset?' Zoe was rubbing her hand up and down Ellie's arm as she laid her head on her shoulder.

'I just feel like I need to concentrate on me and the baby right now – I feel like I need to get my head around things

273

and then I see Chris and everything gets jumbled up in my head again. I just can't focus on me and him right now; I need to focus on me and the baby. I can't cope with anything else – one thing at a time.'

'Honey, that's fine. If that's what you need, then that's what we will do. But just remember that he will always be a part of this – whether you acknowledge it or not. So by all means take some time out for you now, but sooner or later, you need to work out a plan that involves Chris and moving forward. Okay?'

Ellie nodded. Life would be much simpler if she didn't have feelings for him.

Chapter 29

'Ellie, you can't just hide away in there forever.' Ellie ignored Zoe and turned over in bed. 'You've been in there for like a month now.' Another knock.

She pulled the duvet down. 'I haven't been in here a bloody month! Now who's the drama queen?'

'As good as! Ellie, it's been ages. Come on. You can't lock yourself away from the world. You've been missing mums' club and I'm not running around for you if you won't pull your weight in the shop. I let you have a couple of weeks off, but this is just silly!'

'I'm not locking myself away. I'm just taking some time to myself while I can, before the baby comes.'

Zoe unlocked the door from the outside and came into the room, followed by Imogen. 'I'm afraid that time is up. Come on, get up.' Zoe pulled the cover off Ellie and tickled her foot.

'Hey!' she squealed, retracting her foot rapidly. 'So much for having a bloody lock if you can open it from that side! What are you doing?'

'We are stopping you from wallowing.' Imogen picked up

some clothes from the dresser and threw them onto the bed. 'Come on, get dressed!'

'Girls, I'm not bloody wallowing, I'm relaxing before the baby comes.' She rolled out of bed and stood up. Where are we going?'

'You'll see. Just get dressed.'

An hour later they were all in Zoe's car, pulling into the driveway of a huge manor house. As they entered through the gates, Ellie took in the sign as they passed it. 'Green Acre Spa?'

Zoe squealed. 'Yes! We are having a spa day!'

Ellie looked at each of the girls in turn. 'Are you serious?'

'Great idea, huh?' Imogen asked.

They parked up and made their way across the gravel car park to the front door. As they approached, Ellie couldn't help but smile. 'Pippa?'

Pippa turned around at the sound of her name and squealed in return. 'Eeek, you're here!'

She pulled each of the girls in for a hug, finishing with Ellie.

'I can't believe you're here too – this is awesome.'

'Come on, let's get inside.' Zoe led them inside and within minutes they were in their white gowns and slippers and heading to the swimming pool.

Ellie looked around at her friends. Just a few months ago she didn't even know these girls, and now they were doing things like this. It was alien to Ellie. She spent her time back at home going out with clients and to launch parties and stuff like that, which was great, but they weren't real friends, they were just colleagues. She had never really had girlfriends like this before. 'I just want to say thanks, girls.' She smiled at them all in turn.

'What for?' Pippa poured them all a glass of sparkling water.

'For being there for me. I know you all have stuff going on it your lives, but you've all taken the time to do this for me.' She looked away, embarrassed, 'It's nice.'

'We can't all take the credit for this. It was Zoe's idea.' Ellie turned to her sister. 'Really?' Zoe nodded. 'Why?'

'What do you mean 'why?', because I love you and I hate seeing you so down.'

'I'm not down – just a bit stressed out.'

Imogen stood up. 'I'm going for a swim, Pip, fancy joining me?' She gave Pippa a knowing look and Ellie could see what they were doing. And she really appreciated it. They made their way into the pool, leaving the two of them at the table.

'Why are you so stressed out? Talk to me, Ellie. I feel like you are just covering over everything and pretending it is all okay when I can see you suffering. You've been holed up in your room every day since you had your scan.'

'I have been doing research online and drawing up some ideas for work – I haven't just been sitting on my arse doing nothing, Zoe.' Ellie's face flashed with frustration.

'I didn't say that.'

'Look, seeing the baby in the scan again just brought it all home. I have to be realistic and start thinking about the future. I have been working on creating a brand – something to go forward with after the baby is born.'

'Like what?'

Ellie turned to face her sister. 'Okay, don't laugh.'

Zoe shrugged. 'Why would I laugh?'

'Because I know what you will be thinking when I tell you.' Zoe looked confused, so Ellie carried on talking. 'I love doing my make-up jobs, right? Creating these masterpieces are my life and when the baby comes, I don't want to just give up on it, but equally, I will not have as much time to indulge in doing it and then there is childcare to think about and it all just gets a bit murky.'

'I can help with childcare!'

'I know you can, and I am sure I will take you up on that idea on many occasions, but I can't live my life pushing this little one from pillar to post just so I can work. Not when there are ways around it.'

Zoe raised her eyebrows. 'What do you mean? Are you going to sort things with Chris?'

Ellie exhaled. 'Oh my God, can you just forget about Chris for a minute and concentrate on me? I have found a way to still work creatively, but involve the baby too.'

Zoe's face was creased in confusion. 'You're going to do ... baby make-up? Ellie, I don't think that will take off.'

Ellie threw her head back. 'No! I have been researching online and,' she paused for effect, 'I am going to do face-painting alongside the make-up.'

'Face-painting?'

'Yes! I've been watching lots of tutorials on YouTube and I think I could be *really* good at it. I can do children's parties and then also do things like prom make-up, occasion make-up ... all stuff like that. I mean, it's no film set but Zoe

– this could be the answer.' Zoe was staring at her open-mouthed. 'What? Is it a stupid idea?'

'Not at all.' Zoe smiled. 'I'm so proud of you.'

'Oh, be quiet,' Ellie said as she looked away, embarrassed.

'I'm serious. You have proper grown up – taking responsibility, adapting your life, changing your job, moving to a different area – what the hell happened to my wild little sister?'

They both laughed and Ellie stood up, dropping her robe, ready to enter the water.

'You do need to give Chris a break, though, he's struggling with it all a little.'

Ellie sat back down. 'What do you mean?'

'He has texted me a few times just to say that he wants to be more involved, but you aren't really listening. He's trying to give you space because he can see that you are – well were – struggling too. But you seem to have got your head around things and you have a plan sorted ... just remember that he deserves to be included in all this too.'

Ellie felt the guilt weigh down in her stomach. 'I know he does. And he will. I just needed to sort myself out first. I don't need to rely on him – I've always supported myself and having this baby doesn't change the fact that I can cope with this by myself.'

'No one is disputing that. It's not a case of not coping; it's a case of him being that baby's dad, and he actually wants to be involved. Like, genuinely wants to have this baby. What are you so worried about?'

They sat in silence for a minute. Ellie wanted to scream at her sister and tell her to stop making a big deal out of nothing.

To stop going on all the time. But she knew it was only a matter of time before she had to face up to things. She inhaled before saying, 'Okay, I'm scared. There, happy?'

'No, I'm not happy. I don't want you to be scared. I don't keep on at you to make you sad; I do it because I care. And I'm not the only one who cares, Ellie.' She raised her eyebrows at her and Ellie knew exactly what she was getting at.

'What are you talking about?' Ellie guffawed.

'Come on, you can't tell me you don't see the way he looks at you. He wants you – he always has.'

'Don't talk rubbish.' She dismissed the comment, ignoring the rush of feelings that erupted at the thought of her and Chris actually being together.

'Okay, I'm talking rubbish? Really? You're telling me you don't think Chris has feelings for you? Why do you think he slept with you in the first place?'

'Because he was drunk, we both were. Shit happens.'

'No, Ellie, because the guy cares about you. It's obvious. And I think he always has. And I know you feel the same.'

'Pfft, don't be silly. He's a friend. That's it.' She couldn't keep eye contact and that annoyed her even more.

'Ellie, come on—'

Ellie groaned. 'Zoe, stop it. Let's just enjoy the day, please.'

Zoe exhaled and stood up, taking her robe off ready to go into the pool. 'Fine. But, for the record, I think you're being stupid.'

* * * * *

'What do you think about it all?' Imogen asked as she bounced around in the pool, creating ripples that crashed off the side and dispersed. It was nice to be in the water with her huge bump, especially with the new two-piece she had bought especially for this spa day. She was matching the other girls in bump size because of carrying two. The water made her weightless and it felt amazing. She wanted to stay there forever.

'I don't know, it's all so complicated.'

'You're telling me. But then again, whose life isn't?' She let her thoughts drift back to her own issues at home but rapidly pushed them aside. She needed to try and keep the stress at bay.

'True.' Pippa nodded as she bobbed around.

'How's everything at home with you guys?'

'Oh, you know, the usual.'

Imogen watched Pippa stretch her arms out to fully appreciate the water surrounding her, mirroring her and feeling as if she was floating on clouds. The babies were so heavy already. 'Are things still off with you and Jason?' She pressed. She didn't like to pry, but what better time to talk about stuff than when there's no one else around.

'Yeah, a little bit.' Pippa looked sad as she spoke.

'Have you tried talking to him?' Imogen glanced over at the other two as they spoke.

'Kind of, but to be honest, I just don't want to rock the boat. I feel hormonal enough as it is and everything just seems to set me off at the moment. He only has to do the smallest thing and it makes me cry!'

'Well, that's understandable. You *are* pregnant.'

'Yes, but I don't see you and Ellie crying at the drop of a hat.' Pippa dunked her head under the water to wet her hair, using her hands to smooth it back.

'Hey, we have our moments.'

'Yeah, but still. I think I'm just over-sensitive to everything. He said to me the other night how he feels like he can do nothing right and that I'm always having a go at him.'

'And are you?' Imogen turned onto her back and swished her arms, moving her along very slowly.

'I don't feel like I am. But I probably am. I just miss him, you know? I hardly get to see him these days. I feel like a single parent before the baby is even here. He said he was going to try and work less, but that didn't last long.' She protectively gave her bump a stroke.

'He's still working loads?' Pippa just shrugged.

'Well, you know you have us lot, don't you? We'll always be around to help.'

'I know. I just feel a bit deflated about it all.'

'What do you mean?'

Imogen looked over her shoulder to see Ellie climbing into the water, closely followed by Zoe. 'All right?' she asked. Zoe simply rolled her eyes and the girls knew to say no more. It was clearly a sister thing.

'What's up?' Zoe asked Pippa, who was looking a little concerned.

'I was just saying to Imogen that I feel a bit deflated at the moment.'

'Is this to do with him at home?' Zoe rolled her eyes and Imogen immediately pressed for more info.

'What's happened? What have I missed?'

'You know when all that happened a couple of weeks ago with Patrick not being at work and stuff?'

Imogen nodded, wondering where this was going.

'Well, when he got home that night we spoke about it and Jason admitted that he was struggling to deal with the whole baby thing.'

Imogen gasped. 'Now he tells you this?'

'I know. We spoke about it on and off over that following week and he has reassured me that it was just a case of cold feet and that it is normal, blah blah blah ...'

'You don't sound convinced, Pip,' Imogen laughed.

Pippa shrugged. 'I guess I am. I just worry what he will be like when the baby is actually here. I can't be looking after a baby and dealing with him being flaky and wondering whether it is what he wants.'

'So what do you plan to do?' Ellie said as she bobbed around in the water.

'I don't know yet. I'm not thinking about it – I'm just going to enjoy these last few months of pregnancy and deal with it as and when the problem arises.'

'Sounds like a plan to me.' Imogen said as she lay back into the water, feeling the liquid lift her up and steady her floating body. 'I could stay here forever.'

* * * * *

At dinner that evening, the girls ordered a feast. There were plates of tapas and crudités, a huge bowl of salad and some side accompaniments to flesh it all out a bit. Being a table of pregnant women, and Zoe, they took it upon themselves to order whatever they wanted and purely indulge. Although it just turned into a case of eyes bigger than their bellies – which was a hard thing to do!

'I honestly don't think I'll be able to fit any more of this food into my stomach. I blame the babies taking up all the space.' Imogen put down her knife and fork and leant back in her chair. 'I'm out!' she declared.

'I think I'll have to join you on that one, my friend.' Pippa placed hers down too.

Imogen glanced over at Zoe, who was still eating. 'How? Just how are you still eating?'

'It's clearly a baby thing – she has more space in her tummy than we all do!'

Imogen and Pippa both laughed at Ellie's remark as Zoe picked up her glass of wine. 'Yes, true, and I get to do this.' She took a sip.

The other girls both kicked up a protest of how it was unfair, but Imogen turned her nose up. 'Honestly, I couldn't drink it even if I wanted to. Just the smell of it makes me feel sick.'

'Oh sorry, I didn't realise.'

'No, it's fine. I can't smell yours. I just meant if I sipped it I would smell it. I can't stomach any alcoholic smell.' She said, her face contorted with disgust.

'Well, it's a good job you can't drink any, then! I, on the other hand, could do with a few shots right about now.'

'Ellie!'

'What? I'm not allowed to say it? It's not like I'm actually sinking shots of Sambuca, is it!' She looked at Imogen and winked. 'Although I do love a Sambuca shot.'

'Were you a big drinker before you fell pregnant?' Imogen laughed and picked up her fork to spear one last olive into her mouth, then instantly regretted it. 'Urgh, why did I do that? I should've just stopped,' She dropped the fork back down, indicating for the conversation to continue with her hand whilst the other hand pressed on her ever-growing belly.

Ellie pushed her bottom lip out as she nodded. 'Yeah, I didn't mind a drink or two.'

'Or five,' Zoe said under her breath and Ellie shot her a look.

'I enjoyed a night out, what's wrong with that?' Ellie seemed to throw up her defence, so Imogen calmed the situation before it got worse.

'There's nothing wrong with that. I suppose with your job there were lots of glam nights out?' She nodded at Ellie to encourage her to agree and move the conversation on.

'Yeah, there were a few. I remember this one night, it was for a client of mine who was having a birthday celebration and she invited me along. I did her make-up and then totally let my hair down. It was a free bar all night and, boy, did I make the most of this free bar. Only I shouldn't have done because halfway through the night she pulled me aside and asked me to top up her make-up. I thought it was fine, but she wanted more – she liked the full-on look. I was so hammered I could barely see straight, but I had to blag it because she was a regular and I didn't want to piss her off. It was literally half an hour of looking through one eye so that I didn't see double!'

Zoe began laughing. 'Remember when we were little and you did my make-up for Christmas one year?' Ellie's face lit up as she obviously remembered it.

'What happened?' Imogen pressed, desperate to hear what had them both giggling. She ignored the vibrating in her robe pocket, knowing full well that it was probably a message she didn't want to read.

'I showed her into the living room, on Christmas Day ...'

'With all the family there!' Zoe added.

'Yeah, we literally had everyone there. And I made some big announcement about her coming in so everyone was looking. And in she walked, looking like, what could only be described as a drunken hooker!' The girls burst into laughter as Imogen and Pippa sat open-mouthed.

'No you didn't?' Imogen gasped.

Ellie nodded. 'Mum asked us to quickly to get it off and it wasn't until years later, when we were looking at the pictures, that Mum admitted how horrified she was seeing her little Zoe looking like that. It was hilarious.'

'Oh and remember that time that I let you do my make-up for the prom?'

'Oh no, Dad wouldn't let you out the house!'

'So do you specialise in make-up for call girls?' The table erupted in laughter. Imogen smiled. It was so nice to be able to see everyone so happy and relaxed. She really did fit in with these girls. After spending a life trying to hide who she was, it was nice to let go and fully be who she wanted to be. It wasn't as if she felt this relaxed at home, with all the secrets at the moment.

'Girls, I need to talk to you about something.' Pippa looked nervous and Imogen instantly felt a twinge of sadness at seeing her friend looking so sad. 'The other night when Jason and I had an argument ...'

'Another one?' Ellie stated. 'These are getting really frequent now, aren't they?' She pulled a face. 'Not that I knew what you were like as a couple beforehand, but it seems like you two are always having words at the moment?'

Pippa nodded. 'No, you're right. Things are a bit shit. But I mean when he said about the struggling with having a baby thing ...' Pippa took a deep breath before saying, 'I have been thinking about it a lot. It's always on my mind, but lately it has totally consumed my brain ... I don't think he wants it.'

Imogen gasped and then apologised. 'Sorry, that sounded really dramatic.'

Pippa smiled and it was nice to see her face brighten again, albeit short-lived. 'I just don't know what to do. When we got together, all we spoke about was one day having a family. And then we split up because I found out he had been having an affair.'

Imogen gasped again.

'Jeez, love, it sounds like you're watching a TV drama.' Ellie laughed and so did the rest of the table.

'I'm so sorry!' Imogen quickly said, feeling awful. 'I didn't mean to make your life sound like a television programme – I just, I can't believe it. You poor thing.'

'I'm fine.' Pippa smiled, but it didn't reach her eyes.

'You have to stop saying that, love, it might fool everyone else but not us.' Ellie raised her eyebrows and clearly meant business.

'Can we just take a moment to appreciate the fact that my baby sister is totally embracing our little friendship circle?' Zoe smiled cheekily in response to Ellie poking her tongue out. 'Anyway, back to more important things, Pip?'

'I just ... I'm starting to wonder what to do for the best. All these years I have wanted to prove myself and build this perfect little family unit that I've dreamed of for so long. But now, it's all ... falling apart.'

'Do you love him?'

'Ellie!' It was Zoe's turn to gasp now.

'What? She needs to be honest with herself.' Ellie looked to Pippa. 'Is he worth all this stressing over?'

Imogen was going to put forward her thoughts but decided against it as she watched Pippa's face betray her real feelings. Pippa eventually said, 'I can't just give up. The baby deserves for me to at least try. Surely I owe it that?'

'Honey, it's not like you haven't been trying already?' Imogen added, trying to keep her comments as neutral as possible. She could see the strain on Pippa's face.

'I know,' she finally conceded. 'I just don't think I could bear it if it all went wrong again. I really want this to work.'

'Because you love him, or because you are scared to be alone?'

'Jeez, Ellie, rein it in a bit will you?' Zoe said under her breath.

'It's fine,' Pippa said, running her finger around her glass and avoiding eye contact.

'Just think about it and make sure you are doing it for the right reasons.'

'Zoe's right. You know we are here for you, right?' Pippa nodded at Imogen. 'So just don't ever feel pressured into doing anything you don't want to do. There's always a way out.' A bit hypocritical on Imogen's part seeing as she was harbouring all these secrets herself, but as always, it's easier to give advice than it is to take it.

'You're right. I just need to give him time, I think. It's a big change in our life, so maybe he just needs a little longer to adjust to it, that's all. He said he wants the baby and, who knows, once it is here, things could be different.'

'And you're happy to wait and see if that's the case?'

Pippa shrugged. 'For now, I guess.'

Imogen watched her friend as she poured herself another drink and she felt a wave of sorrow, knowing that she was struggling so much. 'It's really good that you're talking to us, though, Pip, don't suffer in silence. We are all here in the same boat; we just want you to be happy. Never feel like you can't talk to us.'

Zoe put her hand up. 'Technically I'm not in the same boat as I'm not hiding a watermelon up my shirt, but I'm there in spirit and will always be on hand for support – and babysitting!'

They all laughed. 'Thanks, girls,' Pippa said, a smile spreading across her face. 'What would I do without you lot?'

After dinner they went back to the locker room to change

into their clothes and get ready to leave. Imogen quickly changed into her outfit so that she had time to check her phone without anyone looking over her shoulder. She was right to be worried because she had another message from her mum.

Please, I just want to talk? I can't bear the silent treatment.

She chose to delete it. She had had enough negativity from her to last a lifetime. It was now just her and Alice. That was all she needed. If she kept telling herself that, maybe she would start to believe it.

'Everything okay?'

Imogen spun round to face Zoe. 'What? Oh ... yeah. It's fine.'

Zoe gave her a look. 'From your mum?' Imogen nodded. 'Have you told Alice yet?'

'No, I've got it all under control.' She waved the remark away.

'Well, if you're sure? I won't keep on at you, but you know I'm always here, don't you?'

'I do.' She gave her a hug. 'Thank you.'

They all walked out of the spa together, down the steps into the moonlit car park. Zoe ran off to get the car and bring it round the front so that the others didn't have to walk too far. As they waited, Imogen stepped forward and sat on the steps, looking out over the grounds. It looked truly mesmerising. The moonlight was glistening over the crisp grass and it smelt fresh, clean and cold. She took a deep breath and then shuddered. She thought about the message her mum had sent. She was really struggling to shake it off. Maybe she should give her one more chance. This latest message was a lot less negative than her previous ones, so maybe she should give her a chance to make things right? If she didn't, then she would regret it – she knew she would. One more chance and then maybe she could speak to Alice and tell her something positive about her mum for a change.

She acted on impulse and typed out a message.

Meet me Monday afternoon at 2 by the lake.

That was it. She was committed now. She just hoped this time it didn't backfire – it was her last chance to make it work.

* * * * *

As the car pulled away from the spa, Ellie looked around at the other girls in the back, who were engaged in a conversation about birthing plans. Zoe took the moment to quietly say to Ellie, 'I know I always go on, and I don't want you to think I'm nagging. I just care about you, that all.' She swapped between looking at the road and stealing glances to Ellie.

'I know,' Ellie admitted.

'And I know you'll make the right decision in the long run.'

So much for not nagging. That was just an indirect way of nagging. But Ellie didn't bite on it, she just smiled and looked out of the window. She then she remembered what day it was tomorrow. She took out her phone and typed a short message.

Happy birthday for tomorrow xx

Chris' reply pinged back almost instantly.

Thank you. I miss you xx

She closed the message and sighed. She missed him too.

Chapter 30

Imogen stood at the side of the lake watching the ripples as a family of ducks swam by. As if it wasn't nerve-racking enough to be seeing her mum for the first time in ages, she was really suffering with a headache today. She took another deep breath as she closed her eyes. She hated having to lie to Alice this morning, yet again, telling her she was meeting some mums she met at the mums' club for lunch. But Alice would understand once she knew everything was going to be okay. Imogen just needed to sort things with her mum and then they could all start to build their future. She would talk to her mum today, and her mum clearly wanted to make things right. Everything would work out fine. She might finally get the happy family that she always wanted. Today was going to be the start of a new beginning. No more lies to Alice.

'Imogen?'

She opened her eyes but didn't turn around straight away. She hadn't heard that voice for ages and it created a whole world of emotions just with that one word. After reminding herself to breathe, she slowly turned around, lifting her eyes to look at her mum. She looked ... different. She no longer had the long blonde hair that she always wore in the same side plait Imogen remembered from growing up. Her hair was now shorter and really dark. And she was wearing a dress, which wasn't like her at all. It was long and flowy and just not the sort of thing her mum would usually wear. Imogen wasn't sure why this mattered to her, but it made her feel a little more uncomfortable. As if she was looking at a stranger.

'Oh my!' Her mum looked down at Imogen's bump. 'I can't believe it.'

Imogen stayed quiet. She couldn't tell if her mum was happy or sad at the sight of her tummy.

'How are you feeling?' Her mum took a tentative step towards her, but immediately stopped when Imogen shuffled backwards.

'I'm okay.' She managed to squeak out. She brushed her feet along the gravel, watching the stones trickle away from her feet, down towards the pond. Why was this so hard? This was her mum – things shouldn't feel so unnatural. She felt like a child again.

'Listen, Imogen. I should say sorry.'

Of all the things she thought they would talk about today, her mum apologising wasn't one of them. She gave the comment the respect it should have by looking at her. She looked sad. She looked tired.

'I hate that we don't talk any more. I ... I miss you.'

'I know. I miss you too.' This was the most truthful thing she had said in ages. 'But, I just can't have you being so negative about my life all the time, Mum, it's making me ill.'

Her mum exhaled. 'I know, I'm sorry, but it's just so hard. I want you to be happy.'

'I *am* happy!' She couldn't stop herself from sounding like a spoilt teenager. Short of stamping her feet, she felt practically fifteen again.

'I want you to have a family ...'

'I *do* have a family.' She rubbed her stomach.

'Not like this.'

'What do you mean?'

The tension was already building between them. Her mum seemed to be trying to find the right words and eventually said, 'I want you to have a *normal* family.'

The words stung. 'Normal?' she whispered. 'Mum, this is normal. I am with the person I love and we are having a baby. Why does it matter that we are the same sex?'

'Because, Imogen, it's not natural.' She looked around her, wary of people hearing, Imogen guessed.

That fact alone made the anger inside her burn. Her heart raced as the fury rose up inside her. 'Who are you to decide what is fucking normal!' The words not only took her mum by surprise, but she shocked herself too. She wasn't normally one to swear, but her mum triggered something inside her, which changed who she was. She didn't like this person; lies, swearing, feeling stressed ... this wasn't what she wanted from her own family.

'Imogen!'

'No! You can't play mummy to me just because you don't like what I do or how I speak. You lost that privilege when you disowned me.' Her heart was pounding. She thought she wanted this, but now that her mum was standing in front of her, still speaking the way she was, she didn't want it any more.

'Imogen, that's not fair.'

She laughed. 'No, shall I tell you what's not fair? It's not fair that I've had to go through my first pregnancy without my mum. It's unfair that I had to have my wedding day without my mum. It's unfair that I can't even *talk* to my mum without her badmouthing my wife!' Her mum noticeably flinched when Imogen referred to Alice as her wife. 'See! You can't even hear me talk about it.'

'Imogen, try to see it from my point of view. I have the neighbours on my case all the time asking where you are and why they never see you come over any more.' Her voice was quiet and she was still clearly uncomfortable with being out in public and talking about something so personal.

'And whose fault is that?'

Her mum exhaled heavily. 'You just want to hurt me, don't you?'

'What?' Imogen's voice rose an octave the more upset she got. 'I can't believe you. Why can't you just be happy for me?'

'Because, Imogen, I want you to be normal. To have a normal relationship – with a man – and have children, so that I can be a grandma.'

'You *will* be a grandma! In case you haven't noticed, there's a baby in here.' She pointed at her stomach. 'Actually, there are *two* babies in here!'

'Two!' Her mum gasped.

'Yes, mum, two.' She threw up two fingers in exasperation. 'Twins!'

'Do you know what you will be doing to those children?'

Imogen saw red. She no longer felt the yearning to have her mum around; she couldn't even bear to be looking at this woman right now. 'How dare you?' Her voice was calm and steady. 'These children will be loved a hell of a lot more than you have ever loved anyone.'

'Oh don't be so dramatic, Imogen. I do love you! You are my baby. But I just cannot get on board with all of this.' She waved her arms about to highlight her words. Imogen turned to walk away, but she had taken just a few steps when her arm was pulled back. 'Don't walk away from me, young lady.'

She snatched her arm back, losing her balance at the sheer force she used. She stumbled and her mum reached out to help her, but she screamed, 'No! I don't need your help,' a little louder than she had meant.

'Imogen, look what you are doing to yourself. It's that woman. Ever since you started,' she seemed to be searching for the right words to use and settled on, 'messing around with that girl, you have turned into a rude, disrespectful, horrible person.'

'No, you're wrong,' she took a step closer to her mum, pointing at the ground. 'Ever since I've been with Alice, she has made me a better person. She loves me for who I am. She doesn't try to change me. She is the most caring, supportive, beautiful person, inside and out, and I would do anything for her.'

'You can have all of that with a man, you know! You just need to find him. Get yourself out on the market again. We can sort the whole baby situation. I'll be around to help and—'

'No!'

'Imogen, come on.' She was pleading with her now. Desperation laced every word.

'No, Mum. You've had your chance to be involved in the babies' lives, but you've blown it.' Her hands were shaking with anger, but she was determined not to let her mum see that she had got to her.

Imogen thought she would feel sad or upset but, actually, she felt empowered. She didn't need the kind of negativity in her life that her mum brought. Alice was right; she should've made this cut a long time ago. 'Do you know what, Mum?' her words were laced with sorrow. 'I'm done.'

'What do you mean, you're done? Don't be so dramatic, Imogen.'

Imogen stopped again, having already started to walk away. She turned slowly and stood, with every ounce of confidence that she didn't feel, and said, 'I'm done with all this. You, me, all your nasty messages. I'm done. And you know why?' Her mum looked uncomfortable and shuffled on her feet to try and hide it. 'Because I don't need you. I have Alice and I love her and nothing will change that. You can't change me, this is me.' She jabbed herself hard in the chest. 'And I am about to become a mum to our babies – mine and Alice's – and if you don't like that, that's fine. But it's going to happen. So you can carry on being negative and stressing about it, I don't care. Because no one else matters. They are my family now.'

And with that, she walked away. Head held high and heart racing, but with a big fat smile on her face.

* * * * *

'Imogen, what's wrong?'

'We need to talk.' She stormed into the office where Alice worked and walked up to her desk. Her heart still pounding and her eyes feeling fuzzy.

'You look awful, is everything okay? Is it the babies? What's wrong?' Alice's face was contorted with fear and she was now standing up, leaning on her desk with her hands.

'The babies are fine.' Alice's face noticeably relaxed a little. 'Please, it's important.' She didn't feel confident any more. Every ounce of confidence had seeped out of her during the walk from the lake to here. She had expected her mum to at least try to follow her, but she didn't. She wasn't sure if she was relieved or sad that her mum clearly didn't care. Her voice broke as she added, 'please.'

'Of course. Come through.' Alice looked at her colleague, who simply nodded, silently agreeing to cover her desk. She walked Imogen through to the back room. 'What's going on?'

'Alice, it's all messed up.' The tears were already falling. Alice immediately moved forward to hug her, but Imogen stepped back. 'No, I don't deserve a cuddle. I haven't been honest with you.' The guilt weighed her down. 'I should've told you about everything before.'

'What do you mean?' Alice took a step backwards. She looked a little frightened.

'I've just been to see my mum.'

'Oh shit. Why didn't you tell me?' Her face softened now that she knew it wasn't anything about their relationship, which Imogen had guessed was her first worry.

'Because it was a last-minute thing and I was hoping to be coming to you with better news. But it's all just gone wrong.'

'What do you mean? Is she ill?'

'No, she's not ill.' She laughed a little. Not a genuine, happy laugh, but a *what is happening* laugh.

'Well, what? Imogen, I don't understand?'

'Mum's been texting me ... a lot.' She moved about on her feet as she spoke, feeling jittery because of the adrenaline.

'I know, we spoke about this.'

'No, after that. After I said I wasn't speaking to her any more. I was, I have been.' She felt ashamed.

'What?' It came out like a whisper, which made Imogen feel even worse. 'And you didn't feel like you could tell me this?'

She stopped moving and looked at Alice sadly. 'I wanted to, I really did.'

'But ...?'

'It's not that easy, Alice.'

'Oh, because I'm so unapproachable. Imogen, I've done everything for you, my whole life is for you. Why would you keep something like this from me? I thought we spoke about it, I thought we agreed.' The hurt on her face was more painful than anything Imogen had felt before. She felt like a monster.

'Alice, please, try to understand.' She moved towards her but Alice now backed away. 'Listen, she's been texting for ages, but her last one seemed a lot nicer. I thought she was coming round to everything.'

'I don't understand.' Alice sat down on the table opposite to where Imogen was standing.

'She's been sending me nasty messages, basically telling me ...' she hesitated. How could she say this to Alice? Not telling her was strictly because she didn't want Alice to hear these horrible things. She exhaled in defeat, 'I didn't want to tell you because she's not been very nice about us.'

'She never has, what's new?' Alice said, almost under her breath.

'She's been trying to get me to leave you, telling me I have brought shame onto the family. She heard about the babies and flipped.'

'Are you serious?' Imogen nodded, ashamed. 'Why didn't you feel like you could tell me, Ims? I'm supposed to be your wife. Have I ever given you reason to think I'd go mad at you?' Alice had softened a little and seemed more sad than angry.

'I was trying to protect you.'

'By making yourself ill over it?'

'I know it sounds stupid. I was trying to do the right thing, honest.'

Alice stood up and closed the gap between them, throwing her arms around Imogen and pulling her close. 'It's okay. I know you were. I just wish you'd have been honest with me. You really frustrate me sometimes.' They stood for a moment in the embrace. Alice was stroking the back of Imogen's head and she silently sobbed into her shoulder. After she had calmed a little, Alice said, 'So why were you meeting her after she sent you all those horrible messages? It doesn't make sense.'

There was a knock on the door and one of Alice's colleagues walked in holding two mugs of tea. 'Sorry,' she grimaced as she saw Imogen's tear-stained face. 'I just thought you might need these?'

'Thanks.' Alice took the mugs and closed the door again with her foot. She passed a mug to Imogen. 'She blatantly just wanted to have a nose. I wouldn't be surprised if she was lying on the floor out there with her ear pressed up against the gap underneath.'

Alice pulled a face to pretend to be the colleague and Imogen smiled at her, recognising her attempt to lighten the mood and appreciating it. She took the mug and sipped at the sugary liquid. It tasted amazing and gave her the moment she needed to regroup. 'I wanted to meet her because I thought I could make her see sense. She seemed to be easing up on the messages and I thought, if I just spoke to her, she would see how much I love you and accept the fact that we were together.'

'I'm guessing she didn't?'

Imogen shook her head. 'Nope. She just tried to convince me that life would be better with a man.'

'She's unbelievable.' Alice shook her head in disbelief.

'I know. But I just basically told her that I loved you and that she wasn't welcome if she was going to be so negative.'

'You really said that?' Imogen nodded, giving way to a little smile. 'Who are you and what have you done with my Imogen?'

They both laughed. 'I know. Get me, being all bossy!'

'You couldn't be bossy even if you tried, Ims, it's just not in your nature. You're too lovely.'

'Well, I did. And it felt great.'

'Did it?' She looked shocked.

'Well, for all of two seconds.' She pulled a face 'Then I felt scared, so I just walked away.'

Alice laughed but it was laden with love. 'Well, what do you want to happen now?' This was a huge question. Because the truth was, she wanted her mum to be around. But she knew that wouldn't happen. But it was the one thing in her life that she was missing. Instead of saying that, though, she just shrugged. 'You know, you'll always have me, don't you? I love you so much, Imogen, don't ever lose sight of that. And whilst I understand why you didn't tell me, please promise that in the future you will keep me in the loop? I am here to be your shoulder to lean on. Let me take the stress so that you can concentrate on being mummy and growing those beautiful babies.'

'I promise.' She took a deep breath. 'There is one more thing I should tell you, though.' Alice nodded. 'I've been signed off work for a while now. The doctor said I was suffering from stress when I went to see him and he signed me off.' She saw Alice's face fill with sorrow. 'I'm sorry! I wanted to tell you, but I didn't want you to be disappointed in me. I didn't want you to think I wasn't capable of this pregnancy, and I am! I swear I just let things get on top of me for a bit, but I'm sorting it, I promise.'

'Imogen,' Alice tilted her face back up to look at her again. 'You would never disappoint me. Ever. Okay? I love you so much and we are going to get through this and at the end of it all,' she rubbed a hand on her tummy, 'we will have these little people to love forever too.'

Imogen placed her hand on top of Alice's for a second

before Alice pulled her into a cuddle. 'You are silly sometimes. But I love you.'

'I love you too.' She felt every ounce of her worries melt away into Alice's arms. So long as she had Alice, she would be okay.

PART THREE:

Third Trimester

Chapter 31

'It feels weird not being at Zoe's – I feel like we are betraying her.' Pippa looked around at her surroundings. The coffee shop they were in at the park was not as nice as Zoe's. It had dingy wallpaper that was peeling at the edges and a weird smell coming from the far corner.

'I know, I feel on edge, like I'm about to be caught doing something I am not supposed to be.' Imogen looked nervously over her shoulder.

'Oh, will you two give it a rest?' Ellie sipped at her coffee and pulled a face. 'It's not *that* bad.' Pippa raised her eyebrows at Ellie's disgusted expression. 'Okay, fair enough, the coffee isn't great but we are doing Zoe a favour. She's hosting that over-sixties lunch thing, so it wouldn't be fair on us to take up tables. She won't mind us being here. Treat it like we are scoping out the local businesses for her.'

'Well, she hasn't got anything to worry about, that's for sure,' Imogen whispered.

'I cannot believe it's nearly the end of April. This pregnancy is going far too fast for my liking.' Pippa looked at her friends in disbelief. 'You must be thinking the same, Ellie, you're a couple of weeks ahead of me!'

'Tell me about it! I have spent the last month walking around like an eighty-year-old woman – my hips are killing me! Maybe I should be at that OAP meeting today.'

Pippa's phone beeped and she opened the message from Jason.

I'm here xx

Pippa frowned and then Ellie said, 'What's up?'

She spoke, not moving her eyes away from the text. 'It's from Jason, he says he's here.'

'Where, here?' Imogen asked, pointing at the floor to indicate the café.

Pippa looked up and shrugged. 'I don't know. I'll ask him.' She began to type a response when Ellie suddenly said. 'Oh wait, there he is!'

Pippa looked up and could see Jason walking past the café, a huge smile on his face. He wasn't walking towards the café, though, he was strolling straight past. 'I'll go and let him know we are in here.' She went to stand up, but Ellie placed her hand on Pippa's arm to stall her.

'Hang on a minute; did he know you were coming here?' Pippa shook her head.

'Did you arrange to meet here?'

Another shake.

'Then why would he say 'I'm here'?'

Pippa sat back down, confused. 'I ... I don't know, actually.'

'Look, he's going over towards the toilets.' Imogen was pointing out of the window.

'Just wait and see where he goes.' Ellie pulled on Pippa's arm, so she sat back down in her chair again.

The girls watched for a couple of minutes and saw him go over to the toilets and wait outside. Pippa felt uncomfortable. Her heart was racing and she started to panic, although she wasn't sure why. 'This is stupid; I'm going to text him.' She ignored the protests from the girls and sent a quick text asking what he meant. She then watched him out of the window, take out his phone and type a reply. Seconds later, her phone beeped.

Sorry, that wasn't meant for you – I'm meeting the guys at work for a bite to eat. We just mess around with the kisses on texts. It's a guy thing. Xx

'What a load of bullshit!' Ellie stated and Imogen shushed her, nervously looking over her shoulder at the rest of the coffee shop. 'I'm sorry, but you aren't stupid enough to believe that pile of crap, are you?'

Pippa looked over her shoulder and out of the window again. He was leaning up against the toilets, leg bent at the knee, with the sole of his foot flat on the wall, striking a very questionable boyband pose. He looked relaxed, almost happy.

'He lied.' Pippa said, almost to herself.

'Yes, but the question is ... why?' Ellie sipped her coffee again and frowned. 'Why do I keep drinking this?' she pushed it away.

Pippa watched for what felt like hours, but it could have

only been about ten minutes. But nothing happened. He stayed up against that wall the whole time. Not moving at all. Just occasionally looking at his phone. Eventually, Pippa stood up. 'I can't take this any more, I'm just going to ring him and see what he's doing.' The girls didn't argue, so Pippa took her phone and dialled his number. She watched him intently as she listened for the ring tone. It began and Jason moved instantly, lifting the phone into view and looking at the screen. Pippa was preparing herself to speak when she saw Jason put the phone back into his pocket.

'The bastard just ignored you!' Ellie squeaked.

Pippa watched in confusion and ended the call. Slowly she lowered herself back into her chair. 'Why is he ignoring me?' she asked, not taking her eyes off him.

'I don't know, honey.' Imogen gently rubbed Pippa's arm, but she hardly felt it. She felt a little numb, actually.

'I'm going to try again. Maybe he didn't realise it was me. I know he doesn't like to answer anonymous calls, so maybe I withheld my number without realising.' She didn't miss the looks the girls gave each other but she didn't care. She would give him the benefit of the doubt and try again. She listened and again, watched him acknowledge the fact that it was her and return the phone to his pocket, unanswered.

'For fuck's sake!' Pippa hissed, slamming the phone down onto the table.

Both Ellie and Imogen watched her, eyes wide. 'Jeez Pippa, I've never heard you swear like that.' Ellie was almost laughing.

'Why is he ignoring my calls? I don't get it.' She whipped her phone up and typed a message.

Why won't you answer my calls?

She snapped her head back up to the window as she sent the message and silently dared him to ignore it. She was fuming. She watched him take the phone out yet again and read the message.

'Come on, you bastard, reply.' Ellie said, picking up her coffee and then spitting it back into the cup. 'Urgh, Imogen, take this cup away from me!' Imogen did as she was asked, laughing.

Pippa felt relief flood her body when she saw that he was typing and then her phone beeped in response. 'Oh, thank goodness for that,' she said, laughing nervously and smiling at the girls. How would she still keep her head held high if he had ignored her text too? Thankful that he did reply, she opened the message, but straight away felt the fury rise up again. The girls clearly saw Pippa's change in mood because they immediately said, 'What's wrong?'

Pippa slid the phone across the table to Ellie and resumed her stare out of the window at her lying husband.

'Sorry, Pip, I'm just in a meeting at the moment. I'll call you later.' Ellie looked up at Pippa. 'Oh dear.'

'That's it. I'm going to go over there and give him a piece of my mind. I am bloody pregnant with his child and this is what he does to me. It's not on, girls.' She looked at them for reassurance. 'I'm not overreacting, am I?'

'Of course not!'

Pippa stood up, but this time Imogen placed her hand on her forearm to stop her. 'Hang on, Pip, who's that?'

Pippa and Ellie followed Imogen's pointing over to Jason again, but this time they could see someone approaching him across the grass. 'I don't know who that is.' Pippa said, noticing her breathing had rapidly increased in speed.

They watched as a woman approached Jason. They could only see her from the back, but she was wearing a dress and had vibrant red hair trailing down her back.

'Maybe this was who he was meeting, then?' Imogen questioned, but none of the girls adjusted their stare.

They watched the woman gradually get closer to him until she reached him and he leant forward and kissed her.

Not just a peck on the cheek, but a full-on passionate kiss.

Chapter 32

Ellie ushered Pippa through the door of the café, closely followed by Imogen. The girls sat Pippa down at their usual table at the back in the corner, which was actually still free, and Ellie left Pippa sobbing with Imogen and ran out the back to get Zoe.

'What's the matter?' Zoe asked, drying her hands on the pink tea towel that she grabbed from the side as Ellie ran in. 'You need to slow down. It's not good for you to be running about all over the place with that belly.'

'It's Pippa,' Ellie said breathlessly. A mix of walking really fast and adrenaline – with a good splash of anger thrown in – had made her really out of breath. But at this moment in time, that was the last of her worries.

'What is it?' Zoe's face drained of colour. 'Is it the baby?'

Ellie shook her head. 'No, the baby is fine. It's that dickhead, Jason.'

'Oh God, what's happened?' Zoe went to leave the kitchen but Ellie stopped her. 'Let me fill you in first. I don't think Pippa will want to hear me talking about it again in front of her.' Zoe stopped as she listened to Ellie unfold the drama that had taken place in the park.

'Oh my God, you're kidding?'

'Nope.'

'Well, where is she now? Is she okay?' Zoe's eyes frantically darted out to the café.

'What do you think?' Zoe nodded in response to Ellie's rhetorical question. 'She's outside. We brought her back here. I didn't know where else to take her and I figured you're her closest friend so she would want to see your face.'

Zoe nodded and made her way out to the café, immediately rushing over to the table, where Ellie had left the girls and, dropping to her knees, she held out her arms for Pippa to fall into. They sat there for a few minutes, Zoe letting Pippa cry into her shoulder. Ellie went back out into the kitchen to make some coffee. Shortly after she did so, Imogen appeared.

'You okay?' she asked Ellie, still peering around the door.

'Yeah, just thought everyone could do with some coffee.' Imogen nodded in agreement. 'You can come back here, you know. You don't have to hover in the doorway.'

Imogen walked in and took one of the cups from the side as Ellie finished putting some milk in. 'Whose is this? I'll take them out.'

'That one's Pip's and this,' she slid another cup over, 'is Zoe's.' Imogen took the cups out and reappeared.

'Um, there's a woman at the counter. Shall I get Zoe?'

'No it's okay, I'll see to her. Can you finish this cappuccino for me? Help yourself to whatever drink you want.' Ellie walked up to the counter and served the woman, all the time glancing over to Zoe and Pippa in the corner. Pippa looked awful. She had initially been stunned into silence when she realised what Jason was doing. But all of a sudden it was as if a fog of emotion had engulfed her and she was hysterical. The girls had to quickly move her away before she went storming over to him. He would find out that Pippa knew, but not yet. Ellie wanted to make sure he got what he deserved, the lying, cheating bastard. It was a weird feeling, though, seeing Pippa lose it. She was normally so together and had everything under control. Seeing her fall apart felt wrong – it wasn't Pippa.

She caught Zoe out of the corner of her eye and she smiled her thanks to Ellie for taking over the shop. Ellie saluted in response and continued with the customer.

After an hour had passed and the shop had quietened down, Ellie was finally able to join the girls back at the table. Pippa had calmed by now, but she seemed very subdued. Ellie smiled sympathetically as she sat down. 'How you feeling?'

'I'm okay,' Pippa replied, sipping at her latest hot drink. 'I'm sorry for turning into a complete mess earlier.'

'Hey, you don't need to apologise. You had every right to react how you did. I'm just really sorry you have to go through it at all.' Ellie felt so sorry for her. Her mind temporarily flicked to Chris and how things had been starting to feel good between them lately and then what it would feel like if he did something like this to her.

'We've made a decision.' Zoe was focusing her attention on Ellie now, filling her in on what had been spoken about over the last hour.

'And you're happy with this?' Ellie directed the question at Pippa, who just shrugged and said, 'What have I got to lose?'

'Okay, when?'

'Tomorrow. Pippa will stay here with us tonight and just tell Jason she's having a girly sleepover with us lot, and then tomorrow it's all systems go.

Chapter 33

Tonight was the night and Pippa felt sick. All last night she had gone over the plan in her head, trying to stop herself from thinking it was a bad idea. But she couldn't avoid the fact that something needed to be done – she wasn't going to be made a fool of again. She had asked the girls over and over again whether it was right to talk to him first, that there might have been an explanation, but as Ellie said, there would be no explanation in this world that would mean it was acceptable to be acting the way he was with that woman. It wasn't just the thought of her marriage ending that upset her, or the fact that her baby would be growing up without its mum and dad being together, but more to do with the realisation that after all these months, her suspicions have been right. All those times she doubted herself and cursed herself for being paranoid – all the while she had actually been spot on. She had spent hours going over in her head whether she had done something wrong to push him away, but the girls had not let her dwell on that fact for very long. And then there was the fact that pretty soon everyone in town would know what had happened. There was no covering this one up – she had failed as a wife and the whole town would be talking about it. What a mess.

Jason's keys in the front door yanked her back into the here and now. *Shit*, she thought, as her heart began to pound. She had been so caught up in the plan, she hadn't even given a second thought to how she would actually feel seeing him again. Her nausea crept up a level and she could feel her throat clogging up. She mustn't let on to him that anything was wrong. Yet this was a hell of a lot harder than it seemed!

'All right?' he said as he entered the living room and dropped his bag onto the floor.

'Uh-huh,' Pippa replied, feeling safer with sounds than words. She kept her gaze fixed firmly on the TV, not taking in a single word of what the chefs were saying to each other, but thankful for the distraction.

'Good day?' He seemed really cheerful, which was initially calming, but then she realised why he must've been so cheerful. She then found herself wondering what he did last night when she was staying at Zoe's. The thought hadn't crossed her mind at the time because she just saw it as her needing time to calm down, but of course, free house, no wife, maybe he was cheery today for another reason. She couldn't stop the scenario playing out in her mind and she felt herself panicking.

She nodded in reply to his question, still unable to form any words and avoiding his eye contact.

'Well, aren't you a great conversationalist today?' he said sarcastically and walked out into the kitchen. Pippa tried so hard to bottle up the tears that were forming at an alarming rate and beginning to pool in the corner of her eyes. She mustn't ruin this now. She just needed to get through the next couple of hours until he fell asleep and then she could start sorting all this out.

Typically, it took Jason a lot longer to fall asleep than normal. The one night she wanted to just get out the way and he was on top form. He spent the whole evening being chatty, engaging in conversation with her and even snuggling up on the sofa with her whilst they watched TV. For her part she didn't take in anything that was going on in the programmes and when he snuggled up next to her with his arm around her, she felt awkward and uncomfortable and just wanted to scream at him to get his filthy hands off her. But she couldn't, not yet. So she endured an hour and a half of him being like that before his breathing finally slowed to a soft snore. She left it for another half an hour to make sure he was fully asleep before sliding off the sofa – as smoothly as she could with her huge baby bump – and pocketing his mobile phone, which had been switched off and left on the side. He had taken to switching his phone off when he got home recently. She didn't think anything of it before, but now she realised it was probably because that woman might text or call him and give the game away.

She hurried into the bathroom downstairs and locked the door. Sitting on the toilet, seat down, and her hands shaking intensely, she pressed hard on the power button to turn it on. Annoyingly the phone played a tune as it started up and she was forced to quickly sit on it to muffle the noise. Her heart raced even more at the risk of being caught out with his phone. What would he do? She guessed he would go mad, like he did before. She couldn't risk that because if he started shouting at her for snooping she wasn't sure she'd be able to hold in the fact that she knew.

Pulling the phone out from under her bum she was faced with the pin request. She tried the number from before, but it didn't work. 'Damn it!' she cursed. Of course he had changed his pin. He wasn't as silly as he looked. She tried a few combinations and ended up locking the phone. Just the thought that he had changed his pin after last time made her angry. She sat for a further minute, waiting for the pin request to be ready for another attempt. She then tried another attempt before it locked her out again. 'Bloody phone!' She put it down on the side, now having to wait a little longer to try again. She whipped out her phone and texted the WhatsApp group she had set up with the girls.

I can't bloody get into his phone! Pin!!!

In quick succession she received replies from all three.

Ellie: Fuck!

Imogen: Oh no!

Zoe: You need to think. What would he use?

Pippa replied:

I've tried all the things I can think of, nothing is working!!

Imogen: What about birthdays?

Ellie: I'm guessing your anniversary isn't one the bastard would use!

Zoe: Think outside the box. He won't want you to get in, so what would he use ... anything at home he uses locks for? Or work?

Pippa frantically tried again, but still nothing. Then it came to her. She grabbed the phone again and typed in the code for the office back door. She had only ever used it once when visiting him at work after hours and she was actually amazed that she remembered it. The phone jumped into life.

OMG IM IN!!!

Zoe: What was it???

His bloody work code for the door!

Ellie: Ha-ha! Result! Okay, do your thing. Xx

Pippa put her phone down and went into his messages. Blank. Of course he deleted them all. Just as she was about to move onto contacts, a new message pinged into his inbox.

It was from 'Patrick'. 'Oh shit,' she whispered as she clicked on it to open.

Hey, last night was amazing. I miss you. Call me when you land.xx

Heart doing a million beats per second, she quickly took a picture of this message and added it to the group with the caption 'WTF?'

Imogen: Land?

Ellie: Where the fuck is he going?

Imogen: Are you going to reply??

Pippa looked at his message over and over again. It wasn't the 'land' part that had made her feel so ill. 'Last night was amazing', he had been with her whilst Pippa was at Zoe's. Just that thought alone made her feel empty.

Zoe: Don't dwell on the 'last night' aspect; I know what you will be thinking. Just take a deep breath and do what you need to. It'll soon be over.

She smiled at Zoe's message – she knew her so well.

Okay, I'm doing it!

Pippa put her phone down and typed the response that she and the girls had agreed on yesterday.

I need to see you, it's important. Meet me at the park at 10am?

She didn't need to wait long for a reply.

Tomorrow? I thought you went back to work today? Is everything okay?

So he told her he worked somewhere where he presumably needed to fly to ... this was just getting more and more confusing. She typed a response, which she hoped would end this conversation.

I couldn't go. Need to talk. Tomorrow?

'Patrick' replied with an 'okay' and a ton of kisses. Pippa couldn't bring herself to reply again so she turned the phone off and put it in her pocket. She then sent another message to the girls confirming she had carried out the task as planned and that she was going to bed.

As she stood up, there was a knock on the bathroom door. 'Pip? You okay?'

Panic rapidly spread through her body. He was awake! How long had he been awake? 'Yeah, I'm fine,' she squeaked.

'You've been in there a little while, you sure you're okay?'

Shit! 'Yeah I'm fine, just a bit of an upset stomach, that's all.' She flushed the toilet for authenticity and turned the tap on.

'Okay, well I'm going up now. See you up there.'

'Okay!' she called, frantically washing her hands, trying to wash the deception off her fingers. A minute later he was at the door again.

'Babe, you seen my phone?'

All of a sudden his phone in her pocket felt as though it was a lead weight. The guilt bearing down on her left buttock. 'No,' she replied, instantly disliking herself for lying.

'You sure? I swear I put it on the side earlier, but I can't find it.' He sounded a little panicked and that made Pippa feel a bolt of anger.

'Sorry, I haven't seen it. You sure you came home with it? I don't remember you having it earlier.' She relayed the lines that the girls had thought up for her. She needed to try and convince him that he didn't come home with it so that he would go into work tomorrow without it. She needed to keep hold of his phone now.

'I'm sure I did.' He paused. 'Maybe I left it at work, then.' He didn't sound convinced.

She heard his feet pad away to the stairs and then climb up them.

She just wanted it to be the morning now.

* * * * *

'I feel like I'm going to be sick.'

'It's okay, you'll be fine, and we are all here with you.' Pippa felt a hand on her shoulder as Zoe spoke to her. 'Just take deep breaths.'

Pippa waited at the bench in the park she'd been at not twenty-four hours previously. It felt like a million years ago, though. So much had happened since she'd seen Jason and that woman here. Her mind was shattered after running a million miles all through last night. She didn't get any sleep, not even five minutes, and she was really feeling it today. 'What time is it?'

Ellie looked at her phone. '9.55.'

'Oh, bloody hell,' Pippa's leg began to jump up and down in anticipation. 'What if she doesn't turn up? How long do we wait for her?'

'Oh, I think she'll turn up. She probably thinks she will get a replay of yesterday.' Ellie's face said it all. She was fuming.

'I don't even remember what she looks like!' Once she had seen Jason's face, she found it hard to look at anything else but his face. She didn't get a good view of the woman.

'Nor do I, if I'm honest,' Imogen added.

'It's okay; I remember.'

'Ellie, you need to chill out, okay, you behaving like that doesn't help calm the situation.' Zoe gave her sister the look, to which Ellie poked out her tongue.

'It's okay, Zoe, I'd rather someone was on the ball because I sure as hell am not.' Her leg began to bounce up and down as the time got closer and her anticipation grew.

'Wait, is that her?' Imogen pointed to a woman standing by the toilets alone, looking at her phone. She had her back to them, but they could tell she was typing so they took Jason's phone out of the bag and all looked at it. Sure enough, a moment later, a message pinged onto the screen. The phone was on silent so as to not draw her attention to them if she rang. Pippa opened the message and the words; '***I'm here xx***' flashed up. They all glanced up at Pippa for a reaction before then all looking over to the woman.

'You ready?' Zoe asked, rubbing Pippa's arm.

'No, but I guess it's time.' She swallowed hard to push down the bile that was creeping up the back of her throat.

'It'll be okay. Remember, we are here and we will go at your pace.'

Pippa nodded and stood up, making her way over to the woman with the girls following closely behind. The feeling as she approached this woman was nothing like she had ever felt before. She was angry, upset, scared and confused all at the same time and the feeling made her jittery. Her legs felt like jelly as she approached the woman.

She took a deep breath as they reached her and said, 'Excuse me?' But she wasn't prepared for the sight she saw when the woman turned round, because it wasn't the woman's face she saw first, but her huge, pregnant belly.

Chapter 34

'Holy Cow!' Ellie couldn't stop herself before the words come out. She quickly looked to Pippa, who was standing open-mouthed, staring at the woman's stomach.

'Can I help you ladies?' The woman asked, seeming disgruntled by the rude reaction she received from the girls as she turned around. 'Only I am meeting someone.' She was only a young woman, probably their age if not a little younger. She had beautiful long, red hair, which she wore down and over one shoulder. She was a very pretty lady, which Ellie didn't want to admit. But even though she thought Pippa was very pretty too, this girl in front of them couldn't be more opposite to Pippa. She noticed how good her make-up was too – this woman knew what she was doing in that department.

'Yeah, and don't we know it!' Ellie had regained control of her mouth once again and was now seriously pissed off.

'Excuse me?' The woman frowned at Ellie, mimicking her tone and putting a protective arm around her belly as she spoke.

'Okay, let's not get carried away,' Zoe spoke up, holding a hand out to try and calm the situation. 'Pip?'

Pippa couldn't speak. She just stood frozen to the spot and

Ellie felt the overwhelming urge to hug her right now. Poor woman.

'Okay, here's the thing.' Zoe was directing her words to the woman now and Ellie stared at her hard in the face; there was no way she was going to lie to them. 'We know you are here to meet someone, but that person is us.' Zoe paused as the woman looked around at each of them.

'I ... I don't understand.'

'You're here to meet Jason?' Zoe asked and the woman's reaction changed.

'Yes, what's wrong? Is he okay? Has something happened?' She looked genuinely worried.

'He's fine, but unfortunately his wife isn't.' Zoe indicated to Pippa and the woman's gaze followed. First to Pippa and then to Pippa's baby bump.

'What? Um ... I don't understand.'

'This is Jason's wife.' Imogen added, making sure it was crystal clear.

'Wife?' It came out like a whisper and Ellie, along with the others, clocked on to what was going on.

'You didn't know he was married?' Zoe asked. But she didn't have to; the woman began to cry.

'Shit.' It was the first time Pippa had spoken since they had approached the woman. All the girls looked at her as she walked forward and hugged the woman. Ellie looked over to Zoe and Imogen, who both shrugged. They waited a moment, until Pippa broke the embrace and wiped the woman's tears. 'Don't cry,' she said, 'he isn't worth crying over.'

Amazed by the sheer strength of her friend, Ellie felt

emotional too. 'Maybe we could all go back to the café and talk?' Zoe asked, receiving nods from everyone in agreement.

'What café?' the woman said, through sobs.

'I own the café on Hamilton Drive. It won't be busy and you can talk in peace. I'm guessing there's more to this story than we anticipated.'

A short while later and they were all round a table in the café and Zoe was bringing over tea and biscuits. The girls had shown proof in the form of Jason's phone and wedding pictures on Facebook to prove they weren't lying.

'How long have you been married?' The woman, who they now knew was called Jenna, asked as she sipped her tea for a much-needed sugar hit.

'Nearly nine years now.'

Jenna exhaled, 'Jeez.'

'You really didn't know about Pippa?' Ellie was still suspicious of this woman. Jenna shook her head. 'Did you not wonder where he went every night?'

'He told me he worked abroad and stayed with his mates when he came back. Said he was looking for somewhere to rent for when he was working over this way.'

'Worked abroad? Doing what?' Ellie glanced at Pippa, aware this conversation must be hard for her to hear, but also aware that she needed to hear it.

'Something in property. Buying property abroad for people here. He said he was waiting to settle down to find somewhere so he could have a family.'

'He has a family!' Pippa shouted, more to herself than directly at anyone. She then apologised.

'It's okay; I can see why you would be upset. But I swear I had no idea. I thought he wanted to settle down with me and have a family.' Sadness filled her eyes again but she held it back.

'So I take it that's his?' Ellie nodded her head towards Jenna's stomach, asking the question that no one wanted to, though she already knew the answer.

Jenna nodded and welled up. 'I'm so sorry,' she said to Pippa, who had tears in her eyes too.

'I just can't believe it.' Pippa hadn't spoken much throughout the whole time. 'How could he do this, not just to me, but to both of us?'

Imogen's phone beeped and she apologised, pulling it out and switching it to silent. She placed it on the table.

'It's fine, you can read your message.' Pippa laughed half-heartedly.

'No, it's okay, it's a voicemail. I'll check it in a bit. So what's going to happen now?'

Pippa shrugged and Jenna shook her head. 'I have no idea. I can't take it all in. It doesn't feel real.'

'Well, you'd better start believing it because this shit is happening and that lowlife needs to be put in his place.'

Jenna looked shocked and Pippa added, 'You'll get used to Ellie.' She then threw a sideways smile at Ellie.

'Okay, what have I missed?' Zoe sat back down. 'I can't believe there are all these people in here. It's never normally busy at this time.'

'It's fine, you don't have to sit down.' Pippa smiled at Zoe, but Ellie could see it was strained. Her features were soft and friendly but behind her eyes she could see the pressure of recent events debilitating her.

'Oh no, its fine. Sarah is here now, so she can take the reins for a bit.'

Ellie clapped her hands to get the attention back on the matter in hand. 'So, come on then, what's the plan of action?' Silence ensued around the table. 'Okay, so are we in agreement that Jason needs to be confronted?'

Everyone waited for Pippa and Jenna to answer first. They looked at each other and slowly, together, nodded.

'Okay, great, so we are on the same page. Next question is,' Ellie actually felt a bit nervous about asking this as it was such a huge question, 'Do either of you want to still be with Jason and work things out?'

The atmosphere changed and became very tense. Neither woman answered. They glanced at each other but then both looked into their hands. Finally, Pippa said, 'I don't know what I want to do.'

'Are you serious?'

'Ellie, this is a huge thing, it's not simply black and white.' Zoe was always the mediator in everything. Even when they were growing up she always had a sensible head on her shoulders. Ellie envied her that sometimes. Although sometimes she did think her sister just needed to lighten up.

'I think we need to tell him,' Jenna spoke up. All the girls stopped and looked at her. 'I don't think anyone can make a decision for the future until we speak to him.'

'Jenna's right.' Now it was everyone's turn to look at Pippa. 'We need to tell him.' She looked at Jenna, 'but we do it together. So he knows we are on the same side and doesn't try to spill any more crap to us.'

Jenna nodded. 'Agreed.'

'Right, so when?' Imogen said.

'No time like the present.'

'Are you sure, Pip?' Zoe put her hand on Pippa's back and once again, Ellie was reminded just how close these two were. They had a beautiful friendship. Pippa was lucky to have that. Ellie had that once, with Chris. She missed it.

'I'm sure. Let's just get this over and done with. You okay with that, Jenna?' She nodded in reply.

'Okay, well, I'll make sure Sarah can stay for the afternoon.'

'You don't have to.'

'I want to. You aren't doing this alone.'

'Thanks, girls,' Pippa directed this to all of them.

As they made their way out of the shop, Imogen suddenly stopped them by saying, 'Oh my God!'

The girls turned to face her, looking over their shoulders mid-stride and Ellie noticed that the colour seemed to have drained from her face. She looked as if she was about to fall over. Ellie ran back to steady her with her arm. 'Hey, steady. What's wrong?'

'It's Alice, she's in hospital.'

Chapter 35

Imogen rushed down the winding hospital corridors as fast as was possible with her baby bump in tow. She had called on her way to see what was going on. They couldn't tell her much but she did know that Alice has been knocked over by a car.

All the corridors looked the same: white and clinical, with a few posters dotted around and random sets of chairs outside numerous doors. She couldn't focus and more than once stopped, regained her composure and carried on.

She rounded the corner to the ward she had been directed to and came to a reception area. 'Hello ... excuse me?' She called as the receptionist got up to leave the station.

'Oh, sorry, I didn't see you there. How can I help?' The woman had an enormous smile and it kind of relaxed Imogen a little seeing a friendly face.

'I'm looking for Alice Armstrong?' Her voice was shaking as she spoke. The woman looked on the wall and directed Imogen to cubicle 4b. She gave her thanks and set off. It didn't take her long before she was walking up to the cubicle. As she approached she could see Alice lying in the bed, leg in a cast with an array of cuts and bruises covering her face and arms. She stopped at the end of the bed and let out a small sob as she covered her mouth. Alice opened her eyes instantly and a smile crept across her face.

'Hey, beautiful,' she said, holding her arms out for a hug. Imogen let another sob escape as she lunged forward, wrapping her arms around Alice and squeezing her tight. She let the tears fall as she held onto the woman she loved so much. 'Hey, shh, it's okay. I'm okay.'

Imogen pulled back and sat on the edge of the bed. 'What happened?' she cried.

'Okay don't be mad ...' Alice took her hand and rubbed the top with her thumb. 'I went to see your mum.' Alice pulled a face in response to Imogen's shocked expression. 'I know, I shouldn't have interfered and I know you didn't want me to get involved, but I couldn't just leave it. She had really upset you and it was time she heard a few home truths about our relationship.'

Imogen stayed quiet, stunned by her revelation.

'I was doing it for you, for us. I just wanted to make things right.' She paused. 'Please don't be mad at me.'

Imogen let the information settle before saying, 'I'm not mad at you. I'm just, well, I don't know how I feel.'

'She's a lost cause, you know that?' Alice tried to smile, but Imogen could see the sadness behind her eyes. 'I'm sorry.'

'It's okay. I knew she would never come to terms with us.'

'I know. But I thought if I could speak to her, you know, show her how much I love her daughter that she would understand. But she just ... she doesn't want to listen to anything.'

'I know.' She moved a stray hair away from Alice's face and brushed her thumb down her face. 'You look so bruised. What happened?'

'Well, your mum and I argued and she told me I had stolen her daughter away from her and that she would never forgive me for it.'

'Oh Alice, I'm so sorry you had to listen to that.' She hated that her family made the person she loved feel so inadequate and disliked.

'It's fine, it will take a lot more than a few harsh words to get to me. You know that.' She smiled and gave Imogen a wink. A wink that still, to this day, sent tingles down her spine.

'So, I'm sorry, but I don't understand how it's gone from that, to you lying here with, I'm guessing, a broken leg?'

Alice nodded. 'Well your mum stormed off saying something about talking to you and making you see sense. I saw red and ran after her to have it out with her and I didn't look before running across the road. And, well, you can figure out the rest.'

'Oh, you idiot!'

'Thanks, I love you too.' Alice smiled.

'Honestly, I can't believe this has happened. This is crazy. Why can't she just accept that I am happy and we are about to have the babies and—' she halted as she saw the figure appear in the doorway to the ward. 'No way!'

'What?' Alice tried to look where Imogen was, but her view was blocked by the curtain.

'What are you doing here?' Imogen said, through clenched teeth. Her mum came closer and stopped when she was in full view of both Imogen and Alice.

'I came to see if Alice was okay.' She hovered, not coming any closer. She looked pale and defeated, and really ashamed.

'How dare you? You are not welcome here.' Imogen felt a hand on her arm and flinched before realising it was Alice.

'Look, I understand why you might not want me here, but I am trying to do the right thing,' she begged.

'The right thing? The right thing would've been to support me in my life decisions. The right thing would've been to be there for me when I needed you.' Her voice was getting louder the angrier she got. 'The right bloody thing would've been to get your head out of your arse and see how much I love this woman and realise that it doesn't matter if she is male, female, black, white or bloody green! You wouldn't know the right thing if it slapped you round the face!'

'Alright, Ims, calm down. This isn't good for the babies.' Alice had sat up and was trying desperately to comfort Imogen from her awkward position in the bed.

'I'm sorry. I didn't want to upset anyone by coming here. I just wanted to make sure you were okay.' She directed the comment at Alice and this enraged Imogen further, but she concentrated on taking deep breaths and calming herself for the sake of the babies.

'And Imogen, you're right,' her mum said, with sadness in her eyes. 'I should've been there for you and I should've tried to understand. That was wrong of me. And I'm sorry.'

She didn't know what to say. She was so full of fury that she was struggling to form any words that weren't shouting or swearing, so she opted to stay silent for the time being.

'I know you may never want to forgive me – and to be

honest, I wouldn't blame you – but I did need to come and say this to you. It was the least I could do after ...' she indicated Alice and her leg.

Alice didn't say anything, but instead looked at Imogen. But she didn't know what to say or do either. This was so completely out of character from her mum and she wasn't completely convinced it was sincere. It was as if her mum had read her mind because she then added, 'You don't believe me?'

'What do you expect?' Imogen spat out the words with venom.

'I am trying to make things right now, Imogen, you have to believe me.'

'Why? Why do I *have* to believe you? Why do you deserve another chance? God knows I've given you enough in the past.'

'Yes, that's true. But I realise now that I was wrong.'

'Why?' Imogen threw back at her. 'What's changed?'

She was silent for a second, but then simply said, 'I have.'

'Oh don't make me laugh,' Imogen guffawed. 'You couldn't change even if you wanted to.'

'Look, you don't have to believe me. But I've had time to reflect. It's hard coming to terms with something like that and then I spoke to you and it made me angry. You came at me all guns blazing, shouting about me doing this and me doing that.'

'I came to tell you how much I love Imogen and you were hell bent on defending your nasty messages.'

'Yes, I know. I guess we were both in the wrong.' She turned back to face Imogen. 'But I mean it. Seeing Alice hurt uncovered a whole world of feelings I didn't know I had. I felt awful that Alice had hurt herself, but I felt even worse thinking about how upset you were going to be when you found out she was hurt. It made me realise how much you ... love her.' She looked awkward saying those last words. Imogen studied her face and even though she was the same woman, with her stern exterior, she seemed different behind her eyes.

Her mum sighed. 'Look, all I can say is I'm sorry and I am willing to try and make this work. I can't promise anything. I've spent my whole life feeling a certain way and never did I ever think your sexuality was going to be something I would have to come to terms with. But I do have to. It's not an easy transition for me, Imogen, and I'm not saying that I am happy about this,' she gave Alice a sideward glance and looked completely uncomfortable about it. 'But all I can do is try. It will take time and I'm not even sure I can do it but ... well ...' she sighed again, but louder this time. 'I am willing to try.' She tried to smile. 'I'll leave you two to it; I just wanted to say my piece. I would never have forgiven myself if anything had happened to ... you,' she looked again at Alice from the corner of her eye, 'So now I know you're okay, I'll leave.'

She didn't wait for a response before walking out of the ward, without so much as a glance back.

Imogen was stunned and after a few minutes, looked at Alice. 'What the hell just happened?'

Alice looked back at her, equally stunned, and simply said, 'A miracle.'

Chapter 36

Pippa felt sick. Not just a little nausea – full on, I'm-going-to-throw-up-at-any-minute, sick. She walked the short distance from the car park to the back of Jason's office in silence. His office building was large in comparison to the other buildings surrounding it. It was actually part of an industrial unit on the outskirts of their village, so whilst there were lots of buildings around his, beyond that there were fields and countryside. The building itself was square-looking with multiple stories. It wasn't a very attractive set of offices, but it did the job it needed to.

Jenna, Zoe and Ellie were close behind. Everyone must be feeling similar to her as no one was saying a word – the silence was uncomfortable, but not as uncomfortable as the next instalment of her life would be.

No one spoke in the car either, which Pippa kind of appreciated. She couldn't stop the recent events replaying in her mind and, as a result, flashbacks to when she caught Jason out before were resurfacing and bringing with them a tirade of old emotions she thought she had buried deep inside her forever. But no, here they were, screaming *I told you so* and making her feel like the biggest fool in the world.

They approached the big, glass-fronted building and Pippa gazed up towards where Jason's office was. He wasn't too high up, which she was thankful for today as she didn't fancy traipsing up all those stairs and no way was she getting in a lift. She walked the steps up to the reception door and froze. Almost instantly she felt a hand on her back. 'You okay?' It was Zoe. Pippa turned and looked at her, but still no words came out. 'It'll be okay, I promise. We are all here. Just take it at your pace; we don't have to go in right now if you aren't ready.' Pippa swallowed hard, trying to pass the lump that had formed in her throat. It wouldn't budge. She tried again and gave in to a small cough.

'Here,' Ellie pushed her hand between Pippa and Zoe, offering a bottle of water. 'Take this.' Pippa took the bottle and drank half of it in one go. 'Bet you wished that was vodka, hey?' Ellie laughed, but nobody else did.

Another deep breath and Pippa finally said, 'Let's do this.' She glanced at Jenna, who looked as pale as a ghost, her eyes dark and sunken. She held out her hand to take hers. 'You ready?' she asked. Jenna simply nodded. She squeezed her hand reassuringly, pretending to be a million times stronger than she actually felt.

They walked in, hand in hand still, and Pippa walked up to the desk – not taking in any of the surroundings in the foyer, just concentrating hard on getting to the reception desk without falling over. Betty smiled back but immediately her face dropped when she saw Pippa's expression. 'Hi Pippa, is ... everything ... okay?' she asked, haltingly.

'It will be. Where's my husband?' She was aware she

sounded sharp and rude, but right now it took all her energy to not throw up, so this was the least of her worries. Betty would understand soon enough.

'Erm, well he's in a meeting, I think. Do you need him right away?' Betty glanced round at the other girls surrounding Pippa and then settled back on Pippa's face. She turned and looked at the others. 'I didn't account for him being in a meeting. What am I supposed to do now, wait?' She wasn't sure she had the strength to wait; she was on edge as it was. She was thankful when Ellie stepped forward, leaning on the reception desk and said, 'We'd like to see him now ... please,' she added as an afterthought.

Betty looked a little shocked at Ellie's comment and stood up. 'Oh, okay. Well, I'll just go and get him. Would you like to wait in his office?' She directed the question at Pippa, but then her glance did another full circle around the others, too. Had it not been such a stressful time for Pippa, she would've found this amusing.

Pippa nodded and as Betty began to direct her, she interrupted with, 'I know where his office is,' and then, realising her snappiness was uncalled for, she added, 'But thank you, Betty,' with a smile for good measure.

Betty scurried off as Pippa showed the girls towards the stairs and subsequently into Jason's office.

'Did you see her face? We must look like the pregnant mafia or something.' Ellie plonked herself down into Jason's seat behind the desk and began rifling through his drawers.

'What are you doing?' Pippa squeaked, horrified at the sheer invasion of privacy.

'Looking for anything dodgy,' Ellie looked up at them all. 'What?'

'Maybe you should just leave Pippa to the detective work. Let her do things *her* way.' Zoe gave Ellie the look and she closed the drawer she was rummaging in and stood up. 'You still doing okay?' Zoe asked.

'Yeah, I guess. I just want it to be over already.' Pippa looked at Jenna, who was going paler by the second. And then she had a thought. It must be so hard for her right now, having this dumped on her, being pregnant too, and not having the support network of friends that Pippa had. It was easy to get wrapped up in this moment of self-pity when, really, she had the girls behind her. Who did Jenna have right now. She walked over and put her arm around her shoulder. 'How are you holding up?'

Jenna seemed shocked by her friendliness but then smiled. 'I'm okay. How are you coping?'

'I'm okay. Look, I know this has been really hard on you and some moments I forget that you don't know us. I just feel like we are a group of friends going to sort this out and I forget that, actually, before today, you didn't know who I was. I am so lucky to have these girls behind me and I want you to know that we will be there for you too. He doesn't deserve to ruin our lives, don't let him.' Jenna smiled, but didn't say anything. Pippa moved away slightly and took another deep breath. She walked over to the window and sighed. What the hell happened to being happily married with a child on the way? A child they had both longed for, for what felt like a lifetime. But now, that all seemed so far away. Pippa could hear Ellie and Jenna chatting when she felt Zoe step up to the window next to her.

'That was a really nice thing you did there. You didn't have to do that.' Pippa shrugged. 'Even in the midst of all this anguish, you still find time to be as lovely as you are. I'm proud of you.'

The moment was cut short by a door slamming outside. All four girls snapped their heads to the office door and then back at each other. They could hear Jason's voice approaching and Pippa felt her legs turn to jelly as her blood pumped through her veins rapidly, causing her to temporarily hear a ringing sound in her ear. She glanced at Jenna, who also looked as if she might keel over. This was it. This was the moment Pippa's life changed forever – no more being walked over. She stared at the door as she heard him approach. The handle twisted and, before she knew it, he came strolling in. He was smartly dressed today in his dark-grey work suit with a pink tie. She always loved this particular suit as it made his bum look amazing. But she couldn't see past the betrayal now and where before she would see her gorgeous husband, now all she saw was a lying, dirty rat.

He saw Pippa first, standing with Zoe. Jenna and Ellie were next to the door, so as he opened it, the door shielded them from view initially. 'Pip, what's wrong? Betty said you were here and it looked like an emergency. Is it the baby?'

'No, the baby is fine.' She actually surprised herself with the calmness of her voice.

He stood in front of her and flung his arms out to the sides in exasperation. 'Well, what is it? I was in a meeting.'

He sounded frustrated with her and this spurred her on to show him for the lowlife that he was.

'Have you got something to tell me?' she asked, her outer self projecting calmness and control whilst inside she was flapping massively.

'Oh for God's sake, Pip, stop talking in riddles. I have work to do. What do you want?' Pippa saw the expression on Zoe's face turn to hatred as Jason spoke to her the way he did when people weren't around. Pippa looked to Zoe briefly and Zoe gave the slightest of nods, just to show she was there and it was okay. 'Well?' Jason pressed.

'You lying bastard.' The words were not what she had planned to say. They just came out. She even shocked herself a little bit, and it was clear she shocked Jason because his face crumpled into confusion.

'What are you on about?'

Jenna chose that moment to walk out from next to the door and take up her place next to Pippa. Jason's expression rapidly revealed a multitude of emotions, ranging from confusion, to shock, to realisation and then to guilt. Neither woman said anything. They simply watched as Jason lifted his hands to his head, rubbing them through his hair and then resting them over his mouth.

'Nothing to say?' Jenna spoke up, but even Pippa could hear the tremble of despair in her voice.

He stood in silence. Dropping his hands to his side, he looked defeated. Pippa wasn't sure if she was glad about that or annoyed. Why wasn't he pleading with her to understand?

'Are you just going to stand there ...? SAY SOMETHING!'

Every person in the room snapped their heads to Pippa as she screamed the words. But she didn't care. Her whole body was trembling with anger. She wasn't feeling in complete control of herself and that scared her – she didn't like not being in control.

'Pip, don't get yourself worked up,' he held out his hand to touch her bump, 'It's not good for the baby.'

'Get your hands away from me.' She whipped her hands protectively in front of her bump, whacking his hand away as she did. 'How dare you tell me not to get worked up? The only reason I'm worked up is because of you!'

'Okay, okay, calm down.' He turned around and closed the office door. It was then that he spotted Ellie. He didn't say anything to her, but Pippa didn't miss the sneering look Ellie gave him. It lingered in the air for a second before Jason pulled his attention away. He turned back, holding his hands out. 'Can we please talk about this?'

'I'm listening.' Pippa crossed her arms defensively.

He looked around at the other girls, but lingered a little too long on Jenna. He then said, 'Can we talk in private?'

'No.'

'No?' He seemed shocked by her answer. 'Why not? It's nothing to do with anyone else.'

Jenna coughed. 'Ahem?'

'I meant those two.' He indicated Ellie and Zoe and Pippa noticed that he spoke to Jenna in the same way he had started to address Pippa. Short, sharp and disrespectful. Jenna was clearly shocked and Pippa wondered if this was the moment when she realised the honeymoon period was now over and shit was about to get real *very* quickly.

'Do you want us to go?' Zoe asked Pippa but she shook her head.

'Oh for God's sake, come on. I don't want half the town knowing our business.'

'Then you shouldn't have bloody done it, should you?' Pippa wasn't giving in. Plus, she needed those girls. Having them here made it easier to keep up the strong façade. Without them emotionally holding her up, she would fall. And fall hard.

'Okay, here's the thing ...' he trailed off and looked to be searching for an excuse.

'I don't want to hear your excuses, Jason.'

'I'm not making up excuses. Pip, I love you.'

'Pfft!' She shook her head and laughed in disbelief. 'Love me? You don't know what the word means. And what about Jenna?' She looked at the woman next to her who she felt incredibly sorry for right now. 'You've knocked her up too, no 'I love you' to her?'

He glanced over to Jenna and then back to Pippa. 'I don't know what to say.'

'You're a coward.' Jenna said, softly but loud enough to make an impact. 'All that stuff you told me, all those promises you made me, they were all lies.' Her eyes rapidly filling with tears, Jenna stopped talking.

'Do you actually want to be with either of us?' Pippa asked the question that she wasn't sure we wanted the answer to. What if he said no? She would feel like absolute shit. But equally, what if he said yes? Would she even take him back? Never before had she been so confused.

346

'Of course I do.'

'Care to elaborate which one?' Ellie chipped in from behind him. Jason turned and shot her a filthy look. 'Hey, no use giving me those looks, mate, I'm not the one who fucked up.'

'This has nothing to do with you. Why are you even here?' He threw out the words viciously and glared at her.

'Because, Pippa deserves to be treated better than this – and Jenna, for that matter – so I'm here to make sure you don't squirm your way out of this.' Ellie squared up to Jason and Pippa actually felt as if she wanted to laugh. Not that she wasn't falling apart internally from all this, but because if she didn't laugh, she would cry. And she was scared that if she let that happen, she wouldn't pull back from this and he would know that he had got her.

'Jason?' He turned to face her, his expression softening. 'Let's face it, you've messed up. Catastrophically messed up. And the real question here is what happens next?'

'I'll make it up to you, I swear. It was a stupid mistake and I promise it will never happen again.'

Jenna let out a sob as she stormed out of the room. Zoe made a movement to go but Ellie called out, 'Its okay, I'll go. You stay here.'

Pippa was so grateful that the girls had taken Jenna under their wing too. Because the truth of the matter was, he'd played them both. 'How can you even say that? Jenna had no idea you were married. The poor girl thought she was settled in a long-term relationship with you and you get her pregnant too and then drop her, just like that? What kind of a man are you?'

'I don't know what you want me to do?'

'What I want you to do? You don't know what I want you to do?' She gave in to a laugh. An exasperated, *I can't believe I'm having this conversation,* laugh. 'I want you to have not fucked up in the first place!'

'But I can't change that now.'

'You shouldn't have done it at all.'

'I know that!' He raised his voice.

'No ... I'm done.' She picked up her bag and tried to walk out of the door, but Jason grabbed her arm. 'Get off me,' she spat through gritted teeth.

'You can't just walk out. That's my baby in there.' He pointed to her stomach.

'Yeah, and that's your baby in there too!' She pointed out the door towards the direction that Jenna had rushed in. 'But I don't see you fighting for that one.'

'I can fight for it if you want. Or I'll just walk away. What do you want me to do?'

Pippa paused and slowly took a step forward so that she was just inches from Jason's face. 'I want you to leave me alone. I'm done. Not just done for today, done for good. I don't want to see you ever again.'

'Pip, you don't mean that.' He even had the cheek to look emotional.

'Don't I?'

'What about my baby?'

'What about it? You're telling me you actually care? It wasn't that long ago you were saying you didn't want it. You were 'struggling' with it.' She used air quotes and put her hand on her chest.

'Of course I care!'

'Then why do this? Why, not only have an affair, but get her pregnant too?'

'I didn't mean to – it was just a bit of fun. You sucked all the fun out of us.'

And there it was. 'I sucked the fun out?'

'Yes! It was all planned sex and let's do this position and let's have sex now because I'm ovulating and, no touching yourself for however many days before we can have sex so that the sperm is at its optimum. Pip, you made sex into a chore! And that's saying a lot when a man feels like it's a chore!'

She stopped, to take it all in. She knew she had been very regimented with it all in the run-up to her falling pregnant, but to hear him use that against her was hard to listen to. 'I did all of that because I wanted this baby so much. It wasn't happening for us, Jason, and this was our last chance. I had no choice but to make sure everything was right.'

'But it was too much. You took all the fun out of it and I had to look elsewhere.'

She stood up tall again, anger building her up. 'Are you seriously blaming me for making you have an affair? Did you not think to just talk to me about it and make things right, instead of going behind my back!'

'I know, I handled it wrong. I can't change it now.' He looked exhausted. He watched her for a minute and she maintained her stance. There was no way she was backing down now. She had to face the fact that she was going to have to be the strong, independent woman she was so scared of being. 'You're really leaving, aren't you?' he asked, sadness deflating his body and making him look so small. Pippa nodded. 'I want to see my baby ... please?'

'Fine. You can see the baby whenever you like. Not because you deserve to, but because this baby deserves to know its father. And when it's older, it'll soon realise what a lowlife its father is.' And she turned around and walked out of the office with her head held high. As she rounded the corner of the corridor, she passed the reception, with Betty still sitting at the desk. 'Thanks, Betty,' she said as she marched by. Having second thoughts, she stopped and doubled back. 'Betty?'

She looked up at Pippa with the guiltiest face. Pippa knew the answer before she asked the question. 'Did you know my husband was having an affair?'

Betty nodded. 'I'm sorry, Pippa. I just didn't want to have to keep something like that to myself, so I thought it was better to leave. I caught them in his office. But, I needed the money and he told me it was over. I swear I didn't know he was still seeing her.'

Pippa laughed, thinking about just how many people Jason had done over. 'It's fine, Betty, honestly.'

She turned and pushed the doors open, welcoming the breeze on her face as she marched towards the car.

As she approached she saw Jenna and Ellie sitting inside talking. Jenna was crying. She opened the door and sat down in the passenger seat. 'You okay?' she asked Jenna.

'Yeah. I'm sorry. I just couldn't listen to it any more.'

'It's fine. I've told him where to go.'

Zoe jumped in the driver's seat. 'You okay?'

'Not really, but can we just drive.'

'Of course.' Zoe started the engine and did as she was asked.

Pippa leant her head against the window and closed her eyes, terrified of the next chapter in her life. Single, divorced, with a new-born baby. Shit.

Chapter 37

'He's still sending me messages.'

Ellie chose to ignore her sister's comment and continued rubbing the stretch-mark cream into her ever-growing belly. Zoe was sitting next to her on the sofa, watching her closely. She leaned forward just a little and said, 'I know you heard me.'

'Nope, didn't hear you. Not one bit,' she chirped.

'Hmm, I'm sure.' Zoe placed her hand on top of Ellie's to stop the circular motion and to get her attention. 'He really misses you.'

'He can see me whenever he likes. I saw him a couple of weeks ago.'

'You know what I mean. He hates not being with you. He's missing out on all the baby-related things and—'

'Zoe, let me save you time.' She held her hand up for her sister to listen. 'I've already told him and I've already told you. He can be as involved as he likes with the baby. I'm not that far away.'

'But why don't you just talk about maybe, you know, getting together on a more official basis.'

'No, Zoe.'

'Why!'

'Because I said so.'

Zoe crossed her arms. 'That's not a valid answer.'

'I'm a mum now. I'm allowed to use that answer. I can also use 'just do as I say', 'if the wind changes your face will stay like that,' and my personal favourite, 'just, because'.'

Zoe laughed. 'Yeah, well, that stuff doesn't work on me.'

Ellie shrugged. 'Not my problem, I'm afraid.'

'But Chris *is* your problem.'

'He's not a problem.'

'Exactly! And he can be so much more. You like him like that, I know you do. I don't know why you don't just let it happen between you guys.'

'Because we are friends, Zoe, that's it! We don't work as anything else.' Ellie stood up as the buzzer went on the front door. 'Chris has agreed this too; I don't know why he keeps texting you about me being all the way up here. Nothing can change that. We need to just deal with it. Chris and I have an amazing friendship and I don't want to risk everything just because society dictates that because we are having a baby together, we need to be together as a couple.'

'Society dictates? Are you serious? You're not giving this a shot because you don't want 'society' to dictate to you? Man, Ellie, I know you're always the one who hated being told what to do as a kid, but this takes it to a whole new level!' Zoe stopped behind Ellie, one foot still on the steps.

'Anyway, you should be being nice to me – it's my birthday!'

Ellie poked her tongue out at her sister before opening the door and being faced by a floating bunch of flowers. 'Um ... hello?' she said, peering round the side.

The man held out the flowers for Ellie to take. 'These are for an Ellie Samson?'

'Yep, that's me.' She took the flowers and looked at Zoe. 'Who are they from?'

The courier thought she was talking to him and replied, 'There's a note attached somewhere in there.' He pointed into the centre of the flowers before smiling and walking off back to his van.

'Can you see the note?' Ellie asked, peering over the top of the huge bunch. 'I need both hands to hold this.'

'Here, let me carry it upstairs and you can sit down.' Zoe took the flowers and walked off up the stairs and Ellie couldn't help but think that Zoe knew what these flowers were about. And if that was the case, then she knew who they were from.

'They're from Chris, aren't they?' She gave Zoe a raised-eyebrow look, but inside she found herself secretly wanting them to be from him.

'What makes you think I know?' Zoe couldn't look her in the eye. She placed the flowers down on the coffee table and sat back on the sofa, waiting for Ellie to read the note.

As much as Ellie wanted to keep her sister in suspense even longer, she desperately wanted to know herself. She whipped the card from between the sunflower and the rose and sat down to read it. Huge letters spelling *Happy Birthday* adorned the front and Ellie smiled as she opened it.

Ellie,

From the second I met you, I knew that I had met an amazing person. You are funny, loving, hardworking and one of the most beautiful women in the world (you're still number two to Beyoncé, but let's face it, she's never going to marry me.)

Ellie smiled and looked up at her sister, who was watching her closely. Zoe smiled back and nodded for her to continue.

The reason I am sending you this letter is because I know you won't take me seriously otherwise. I wanted to tell you this in person, but every time we meet up you change the subject or you walk off and I never get the chance to say exactly what I have been desperately trying to tell you. So I wrote it here – I hope you are still reading it and if you've discarded it on the floor and walked off in a huff and Zoe, you've picked this up, please take it back to Ellie and, if she won't read it, read it out loud for her to hear.

Ellie found herself chuckling at Chris's stupidity. And also at how well he knew her. She did have the overwhelming urge to throw the message down and pretend it wasn't happening. But she couldn't.

Ellie, I know us sleeping together happened when we were both drunk – it always does – and I know it has freaked you out. It freaked me out too, initially. But not because I slept with you, because I couldn't understand the immense rush of feelings I had for you after it happened.

Ellie swallowed the lump that had formed in her throat. Her heart was racing and she could feel her hands shaking.

We have always been 'Ellie and Chris'. Inseparable. That's what caused so many problems with all the girl-friends I've ever had. None of them could understand the closeness I had with you and every single one of them asked me to spend less time with you, and you know what? I couldn't. Because I couldn't ever imagine my life without you in it.

Ellie paused, folding the letter up and placing it back on the table, unfinished. She put her head in her hands.

'Ellie, what is it?'

'I can't do this.' She said, calmly. 'Take it away.'

'What?'

'The letter. Take it away. I don't want to read it any more.' She pushed the piece of paper away further and stood up.

'Ellie, where are you going?'

'I need to just ... I need ...' she couldn't finish her sentence.

Zoe walked over to her and stopped her. 'What's going on, why are you being all weird?'

'Zoe, it's too much. I can't be with Chris – not like that.'

'Why? I know you want him like that and, clearly, by the sounds of that letter, he does too. Why keep fighting against it?'

357

Ellie exhaled sadly. 'Zoe, I have you in my life, yes?' Zoe nodded. 'And I have Chris?' Another nod. 'You are both the most important people in my whole world,' she rubbed her belly, 'until this one comes along.'

Zoe smiled. 'So I don't understand what the problem is?'

'If I was to make things happen between Chris and I, like proper relationship things, and if it went wrong then I've messed it all up. And I lose him. For good.'

'But that's a huge 'what if' moment, Ellie. How about you look at it as, what if it turns out amazing and you live happily ever after?'

Ellie laughed. 'Sis, those things only ever happen in fairytales.'

'You're wrong,' she challenged.

'Yeah, well, I'm not willing to risk finding that out. Chris and I are friends, and bloody good ones at that. And that's how it is going to stay.'

Chapter 38

'So, it's been two weeks since Jason moved out. How are you feeling?'

'Tired,' Pippa decided she could no longer hide the fact that she was suffering and putting on a brave face. She was miserable and it was time she leant on the girls for support, not pretend everything was hunky dory.

'Are you not sleeping?' Zoe poured the coffee and Pippa noticed that she also looked tired and run down.

'Not really. He keeps calling me, begging to come back.'

'And how do you feel about that?' Imogen took the coffee Zoe had poured for her and picked up a slice of Bakewell.

'I know I've done the right thing, but it's just so hard. I keep thinking about when the baby is here and having to do everything alone.'

'You're not alone, you have us.'

Pippa smiled. 'I know, but it's not the same, is it?'

'Plenty of people are single parents and they cope. And that's how you have to look at it. It will be tough, and you will have moments when you think it would be easier to have him back, but always remember that it won't be hard forever and we are here every step along the way to make things as easy as we can.'

'Zoe's right. You'll have me, too.'

'Imogen, you'll have enough on your plate with your new-borns.' She felt a pang of jealousy as she thought about the amazing relationship Imogen had with Alice. 'Anyway, how's Alice doing?'

'Yeah she's doing okay. She's back at work.' Imogen raised her eyebrow, clearly disapproving of Alice's choice to return to work so soon. 'But she said she wants to save her time off for when the babies come, so she'd rather be there at the moment.'

'Surely she's entitled to have time off in both instances? Hasn't the doctor signed her off?' Pippa took a slice of cake, but after the first nibble, realised that she wasn't that hungry and left it on her plate.

'Yeah she is, but being at home is driving her mad. She likes to know she's looking after me and by going to work she feels validated – her words, not mine,' she added quickly.

'If I was her boss, I would insist she was at home.'

'The boss is an idiot. Alice practically runs the place whilst he sits at a desk somewhere else, so to him, if she's in then it means he doesn't have to be. She's just sitting at her desk all day, so it's not strenuous on her leg or anything. She can get herself around; she just can't stand for very long. I've been driving her into work.'

'Are you off on maternity leave now?' Pippa longed to have the comfort of maternity leave, but as she was self-employed and had relied on Jason for so many years, she wasn't able to take a break from work just yet. She was exhausted.

'Well officially, as of Friday. I took it a few weeks earlier because I wasn't feeling great and Alice didn't want me to be stressing. The school was really good about it, actually considering I hadn't been back that long after being signed off. I was half-expecting them to tell me to not bother to come back at all!'

'And what about you?' Zoe turned her attention back to Pippa. 'Have you decided what you want to do workwise yet?'

Pippa shrugged. 'Who knows? I am taking one day at a time right now. Jason has agreed to pay the mortgage while I look for a smaller place and I have some savings to tide me over for a few months. But really I need to find somewhere ASAP. I can't afford to stay at the house now that he's gone.' She looked down into her cup. The brown liquid churned as she stirred it.

'That's pretty rubbish,' Zoe said, standing up to go and see the customers. 'You know, you can always stay with me?'

'Thanks, but I think you've got enough going on at your place, with Ellie staying, and I wouldn't want to overcrowd you both. I'll work something out.' She smiled, but it didn't reach her eyes.

'Where is Ellie anyway?' Imogen asked, just before Zoe walked off.

Zoe rolled her eyes. 'Don't ask. Man problems.'

Pippa looked at Imogen. 'Oh dear, that doesn't sound good.'

'It's just getting stupid now. I've a right mind to get their heads and bang them together.'

'What's happening now, then?'

'Well, Ellie is saying that she's not interested in being with

Chris because he only wants to be with her because of the baby. He keeps saying it's what they should be doing and it's the right thing and she's taking it that he's settling for second best because of the situation.'

'And is he?' Pippa asked.

'No, I don't think so. He loves her, he always has – she just can't see it.'

* * * * *

'Thanks for picking me up.'

Imogen tutted at Alice's comment. 'You know you don't have to say that every time I pick you up. I honestly don't mind and I don't feel as if you're a burden and all the rest of the stuff you say all the time.' She smiled knowing she had covered everything Alice was about to say.

'All right, smart arse. I was just saying.' Alice peered out of the window thoughtfully.

'Look, I know you like to look after me and you are feeling inadequate at the moment but honestly, I'm fine. I like looking after you.'

'But it's my job to look after *you*, Imogen. You are the one carrying our babies. I'm just useless.'

'Alice, you are so far off the mark, it's unreal. You have been so completely with me the whole way. I have had the kind of commitment from you that hardly anyone else gets. You understand me like no one else can. When I'm in pain, you're there to massage me or run me a bath. When I'm sick, you're there holding my hair back and telling me it's okay.

When I needed Haribo and cucumber at 3am ... you were there with me, eating it as well!'

They both laughed. 'Yeah, well, I couldn't let you sit up and eat on your own – although I still can't eat the two together; you're just a freak of nature.'

'Hey, don't knock it until you've tried it.' She smiled at Alice and then took her attention back to the road. 'I mean it, though, Alice, you are my life. I wouldn't be the woman I am today if it wasn't for you. When you were in hospital last week, I felt like my world had fallen apart. Nothing else mattered in the whole universe; I was just praying that you were okay.' She felt the emotion catch in her throat as she pulled onto their drive. She parked, pulling the handbrake up, and turned to Alice. 'I don't know what I'd do if I ever lost you.'

'Hey, you don't need to think about that; it's not going to happen. I'll always be here for you. Always.' Alice slowly rubbed her thumb down Imogen's cheek to her jawline.

'Please don't ever feel useless. You're not useless; you're everything.'

Alice smiled lovingly. 'I love you, Imogen.'

'I love you, too.' She squeezed her in her arms. 'So much.'

Chapter 39

'What do you think?' Pippa held out her arms, show-casing her new flat. 'Signed the tenancy this morning. First of June, first day of the rest of my life.'

'Wow, I can't believe you found somewhere so quickly.' Imogen walked around the empty space that would soon be Pippa's living room. 'I love it.'

'It's great! Why couldn't I find a place like this?' Ellie put her hands on her hips. 'It's so not fair.'

'Oh you look just like the seven-year-old I remember!' Zoe laughed. 'Seriously Pip, I'm so proud of you. This place is great.'

'Really?' Pippa looked around the room again. 'This place scares the life out of me.'

'Why?' All the girls stopped to look at her.

'Because it's just me. No one else. Me, myself and I.' She rubbed her bump. 'What if I mess things up?'

'You won't mess things up. You've got this.' Zoe rubbed her arm.

'I guess.' She walked to the hallway and opened another door. 'Come and look in here.' The girls followed and one by one entered the small room. 'This'll be the baby's room.' She turned and smiled at the girls, waiting for their approval. 'Do you think it's okay?'

'It's perfect.'

'Come on, let's set up in the living room.' Ellie walked off and Imogen followed.

'Set up what?' Zoe didn't reply to Pippa's question, but just smiled and walked back through to the living room, urging her to follow. When she arrived in there, the girls were busy unpacking a cool box. Paper plates were lined up on the floor, a picnic blanket was laid out and the girls were unloading little Tupperware boxes of sandwiches, fruit, salads and chocolate onto the mat. 'Oh my God, what's this?'

'Well, you said you had a surprise and we figured it was this, so we set up a little celebration tea party. It's our way of christening your new home.' Imogen smiled and continued to lay out the little extras.

'Plus, this just means that when you're in and settled, it'll be your turn to host a dinner party, because, technically, we've already done ours.' Ellie picked up a strawberry and popped it into her mouth.

'You guys are so sweet. Where did you hide that cool box ... and the blanket ...?'

'We left it outside the front door as we came in. Didn't you notice us pushing you to the front as we walked in?'

'Yes, but I just assumed you wanted me to go first because it was my place.'

'Nope, we just didn't want you to see that Zoe was holding the cool box.' Ellie took another strawberry.

'Ellie, stop eating all the strawberries!'

'Well, will you all stop the talking and get started? I'm starving.'

One by one they manoeuvred themselves down onto the floor. Very slowly, and with great difficulty.

'Whose great idea was it to put three pregnant ladies on the floor?' Imogen whined as she squirmed on her way down.

'I'd say that was the super-slim Jim over there!' Ellie said, nodding her head towards Zoe, who had plonked herself down nice and easy.

'Sorry girls, I didn't think this through. So, come on then, how many weeks have we ticked over onto now? Ellie, I know you're thirty-six weeks.'

Pippa lifted her hand up and said, 'thirty-four.'

'A very uncomfortable and miserable thirty-two!' Imogen lay back on the floor and spread her arms out to the side. 'Right, that's it. I'm staying here like this forever.'

'Hey, wouldn't it be funny if we all, one by one, started to go into labour,' Pippa laughed as she looked at Zoe's face, 'You wouldn't know who to deal with first.'

'That's not even funny to joke about.' She eyed them all suspiciously. 'None of you are feeling twinges, are you? Because I don't think I could handle three labouring people. Ellie's going to be hard enough on her own.'

'Hey!'

'What? You're telling me you are going to be as chilled as a cucumber during labour?'

'Ah! Cucumber. That's what I forgot,' Imogen huffed. 'Now what am I going to eat with my Haribo?'

'Urgh! You are something else, Ims.' Ellie turned her nose

Lucie Wheeler

up at the thought of Imogen's craving. 'So, has Jason seen the place yet?' Ellie asked the question that Pippa had guessed none of the others wanted to ask.

'Not yet. I will send him the details when I'm properly in. I don't think I can face him just yet.' She paused and then decided it was now or never. 'There's something else, too.'

'Oh my God, you're not taking him back, are you?' Zoe's eyes were wide with anticipation. 'Because you know you don't have to do that. I know it seems hard now, but you've done the hardest bit, you've left. You have your own place now – and this is lovely – so please don't let him trap you into letting him wheedle his way back in and—'

'Will you breathe, woman? I'm not taking him back.' Pippa laughed as Zoe exhaled in relief. 'However, I can't say the same for Jenna.'

'No!' Ellie gasped and the others all followed suit. 'Are you serious? I thought she was done with him too?'

'Yeah, so did I. But she came to the house the other day and asked to speak to me. She told me she loved him and really wanted to make it work, but she wanted me to say it was okay first.'

'So you gave her your blessing?' Ellie was shovelling in more strawberries as the story unfolded.

'More than that, I gave her the house.'

'What?' This time the girls spoke in unison.

'I told her that she and Jason were welcome to the house and that I hoped they could work through things.'

'Pip,' Zoe shuffled on the floor. 'I don't understand. Why would you do that?'

'Because I'm tired.'

'If you're tired, you take a nap! You don't give away your house.' The more worked up Ellie got, the more strawberries she ate. Pippa found the girls' reactions amusing.

'Look, girls, I know you're worried about me, but you really don't have to be. I'm okay. I know what I'm doing. The house was never going to be my home any more. Even if I took Jason up on the offer of staying there, it would always be the place where Jason and I argued. It was full of sad memories and betrayal. I didn't want to be there any more. This way, he is off my back and I get to start fresh. In somewhere that is mine.' She looked around the room. 'Yes, it's going to take time to get it looking cosy and then baby will probably be here before I have a chance to do anything substantial with the place, but do you know what?' The girls all waited in silence. 'It already feels like home.' Pippa smiled, knowing that every word she said was true. She meant it.

'Are you sure you're doing the right thing?' Zoe looked uneasy, but Pippa placed her hand on Zoe's knee and nodded. 'Well, in that case, you know we will always support you. And we will help you make it cosy before the baby comes, won't we girls?'

A general agreement ran round the circle and Pippa nodded again. 'Great, now let's eat before Ellie demolishes it all.'

'Actually, there's something I want to talk to you girls about.' Ellie put another strawberry in her mouth and pulled out a few pieces of paper. Pippa leaned over to take a look, but couldn't make sense of Ellie's scrawl. 'I have been doing a lot of thinking lately – business-wise.'

'Oh excellent! Have you decided what you are going to do once the baby is here?' Pippa picked up a sandwich and nibbled at the edges.

'Yes, kind of. And it involves ... you girls.'

They all looked to each other and then back to Ellie. 'Care to elaborate?' Zoe questioned.

'What, you don't know either?' Pippa asked Zoe, who shook her head. 'Blimey, this must be big.'

'Well, I was talking to Zoe a while back about branching out to face-painting to widen my client base once the baby comes. I can do children's parties, it works around childcare, it's alright pay, actually, and I am only required to do as much or as little as I can manage – it's perfect.'

'Sounds great,' Imogen agreed. Moving uncomfortably on the floor.

'Ellie, it does sound great – don't get me wrong – but face-painting alone won't bring in much of a wage.' Pippa knew how hard running a business is and she didn't want Ellie to go in naively.

'You're right; face-painting alone won't bring in much. That's where you girls come in.'

Confusion seeped round the circle. 'I don't understand.' Zoe frowned.

'Pip – what do you love to do?'

'Bake,' she replied in a heartbeat.

'Exactly. Imogen – what do you love to do?'

She looked worried, as though she might get the answer wrong. 'Well, I love working with children. You know, things like playing games, doing activities, hearing them laugh ...'

she trailed off, smiling at the images her words conjured up.

'Perfect. And Zoe?'

'Well, I seem to be the odd one out here. I just love to be social, make food; design new menus ... stuff like that.'

Ellie smiled. 'You are not the odd one out – you are a key cog in my idea.' Ellie was smug and the others had no idea what was going on in that head of hers.

'Ellie, come on. Stop talking in riddles – what are you talking about?' Pippa laughed, pressing for more information.

'Well, I wanted to propose that you girls go into business with me – as a party-planning company.' Ellie waited for an initial reaction.

'I don't understand where we fit into this?' Imogen asked.

'Think about it. To run this business successfully we need someone who loves to create things – themes, menus, designs, invitations ... Zoe loves doing this – did you see the flyers she made for the mums' club?'

Agreement hummed around the circle.

'And if, as a business, we can offer the whole thing – even better. We can plan the party, design the invitations, and create a theme and food to echo that theme. Pippa, you can bake the birthday cakes and I know you are super-organised, so you can sort of project-manage. Imogen, you will be perfect for entertaining the children, creating activities and games to reflect the theme. You can coordinate everything related to the fun parts. And me – I can be face-painter extraordinaire. I will also be helping out more in the café, especially if Zoe is doing more on the party-planning business. And I am sure,

371

between us, there are other avenues we can go down, too. It could be the answer to all our work predicaments.' She paused and looked at the shocked faces around the group, and added, 'And I would get to work with my best friends.' She held her hands out to the side. 'What more could we ask for?'

'Wow, you've really thought this through.' Pippa picked up the various bits of paper that Ellie had laid out on the floor.

'So what do you say, girls? You want to go into business with me?'

Chapter 40

'I've got a surprise for you!'

Ellie glanced up from the magazine she was reading and eyed her sister suspiciously. 'What are you up to?' Zoe started jumping up and down on the spot and squealing, followed by rapid clapping of her hands. 'Seriously?' Ellie asked, raising an eyebrow and stifling the smile that was creeping up.

'I'm so excited. I've been sitting on this for almost two weeks now and the anticipation is killing me!'

Ellie waited for Zoe to continue, but she didn't. She just stood, smiling manically at her.

'So ... am I supposed to be guessing or ...?' she trailed off.

'Oh right, yes, sorry. Get your coat.' She ran out of the living room.

'My coat? Where are we going?' Ellie called out into the hallway. 'I've got to tell you, Zo, this bump isn't getting any lighter, do I really have to walk somewhere?'

Zoe poked her head around the door. 'I'm driving; you've just got to walk to the car. You can manage that, right?' She disappeared again.

Ellie shuffled to the end of the sofa, mumbling 'Doesn't

look like I have a bloody choice, does it?' She took a deep breath and hoisted herself up to a standing position. She was just about done with this pregnancy now. Her feet hurt, her back hurt, her boobs hurt ... she wasn't glowing, she was ballooning.

'Come on, slow-coach,' Zoe chirped, as she bounced back into the room.

'I'd like to see you carting around a lump like this!'

'Oh, someone is a grumpy-pants today.'

'And someone has taken too much caffeine today!' Ellie shot her a look and waddled over to the front door.

'Come on, less than two weeks until due date. Then it'll all be over and you'll be holding that bundle of joy in there.' Zoe rubbed Ellie's tummy and she recoiled in discomfort.

'Get off.'

Ellie and Zoe's phone's beeped at the same time. They looked at each other. 'How's that for synchronised texting!' Zoe laughed and read hers first. 'Oh it's Alice – Imogen went into hospital in the early hours of this morning and they are going down for an emergency C-section in the next hour.'

'Oh God, I hope she's okay.' Ellie rubbed her tummy again; it had become a sort if instinct thing now.

'I'm sure she's fine. I'll reply in a bit. Let's get going, otherwise we will be late.'

'Come on, then, let's get this over with.'

'It's a surprise; you're supposed to be happy, not wishing for it to be over.' Zoe jumped up and down again. 'I can't wait to see your face.'

'This wants to be good. I had a day planned on the sofa

today, so whatever it is needs to top that otherwise you're getting it.'

'Oh don't worry,' Zoe smiled. 'It'll top it tenfold.'

Twenty minutes later, Zoe pulled up and parked on the side of the road. Ellie glanced at her surroundings. She then looked at Zoe, unimpressed. 'You've driven me to ... a road. Seriously, Zo, this needs to get better, and fast. I need to pee again.'

'We're not there yet. Just wait.' She pulled her key from the ignition and got out.

'Where are you going? You said I would only have to walk to the car.'

Zoe walked round and opened Ellie's door. 'Yes, to the car. And then from the car.' Ellie groaned. 'Come on, it's not far!'

Ellie shuffled herself out of the car and looked at Zoe. 'Well?'

'This way.' Zoe skipped off across the road and stopped at a gate. 'Come on.'

'Are we visiting someone? You should've told me before we left; I would've done my make- up! Look at me! You're out of order, I'm not going in.'

Zoe walked back across the road and looped her arm into Ellie's, guiding her across the road. 'Don't be silly, you look beautiful. Anyway, we are not visiting anyone. Well, not exactly.'

Ellie stomped up the steps to the front door behind her sister. She longed to be sitting on the sofa again, reading her magazine and getting ready to nap. Ellie lifted her arm to knock, but Zoe gently placed her hand over hers and lowered it. When Ellie looked at her, confused, Zoe held up a key. Ellie pointed to the key and frowned. 'What's that?'

'This, dear sister, is a key.' Zoe winked and unlocked the front door, opening it up to a beautiful grand hallway. 'You coming in or shall I just wait for you here?' Zoe's face was as smug as you could get – she was loving every minute of this. Ellie, on the other hand, was confused.

Ellie walked past her sister and into the room on the right, which was clearly a living room. Ellie knew this because the grand fireplace and bay window kind of gave it away. She turned to Zoe, who was now hovering in the doorway to the living room. 'It's empty?'

'Wow, there's no getting past you, Sherlock.' Zoe smiled excitedly.

'Zoe, I'm confused and hungry and I need a pee. Would you just tell me what's going on?'

'I can do one better than that.'

'What?' Ellie's voice was high-pitched now, frustration starting to creep in because of the constant riddles. Zoe left the doorway, so Ellie walked over to the fireplace and ran her finger across the mantelpiece. It was a beautiful, carved wood effect in the most gorgeous cream colour. She sighed.

'Hey, beautiful.'

She froze, knowing that voice so well. Her heart pounding against her chest wall, she slowly turned to look over her shoulder. And there he was. Standing in the doorway with Zoe by his side.

'Chris?' He gave the smallest nod. His smile was spread across his face and he looked genuinely happy to see her. He also looked as though he was taking some pleasure in seeing her so shocked to see him. 'I ... I don't understand.'

Zoe squeezed Chris on the arm and said to him, 'I'll leave you to it.' She then looked at Ellie, 'I'll be in the car. Just ... listen to him.' Zoe gave Chris one last smile before leaving the pair of them standing in the empty room, staring at each other.

'Chris, I don't understand. I thought you were coming up here next weekend?'

'Just listen.' He held his hand up to quieten her. 'Let me say what I need to say and then I promise I will listen to you and whatever you decide, I will accept. But please, just hear me out this last time?'

Ellie nodded her acceptance of the terms, rubbing her belly as it tightened a little.

Chris walked further into the room so that he was a little closer to her. 'Els, you haven't made this easy for me – or yourself, for that matter – but I need you to understand how I feel.' He paused as he gazed into her eyes. His beautiful deep-blue eyes searching for hers to reciprocate. 'What happened between us, that night, was the best thing that ever happened to me.'

'But Chris ...'

'No, let me finish.'

She nodded and held it in.

'I felt completely connected with you. It was right, we fit together perfectly.'

Ellie snorted as she laughed at his poor expression. The serious face he had also broke into laughter. 'Okay, bad choice of words. But you know what I mean. Stop it, let me get this out.' He smiled at her. 'That night was great, all the nights we have had together have been great. But then it's over and we go back to being just us. But the truth is, it isn't just meaningless one-night stands for me – it means something, you mean something.'

Ellie began swaying her hips to relieve some of the pain in her stomach as her belly tightened and relaxed. She'd been getting pains for the last few days. She wasn't impressed. She saw him take in the way she was moving and reassured him. 'Braxton Hicks. It's fine.'

He nodded and continued. 'When you were acting weird around me after last time, not texting and being off with me, it really wound me up. Not because of what you were doing, but because I had let myself get attached to you when I knew there could never be a future with us.' Ellie felt disappointment drop as she heard him say there was no future. Yes, it was what she had been saying for months now, but she started to realise how wrong she was about how she felt.

Chris moved a step closer to her, but then seemed to stop, keeping enough distance between them to act as a barrier.

'But then you told me you were pregnant. And my world fell apart. Because you had been seeing that guy and told me it wasn't serious, but now you were pregnant with, what I thought was his baby, it would have to get serious and I had really lost my chance. All those years of bottling up my feelings and I had missed my opportunity.'

'Feelings?'

He nodded. 'And then you told me the baby was mine.' He

exhaled, blowing through his cheeks, 'That was huge!' Another laugh. 'It was the best news I have ever been given.'

Ellie creased her brow. 'Chris, I don't understand where you're going with this.'

He stepped forward to close that gap between them and placed his hand on her face. Ever so gently he stroked his thumb down her face and then over her bottom lip before saying, 'Ellie, I'm in love with you. I always have been.'

She was speechless. She wanted to say something, but couldn't find any words. It was as if his stare, his eyes, had immobilised the use of her mouth as she stared back into them.

'Do you love me, Ellie?'

'Chris, this is stupid, you know I love you to pieces, you're my best friend and—'

'No,' he stopped her mid-sentence, 'I don't mean like a best friend, I mean, do you *love* me?'

She wanted to cry. There and then, she wanted to curl up into a ball and sob her heart out. Because, the truth was, she had never loved anyone as much as she loved this man. Slowly she nodded, her chin twitching with emotion as her eyes filled up.

'Then why can't you let us be together? Why are you fighting against this so much?'

'Because I don't want anyone to get hurt!' The words came out before she even realised she was going to speak.

'No one will get hurt, Els.'

'You don't know that for sure – I don't want to take the risk.'

'What are you talking about?'

'Chris, I have only got you and Zoe. If we mess things up by doing this, then I lose you forever. I love how we are together – why have we got to mess around with it? It works!'

'But it's not enough any more! I love you, Els,' he rubbed her tummy, 'and I love this little one too, so much.'

She gave in and let the tears slide down her cheeks. He closed the last gap between them and lifted his hand to her chin, pulling it up so that their heads were touching. He was so close, she could feel his sweet breath heating up her lips as he whispered, 'I will never hurt you.'

He pressed his lips against hers. His kiss felt soft, yet full of passion. She thought about moving away but she found she couldn't. She wanted to stay here forever, feel his arms holding her tight, safe. She reciprocated the kiss, pressing hers back against his. It felt ... right. Slowly he moved both hands so that they were holding her face on either side and his tongue gently prised her lips apart, deepening their kiss. They had kissed on that night but this time it felt different. It meant so much more and the more they kissed, the more she realised that she didn't regret this. He pulled away from her, giving her one last gentle kiss on her forehead before opening his eyes.

'Come on, what do you say?' he asked, holding onto her head. 'Will you be my girlfriend?'

She couldn't stop herself from smiling. 'That sounds really weird coming from you.'

He nudged her gently on the arm, but couldn't hide the grin. 'Hey! So, what do you say?' She took a deep breath and nodded. 'You have no idea how happy you've made me.'

'I promised Zoe she could be at the birth, here in Shropshire, but afterwards we can look into what to do about being so far apart and—'

'No need.' He stepped back and threw his arms out, walking round in a circle and finally stopping to say, 'We're home.'

Ellie paused and then said, 'What?'

'This place. It's ours. Zoe and I have been chatting for weeks. She told me what you said, why you weren't letting yourself be with me. So I took the plunge and found this place, so you could be near to your sister after the baby comes, but we could, you know, live together.'

'What about your work? You can't commute from here every day.'

'It's all sorted. I'll go into London Monday morning, stay until Thursday evening and travel home. I'll work from home on the Friday and then we have the weekend together as ... a family.' He smiled as he held his hands out, 'Problem solved. That's if you don't mind me being away Monday to Thursday.'

'But where will you stay?'

'At the moment, back at mum's, but I'm looking for a smaller place to rent near to work. I got a promotion last week, so the extra money will more than cover it.'

'A promotion! That's great, why didn't you tell me?'

'Because I wanted everything in place before I told you. Kind of added to the drama – and I know you love a bit of drama!' He winked at her and she found herself feeling a little embarrassed. 'So, what do you say? You want to give this family thing a go?'

She stood, stunned to silence.

'I'm taking this silence to be a good thing ... you're not telling me to go take a dive off a cliff? This is progress.'

'You've sorted everything ...' she couldn't take her eyes off him. 'What if today had gone really badly and I had said no?'

'Well, Els, I'm not going to lie to you, it would've really sucked. But, it was worth the risk ... you were worth the risk.'

'Fucking hell,' she whispered under her breath. 'I don't know what to say.'

'Say yes.'

She laughed at his quick answer. 'Yes.'

'Are you serious?' His eyes were wide with excitement. 'This is happening?'

'I guess so.' She was terrified, but she didn't have much time for the terror to take hold because he wrapped his arms around her waist – all forty inches of it – kissing her hard on the lips again. She giggled under his lips and he kissed her over and over again. But then she felt weird and she stopped laughing. He sensed her change in mood and stopped, looking at her face, which she felt had drained of its entire colour.

'What's wrong? You haven't changed your mind already?'

'No,' she croaked. 'I think my waters have just broken.'

Chapter 41

'Just breathe, Ellie, remember to breathe.'

'I am bloody breathing,' she gasped and Zoe took a step away from the bed. 'Argh God, when will it be over?'

'Soon, it'll be over before you know it.'

'That's all right for you to say, you aren't the one who has to push this thing out!' She clenched her teeth and reached for a handful of bed sheets. 'Argh!'

Chris unpeeled her hand and slipped his inside. 'Squeeze my hand, Els, come on. You can do this.'

'How is it this painful? I didn't sign up for this.' She continued to take steady breaths as the latest contraction eased. 'I must be ready to push now, surely? I've been here for days!'

'Ellie, you've been here for like six hours,' Zoe laughed, but Ellie shot her a look and she soon silenced.

'I am just going to examine you, Ellie, okay? Let's see if this baby is ready to come out.' The midwife smiled, but Ellie was too far into her breathing to reciprocate. She looked up at Zoe, who was standing next to Chris, right next to her face.

'I can't do it, Zo.'

'Yes, you can, you've got this. You're almost there and soon you'll have your little baby here to hold forever. You just need to stay strong and keep breathing.' Zoe wiped the flannel over Ellie's forehead again as she closed her eyes.

'Chris?' She croaked.

'Yes, Els, I'm here.' He squeezed her hand to reassure her and she asked him to come closer. He did as she asked and when his face was just inches away from hers she said, 'If I ever say I want to have sex with you again, remind me of this pain.'

Chris and Zoe both laughed. 'Even in labour you find the strength to make jokes, that's what I love so much about you.'

'I'm not joking,' she said, her expression deadly serious. 'If this is what happens when you have sex, I'm becoming a nun when we get out of here.'

'Yeah, we'll see how long that lasts when Chris puts on the charm, hey?' Zoe nudged Chris in the ribs and Ellie couldn't help but spare just a small crack of a smile before the next contraction took hold.

'Okay Ellie, you're ready to push. Just take a deep breath and push down into your bottom. Let's have your baby.'

'Oh my God,' she gasped and reached out for Chris's hand, eyes wide in terror.

'It's okay, Els, I'm here. You can do this. I'm not going anywhere.'

* * * * *

Imogen looked down at the two faces looking back up at her.

She looked at their perfect little noses and their perfect little lips and smiled. Both sleeping soundly in her arms after having just been fed for the first time. She was exhausted, but she didn't want to close her eyes and miss looking at them. Alice came into the room holding two coffee cups and a packet of biscuits.

'Here,' she said, putting the cup down on the side. 'I got you some gingernut biscuits too.'

'Thanks.' Imogen's stare was fixed on the babies. 'I can't stop looking at them. They're just ... perfect.'

'I know, you were amazing.'

'I couldn't have done it without you.' She looked up and Alice placed a soft kiss on her lips, followed by two more, one for each of the babies. 'Have you texted the girls?'

'Yeah, Pippa replied saying good luck and to keep her informed. The others haven't replied yet.'

'Okay. It was quite early.' She lifted up her right arm with twin number two in. 'Here, go for cuddles with mummy.' Alice beamed with pride as Imogen handed over the little girl.

'Hello, beautiful,' Alice said as she sat down on the chair next to the bed, 'You are just so gorgeous. Look at those little fingers.'

Imogen was watching her with a huge grin. This was what it was all about. All her worries just melted away as she lay in that bed with all her favourite people around her. 'I don't want this moment to ever end,' she said, reaching out her free hand to Alice, who then reached out to hold it. 'Can we stay here forever, just like this?'

'We'll always have this, wherever we are, baby.' Their moment was interrupted with a knock on the door. Alice moved to stand up, but before she could, the door opened anyway.

'Mum!' Imogen gasped. 'What are you doing here?'

Her mum looked over to Alice and smiled. 'A little birdy told me you had had the babies.'

Imogen whipped her head round to look at Alice, who just smiled and said, 'I'll leave you two to it.' She handed the baby back to Imogen and then left the room, taking one last glance at Imogen before closing the door. Imogen smiled back and mouthed thank you, receiving a nod in response. She turned back to her mum, who was standing by the bed, peering at the babies, tears in her eyes.

'Oh my goodness, Imogen.'

'I know, aren't they perfect?' She looked back up to her mum, 'You want to have a cuddle?'

Her mum looked shocked and then as if she was about to cry. 'Can I? Is that okay?'

'Of course it is, here.' She held up twin number one this time and felt a swell of pride as her mother took the baby. She watched as her mum fell in love and then looked down to her other little girl. She would never push her girls away the way her mum had with her. But now, seeing how she was being with her little girl, she couldn't help but pray that her mum was finally coming round to the idea that Imogen was happily married, to the woman of her dreams. She was so far into her thoughts that she jumped a little when she felt her mum take her hand. She looked up and felt like a six-year-old again, looking up to the woman she loved so much.

'I'm sorry, Imogen, for everything.' Her mum had never looked so sincere.

Imogen began to shake her head. 'You don't have to—'

'Yes, I do. I have been awful over the past few years and I got carried away with what other people thought and what I felt as if I should be feeling when actually, this is all I've ever wanted for you.' She smiled, looking at the baby and then back at her daughter.

'It is?'

She nodded. 'Yes. My whole life, all I've ever wanted was for my daughter to find someone she loves, who loves her back, and for her to experience the amazing gift that is parenthood. And you did it. But I was too selfish to realise, all because it was wrapped up in a package that wasn't 'the norm'.' She tried to do air quotes with one hand, but it didn't really work. Imogen smiled to herself and let it pass. 'And she does, you know?'

'Who, does what?'

'Alice. She loves you so much. I can see it in the way she looks at you, and the way you look at her. It's beautiful what you two have.' She nodded slightly, almost reassuring herself.

'I've been trying to tell you that for years.' Imogen placed her finger inside the baby's hand, running her thumb over the soft skin.

'I know. But I chose not to listen. But honey, I'm listening now, and I hear it.' She took Imogen's hand and squeezed it. 'I'm sorry to have put you through what I did. Can you ever forgive me?'

'Of course I can. You're my mum. All I ever wanted was to have my mum around – I've really missed you.'

'I know, and I've missed you. And I can't thank Alice enough for making this possible. She's a good girl.' Another nod. 'We've had a chat, I've apologised to her too. When she contacted me, she told me how much she could see you were missing me.'

Imogen wiped the tear that had fallen with the back of her hand. 'I never could get anything past that one.' She laughed as she fondly thought of her wife. 'Speak of the devil ...'

Alice froze as she walked in. 'Are you guys talking about me?' She laughed and immediately made her way over to the bed, handing over some Haribos. 'Look what I found.'

'Oh, my word, you are amazing.' Imogen took the bag and looked at her mum's confused expression. 'Pregnancy craving.' Her mum nodded and turned her attention back to the baby in her arms.

'And I have news. The reason the other girls didn't reply was because Ellie is in labour!'

'What! You're joking!'

'Nope. At the hospital as we speak. And even better news, she and Chris have finally got it together.' Alice did a little *whoop* in the air with her fist.

'Oh, about time. This is amazing; their baby will have the same birthday as these two if it's born today.'

Alice popped a few Haribos into her mouth and said, 'Now we just need Pippa to squeeze hers out, hey?'

Imogen laughed as she passed her daughter to Alice for more cuddles. Today actually couldn't get any better.

* * * * *

'Oh my God, she's beautiful.' Ellie looked down at the little wrapped bundle in her arms. 'I can't believe I made you.'

'She's perfect, just like her mummy.' Chris bent down and planted a soft kiss on Ellie's forehead.

'This is so surreal. I really didn't think, this time last year, I would be here, holding my baby, with you being the dad.' Ellie found herself giggling and then unable to stop.

'I think someone is still high on the drugs.' He raised an eyebrow, pretending to be concerned but couldn't keep up the charade for very long.

'Are you kidding? I hardly had any of that gas and air stuff and it wore off pretty much as soon as I stopped breathing the damn stuff. It was useless.'

'I think it did more than you realise. You definitely squeezed a little less after taking that stuff. I actually think you would've broken my hand if you hadn't had any.'

'Aw, I'm sorry, is your hand hurting?' She said, sarcastically. 'At least you didn't have to squeeze a baby out of your private areas.' She looked at her daughter and smiled. 'But it was totally worth it.'

'It totally was,' he agreed.

Zoe came back into the room holding bottles of Coke, Sprite and Fanta. 'I didn't know what kind of fizzy you wanted so I grabbed these.'

'That's perfect, thanks Sis.' She watched her put the drinks on the side and called her over to the bedside. 'Here, go see Aunty Zoe.'

'Oh, I am never going to tire of hearing you call me that.' Zoe took the baby and squealed. 'Oh my goodness, I didn't think I could love you any more than I did when you first came out, but I just do. Look at that perfect little button nose. And those tiny feeties.'

'We've decided on a name, Zo.' Ellie enjoyed watching Zoe's face light up.

'Oh my goodness, okay ...?'

Ellie looked at Chris and smiled, and then returned her gaze to Zoe and said, 'This is Scarlett Gracie Wright.'

Zoe gasped. 'Gracie – you gave her Mum's name.'

Ellie nodded and decided that she didn't have the strength to hide the tears and just let them fall. Chris perched on the side of the bed and wrapped his arms around her, pulling her close so that her face was buried in his chest. And feeling as safe as she did in that moment, she dropped her barriers and sobbed.

'I don't know what's wrong with me. I just feel so emotional.' She half laughed and half cried. 'I'm a mess.'

'Well, you don't look a mess. You look amazing.'

'You're just saying that.' She lifted her head and looked at him. 'See, bags under here,' she pointed under her eyes. 'And snot around here,' she indicated her nose and Chris laughed.

'You're an idiot.'

'That's better. That's the Chris I know.'

'Here, go see Mummy so I can take a picture.' Zoe handed the baby to Ellie and ordered Chris to sit closer to Ellie. 'Come on, budge in. This is your first family photo, smile!'

Ellie smiled the most genuinely happiest smile she had felt in a long time. The phone clicked and she bent down to kiss her daughter's head.

'Oh shit!' Zoe gasped.

Ellie snapped her head up. 'What's wrong?'

'It's Pip, she thinks she's in labour!' Zoe laughed in disbe-lief.

'Are you serious?'

Chris laughed. 'You honestly couldn't write this.'

'Well, go!' Ellie shooed her away with her hand.

'What? No, I can't leave you. You've only just had the baby.' Zoe started tapping away on her phone.

'Are you kidding me? Zoe, your best friend is in labour and she has no one else around her. You have to go.'

'But—'

'Zoe, I've got Chris. We'll be fine.' She paused, waiting for Zoe to move. 'Go!'

'Right, yes, gotcha. I'm off.' She ran over and kissed Scarlett, then Ellie on the cheeks. She paused at Chris and then saluted him before running out of the room.

'She's a nutter,' Ellie said, looking back down at her daughter. She just couldn't get enough of her.

'Your mum would be so proud of you.' Chris said softly, as he stroked his daughter's head. 'I love you, Ellie.'

Ellie looked up at him and embraced the kiss he gave her on her lips. 'I love you, too.' She whispered back.

Chapter 42

Pippa took another deep breath as she moved her hips back and forth on the birthing ball. With her eyes tight shut, she concentrated on counting to get her through the pain. Every ounce of her energy was concentrated on the inhalation and exhalation of air. Which is why, when there was a knock on her front door, she jumped and stopped rocking.

'Who is it?' she called, screwing up her face in pain as the contraction wore off.

'It's Zoe.'

'Oh thank God,' she gasped as she pulled herself to standing. The pain hadn't died down enough yet so she called out, 'Just give me a minute' and waited until it had subsided enough for her to walk to the front door. Sheer relief flooded her body when she saw Zoe's face. 'I'm so glad you're here first.'

'I'm sorry it took me so long, I was at the hospital with Ellie and then the damn parking meter wouldn't take my money quick enough.' She stopped on the spot on her way to the living room and spun back on her heels. 'Hang on, did you say here 'first'?'

Pippa nodded. 'I called Jason.'

'Oh,' Zoe responded, clearly not impressed by this. 'And?'

'He said he would be here soon.'

'And that's what you want, is it? Him here?'

Pippa huffed as she sat back down on the ball. 'Not really my choice, is it?'

'What do you mean; of course it's your choice. If you don't want him here, he doesn't have to be.'

'Yes he does, Zo, he's the dad. I wouldn't hold him back from the moment his child was born just because he's a total arse. He might be an idiot to me, but as long as he does the right thing for the baby, surely that's all that matters?' She wasn't sure if she was trying to convince Zoe, or herself.

'Fair enough, it's your choice. So what's the latest?' Zoe began pottering around the flat already, moving things from one place to another. It was obvious she just wanted to be helpful. Pippa found it sweet.

'The contractions aren't close enough together yet to go into hospital, so I've called the midwife and I'm to go in when they are about five minutes apart.' She breathed slowly

'And how far apart are they now?'

'About ten minutes.' She said between breaths.

'Okay. What do you want me to do? Have you got your hospital bag ready? Anything I need to put in there?' Zoe had her hands outstretched, ready for action. She looked so nervous.

Pippa shook her head. 'Nope, it's all done and by the front door.' Pippa hesitated before asking the next question. 'Can you call Jason?'

Zoe hesitated. 'Sure, why?'

'I just want to know how far away he is and see whether it's worth him going straight to the hospital or not.'

'How close together are your contractions now?'

'I don't know. I feel like it's going really quick, but I just don't know. Here,' she gave Zoe her phone, 'Stick it on speaker-phone so I can talk to him.' Zoe did as she asked and the phone began to ring. It rang and rang, but he wasn't answering. Pippa looked up to Zoe, trying to hide the worry. 'Maybe he's driving.'

Zoe raised an eyebrow. 'Hasn't he got a hands-free?'

Pippa nodded. 'Try it again.' Zoe did it for a second time and still it continued to ring and Pippa couldn't help but feel nervous. But she didn't feel like it for long because just as Zoe was putting the phone down, the door went again. 'Oh, that's probably him.'

'Okay. I'll go, you just chill.' Zoe jumped up and went to the door, opening it up to Jason, as expected. 'Alright?' she asked him, but Pippa could sense the frosty atmosphere between the two of them already.

'Fine thanks, you?'

'Fine.'

'How comes you're here?' He walked in and saw Pippa, smiling at her as he took his coat off.

'Pippa asked me to come.'

Pippa could feel that Zoe was on the brink of telling Jason exactly what she thought of him, but was grateful that she didn't. She continued her rocking, trying to breathe as she felt the next contraction take hold. She inhaled hard, increasing her rocking so that she was going a little faster, the more the pain increased, the faster she went.

'Hey, it's okay, I'm here now.' Jason bent down in front of her, taking her hand into his. Unexpectedly, anger shot into her body and she jerked her hand away. 'Pip?' he questioned.

'Look, just because ... *breathe* ... I asked you to be here ... *breathe* ... doesn't mean I need you here ... *breathe* ...'

'I don't understand. You said you wanted me here at the birth. I thought you wanted me here so we could do this together.' His face oozed confusion. Pippa would feel sorry for him if she didn't hate him so much.

'And we are, we can do this together ... *breathe* ... but you don't need to touch me ... *breathe* ... just be here!' Talking was too hard, she needed to stop. She pressed her chin into her neck as her pain intensified. Jason stood up like a stroppy teenager and walked over to the sofa, plonking himself down on it.

'Pip? Your contractions are getting closer together, I think maybe we should make our way to the hospital, just to be safe?' Pippa nodded and Zoe took her arm, lifting herself up to standing. 'Just take it easy, there's no rush. I'll walk when you walk.'

She took her first step and stopped. 'Not yet,' she said, breathlessly, 'in a minute'. She stood and leaned on Zoe, puffing as she did. After a minute, she was able to walk slowly.

'Can you carry the bag down to my car?' Zoe asked Jason, who was immersed in his phone already and simply stood up to acknowledge hearing her. Pippa could see Zoe clenching her jaws but she gave her credit, she didn't say anything.

Walking to the car was the hardest thing she had ever done. With every few minutes she had to stop and compose herself. 'I think they're getting closer together,' she said as she leant against yet another wall.

'It's okay, we are nearly there and the hospital isn't far.' Zoe looked over her shoulder at Jason.

'Okay, just get me in the car.' Pippa used her energy to make the last few steps to Zoe's car and slide into the front seat. The pain increased as she sat down. 'Oh, hurry up, Zo!' She looked out the window to see Jason opening the back door and throwing the bag in, closing it without getting in. 'What are you doing, get in!'

'Pip, I've got to go.'

Both Pippa and Zoe looked at him, horrified. 'What do you mean you have to go, go where?'

'It's Jenna; she thinks she may be having contractions.' He at least had the decency to look ashamed at his comment.

'Are you for real?' Zoe shouted from the driver's seat. 'Pippa is in labour here, with your child, and you're just going to go off?'

'What am I supposed to do? Jenna might be in labour too. I'm in a really difficult situation here.'

'And whose fault is that, Jason? Pippa is your wife, for crying out loud, get in the car!'

Pippa couldn't speak. She was stunned by what was unfolding in front of her. She rubbed her hand over her bump as the contraction died down again.

'I'm sorry, I can't. I'll go and find out what's happening and I'll come to the hospital as soon as I can.'

Zoe started to talk, but Pippa got in first. 'Do you know what, Jason? Don't bother!'

'What do you mean?'

'Well, clearly you have your priorities and me and this baby don't rank very highly, so don't bother. I'll let you know when the baby is here, but I don't want you there.'

'But Pippa, you've got to understand the position I'm in.' He was leaning towards the car, pleading for her forgiveness.

'No Jason, I haven't got to understand anything.'

'But—'

She held up her hand to silence him. 'I don't want to hear any more rubbish from you. Now, if you don't mind, I'm off to have a baby.'

Jason punched the side of the car as Zoe drove off and Pippa could see him in her mirror, holding his head with his hands in exasperation.

'Good for you, Pip. I'm proud of you.'

But she didn't have time to dwell on it. 'Oh God, here's another one.'

Zoe put her foot down and reached across for Pippa's hand. 'You can do this – I know you can.'

Pippa looked out of her window at the navy-streaked sky and concentrated on her breathing. There was only an hour left of today – tomorrow, her new life as mummy would begin. And she had never been more ready.

Epilogue

Slashes of deep blue streaked across the sky above, sprinkled with glittering stars and milky residue from the clouds, which were slowly dispersing from earlier in the day.

Zoe looked across at her friends as they sat on the table outside the front of the café. 'Can you believe it's been a whole year?'

Ellie shook her head. 'It doesn't seem real, does it?'

'So much has happened.' Pippa rocked Henry in her arms as he stirred. 'One year old. I feel like he was only born yesterday.'

Imogen nodded as she rocked the pushchair with her foot. 'Tell me about it. These two certainly keep me young. I feel like I've blinked and they turned one!'

'So what's the plan for the next year, girls? We've managed to survive a whole year of being parents. We can do anything!' Ellie was leaning against the wall and she shivered slightly from its cold surface.

'Sleep would be nice. I've heard that some people get to do it every night! Maybe we should try it?'

'Imogen, I don't know how you do it with two. Henry is more than a handful!'

'Alice has been amazing; I couldn't do it without her. And Mum. She's been great, too. She even offered to have them for a day whilst Alice and I celebrate our wedding anniversary.'

'Who would've thought that would happen?' Pippa sounded as gobsmacked as Imogen was when her mum had offered.

She gave a little laugh. 'Don't get me wrong, it's been hard. This year has been a real rollercoaster and I don't think Mum is totally on board with things, but she's certainly trying. That's all I can ask for at the moment, hey?'

'I'm really pleased you sorted things out.' Zoe made a point of looking at Ellie. 'It really helps when you've got family on your side, hey?'

'I know what you're doing, Zoe.' Ellie chipped in.

'I'm just glad I don't have Jason's mum in my ear any more. Can you imagine what she would be like with Henry? I wouldn't be able to do anything right.'

'Have you heard from him lately?'

'No, he's not interested in Henry now that he gets to play happy families with Jenna and the little one. But do you know what? I'm glad. I don't want Henry growing up thinking that the way his dad behaves is the right way to treat people. I want him to grow up and be a gentleman.' She smiled as she stroked down his nose.

'Do you think you'll tell him about his half-sister?' Imogen leant over as Eliza stirred and replaced her dummy, which quietened her immediately.

'Yeah, one day. I wouldn't keep it from him. But I'm not in any rush to create a link with those three.'

'I think we should also acknowledge the fact that, a year later, the business is going really well.'

Zoe groaned at her sister. 'You only want to acknowledge it because it was your idea. There's nothing like a bit of self-indulgence when it comes to praise, hey, Els?' Zoe laughed, but inside, she couldn't be prouder of what her sister had achieved. 'You know, if you had said to me a couple of years ago that my sister would be loving motherhood, in a relation-ship with Chris and heading up her own child-orientated business – I would've been willing to bet money that it was a joke. But yet, here we are. You are totally rocking mother-hood.'

'Thanks, Zo. I would be inclined to agree with you there – children and settling down was never on my to-do list of life.' She glanced through the café window at Chris, who was sitting with Scarlett on his lap and eating cake, chatting to Zoe's boyfriend, Gregg. 'But I wouldn't change it for the world.'

Zoe jumped up and retrieved a bottle of champagne from just inside the door of the café before returning outside. 'Here, take one.' She held out the glasses to her friends. 'In celebration of the company being such a huge success – here's to many more years of trading.' She topped up the first glass.

'And friendship,' Imogen added, holding her glass out.

'And getting rid of losers!' Pippa held hers out.

'And a happy birthday to Scarlett, Henry, Eliza and Beth,' Ellie smiled, 'who are the luckiest children alive to have wonderful parents like us.'

'Hear, hear!' the girls chorused and clinked their glasses

together. Ellie noticed that Zoe didn't have a glass. 'Where's yours.'

Zoe smiled. 'I want to add one more toast.

The girls' attention all turned on her. She took a deep breath.

To new beginnings. For us, for our children and ... she rubbed her tummy, to this little one.

Acknowledgements

Firstly, thank you to Margaret James and Sue Moorcroft, both of whom played a huge part in my writing journey. Without their unwavering support and encouragement, I wouldn't be the writer I am today. Margaret, thank you for being the very first person to tell me I could write. Your guidance as my tutor at the London School of Journalism was priceless and I'll never forget how much time and patience you put into my early work. And Sue, what can I say? Thank you on so many levels for being by my side over the years. For making me laugh, mentoring me and, most of all, for being my friend.

Heartfelt thanks to my amazing friends, The Romaniacs. Catherine, Celia, Debbie, Jan, Laura, Sue and Vanessa – you mean more to me than I could ever put into words. Thank you for keeping me going through the hard times and shouting the loudest through the high times. You aren't just my friends, you are my sisters, and I love you with all my heart.

To my agent, Kate Nash, who took me under her wing back in 2013 and made me part of her agency family. Thank you for always being on the other end of the phone when I need you and for listening to my constant questions, queries and

Lucie Wheeler

wonderings. For not shouting at me when I text early in the morning and late at night, and for teaching me how to believe in myself.

A huge thank you to my editor, Charlotte Ledger, for believing in me and taking a chance. It feels like a million years ago that we were sitting in that tea shop, eating cake and discussing this book. And now it's here! Thanks also to the rest of the team at HarperCollins for making my dream come true and to Emily Ruston for her excellent editing skills – you really helped me bring this story alive! Thanks for being so patient!

To my online support network of friends on social media, thank you for always being there – you rock and totally keep me sane!

And to my 'real life' friends. Thank you for not shouting at me when I had to cancel things because I had deadlines to meet, and for not disturbing me when I needed to write. Special thank you to Kayleigh, Hannah and Tarnya for pulling me through the hard times and making me laugh when I felt like giving up, and my university friends for keeping me smiling when I had to juggle a million things each semester!

To the staff at Anglia Ruskin University – thank you for the amazing support you give me regarding my writing. It might not be what I am studying at ARU, but you give me time, encouragement and endless opportunities to support my writing passion and, for that, I am incredibly grateful.

To Michelle and Anneka – thank you for sharing your story with me. Sending love and hugs to you both, and especially to little Jesse. Keep fighting!

And finally, to my family. My husband, Craig, and my daughter, Gracie. Thank you for understanding and putting up with my huge workload. And most of all, thank you for always being there.

Printed by RR Donnelley at Glasgow, UK